GAIL HAMILTON
SELECTED WRITINGS

AMERICAN WOMEN WRITERS SERIES

Joanne Dobson, Judith Fetterley, and Elaine Showalter, series editors

ALTERNATIVE ALCOTT
Louisa May Alcott
Elaine Showalter, editor

MOODS
Louisa May Alcott
Sarah Elbert, editor

STORIES FROM THE COUNTRY OF LOST BORDERS
Mary Austin
Marjorie Pryse, editor

CLOVERNOOK SKETCHES AND OTHER STORIES
Alice Cary
Judith Fetterley, editor

HOBOMOK AND OTHER WRITINGS ON INDIANS
Lydia Maria Child
Carolyn L. Karcher, editor

"HOW CELIA CHANGED HER MIND" AND SELECTED STORIES
Rose Terry Cooke
Elizabeth Ammons, editor

THE LAMPLIGHTER
Maria Susanna Cummins
Nina Baym, editor

RUTH HALL AND OTHER WRITINGS
Fanny Fern
Joyce Warren, editor

THE ESSENTIAL MARGARET FULLER
Jeffrey Steele, editor

GAIL HAMILTON: SELECTED WRITINGS
Susan Coultrap-McQuin, editor

A NEW HOME, WHO'LL FOLLOW?
Caroline M. Kirkland
Sandra A. Zagarell, editor

QUICKSAND AND *PASSING*
Nella Larsen
Deborah E. McDowell, editor

HOPE LESLIE
Catharine Maria Sedgwick
Mary Kelley, editor

THE HIDDEN HAND
E.D.E.N. Southworth
Joanne Dobson, editor

"THE AMBER GODS" AND OTHER STORIES
Harriet Prescott Spofford
Alfred Bendixen, editor

OLDTOWN FOLKS
Harriet Beecher Stowe
Dorothy Berkson, editor

WOMEN ARTISTS, WOMEN EXILES: "MISS GRIEF" AND OTHER STORIES
Constance Fenimore Woolson
Joan Myers Weimer, editor

AMERICAN WOMEN POETS OF THE NINETEENTH CENTURY: AN ANTHOLOGY
Cheryl Walker, editor

GAIL HAMILTON

SELECTED WRITINGS

Edited and with an introduction by

SUSAN COULTRAP-MCQUIN

RUTGERS UNIVERSITY PRESS

New Brunswick, New Jersey

Library of Congress Cataloging-in-Publication Data

Hamilton, Gail, 1833–1896.
Gail Hamilton: selected writings / edited and with an introduction by Susan Coultrap-McQuin.
p. cm. — (American women writers series)
Includes bibliographical references.
ISBN 0-8135-1809-1 (cloth) — ISBN 0-8135-1810-5 (pbk.)
I. Coultrap-McQuin, Susan Margaret. II. Title. III. Series.
PS1544.A6 1992
814′.4—dc20 91-35821
CIP

British Cataloging-in-Publication information available

Manufactured in the United States of America

To David
Katherine
Christopher

CONTENTS

ACKNOWLEDGMENTS

Several people and institutions aided me in this project. I would like to thank them here. The Minitex-Interlibrary Loan staff at the University of Minnesota, Duluth—Susan Kesti, Mary Palzer, Liz Benson—cheerfully and efficiently helped secure the books I needed for this project. The University of Minnesota Grant-in-Aid Program provided some much needed funding. Essex Institute in Salem, Massachusetts, which holds the largest collection of Mary Abigail Dodge materials, granted permission to quote from their manuscripts.

For their personal and professional encouragement of this project, I would like to thank Leslie Mitchner and Judith Fetterley; I am pleased to have Dodge's work in the American Women Writers Series. I also appreciate the help of Shawn Burich, who assisted in the initial stages of tracking down elusive quotes. Perhaps most of all, I owe thanks to all those people who patiently compiled the reference works that made the process of annotating these texts possible.

Finally, I thank David, Katherine, and Christopher for the laughter and good times we share.

INTRODUCTION

When Mary Abigail Dodge died in 1896, the United States lost one of its most pungent commentators on political, religious, and social life. Although she was not uniformly admired by her contemporaries, Mary Abigail Dodge—or Gail Hamilton, as she was known to her readers—was always taken seriously. Considered by some to be an "intellectual magnet," "a strong-minded woman," and "the most brilliant woman of her generation," she was also described by one admirer as "the friend of the poor and oppressed in all lands."[1] But her reputation was stronger than that: she was a woman whom few wished to challenge. Her articles and books on women's rights, for instance, earned her the reputation of being "a lady, at whose mention stalwart men have been known to tremble, and hide in corners" (Fern 206). Her civil service reform articles were considered by some to be the "most brilliant and the most widely read series of criticisms ever contributed by a woman's pen to the literature of American politics" ("Civil Service Discussions"). She was a writer who irritated many by her probing analyses, but who also won the friendship and support of leading writers and politicians of her day.

Her essays and books ranged over a wide variety of subjects treated from various perspectives. Edwin Percy Whipple described her as "a writer who takes up all classes of subjects, [who] is tart, tender, shrewish, pathetic, monitory, objurgatory, tolerant, prejudiced, didactic, and dramatic by turns" (qtd. in Pulsifer 172). In 1894 the critic Henry C. Vedder claimed that Gail Hamilton "excels in vivacity and wit. In sarcasm and invective she has hardly a peer among American authors. She is incisive, even combative, by nature, and thoroughly enjoys a good, hot old-fashioned controversy" (Vedder 196). In her obituary, the *Woman's Journal* concluded she was "one of the wittiest and most forcible writers of her day . . . [who] has made her mark in politics, religion and philanthropy ("In Memoriam").

While such evaluations by her contemporaries are impressive, they alone might not justify republication of her work today. What does justify it are its many strengths: especially some of its social critique, its humor, and its rage. The appeal of this work is enhanced by its having been written by a woman who moved beyond many of the stereotypic expectations of women in the nineteenth century: Dodge lived an independent life and refused to confine herself intellectually to woman's sphere. Unlike the many female poets and novelists, she chose to be an essayist and political journalist. Her writings on such topics as women in society, women writers, and author-publisher relations are as thought provoking today as they were in her own time. Furthermore, she is fun to read. Whether she is describing her vegetable garden or examining the relations between women and men, her remarks often spark hearty laughter from readers and encourage them to think about the world in a new way. But she can also be shocking to read. When kindled, her anger is as powerful as any expressed in nineteenth- (or twentieth-) century work. With a quick twist, Dodge's sarcasm reduces opposing views on women's rights or publishing to the ridiculous and insignificant.

The pieces collected here demonstrate these vigorous qualities in Dodge's work. The sample letters reveal Dodge's independence and self-confidence, her usual good humor, and her forceful reactions when crossed. They express her views of women and her attitudes toward authorship as well as her unorthodox approach to literary business. "My Garden," a wholly humorous essay, subtly probes the relations between women and men, even while making the reader laugh out loud about gardening. This piece, like the others, shows how well perfected were Dodge's powers of invention. "Men and Women" and "My Book" are longer essays examining the meaning of womanhood and the ends of authorship respectively. Though primarily serious, these also use humor to make some important points. In addition, they reveal Dodge's discursive style and effective mode of argumentation. Finally, the chapters from *A Battle of the Books,* which chronicles Dodge's dispute with the publisher James T. Fields, show how powerfully and effectively Dodge expressed anger in her work.

MARY ABIGAIL DODGE was born into a relatively prosperous and loving family in Hamilton, Massachusetts, on 31 March 1833. She was the seventh and youngest child of the farmer James Brown Dodge (1788–1864) and the former school teacher Hannah Stanwood Dodge (1793–1868). Her father was admired by the villagers as a kind, sociable husband, and her mother was respected as a good wife, a great reader, and a fine seamstress.[2] They were both members of the Congregational church and raised their children in its ways, but they also allowed them plenty of room for self-expression. Quite early, Abby, as she was called by her family, developed a hatred of housework and a love of leisure and independence and books (*Memorial* 85). She was allowed to romp through the countryside, to help with the gardening, and to have plenty of time to read. Thus, she became, Harriet Prescott Spofford reported, "a ruddy, curly-haired little child, overflowing with vitality, singing, dancing, and full of the joy of life, and of an astonishing intellectual energy" (Spofford, "Biographical Sketch" ix).

One thing, however, marred her otherwise happy childhood. At age two she had an accident, which left her blind in one eye, and made her extremely bashful in social situations thereafter. When growing up she believed she was, as she wrote in a notebook in 1850, "*surpassingly ugly,* ugly in form—ugly in feature." Those feelings, she said, led to her bashfulness—the desire when in a room of many people "to creep under the table or behind the sofa" to hide (Notebook 2: "A Chapter on Bashfulness and Ugliness"). In adulthood she eventually "grew to perfect poise and aplomb," but as a child and young woman her shyness caused her many painful moments (Spofford, *Friends* 100).

Despite her bashfulness, Abby quite early impressed those around her with her intelligence. She began school at the age of two where everyone—teachers, pupils, and visitors—soon realized she was smart and witty. Pupils gave her toys, medals, and other trinkets as tokens of their admiration. One visitor to the school was so taken by her, he left some money with the teacher for the child. By age five she was studying geography. At a school exhibition before she was seven, she was asked to speak any pieces she knew by heart: she repeated nineteen before her mother made her stop (*Life in Letters* 1:8–9). In addition to being precocious, she was conscientious: she thought good students were those who arrived on time, followed the rules, and were always ready to recite (Notebook 1: "The Character of a Good Scholar," dated 1841). Nevertheless Abby feared "that torment of a schoolgirl's life:" the trauma of writing a composition (Notebook 1: "Composition" 29 Apr. 1848).

She was fortunate in her education: not only was she a good student who was encouraged by her parents, but also educational opportunities for women were expanding. At age twelve, she was sent to a boarding school in Cambridge and, then, at age thirteen she began attending Ipswich Female Seminary from which she graduated in 1850 at age seventeen. The seminary, run by friends of her family, stressed intellectual achievement and self-reliance and by academic standards of the time was excellent. Her schoolwork included French, Latin, German, algebra, history, chemistry, and philosophy. Nevertheless, the underlying assumption of her education was that she and the other students would have an essentially domestic future. There would be no college education for them, as there would have been for many of their male peers.

As a result of her own education, she became a youthful advocate of education for women, though at this time in her life she defended it primarily in terms of its making women better wives and mothers. In a composition written in 1850, she protested against the stereotypes of schoolgirls, which showed them as superficial or pedantic. She pointed out that women were usually not given the opportunity to study for as many years as men, or, when they were, they had to fight constantly against negative public opinion. Either way, women were not given credit for their accomplishments. But if women were well educated, Abby argued, they would use their knowledge to improve themselves as wives and mothers: "Let her garnish her own mind with the stories of literature. Let her drink deeply at the fountain of knowledge. . . . Let her make her home the dwelling place of elegance—intellect—purity—affection. There, *there* will she find her true sphere" (Notebook 2: "A Apology for School-girls" 1 Nov. 1850).

While she had come to accept some of the messages of domesticity for women that permeated her society, she also, somewhat paradoxically, had come to believe in the importance for women of self-improvement and self-reliance. She believed that women, like men, were ultimately responsible for the measure of their own lives and could contribute something meaningful to the world by fully developing themselves. She did not believe women needed to sacrifice their own development for that of others. In addition, she envisioned a happy life for women who relied on themselves: "What can be more pleasing than the idea of a quiet life in a vine-clad cottage with plenty of books for companions—an intelligent & affectionate grimalkin, to purr her compliments every morning, & a lively parrot to sing 'pretty Poll?'" (Notebook 1: "Young Men and Maidens," 30 June 1849).

As a young woman, Dodge thought about her future in terms of a career, not marriage. Believing that she was not beautiful, she decided that she should plan on going to work after her schooling. As she wrote in *Gala-Days* (1863), "Now I maintain a woman ought to be very handsome . . . or else she ought to go to work and do something" (64). There were not, however, very many options for women of her time: teaching, sewing, and factory work were among the most common choices. During the 1840s, however, women writers were becoming more prominent on the national scene. Dodge dreamed about becoming one of them and filled her notebooks with poetry, while her schoolmates teased her about such an occupation (*Life in Letters* 1:18). Nevertheless, when she graduated from Ipswich, she turned to teaching because of its regular income, first at Ipswich, then in 1854 at Hartford Female Seminary, and from 1855 to 1858 at Hartford High School. As a teacher she was quite successful, even though she did not always enjoy what she was doing (*Memorial* 126). She had little time for writing. In 1856, however, she did begin sending some submissions to the *National Era,* an antislavery paper, and the *Independent,* a highly regarded and widely circulated Protestant paper. She also sought advice from the popular writer Grace Greenwood (Sara Jane Clarke Lippincott) about the way to proceed with a literary career (letter included here). Slowly she was realizing that she must write; it was "essential" to her happiness.

In 1858 Gamaliel Bailey, publisher of the *National Era,* invited Dodge to live with his family in Washington and to be a governess for his children. This was a turning point in her life because it moved her away from teaching and into the role of political analyst and social commentator. While she lived with the Baileys, she came to know many politicians and public figures. In fact, she attracted quite a circle of admirers, as did Gertrude Stein years later in Paris. As Dodge explained her popularity in 1860, "I circulate and talk wild and make 'em laugh and am natural and so people get round me" (*Life in Letters* 1:279). Those contacts gave her an entrée into political happenings in the nation's capital. Soon she was sending commentaries on what she observed in Congress and elsewhere under the name Cunctare to the *Congregationalist,* thereby becoming one of the first female Washington correspondents (Beasley 89). Furthermore, because she had considerable free time as a governess, she also wrote many opinion pieces and book reviews as Gail Hamilton for the *National Era, Independent,* and *Congregationalist.*

About this time in her life, she resolved never to marry. In a letter to her brother in 1860, she wrote, "I'm not married and I don't think I shall be. I can't afford the time, and besides, the men ought to be given to the women who can't get along without 'em. I can support myself, and so I think I'd better do it." Five years later she reiterated her commitment to this choice in a letter she wrote Henry James, Sr.: "I have friends on every side who delight in me, men and women who come to me for joy, and solace, and strength . . . because I have never been overborne by hard physical labor, nor undermined by the unspeakable disappointments of marriage. God has suffered me to keep my life in my own right hand."[3]

In 1860 after the death of Dr. Bailey, Dodge returned to her parents' home in Hamilton, and began writing full-time under the name Gail Hamilton (she dropped Cunctare). She did not, however, jump at every chance to publish her work: "I would rather write for a *good* paper without pay than for a foolish one *with,*" she told Grace Greenwood in the 1857 letter included here. She soon developed such a good reputation that James Derby, editor and publisher, asked to include her in his book entitled *Women of the North Distinguished in Literature.* Although by the 1850s and 1860s women were prominent as fiction writers, Dodge was unusual as an essayist and political commentator. She refused to give Derby any personal information about her life, however. This established a pattern for the years ahead: she would continue to use her pen name and to avoid public exposure of her private life.

In letters to publishers, editors, autograph seekers, and potential biographers, and occasionally in such published works as the Preface to *Country Living and Country Thinking* (reprinted here), Dodge repeated her desire to maintain her privacy and to be known in public only in terms of what she had written. In her own defense, she stated three themes repeatedly: (1) she values her personal privacy; (2) she can speak more freely in the persona of Gail Hamilton; and (3) she wishes that her work be evaluated on its own merits, not on the basis of knowledge about its author. How much her desire for privacy had to do with being a woman can be debated. Certainly women were (are) often judged as writers in terms of their sex or personality. The experiences of Fanny Fern (Sara Willis Payson Parton) after she wrote *Ruth Hall* testify to that.[4] Dodge did not hide her sex with her pen name, however, and most people learned who she really was fairly early in her career. Furthermore, though she may initially have felt some self-doubt—a common reason for women to choose a pen name—she certainly did not continue to use the name because of it. Instead, her choice was motivated by propriety, pride, and wit; she wanted to deter printed gossip about herself and her relations with others, and she believed her works could stand on their own merits. She also thoroughly enjoyed the game playing that accompanied having a pen name. She continued to use it throughout her career.

Despite her reticence in public about herself, throughout her adulthood she maintained a lively and revealing correspondence with her family, friends, and publishers. Some of it was published after her death in *Gail Hamilton's Life in Letters* (1901), edited by her sister Augusta. These letters disclose much about Dodge's private life and personality.[5] They describe her daily life, the people she intereacts with, and the places she goes. Many of them, written from Washington, provide behind-the-scenes views of people in Congress and the White House during the second half of the nineteenth century. Dodge discusses topics ranging from her religious views to her attitudes toward individual politicians. The letters also report on her social and literary accomplishments, including the praise and criticism she hears about herself. They are often unabashedly egotistical as she brags about her teaching, writing, or social triumphs. The tone is always lively, usually assertive, frequently playful and witty, sometimes serious, and occasionally viciously angry.

The sample letters reprinted in this volume are taken from *Gail Hamilton's Life in Letters* and relate primarily to Dodge's literary life, although some were included to illustrate her views of slavery and her attitudes toward women and men. Several letters are addressed to publishers and editors, whom she considers to be of equal status to herself. Even at the beginning of her career, her approach to them is not one of a fearful or submissive woman; rather, she uses teasing, self-mockery, exaggeration, and bold assertion in addressing these men. Occasionally she plays the country bumpkin in her letters or is submissive in a mocking way, but she always maintains an aura that suggests her confidence and pride. After her dispute with Fields in the late 1860s, however, the tone in her letters changes. While earlier in her career the humor is wholly good-hearted, after their dispute over compensation there is a cynical edge to her wit in letters both to and about publishers.

Interesting to note in the letters is the way Dodge's attitudes toward authorship and earning money for her literary work evolve over the course of her career. In the beginning she is ambivalent about making money and is much more concerned with establishing a reputation as a good writer. She does not want to put her "brain in pawn," she claims in a letter reprinted here, to earn a lot; elsewhere she asserts that "excellence is far more valuable to me than money" (*Life in Letters* 1:411). Nevertheless, she definitely is pleased when she is paid well: "if Gold and Grandeur are to be my fate, I will endeavor to bear it," she writes playfully to Gamaliel Bailey. Her later letters, however, are much more insistent on her wanting a good price for her work. By that time she has come to believe that compensation is a measure of worth. She also knows that money helps her maintain her independence. Her later letters reflect the philosophy Dodge adopts after her dispute with Fields: "One ought not to *write* for money, but I consider it a first duty after one has written to exact the highest possible price. It is not a matter which concerns only the writer, but all writers" (*Life in Letters* 2:1065).

Her letters provide other insights about Dodge. They show how deeply she felt a calling to authorship, even in her earliest letters seeking advice from Grace Greenwood. They also reveal an ever-increasing confidence in her own powers as writer. And, significantly, they show how wide ranging were her interests; in her letters she discusses abolition and women's rights, contemporary literature and even housework. Over the years Dodge developed many good friendships with literary persons and Washington politicians; descriptions of those people also found their way into her correspondence. In letters to such male friends as George Wood and Henry James, Sr., there is a candor and a closeness that seems remarkable in an era of separate spheres.

Particularly striking as revealed in Dodge's letters are her independence and self-confidence. She truly believes in herself: "If I once get my name up you know I can do anything." She also seems to like herself. Although she is probably chuckling when she writes the following, she seems sincere: "When people say they like me, it seems so natural that they *should* like me that I have not the smallest hesitation in giving them full credence. If they say they do not like me I always think it is prejudice, or they do not know me, or something" (*Life in Letters* 1 : 368). Even when she admits some faults, she insists, "I am very glad that 'I am what I am'" (*Life in Letters* 1 : 398).

After her parents died in the late 1860s, Dodge lived at least part of each year in Washington with her cousin Harriet Stanwood Blaine, who was married to the politician James G. Blaine. In addition to her writing she helped with the Blaines's children and with their entertaining, as well as aiding James with speeches and a book. Although she also did some traveling around the United States and Europe, the rest of the time she stayed in Hamilton with her sister Augusta, to whom she was very close. Augusta shielded the author from many household responsibilities so she could have as much time as she wanted for writing. And her writing kept her very busy.

During her career Dodge wrote uncounted numbers of newspaper articles on political and social issues as well as more than twenty-five books on topics ranging from religion to education, women's issues and country life to authorship. Her works on religion, for example, argue for a more humane understanding of people and the ideals of the church (*Stumbling-Blocks* (1864)), discuss the divinity and humanity of Jesus (*What Think Ye of Christ?* (1877)), and show the compatibility of Herbert Spenser's views with Christianity (*The Insuppressible Book* (1885)). *A Washington Bible Class* (1890) is a compilation of lectures she gave in a Bible study class conducted for well-known politicians and Washingtonians. She also wrote several books of stories for children, a book of advice on progressive approaches to child rearing (*Nursery Noonings* (1875)), and an educational analysis entitled *Our Common School System* (1880). Her only novel, *First Love Is Best* (1877), which contrasts urban and rural values, was not a success.

Dodge's major statements on women's issues were published between 1862 and 1872, and at the end of her career when, in "An Object Lesson in Woman's Rights," she was defending a woman accused of murder. "Men and Women" (abridged here), from *Country Living and Country Thinking* (1862), was Dodge's earliest analysis of the relations between the sexes. First printed as a nine-part series of articles in the *National Era,* this long essay laid out Dodge's attitudes toward women's rights agitation, woman's sphere, authorship, and women's self-development. Other books focused on marriage—its prospects and its problems (*A New Atmosphere* (1865))—, on suffrage (*Woman's Wrongs: A Counter-Irritant* (1868)), and on Dodge's increasing apprehensions about the women's rights call for more work opportunities and suffrage for women (*Woman's Worth and Worthlessness* (1872)).

Her essays on rural life and social issues were often humorous. *Country Living and Country Thinking* (1862), which includes "My Garden" (reprinted here), *Summer Rest* (1866), and *Twelve Miles from a Lemon* (1874) contain philosophical and humorous essays on the joys and frustrations of life in rural New England. *Gala-Days* (1863), another collection, examines such topics as travel, aging, and the unreasonableness of mothers' subordinating themselves to their children's needs. Essays in *Skirmishes and Sketches* (1865) analyze religion, famous people, biography writing, and critics' reactions to her literary work (in "My Book," reprinted here). *Wool-Gathering* (1867) is an account of the people she met and places she visited on a trip to Minnesota. In contrast to these more philosophical and lighthearted works, *A Battle of the Books* (1870) (excerpted here) was Dodge's angry response to a dispute over compensation and business practices in publishing.

Many of her works were controversial. In the 1860s her books on women challenged the arguments of both the antisuffragists and the suffragists, while advocating many reforms for improving women's opportunities in society. In 1870 *A Battle of the Books*, prompted much debate by writers. In 1877–78, a series of articles on civil service reform published in the *New York Tribune* was widely copied and commented upon. From 1889 to the end of her life, she was known as the champion of Florence Chandler Maybrick, the American whom Dodge and others believed was falsely accused of the murder of her English husband.

Dodge was working on a biography of James Blaine in 1895 when she suffered a stroke, after which she "lay in a sleep" for seven weeks. Although she recovered enough to laugh about the premature obituaries, she died the following year on August 17 at the age of sixty-three. Before she died, she privately published a book on her near-death experiences, which she called *X-Rays* (1896). She left an estate of approximately $30,000 (see Will), not an extraordinary amount for a popular writer. Most of it went to Augusta, who published her sister's two-volume collection of letters in 1901 and the only collection of Dodge's poetry, *Chips, Fragments and Vestiges,* in 1902.

ORIGINALLY published in the *Atlantic Monthly,* "My Garden" is a good example of the humorous essays that are scattered through Dodge's collections. These essays on social issues and rural life, are not autobiographical, though they are often written in the first person; the persona is more simple and countrified than Dodge herself was. The humor is based upon contrasts between urban and rural and male and female perspectives. She makes effective use of such techniques as exaggeration, sarcasm, and self-mockery to inspire laughter, while encouraging readers to look at life in a new way.

"My Garden" is a delightful discourse on the experiences of the narrator with her first garden in the country. To start with she has some unrealistic expectations about rural life. When she moves to the country, for instance, she imagines becoming a Lady Bountiful and producing an abundant harvest of vegetables, flowers, and fruits (cf. Fetterley 424–26). But things do not work out that way. Expecting to send heaping baskets of cherries to her city friends, she is shocked to discover how bad the cherries really are. In fact, almost everything is a disaster: "The bugs eat up the squashes. The worms eat up the apples. The cucumbers won't grow at all. The peas have got lost. The cherries are bitter. . . . Everything that is good for anything won't grow, and everything that grows isn't good for anything." Her failures are matched by the successes of her neighbors, whose gardens yield "baskets of apples, and pears, and tomatoes, and strawberries,—squashes too heavy to lift." At this level, the essay explores the timeless problems of gardening—soil conditions, weather, and bugs—while it also suggests that city folk do not have enough appreciation for the knowledge and skills of farmers.

Although this essay is not a straightforward approach to the relations between women and men in American society, a good deal of its humor plays with assumptions about gender roles in the nineteenth century. Clearly this was the author's intention from the beginning of the essay where the narrator declares herself to be a woman, even at the risk of thereby inviting prejudice against herself. Having alerted readers to this fact, she proceeds to tell the story in which she and the male character Halicarnassus embody the stereotypic female and male traits in their society. Where he is taciturn, she is talkative. When she is emotional, he is rational. While she is idealistic and impulsive, he is logical and materialistic. She knows almost nothing about farming, while he talks as if his experience with it is vast. He wants corn and potatoes; she desires flowers and fruit. The differences between them, she attributes to age, but the reader can see them as typical variations of each sex. Undoubtedly the author had Adam and Eve, hence gender relations, in mind when she wrote: "Halicarnassus was there before me (in the garden, I mean . . .). It has been the one misfortune of my life that Halicarnassus got the start of me at the outset. With a fair field and no favor I should have been quite adequate to him. As it was, he was born and began, and there was no resource left to me but to be born and follow, which I did as fast as possible."

Their discussions over what, how, and where to plant reveal the dynamics of unequal gender relations from a female perspective. She makes fun of Halicarnassus and believes she is smarter than he. She never once lets him think he has told her something she does not know, and she is constantly working to outwit him. She sneaks behind his back to accomplish her purposes and surreptitiously dismantles his projects that conflict with her own. Yet, she always tries to be pleasant to him. In short, theirs is an ongoing battle of the sexes, fought in this case over the garden plot, and she is determined to win: "when Halicarnassus entered the lists against me, he found an opponent worthy of his steel."

The disastrous results of the narrator's experiments with gardening seem to substantiate the cultural stereotype of foolish woman. She chooses yellow soil over black for her flower boxes because "Gold constituted riches, and this was yellow like gold. . . . Night and darkness belonged to the other, while the very heart of sunshine and summer seemed to be imprisoned in this golden dust." She does not understand soil; neither does she understand how to make things grow. All her dreams come to naught because she does not seem to know what to do.

Her bumbling attempts at gardening yield some important insights into life and human nature, however. From her unresponsive flower seeds she learns, "You cannot suit people or plants that are determined not to be suited." In response to Halicarnassus's insistence that they ought to plant corn and potatoes, she observes that "corn and potatoes are very well in their way, but, like every other innocent indulgence, carried too far, become a vice." When she resolves to raise beets, even though she can not stand them, because they "waxed fat and full and crimson-hearted," she observes, "a beet that will come up is better than a cedar of Lebanon that won't." Her earthy maxims transform the foolish woman into a horse-sense philosopher, a character type popular in nineteenth-century vernacular humor (see Morris).

Unlike vernacular humorists of the period, however, Dodge does not usually rely on dialect, malapropisms, or other regional peculiarities to create a humorous effect. She uses overstatement and other techniques to make the reader laugh. In this essay, for instance, she exaggerates the circumstances of her departure from the city: "My pathway was strewed with roses. Feathery asparagus and the crispness of tender lettuce waved dewy greetings from every railroad side." Similarly, her descriptions of her flower seeds are ecstatic beyond reason. She also makes sarcastic remarks, usually regarding her relationship with Halicarnassus. When he asks incredulously what she is doing hauling dirt upstairs, for example, she observes "that, in managing parents, husbands, lovers, brothers, and indeed all classes of inferiors, nothing is so efficacious as to let them know at the outset that you are going to have your own way."

Self-mockery is also a common technique. When the narrator sits down to examine her seeds, she says she looks "as much like Cornelia as a little woman somewhat inclined to dumpiness can." When she begins to tell about her failures she asserts that she "shall endeavor to preserve that calm equanimity which is the birthright of royal minds." Of course, equanimity and royal mind do not spring to mind as descriptions of this narrator. There is, in fact, a tone of self-mockery throughout the essay as time after time the narrator's bright hopes are dashed to the ground. Though she tries hard to be domineering, self-assured, and competent, she simply is not.

Other aspects of style and organization in the essay also contribute to its humor, though on a more subtle level. Throughout the essay the author plays with the notion of "masculine" and "feminine" style. Although at the beginning of the essay she claims to be able to deceive readers about her sex by writing in the style of the "stronger sex"—using "a vigor of thought, a comprehensiveness of view, a closeness of logic, and a terseness of diction"—the description does not fit the delightfully discursive and effusive manner in which she tells about planting her garden. When she adopts what she claims is a more masculine style in the second part of the essay to report on her harvest, the results are equally humorous. Her descriptions are more terse, but the reader laughs as absurd situations are explained briefly and seriously. She organizes the reports on her harvest logically, "beginning with the humbler ministers to our appetites, and soaring gradually into the region of the poetical and the beautiful," but her thoughts do not similarly soar; she progresses from telling about beets that she found "nauseating" to flowers that never grew. When she adopts a comprehensive view of her situation to explain to the readers what she learned, her conclusions are startling and funny, even when revealing truth. They frequently include a twist on a more commonly held view, such as the belief that those who prosper also have their own troubles. In that regard, she discovers the opposite, which she says gave her a victory over her "depraved nature. I saw my neighbor prosper in everything he undertook," she writes. "I had not even the small satisfaction of reflecting that, amid all his splendid successes, his life was cold and cheerless, while mine, amid all its failures, was full of warmth, . . . for he had a lovely wife, promising children, and the whole village for his friends." So much for reassurances to a suffering soul.

Dodge was not, strictly speaking, a vernacular humorist, although her work shares some affinities with that of Marietta Holley and Mark Twain, for example (see Morris esp. 1–22). As mentioned, her central character in this, as well as other humorous essays, is a kind of horse-sense philosopher, but, in contrast to that typical persona in vernacular humor, her language usage is essentially genteel. Like other vernacular humorists, Dodge was concerned with exploring contrasts between rural/simple and urban/sophisticated views of the world. And while not affirming all traditional values, her humor is intent upon examining the (usually negative) impact of urbanization and industrialization on more conservative human values. Finally, her essays explore the meanings of separate spheres, but she neither endorses the inequalities as did Twain, nor as harshly criticizes them as did Holley.

Dodge's humorous essays are a part of the rich tradition of women's humor, which has been traced by Nancy A. Walker in *A Very Serious Thing*. Although her settings are not primarily domestic like most women's, Dodge's persona is female, and female experiences in and views of the world are explored. As in much of women's humor, the female characters are often presented as the "victims of cultural expectations" (Walker 12). While Dodge counters the negative stereotypes of women with the presentation of a sympathetic, often androgynous woman, unlike Marietta Holley or Fanny Fern, Dodge does not overtly endorse social change in her humorous essays (see Curry, Warren). She does make it clear, however, that all is not well between men and women in the "garden." This is a theme that Dodge treats more fully and straightforwardly in other works.

"*MEN AND WOMEN*" is typical of Dodge's more serious writing and is a good example of the way in which she liked to turn readers' expectations on their heads by beginning from one point of view, which she ultimately would abandon, to argue another. This approach effectively engaged readers who might otherwise have shied away from her strong-minded views. In this case, the long essay moves from a humorous, apparently traditional comparison of the strengths of men with weaknesses of women to a conclusion that exhorts women to make the most of themselves. While the essay begins with a humorous anecdote about raising men in New Hampshire, it ends with descriptions of three women who have "raised" themselves up as Dodge wants all women to do. Having begun with the claim that "there is nothing so splendid as a splendid man," Dodge concludes the essay with a vision of womanhood more magnificent yet: "On the fragments of your shattered plans . . . rear a stately palace, whose top shall reach unto heaven."

As the essay progresses, the author becomes less humorous and more serious, even passionate as she discusses such topics as men telling women what to do, the stereotypes of womanhood men propound, the ways in which women conform to those expectations, and the advantages and disadvantages of teaching and writing as full-time careers for women. Her approach to the topics is discursive; that is, she advances her arguments by telling stories, sometimes long ones, to illustrate her points. The result is entertaining and readable, though sometimes longer than modern readers might like. (Because of this lengthiness, a few sections have been cut from "Men and Women" here.) She also uses clear specific details and effective metaphors, and, to a greater degree than in some of her other work, she bolsters her arguments with classical allusions and references to both famous and obscure literary writings.

In this long essay Dodge's principal point is that women ought not to be limited by masculinist views of womanhood, especially by "platitudes about woman's opportunities for self-sacrifice, moral heroism, silent influence, might of love, and all that cut-and-dried woman's spherism." She claims such views are expressed by men who are "thick-headed," and "devoid of sense." In other works she finds these masculine views to be the result of a kind of womb envy (my words) or men's fear of intellectual and economic competition (*Woman's Wrongs; A New Atmosphere*). In any case, she believes men constantly try to tell women how to behave, what to think and to do: "They are continually projecting themselves into our sphere, putting their officious shoulders to our wheels, poking their prurient fingers into our pies." "They ding on doggedly," assuming they know what is best for women, even when they have been unsuccessful in getting women to conform to their idea of true womanhood.

True women, according to such men, are destined for marriage and service to others, particularly to men. Dodge's critique of this popular message here and in other works is extensive. In "Men and Women" she points out that economic and social circumstances do not always make it possible for women to marry and live happily ever after caring for others. Poverty and families with problems are not acknowledged in men's scheme; after all, some women must work. Even in well-to-do families in which women can devote themselves fully to caring for others, they still find extra time on their hands to do other things; they, too, need to be prepared for something else. To keep repeating the same message is ridiculous, Dodge believes, because too many young women are already spending too much time thinking about getting married, rather than preparing for a future that may or may not include marriage. In *A New Atmosphere,* her critique is even more radical as she argues that daughters who are pushed into marriage by their parents are no better off than those bartered in other cultures, and women encouraged to marry for material gain are involved in legalized prostitution.

In "Men and Women" and elsewhere Dodge laments that many women try to conform to popular expectations, thereby limiting their lives. As a result, they pay too much attention to fashion and too little attention to matters of the soul. They are always at the mercy of others' whims. They marry just to be married and devote themselves, at the expense of their own development, to unworthy men; if they do not marry, they assume their lives are ruined. Their education makes them ill prepared for the world, and their movement in society is constrained. Even their language is circumscribed; they must use polite, inoffensive, and often weak expressions: they "must submit to Mrs. Grundy, though the heavens fall. But who can reckon up the loss which we sustain?"

Dodge's message to women is loud and clear: make something of yourself, despite the discrimination and disadvantages imposed on your lives by society. It is up to women themselves, not men, to change women's lives: "Whatever is done for you must be done by you," she advises. She encourages women to improve themselves morally, mentally and physically—in other words, to develop strong bodies, well-trained minds, and deeply felt convictions. To do so, they need as much education as possible. They must not fear either having "muscular power" or being "strong-minded." What she hoped was that women would become more androgynous in their lives and self-expression.

Nevertheless, like most people in the nineteenth century, she did not believe women and men would ever be the same; she thought that they probably were different types of human beings. Though she does not claim to know exactly what innate differences exist, because of women not yet having unrestricted choices about their lives, she does make several suggestions. She most frequently emphasizes spirituality and a desire to nurture as characteristics of women. And, although those characteristics are part of the nineteenth-century stereotype of women, she affirms them as worthwhile in much the same fashion that some feminists today advance an ethic of care. Taking as an ideal the values and emotions expressed in motherhood, she gives them primacy as a way of being in the world. She definitely does not think that expressing this ethic means limiting women to their sphere as men defined it. She argues for expressing the values associated with motherhood throughout society.

Though they are different than men, women are equally responsible for the development of their own individuality. They cannot put their fate in the hands of men. Dodge's emphasis on self-improvement for women is based on the Victorian belief in the importance of character—"the stuff of which [a person] is made,—the texture of her soul." Self-improvement in this nineteenth-century sense was not the acquisition of superficial qualities or image which it has become today. Rather, character was a matter of improving the mind and strengthening moral attributes, as well as helping to improve society. Self-discipline, poise, honesty, integrity and self-reliance were among the qualities Victorians admired. In that spirit, Dodge encouraged women to form the "habits of self-reliance, sound judgment, perseverance and endurance . . . form and accomplish worthy purposes." Such self-improvement was not aimed at making women better wives, although it would do that, she asserts. "Womanhood is greater than wifehood"; women need to improve themselves to be prepared for any role they might assume in the future.

Among the alternatives for women discussed in "Men and Women" are teaching and authorship—two alternatives Dodge herself had tried. She points out the advantages and disadvantages of both careers, but clearly prefers authorship. As disadvantages she points out the various forms of economic and social discrimination against women as women. She is especially strong in her analysis of the negative attitudes of literary critics. Dodge argues that nonetheless women should push forward and assert themselves. She encourages women to try writing if they are "a little inclined to egotism, and tolerably imaginative" or if they are in the "habit of entertaining views of things."

Though Dodge recognizes many problems women face in society, she argues here and in later books that female suffrage is not the solution. While she mentions her reservations in this essay, she explains them in more detail in *Woman's Wrongs.* There, she states her opinion that women already affect political decisions by influencing male relatives who vote. And, she is not convinced that men are trying to oppress or take advantage of women as they make laws. She also does not see that having the vote will expand women's educational opportunities, improve their wages, or end crime in society, as women's rights activists have claimed. Though she thinks female suffrage is probably inevitable, she wants to resist it as long as possible. In the end, she proposes a more restrictive ballot to include some women but also exclude some men: "I would have the ballot made a noble and desirable possession, a sign of sagacity, of ability, of worth, something to be striven for, a guerdon as well as a power. And when it is thus ennobled, let it be open to all who can fulfill the condition—men and women, black and white" (*Woman's Wrongs* 169)

Dodge's views of women and men put her in the middle of the women's rights debates of the nineteenth century (see Kraditor). In fact, during her career both women's rights advocates and antisuffragists claimed her for themselves. While she supported expanding educational and occupational opportunities for women, her writings show opposition to woman suffrage. Even though she encouraged women's self-reliance and independence, she accepted some traditional attitudes about differences between women and men. Despite understanding men's mistreatment of women, she did not believe that men were oppressors, or that nineteenth-century institutions might be perpetuating inequalities. She maintained a firm belief in women's potential capabilities but sometimes came very close to blaming women for their secondary status.

The conservatism in some of her views, especially in her rejection of suffrage, should not turn contemporary readers away from Dodge's compelling, still strikingly modern critique of discrimination against women in society. She presents a clear analysis of the impact of cultural stereotypes on the self-concept and expectations of women. She points out the negative results on women of those stereotypes, including poor health, excessive attention to fashion, and bad marriages. She astutely describes double standards in language usage and literary criticism. She is sensitive to class differences among women and empathizes with the poor. These views alone make her work worth reading today.

"*MY BOOK*," published in *Skirmishes and Sketches* (1865), is important for what it reveals about Dodge herself, her attitudes toward authorship, and her views of literary style. The essay begins with some observations on contemporary biography and a parody of the histories of women writers, provides at its heart a defense of Dodge's literary work, and concludes with a discussion of her aspirations as a writer and her vision of the rewards of authorship. Although less discursive than "Men and Women," "My Book" shares the same pattern of development—a humorous introduction moves to a more serious analysis, concluding with descriptions of the ideal. While "Men and Women" had called for a new understanding of womanhood, "My Book" illustrates the way the new woman as writer responds to a critical world.

Dodge states that her purpose here is to write a history of her own life. But, at first glance, the essay does not seem to be autobiographical at all because no description—chronological or otherwise—of her personal life is provided. Instead, she parodies conventional biographies of women writers, then refutes the criticism she received on her first book. At second glance, however, it is clear that she has consciously chosen to present herself this way; as she points out, "if you write your biography yourself, you can have your choice as to what shall go in and what shall stay out." Apparently she decided to write in a manner that protected the intimate details of her life—an attitude consistent with her using a pen name to maintain her privacy—while presenting important characteristics of her "inner life"—her mind. Because she thought writing a book was the most important thing she had ever done, the meanings of that book and of authorship were the logical focus of her essay.[6]

A reader comes away from this "autobiographical" essay with the strong impression that Mary Abigail Dodge was "monarch of all" she surveyed. She presents herself as intelligent, knowledgeable, and imaginative, willing to express her opinions even when others disagree, yet humble enough to be able to laugh at herself. She certainly does not conform to expectations that women should be submissive and pleasing to others; she wants to be unlimited by any definition of her sphere. She mocks the stereotypes of the writer to which, by implication, she does not conform. In contrast, she shows that she thoroughly enjoys writing and believes it has brought her many rewards; "blessings so rich, so divine, that I sometimes think nothing ever was so beautiful as to have written a book."

The attitudes she expresses toward literary form and style contribute to the image of Dodge as an assertive, self-confident, down-to-earth writer. She has chosen the essay form as preferable to the novel because it is a more straightforward way in which to present her views. But, she does not want to be bound by classical expectations that might prohibit humor in her essays; humor is justified because "like the buoy on the tide" it can still "be moored to foundations firm as the perpetual hills." In this case and in regard to language usage, she does not want simply to conform to elite models; she will be more democratic by using a language she learned in school and from her country environment. Metaphors and illustrations make her work comprehensible to a general public as well as to the educated elite. Her style complements her view of herself as one among many, not above many. Thus, she uses "I" because she thinks it is braver, more honest, and more responsible than "we," "the writer," or the pretense of objectivity in presenting views. This "I" speaks, "not as an isolated individual, but as part of humanity."

The criticisms she receives on her work do not dampen her enthusiasm for writing. She firmly counters charges that she is imitative, unimportant, egotistical, impractical, audacious, irreverent, illogical, inexperienced, and unpredictable. One by one she dismisses those charges as inaccurate or irrelevant and turns each criticism on its head to point to a positive characteristic in her work. In response to the claim that she is egotistical, for instance, she says, "I should be unlike all others of my race, if I were not. . . . Everybody—you, my critic, as well—likes to talk about himself, if he can get other people to listen; and so long as I can get several thousand people to listen, I shall keep talking, you may be sure, and so would you. You are just as egotistical as I am, only you will not own it frankly, as I do." In this passage and throughout her essay, she defends herself not only by counterinterpretation but also by comparing herself favorably to critics whose work, she argues, expresses their own prejudices, strengths, and weaknesses as much as any author's work.

In this essay she does not directly address the impact of sex on a critic's evaluation, as she had in "Men and Women." Nevertheless, she soundly rejects the kinds of criticism that were commonly leveled at women writers in the nineteenth century (Baym esp. 254–58). At that time women writers were dismissed as unskilled and prone to wordiness. Critics assumed women had limited imaginations and criticized them for being unoriginal. They frequently made condescending comparisons between women's and men's works. Many critics urged women to write only on topics appropriate to their sphere, and the most conservative urged women to stop writing altogether. While "Men and Women" had shown that Dodge understood such criticism was the result of critics' discrimination against women, this essay reveals the extent to which such charges were leveled at Dodge herself. But she does not argue the connection between sex and criticism here, not because she fears reprisal, but in defiance of critics who themselves linked their evaluations to her sex. She knew that the only way for a woman to receive fair treatment for her work was to have it evaluated on the same terms as that of men—that is, without attention to the author's sex.

Her defense in "My Book" of literary works, including her own, that critics regarded as lightweight may have had a special resonance with other women writers. Although men, too, were writing what their contemporaries judged to be ephemeral works, women were often singled out for disdain because they were so prominent as authors of bestsellers and as contributors to the popular press. Critics complained that such work was, to use Dodge's metaphor, "ginger-pop beer" rather than "Madeira wine." But Dodge claims not to be bothered by that type of criticism: "I would rather flash and fade in one moment of happy daylight than be corked and cobwebbed for fifty years." She defends popular literature as contributing to a better society, thus benefiting posterity, by quenching the thirst of "thousands of weary wayfarers . . . [who] will be fleeter of foot and gladder of soul because of its humble and evanescent foam." Besides, she points out, who knows what literature future generations will judge to be worthy of immortality. In the meantime, she and other popular writers have expressed themselves and lived more fully because of their literary work. Were she alive today she would enjoy mocking her critics with the republication here of her writings and she certainly would join the chorus of voices now defending the rereading and teaching of noncanonical works.

Dodge's essay itself is an important contribution to our understanding of nineteenth-century women's attitudes toward their literary careers. It demonstrates that not all women writers were anxious about their careers, as some scholars have claimed (Kelley, Gilbert and Gubar). Writers such as Mary Abigail Dodge "pursued their craft with dignity, a marked degree of self-confidence, and style" (Coultrap-McQuin 198). Such writers took their own skills seriously and wished to be judged on the basis of those skills, not on the basis of their sex. They were not amateurish or haphazard in their approaches. They believed deeply in the value of their own work. Though they certainly were mistreated by critics and others who did not take them seriously, many did not allow themselves to be victims.

WHILE "My Book" was Dodge's statement of her value as a writer despite critics' disapproval, *A Battle of the Books* was her declaration of independence from publishers' abuse. Thus, she begins her author's introduction, "When in the course of human events, it becomes necessary for an author to dissolve the bands which have connected him with his publishers, a decent respect for the opinions of mankind requires that he should declare the causes which impel him to separation." But her complaints were not hers alone, as she carefully points out in her book. Her case typifies situations between authors and publishers in the nineteenth-century marketplace that cast authors in "female" roles and publishers in "male" ones.

Relationships between authors and publishers in the nineteenth century were more personal and less businesslike than today. The tone of the "Gentleman Publisher's" marketplace, as it has been called, was set by the major publishers of the time such as James T. Fields, who published Dodge's books in the 1860s (Coultrap-McQuin 27–48). Fields and others like him believed in long-term relationships with their authors that combined friendship and business. In exchange for accepting each new work by an author, publishers expected authors to trust them and not to seek competitive bids elsewhere on their work. To maintain an author's loyalty, publishers assumed caretaking roles toward authors, paying their bills, making purchases, and performing other services. Because honor was expected to prevail in the personal relationship, contracts were not common until after the Civil War.

Gentlemen Publishers also emphasized, as authors of the time often did, their noncommercial aim of contributing to culture by publishing good books. In some cases, publishers made real monetary sacrifices for works they thought important. In others, they neglected their accounts for the more interesting work of reading and advising writers. In any event, publishers wanted to be more than mere businessmen. But most did not forget they also needed to earn a profit to stay in business; they tried to combine both motives. When author-publisher associations broke down due to an author's dissatisfaction over pay, publishers usually defended themselves by asserting their ideal and claiming that they earned much less than authors did by their work.

Dodge's dissatisfaction with the Gentleman Publishers' marketplace began in late 1867 when she read an article in the *Congregationalist* that said new authors were usually paid 10 percent royalties on their books. By her calculation she was earning between 6 2/3 and 7 1/2 percent on hers because she was being paid a fixed sum.[7] Thinking there must be a mistake, she wrote to Fields, of Ticknor and Fields (later in the dispute, Fields, Osgood and Co.). He did not quickly move to allay her concerns. Over the next several months she debated a course of action with her lawyer and friend, William French, and made some discreet inquiries among publishers and authors. Fields offered the excuses that she had agreed to the fixed sum and that he had more printing and advertising expenses than usual with her books. She had almost decided to drop her complaint and quietly change publishers when she discovered that Sophia Hawthorne was similarly disturbed about her deceased husband's agreements with Fields.

Realizing that this was not her problem only but a widespread one in the business, Dodge took up the issue again with renewed vigor. She and the publishers eventually agreed to try to find referees for "friendly, not formal arbitration." While the selection process dragged on, the publishers mounted a public relations campaign in the newspapers portraying themselves as ideal Gentlemen Publishers. In preparation for her defense, the author made many inquiries of publishers and authors about costs and agreements. During arbitration proceedings in April 1869, Dodge presented a lengthy defense of her claims and asked for back payment of royalties, plus 7 percent interest, and expenses of $3000. The referees awarded her only $1,250 and ordered the publishers to henceforth pay her 10 percent royalties, saying they found no intent on the publisher's part to defraud her. Because she was not satisfied with the results, she wrote *A Battle of the Books* and published it at her own expense.

A meticulously documented history of the dispute *A Battle of the Books* is told as if it were someone else's story that occurred a hundred years before. The whole account is prefaced by an editor's introduction claiming the manuscript was found in a ship's stateroom after a rough sea voyage. The editor assures the reader that nothing like this story could happen in the age of such enlightened publishers as Ticknor and Fields who "woo" an author "to receive his dues, [win] open with gentle urgency the hand no longer grasping, but modest and reluctant, and [press] into it the crisp, abundant bills." In the account, names and places are changed but the facts are transparent in the telling. Mr. Dane is Mr. French, for instance, Mr. Hunt is Mr. Fields, Athens is Boston, Corinth is New York City, MN is GH (Gail Hamilton), *City Lights* is *Country Living and Country Thinking,* and so forth. Dodge combines a narrative of the events with copies of actual correspondence and news stories. The repetition and detail contribute to the sense that hers is an honest, if one-sided, account of the dispute.

The range and intensity of emotions she expresses are among the most interesting aspects of the account—emotions much like those of any victim of discrimination who in our day decides to file a grievance or law suit. Initially she expresses confusion and self-doubt and persists in thinking of the publisher as her friend and benefactor. When he puts her off, she becomes sarcastic, but still is reluctant to think ill of him. Somewhat later she expresses sadness over the loss of her friendship with Fields and of the ideals of loyalty and trust that have been shattered. When he still does not answer her accusations, she becomes angrier, more defensive, and more accusatory. Finally, in desperation she wants to let the matter go but feels compelled to push it to completion, not only for herself but for others as well. In retrospect she goes from accusing herself and other writers of being unbusinesslike to expressing extreme bitterness at what she has come to believe is the illusion of the Gentleman Publisher's marketplace.

A Battle of the Books brings to light many problems in the nineteenth-century literary marketplace. Major among them are those concerning authors who expect generosity, honesty, and chivalry from publishers and publishers who take advantage of authors, do not maintain careful records, and misuse their connections to the press. Rather than advising an author to become his or her own publisher, Dodge suggests that the writer "be exact, prompt, methodical, and intelligent so far as possible. He [the author] will thus exert a salutary influence over his publisher, and will be far more likely to receive his dues than if he believes in 'uninquiring trust' and lives wholly by faith." When authors become more businesslike, publishers will have to also. Everyone needs to recognize that the literary marketplace, like any marketplace, operates on principles of supply and demand: "Under this law there is no sex, no chivalry, no deference, no mercy. There is nothing but supply and demand; nothing but buy and sell."

The issue of gender is important in the book, both because Dodge thinks women may be discriminated against by male publishers and because she sees the problems of all writers as analogous to the problems in relationships between women and men. As she describes it, women/authors are in private, expressive roles and men/publishers are in public, instrumental ones. The access to power and influence on the two sides is unequal and is made more so by the women's/authors' lack of attention to important matters presumed to be wholly outside their sphere. The emphasis on maintaining good personal relationships gets in the way of both women/authors and men/publishers admitting theirs is also an economic relationship that demands attention to details. In a relationship that stresses unquestioning loyalty, men/publishers are paternalistic and condescending; women/authors are far too dependent and trusting. Men/publishers use their connections with other men to their own advantage, while women/authors maintain silence about their own lives. While this pattern of expectations had facilitated the access of many women to the literary marketplace in the nineteenth century, Dodge rightly understood that it ultimately disadvantaged both women and men who were writers.

A Battle of the Books may be the most important work of Dodge's literary career. Here, she demonstrated why she was both revered and feared by her generation. Her anger was keen, her analysis strong; the book spoke to her generation and still speaks to ours. More clearly than any other writing of the time, *A Battle of the Books* sounded the death knell of the older way of doing literary business. Though it alone was not responsible for the demise of the Gentleman Publisher's marketplace, it prodded (for better or worse) both publishers and authors to adopt more modern, economic views. As a critique of the literary marketplace, hers is more encompassing than that found in such novels as Fanny Fern's *Ruth Hall* because the treatment moves beyond her personal problems to an insightful analysis of author-publisher relations as a whole. Even today for authors in a vastly different situation, *A Battle of the Books* contains sound advice concerning their working with publishers. Each new author starting out would do well to read it.

NOTES TO INTRODUCTION

1. Sources where these labels are found include Beasley 98; Beale 2:19; Spofford, "Biographical Sketch" xiii; and Pulsifer 215.

2. Pulsifer 166. In addition, good sources of biographical information on Dodge include: Beasley; Coultrap-McQuin; *Life in Letters, Gail Hamilton's;* Langworthy; Spofford; and the Mary Abigail Dodge collection of notebooks, manuscripts, correspondence, and publications in the James Duncan Phillips Library, Essex Institute, Salem, Massachusetts.

3. Both letters from *Life in Letters* are reprinted here. All letters quoted in the introduction and included in the text are from that collection. When a quotation is from a letter that appears in this volume, no citation is given. In regard to marriage, Spofford insists Dodge had many proposals and Albert Mordell claims she asked the poet John Greenleaf Whittier to marry her, but Dodge remained single throughout her life (*Friends* 93; *Quaker Militant* 234).

4. Fanny Fern was severely criticized for this novel. For a discussion of the criticism, see Joyce W. Warren, esp. ix, xx.

5. The tone and content of these letters are typical of Dodge. In the unpublished and published letters I have compared, Augusta made only minor editorial changes, but more comparisons need to be made. Some names are replaced with blanks in the style of the time, and a few letters seem disjointed or out of chronological order.

6. By this time in her career, she had actually published four other books: *Country Living and Country Thinking* (1862), *Gala-Days* (1863), *Stumbling-Blocks* (1864), and *A New Atmosphere* (1865).

7. For a more complete account of the dispute, see Coultrap-McQuin, 105–35.

SELECTED BIBLIOGRAPHY

SELECTED WORKS BY GAIL HAMILTON

Battle of the Books, A. Cambridge, MA: Riverside, 1870.

Biography of James G. Blaine. Norwich, CT, 1893.

Chips, Fragments and Vestiges. Boston: Lee and Shepard, 1902.

"Civil Service Reform." *New York Tribune.* 50 articles. 1877–78. Civil Service Reform Scrapbook. Mary Abigail Dodge Papers. Essex Inst. Salem, MA.

Country Living and Country Thinking. Boston: Ticknor and Fields, 1862.

First Love Is Best. Boston: Estes and Lauriat, 1877.

Gala-Days. Boston: Ticknor and Fields, 1863.

Insuppressible Book, The. Boston: S. E. Cassino, 1885.

Life in Letters, Gail Hamilton's. Ed. H. Augusta Dodge. 2 vols. Boston: Lee and Shepard, 1901.

Memorial. Mrs. Hannah Stanwood Dodge. Cambridge, MA: Riverside, 1869. Mary Abigail Dodge Papers. Essex Inst. Salem, MA.

New Atmosphere, A. Boston: Ticknor and Fields, 1865.

Notebooks 1 & 2 (unpub.). 1841–55. Mary Abigail Dodge Papers. Essex Inst. Salem, MA.

Nursery Noonings. New York: Harper Bros., 1875.

Our Common School System. Boston: Estes and Lauriat, 1880.

Sermons to the Clergy. Boston: W. F. Gill, 1876.

Skirmishes and Sketches. Boston: Ticknor and Fields, 1865.

Stumbling-Blocks. Boston: Ticknor and Fields, 1864.

Summer Rest. Boston: Ticknor and Fields, 1866.

Twelve Miles from a Lemon. New York: Harper and Bros., 1874.

Washington Bible Class, A. New York: D. Appleton, 1890.

What Think Ye of Christ? Boston: Estes and Lauriat, 1877.

Woman's Worth and Worthlessness. New York: Harper and Bros., 1872.

Woman's Wrongs: A Counter-Irritant. Boston: Ticknor and Fields, 1868.

Wool-Gathering. Boston: Ticknor and Fields, 1867.

X-Rays. Hamilton, MA, 1896.

OTHER SOURCES

Baym, Nina. *Novels, Readers, and Reviewers: Responses to Fiction in Antebellum America.* Ithaca: Cornell UP, 1984.

Beale, Harriet S. Blaine. *Letters of Mrs. James G. Blaine.* 2 vols. New York: Duffield, 1908.

Beasley, Maurine. "Mary Abigail Dodge: 'Gail Hamilton' and the Process of Social Change," *Essex Institute Historical Collections* 116, 2 (1980): 82–100.

"Civil Service Discussions." *Daily Tribune* 25 Aug. 1877. Civil Service Reform Scrapbook, Mary Abigail Dodge Papers. Essex Inst. Salem, MA.

Coultrap-McQuin, Susan. *Doing Literary Business: American Women Writers in the Nineteenth Century.* Chapel Hill: U of North Carolina P, 1990.

Curry, Jane Anne. "Women as Subjects and Writers of Nineteenth-Century American Humor." Diss. U of Michigan, 1975.

Fern, Fanny [Sara Payson Parton]. "Gail Hamilton—Miss Dodge." In *Eminent Women of the Age: Being Narratives of the Lives and Deeds of the Most Prominent Women of the Present Generation.* Ed. James Parton et al. 2 vols. Hartford, CT: S. M. Betts, 1869. 1: 202–20.

———. *Ruth Hall and Other Writings.* Ed. Joyce W. Warren. New Brunswick: Rutgers UP, 1986.

Fetterley, Judith. *Provisions: A Reader from 19th-Century American Women.* Bloomington: Indiana UP, 1985.

Gilbert, Sandra M., and Susan Gubar. *The Madwoman in the Attic: The Woman*

Writer and the Nineteenth-Century Literary Imagination. New Haven: Yale UP, 1979.

"In Memoriam. Gail Hamilton." *Woman's Journal* 22 Aug. 1896: 269.

Kelley, Mary. *Private Woman, Public Stage: Literary Domesticity in Nineteenth-Century America.* New York: Oxford UP, 1984.

Kraditor, Aileen S. *The Ideas of the Woman Suffrage Movement, 1890–1920.* New York: Anchor, 1971.

Langworthy, Margaret Wyman. "Mary Abigail Dodge." In *Notable American Women, 1607–1950.* Ed. Edward T. James, et al. 3 vols. Cambridge, MA: Harvard UP, 1971. 1: 493–95.

Mordell, Albert. *Quaker Militant: John Greenleaf Whittier.* Boston: Houghton Mifflin, 1933.

Morris, Linda A. *Women Vernacular Humorists in Nineteenth-Century America: Ann Stephens, Francis Whitcher, and Marietta Holley.* New York: Garland, 1988.

Pulsifer, Janice Goldsmith. "Gail Hamilton, 1833–1896," *Essex Institute Historical Collections* 104, 3 (1968): 165–216.

Spofford, Harriet Prescott. "Biographical Sketch." In *Gail Hamilton's Life in Letters.*

———. "Gail Hamilton," *A Little Book of Friends.* Boston: Little, Brown, 1916. 87–115.

Vedder, Henry C. *American Writers of Today.* New York: Silver, Burdett, 1894.

Walker, Nancy A. *A Very Serious Thing: Women's Humor and American Culture.* Minneapolis: U of Minnesota P, 1988.

Warren, Joyce W. Introduction to Fanny Fern, *Ruth Hall and Other Writings.*

Will. Mary A. Dodge. no. 79671. 21 Sept. 1896. Probate and Family Court Dept., Essex Div., Salem, MA.

A NOTE ON THE TEXT

In most cases, the essays under the name of Gail Hamilton appeared first in a magazine or paper, before they came out in a book. This was true for "My Garden," first published in *Atlantic Monthly* 9 (1862); for "Men and Women," first printed as a nine-part series in the *National Era* (6 Jan. 1859–3 Mar. 1859); and for "My Book," first published in *Atlantic Monthly* 13 (1864). The essays were somewhat revised for book publication. The versions of the essays and books in this anthology are set from the first editions of the books. Capitalization, punctuation marks, old-fashioned hyphenation, and spelling have been preserved, with five minor exceptions: contractions such as "did n't" have been regularized; punctuation marks preceded or followed by a space have been printed without the space; missing quotation marks and periods have been added; missing or incorrect accent marks on foreign words have been corrected and the author's brackets have been changed to parentheses to distinguish them from the editor's insertions.

GAIL HAMILTON
SELECTED WRITINGS

GAIL HAMILTON'S LIFE IN LETTERS

[HARTFORD, CONN.] JUNE 9, 1854.

[MY DEAR PARENTS:]

A few days ago two or three carriage loads of us took a drive to Wadsworth mountain, about seven or eight miles from the city. On the mountain is a tower nearly a hundred feet high, and from the top can be seen one of the most charming landscapes in the world, the Farmington valley on the one side, the Connecticut valley on the other. The river can be traced all along its beautiful winding way by the trees that line its banks. The land is highly cultivated, and the scenery rich and picturesque beyond description. Mt. Holyoke can be seen in the dim distance. A little lake lies quietly almost on the very mountain top, calm as if its fair bosom was never ruffled by the storm king's breath, sheltered on every side by the great forest trees beneath whose shade, and through whose paths, impassable to us, the Indian has doubtless often marched with his tomahawk and war-club. On the shore of the lake is a boat-house, where we carried our refreshments and strengthened ourselves after our five hours' wandering. We started about half-past three and reached home soon after nine.

I wish you would once in a while send me a Kentucky paper—Pro-slavery if possible—I think it is well to look at both sides of the question. My very soul has been stirred within me the last few months by that most unmanly, demoniac Nebraska Bill.[1] I cannot believe that men who have trodden our free Puritan soil, and breathed our free mountain air, can suffer themselves to become the minions of slavery. It is bad enough for the South to "roll it as a sweet morsel under her tongue," but there are mitigating circumstances in her case.[2] The enormity cannot strike so forcibly those who have grown up under its influence, but that men who have never been surrounded by any but free institutions should defend this monster iniquity is indeed incomprehensible! "In their proper position" indeed! If the life, the energy, the hope have been crushed out of them by long years of bondage, is that to be thrown in their face? The very fact that they are happy is the most mournful comment. How degraded must a man be before he can be happy in a life which offers to him nothing but a subservience to the will of another, which takes from him the God-given right to his own conscience, and places him in the power of another. It is a bitter mockery! worthy of Satan himself. I have no doubt that, as a class, the slaves are far below the white man, but let the case be changed, let the white man have occupied the place which the negro has done for centuries, and I have as little doubt that he too would be considered as occupying his "proper position." The early history of the world shows that Africa was prolific of great men.

Before America was ever heard of, Africa was civilized. Her statesmen, her generals, her bishops, her libraries were renowned over the then known world, and because this fallen queen now mourns in sackcloth and ashes, little souls insult her and declare her incapable of being exalted. I believe the time will yet come when she will again sit among princes, "clothed and in her right mind," and glorious in majesty.[3] God speed the day! Certainly our "free Republic" seems not disposed to speed it. I believe we have the sole honor of standing before the world as the champions of slavery and defenders of liberty. I have no patience when I think of it. Even for the Boston riots I cannot be so sorry as I suppose I ought. I lament the loss of life. I lament the lawlessness of mobs, nor do I deem it efficient, but whose fault is it that the passions of our steady and quiet people have been wrought to frenzy? Who is it that has stirred up this agitation? Not the abolitionists certainly, and after all I cannot but hope that out of this present evil the great God is working his own good purposes, that the crisis has at last come, and that the giant of the North will shake off now the chains which have so long bound him, and rise up in the might of his conscious strength, saying to this terrible scourge, "Thus far shalt thou go and no farther." I am afraid I have tired you, but really when I once begin to talk about it, I don't know when to stop.

HARTFORD, CONN., January 17, 1856.

MR. BAILEY: *Sir,*—If you are not in a mood to be disturbed I beg you to take out the postage stamp which I enclose with this—burn the whole package, and send me word immediately that you have done so. Direct, if you please, to Box No. 747, Hartford, Conn.

If, on the other hand, I may be allowed to occupy a half hour of your valuable time—allow me to say at once that I desire to become a contributor to the "Era," if I am worthy.[4] It is quite useless to mention the agency of friends in inducing me to this step, as you have probably heard that a thousand times, and moreover all the friends in the world could not move me to it against my own sweet will. Neither do I write entirely for money, as at this particular juncture I am tolerably well off, though an income of five hundred dollars and an expenditure of one thousand will sometimes produce embarrassment.[5] But I wish to measure myself by a new standard. I have been flattered from my youth up till I have perhaps learned to flatter myself. May I beg that your practised eye glance over the pages that accompany this and see whether they be of sufficient merit to interest your readers, or whether the hand that wrote them is capable of producing anything of real worth?

I hope I am not misunderstood. I do not ask for charity, nor for a friendly judgment, but for a just one. If you think the pieces worthless, you will not hesitate to say so and I promise not to drown myself thereupon. If you think they are good, but not adapted to your paper, I shall be glad to know even that.

If you consider them worth insertion, but not worth remuneration, I shall be glad also and willing to send more on the same terms as long as you think best—or as shortly.

If they are worth being paid for I shall be happy to receive their market value.

I want an end and aim in life, and see no other way to obtain it.

May I request an answer, even if you should decline any farther communication?

I have occasionally "rushed into print," but have never made any stated engagement. The prose article was written more than a year ago and has been seen by several persons. If you print it at all, pray say nothing whatever about it, and of all things do not say anything about this to anybody in public or private, as my happiness in life will be blotted out forever if this circumstance should ever come to the eyes or ears of any of my friends. The utmost secrecy is the only thing which I insist on. I should be very glad to withhold my name, but if it is at all necessary to the transaction of business, I will divulge at once. If you would not deem it impertinent, may I request a reply as soon as your convenience will allow?

I am a woman, twenty-two years old. Direct to Box 747, Hartford, Conn.

Yours respectfully,
SEVEN FORTY-SEVEN.

JANUARY 17, '56.

(P.S.) I do not take the "National Era" and have not seen it for a year. If my articles are published, will you send me a copy? Do not fail to reply privately to this letter even if your engagements give you time only to say "no" and I shall be placed under everlasting obligations.

The printed *morçeau* was printed without my knowledge or consent, but I have seen it copied into four different papers in as many States, which was one encouragement for me to make this attack on you. Will you be so good as to return it to me, as I borrowed it from a friend.

[HARTFORD, CONN.] FEBRUARY 15, 1856.

MY DEAR SISTER: I am going to tell you a story. You know I went to Meriden a few weeks ago. You know also that our cousin is somewhat of a literary person. She wanted me to write—for the public; thought it was a sin that I should not improve my talents, etc. I said Well, what shall I do? She said, "Write at once to Dr. Bailey of the 'National Era.'" I thought upon her words, and after I came home wrote to the gentleman aforesaid. I sent a copy of "Hair," and several pieces of poetry. Well, one, two, three weeks passed away and I came to the conclusion that my letter and its valuable contents were consigned to oblivion, but last night I took a letter from my box addressed to "Seven Forty-Seven" and mailed "Washington, D.C." You see I had not told my real name, but directed him to address

Box 747. I walked leisurely home, went upstairs quietly, lit my gas composedly, and then—I opened the letter and read:

> "Seven Forty Seven" must pardon the delay in answering her delightfully independent letter. My answer will be a short one. Your contributions are acceptable and accepted worthy of a place in the "Era," and filed for insertion. But the compensation is another thing. For cogent reasons, which I need not now specify, I have been obliged for the last year to be rigidly economical. The same reasons compel me to pursue the same course the present year.
>
> After that I shall be easy and be prepared once more to be liberal. If you can afford to wait I will on the first week of next December send you a remittance of fifty dollars, for which you may send me whatever you please in your best style of prose sketches, at any time between this and then. When I tell you that I have on hand articles already paid for enough to fill fifty columns, and that my list of paid contributors is never crowded, you will not wonder at my proposition. But the truth is, your pen is not a commonplace one.
>
> I hope now that "Seven Forty-Seven" will introduce herself to me with her own name, which I am sure must be a worthy one.
>
> With friendly sentiments,
>
> I remain, yours etc.,
>
> G. BAILEY.

This is the substance of the letter. I was quite overwhelmed by such an answer, besides being frightened out of my senses. I never can write fifty dollars' worth between now and December, for I don't have time. I am just as busy as I can be with school duties from morning till night. But don't you think it a generous offer? You see they say I may send just when I please. I ought to send enough to make it about five dollars a column, I think. Now don't tell anybody of this. I hesitated about telling you, but finally concluded I would as a proof of my love for you and confidence in you. I have told Mr. ——— and shall tell A. R., because she induced me to do it. You may send this to father and mother, and upon no account is anybody else to know anything about it at present. I have also entered into an engagement to write for the "Independent," for which they will pay me three dollars a column.[6] The first piece was published a week or two ago. I sent the paper to mother. Mr. ——— says it is too little, but I am perfectly satisfied. A. R. says the honor of writing for the "Independent" is enough without any money. If I once get my name up you know I can do anything. This, too, is a profound secret. I did not tell A. R. Now don't suppose I shall do any great things all of a sudden. With all I have to do it is impossible for me to write much, but it is something to have an outlet provided in case I do overflow. The "National Era" is no mean paper. Grace Greenwood and John G. Whittier write for it, and Mrs. Stowe's "Uncle Tom's Cabin" first appeared in it, and *I* feel quite complimented to be received so cordially on my own recommendation. If I had time I think I could do something in the way of writing.

HARTFORD, CONN., February 18, 1856.

MR. BAILEY:

DEAR SIR: I am astonished! I am overwhelmed! I am on my knees to you (metaphysically)! I am blushing furiously at the savage ferocity of my last letter. I can never write fifty, dollars' worth in the world. I must say, sir, I think you have made a very rash bargain. I don't believe you consulted Mrs. Bailey. Why, suppose now I choose to send only one article between now and next December, don't you see you will have to pay all the same? I have always considered myself a genius. My friends have uniformly cherished the same belief, but now this temple of faith is shaken to its very foundations, and I am under the calamitous necessity of classing myself with the common money-making herd. For, sir, Genius is always repulsed, always Genius goes clad in russet fluttering with rags, only Mediocrity rustles in silk. When Genius is the centre of the wheel of life, gold has a far greater centrifugal than centripetal attraction. But if Gold and Grandeur are to be my fate, I will endeavor to bear it with a very great degree of Christian resignation.

I have not the slightest objection to waiting till next December. I am in no particular need of money. But I am really afraid I shall not come up to what you desire. I have no idea what my "best style" is—in fact I am quite unconscious of having any style at all. The cordiality and kindness of your letter, for which I do assure you I thank you most heartily, have quite banished every thought from my head and left it in the precise state of a squeezed orange, but I will do my best, and if you are not satisfied it shall be all the same as if you had never written—only you won't have poetry—that is too bad, for it is a thousand times easier to write than prose.

If you really have any curiosity to know my name I will tell you, but it is a shocking one. I mean to change it as soon as possible. It is, however, a consolation to reflect that if the name confers no honor on "my family," "my family" make the name respectable.

And I remain, sir, yours very truly,

MARY ABBY DODGE—but don't tell.

[HARTFORD, CONN.] [1856]

[MY DEAR FATHER AND MOTHER:]

Miss Hunt took me aside yesterday and said she had something to tell me—that she had seen two pieces of mine in the "National Era," that her sister knew they were mine because one of them had appeared in the school paper and they both had the same signature. As my articles are printed, or being printed, I shall have to bestir myself to get something more ready for forwarding. One of our old graduates has just called on me. I cannot yet tell how matters and things will go in the school, but at present they wear a promising aspect. I should like a hot brown-bread cake for breakfast, if you please, with good fresh butter melted in and a good deal of it. Good-night, my dear father and mother. The mother of two of our pupils called while I was gone, told how much their boys liked the teachers, and "as for Miss Dodge—she was an oracle."

There's something for you to sleep on.

Yours very affectionately,

ABBY.

[HARTFORD CONN.] JANUARY 2, 1857.

[MY DEAR PARENTS:]

Mr. Curtis brought to school a letter directed to Mrs. Gail Hamilton, Box 747, Hartford, Ct. It proved to be from Mr. Ladd, proprietor of the "Independent." Do you want to read it?—

MRS. GAIL HAMILTON, "Box 747":

MY DEAR MADAM: Your favors of 2d inst. to Editor of "Ind." came duly to hand. Your articles were very acceptable and shall be paid for at the rate of $3.00 a column—*when* we know who you are, for, my dear Mrs. Gail, or Girl, we don't pay "nobodies," we don't— If you will let me into the secret of your name I will be very whist about it, and send your money promptly. Am sorry you have got fifteen children (is that all?) to support at this inclement season of the year, and wonder, as that is the case, you have so much time to devote to literary pursuits.

Hoping you will no longer persevere in your attempts to preserve an incognito,

I am, yours truly,
J. H. LADD.

So this morning I have written him a letter. Want to hear it?—

MR. LADD:

MY DEAR SIR: Awful! awful! awful! To go and put "Mrs. Gail Hamilton" right on the outside of my letter, and the Post Office Clerks know my box, and they will go and tell the P. M. General, and he will go and tell Mr. Buchanan, and Mr. Buchanan will go and put it in his inaugural address, and so you have released grimalkin from her confinement. And then again the Mrs. Why I am not married. Well—really—did I say I had fifteen children? It was a wicked story gotten up for effect—a poet's license. I have only seven—no three—well there, I may as well make a clean breast of it. I have neither chick nor child in the world. Did you ever hear of the "three black crows"?

I have not the slightest objection to telling my name, only it is such a shocking one. It actually hurts my mouth to speak it, it is so rough. But, as there is no prospect of changing it I may as well tell you at once it is— Oh, I wanted to say I am very much obliged and very grateful. I think $3.00 a column is quite enough for such quality of writing. I expected you would say they weren't worth anything, and you wouldn't pay at all. That style does not require thought and labor like some others. It is just like telling stories to little children, and I feel absolutely mean about receiving money for them, but then, oh dear, the flesh is weak, and if I were only rich I would be awfully indifferent and noble about money matters. I shall be rich one day, when I am become famous, and then I will always write for nothing. There! I have not told you my name yet, but I am just on the brink of it. Now—don't you tell, will you? Don't.

Yours very truly,
MARY ABBY DODGE.

"Phebus—what a name
To fill the speaking trump of future fame."[7]

Mrs. Bird said my name was very familiar to her. She had heard a great deal about the Miss Dodge who taught at the High School, but had always supposed I was tall and very dignified and between thirty and forty—so, you see I must have a very dignified reputation, notwithstanding you think I am slightly harum-scarum.

[HARTFORD, CONN.] JANUARY 15. [1857]

[MY DEAR FATHER AND MOTHER:]

Tuesday evening went to hear Mr. Capron deliver a lecture on Ancient Architecture at the schoolhouse to the Sigma Phi Society, formed of some twenty-five of our boys. Received another letter from Mr. Ladd. Want to hear it?—

MY DEAR GAIL: For I do not believe "Mary Abby Dodge" is your true name. However, it matters not. I will send your money, as you insist on your incog. and aliases. You have written thirteen and a half columns, which at three dollars a column, amounts to $40, for which amount I enclose my draft to Mary Abby's order. You need not expect to come any of your "Dodges" over me. Who is T. W. T. C.?[8] I believe him to be your paternal parent. (Mr. C. spoke of his being my literary "pa" in what he wrote to Mr. Ladd.) I am a Yankee and have as good a right to guess as you wooden nutmeg manufacturers. I would like to see you when you come to New York. I have had the honor of an occasional call from some of our lady correspondents—on business of course. Don't fail, at all events, to let me know your address, Mary Abby, when you are in town. Excuse the familiarity of my style. It is no more so than your own. I imagine you a young lady—I won't say how old. I should like to know, as bachelors are, you are aware, very curious about such matters.

I remain, Mary Abby,
Yours faithfully,
J. H. LADD.

Wednesday after school at night found a letter from Dr. Bailey, of Washington. Want to hear it?—

> Will Miss Dodge pardon my delay in remitting? It will be a particularly gracious act on her part, as the only excuse I can plead is negligence. I enclose a draft on New York for fifty dollars. Need I say that I like your contributions? The promptness with which they have appeared is enough. Many have inquired, Who is "Gail Hamilton"?
>
> You will probably continue occasional communications for the "Era," but I cannot offer you a regular engagement. This is my misfortune, not my fault nor yours. But the truth is, I cannot command the means, just now, to commit myself to any stipulated amount for contributions. I may be able to give you something in the course of the year, but I cannot say what, or when. I am sorry, but so it is; the only consolation is, so will it not be always.
>
> Truly yours,
> G. BAILEY.

I heard the other day that "The National Era" had "broke"—and I know they are very poor. It is an anti-slavery paper in a slave State and slave city, and of course receives no local support. I only wonder how it has been able to keep above water so long. It is said to be the only paper published in Washington without any aid from the government. Do you think I ought to send back the fifty dollars? It is too late though, now. It is gone, all gone. "Dear pa," he took it and gave it to Mr. Warburton, and Mr. Warburton put it in some place or other, I have forgotten where, if I ever knew, all but eight dollars, this and the other bringing the whole up to three hundred. I wish to make this statement of affairs, and now you know me possessed of $300 bank stock. Salary, $600 per year, paying $4.50 per week for board. Please after this not try to take my reckoning, or to keep the run of my money matters, as I should be vastly more at ease and more independent if you would exercise your practical mathematics on somebody else's purse than mine. If I don't give you the precise data, therefore, to reason from, you will not think it from any want of confidence in yourselves severally and collectively. I intend to answer Mr. Ladd's letter to-night, Mr. Bailey's to-morrow. Want to hear them? I am afraid the former will be too long, as I want to say "a thing or two."

[HARTFORD, CONN.] JANUARY 16, 1857.

MR. LADD:

DEAR SIR: You do not believe my name is "Mary Abby Dodge," not you! The fleece of the sheep is not to be extended over your organ of vision. Go to the little village of Hamilton, in the State of Massachusetts, ask the worthy priest who presided at my christening what was the name wherewith my parents endowed me at the baptismal font—ask the sober deacon, who holds in his hands the village chronicles, what name was recorded on those Sibylline leaves when my father announced to him, with devout thankfulness, the birth of a seventh child, "Heaven's last best gift," and my word for it you will return six inches shorter, on a moderate calculation, than you were when you left the metropolis of this new world.

Secondly, you believe T. W. T. C. to be my "paternal parent." My dear friend, sit down to a cup of smoking Mocha and find it to be nothing but dishwater. Pop the question to Miss Malinda very tenderly in the twilight, and find when the gas is lighted that you are bound for life to her maiden aunt, "fair, fat, and forty." Sit three hours to witness the unrolling of a pickled princess and "fall to cursing like a very drab-a-scullion" on finding that there is no princess after all, but only a mummy of the baser sort; and in all these you will not be any more out of your reckoning than you were when you drew your bow at a venture and appointed T. W. T. C. my father in the flesh. T. W. T. C. is not my father, but I will tell you what relation he does bear to me. His wife's father's father's brother married my minister's sister. Now you know who *he* is. But you do not know him as one of the best friends a careless, wilful, headlong, headstrong girl was ever blessed with. I sit in sackcloth and ashes every day because I make him so much trouble, and every day I think I will reform and be so docile and calm, and self-possessed; but dear me, when the temptation comes, it seems just as if I could not help it, and generally I do not think how undignified I am until it is all over.

You judge me a wooden nutmeg manufacturer. It is an unmitigated falsehood. Would I stoop to be born in any other State than the one that came out to meet Fremont with 50,000 men.

Fourthly, you want to see me when I come to New York. I am not going to New York, and all the world could not induce me to see you if I were. The very thought of meeting a live publisher, editor, printer, face to face, would drive me "daft, clean daft." I was brought up in the depths of the country, and never saw any one till I was fourteen, and then I was sent to school and never saw any one again till I left it, and I am terribly afraid of people—strangers particularly. You imagine me a young lady. I am not a young lady, by any means. I am twenty-three years old, sir— I almost forgot the very thing I was writing for, to acknowledge the receipt of a piece of paper which you said was $40, but the only thing I saw was my name, and the "Independent," in great flaring letters, so that all the bank people will know that "Mary Abby Dodge" has been writing for the "Independent," and that is the wages of her iniquity. What shall I do with it? I am just as badly off now as I was before. I can't really think I am writing to the Joseph H. Ladd whose name figures so formidably every week at the head of the "Independent." If you *are* the staid gentleman in unexceptionable cravat and gold spectacles, that so prominent an individual ought to be, then I am not writing to you, but to a good-natured man who wrote me an off-hand letter.

Very truly yours,

Well—GAIL HAMILTON

(I think I like that best on the inside of my letters, not on the outside of yours.)

HARTFORD, CONN., April 15, 1857.

YOU DEAR GRACE GREENWOOD:[9] I think you are just as splendid and kind and dear and delightful as you can be. I have just received your letter. If you had not answered mine at all I should not have blamed you in the least; I know your time must be so occupied, and I have no claim upon you, but you have written me, and such a kind letter. I understand what *nous venons* means on a mother's lips. When I was a little girl and used to ask my mother for anything, "I will see about it," was always equivalent to a downright affirmative.

Suppose you were a little bit of a writer—a *very* little bit of one, without a reputation, without much experience, but with the *cacoethes scribendi*[10] strong upon you, what should you do? That is the question.

I have been writing a little for about a year, chiefly for the "National Era" and "Independent." I shall probably continue to do so this year, but that does not use up half my writing material, and I don't know what to do with the rest of it. Is there any good-sense, respectable newspaper that you would like to write for, supposing you were in my place. Perhaps you may think I am too fastidious for a tyro, but I think it is better to have your standard too high than too low. I am poor enough, to be sure, and generally in debt, and would be glad to get money for writing; but I would rather write for a *good* paper without pay, than for a foolish one *with*. If I become a good writer I shall be rich enough one day. Dr. Bailey, of the "Era," made a regular bargain with me, and he expressed himself more than satisfied. He has treated me very generously.

I will send you the only article of mine that I have on hand (out of my scrap-book), and you can judge a little from it. I will follow your advice in anything unless you advise me not to write at all. Write I must. It is absolutely essential to my happiness.

My dear friend,—mine though I never saw you, and dear whether you will or not,—don't write to me again till you can almost as well as not. If you do not write to me again, I shall know you are blessing some one else; and shall not bate one jot or tittle of the regard, the love, I now bear you.

Very truly yours,

GAIL HAMILTON.

On looking, I find two pieces and send them both. You will see that the rhymes are in answer to one of Jenny Marsh's poems.

[WASHINGTON, D.C.] March 12 [1860]

[MY DEAR BROTHER:]

[. . .] Augusta says she never saw anybody *toot his own horn* as I do—that I tell off puffs as cooly as if they were about somebody else and not myself, but I do it because I know if you were here, and I were there, I should want you to do just the same. I don't to anybody else except you and the family letters, only as I write the latter every week, of course they have more of it than you, who only get what happens at the moment to be uppermost in my mind. It's good fun, though. I like to get in a corner and have half a dozen round me and feel a little excited, and make 'em all laugh, and see the women look and wonder what is going on. I tell you, if I *should* give my mind to it, wouldn't I do a thing or two? Nevertheless I get horribly bored. We have so much company evenings. I long for quiet. At a party, when you get tired of one you can go to another, but at home you must entertain people as long as they choose to stay, and the more entertaining you are, you know, the longer they choose to stay. However, it's all very well, and after I am gone home I dare say I shall look back with regret sometimes upon the very things that tire me now. You needn't suppose, however, that I am going to vegetate in Hamilton; not a bit of it. The "Congregationalist" want me to help them; they will give me a salary of from $400 to $600 per annum for work that Mr. Dexter thinks will take only about a day or a day and a half a week.[11] I should go to Boston twice a week. I told him I wouldn't make any engagement about it, but I would see when I got home. I think I should like it. I like *him,* so we shouldn't probably come into unpleasant collision. He wrote me also last week. I think it will give you the best view of the case to copy from his letter, which I will do, leaving out unnecessary episodes. He says the Tract Society were asking him to write books for them, and he couldn't, because he had so much to do, and they began to explain their immense and peculiar need of spicy books when "I said to them, 'If you want books of that sort I can perhaps direct you to a young lady who may do something for you in that line, though her time is, and *is to be,* very much taken up in other directions.' 'You mean Miss Gail Hamilton?' 'Yes.' Whereat I was buttonholed and taken into the private room, and a suction hose applied to ascertain what, how far, etc., I knew of the aforesaid G. H.'s plans, and particularly with reference to the engrossment of her time. I didn't 'run' at all freely, but returned the compliment by applying *my* hose and inquiring what they wanted to know for. They were reticent, whereat I ventured to hint to them that, on further consideration, I doubted whether you would be able to do anything for them, that measures were in progress, that I had, in fact, made you a *quasi* offer, and that negotiations were pending between us which would probably count *them* out. Then they took me into another private room, and Alvord frankly stated that they were after you, and *must* have you, that he had seen Mrs. Cowles and Mr. Bannister, and had interested them in the great work which the T. S. was wanting to have done, and which nobody on earth *but* you could do, and they thought you would be glad to come to New England and have some permanent home and engagements, and he was on the point of writing to you to broach the matter, winding up by a pathetic appeal to me to 'use my influence' and let them have you. I only pumped further. '*How* did they want you?' Well, if they could get the whole of your time to write the books and write for the 'Child's Paper,' etc., they wouldn't probably mind giving you $1,000 or $1,200 per annum if you wanted it. I told them that in all human probability you would not make any such arrangement, that you did not need to tie yourself up in that way, that you could get money enough by your pen without any such hampering, and, further, that I doubted if you would have anything to do with them anyway. I *did* tell him, however, that if anybody could do anything with you I flattered myself *I* could, and that I did think *I* could prevail on you to aid them *some,* that I thought it very possible, in connection with your other work, you might be willing every month or two to write them a little book (in their large type and small pages you could write a book in two or three days any time). He then begged *me* to write you and intercede, and beg, and plead with you on their behalf, and said he wouldn't write to you about it till I had written and heard from you. I said I would write." I wrote to Mr. Dexter that I was amazed at their audacity, that I would do it for $1,200 just as soon as I would for $12,000, and for the Tract Soc. just as soon as I would for the Angel Gabriel or Beelzebub, and no sooner, that the very fact that I was willing to put my brain in pawn would show that my brain wasn't worth pawning, that I would write stories, and if they liked 'em they might have 'em, but I didn't believe they would, and that I would not write to suit them, and I would not make any engagement, and if I did I would break it the first thing.

So the case stands. It would be murder—the idea of my selling myself body and soul to write children's stories! I'd rather have less money and be able to call my soul my own. I haven't said a word of this to anybody but you. I'm afraid if father knew I had refused a salary of $1,200, he would go crazy, so be sure you don't lisp a syllable of it in your letters. I shouldn't tell you only you are so far off. I shall tell mother and Augusta when I go home. For that matter, if I live, it will probably be a great deal better, even in a pecuniary point of view, that I should not make such an engagement, but, good or bad, I won't make it. It will probably not be decided what I shall do till I go home. I mean about the "Congregationalist" and all. I will tell you when it is. I am thinking now of starting for home on the first of April, but I may not so soon. I intend to be about three weeks on the way.

Did you see anything in the March "Atlantic" that sounded like me? I am generally reputed to have written "The Pursuit of Knowledge under Difficulties." I'm not married and I don't think I shall be. I can't afford the time, and besides, the men ought to be given to the women who can't get along without 'em. I can support myself, and so I think I'd better do it. Besides, I have a greater "run" among the men themselves than if I were married. Now I am independent and every man is my "humble servant." If I were married I should be dependent upon the caprices of one. An unmarried woman has an immense advantage over the married woman. You think I "may have seen women on New Year's day, but I make no mention of them." My dear, I like women. In fact, I esteem them very highly, but I bag higher game—when I can. Women do to fall back upon, but for first choice, give me a brace of bearded men.

I don't believe I shall come to Minnesota this summer. First of all, I want quiet and rest more than anything else. Second, there is so much to be done that I don't believe I can get away conveniently. Thirdly, this paper business will be new and I shall want to be on hand in order to see about it. Fourthly, I don't believe I shall have money, for Mrs. Bailey has not paid me a cent since I have been here and I don't believe she will or is able, so I have had to take my C—money.[12] I am afraid I shall have to stay at home and write *one or two books* before I do much of anything. I should like to go very much, both to see you and the country and for the journey's sake.

[HAMILTON, MASS.] May 7

MY DEAR FRIEND [HENRY JAMES SR.]:[13]

. . . Just one word more about the book. Do believe, if you can find it in your heart to do so, that I am better than it. I think I am better than any book I ever wrote, or, I fear, any that I ever shall write. Nothing satisfies me. I catch glimpses of the beautiful Truth. I know I hear her voice and feel her coming, but I only lay hold of the hem of her robe as she passes by, and I have but a fragment and a fragrance. The lovely form escapes me. Nevertheless, I can do no otherwise than seek her, for it seems to me that the search for truth is better than the possession of all other treasures. *You* will surely not do me the injustice to suppose that I launch my advice and opinions from any assumed superiority of character or position. In fact, I do not know that I ever analyzed my motives, or thought much about it anyway. I write because I do write, because I must write, because I will write. Yet nothing that I have ever written has seemed to me adequate when it was accomplished. My life gives me great joy, but also great unrest.

I am not sure that what I have said will indicate to you what I mean, but perhaps your own experience, or imagination, may help you to the meaning. I have talked a great deal about myself in this letter, but then what is the use of writing letters if you cannot talk about yourself. At least this is true, that it is the one subject in the world of which I know more than any one else, and one in which I must confess that I feel extremely interested!

It is the most charming evening possible, and I am going to Boston to-morrow, and to Ashburton Place, which I know, because I once had a friend there, and I shall leave a parcel in the front entry which will be this letter, and a book, and perhaps something else. So will you please stay quietly in the house till I am safely away from it. I suppose I might send a lad with it, and perhaps I will. We will see.

Good-night.

Very truly yours,

MARY ABBY DODGE.

[HAMILTON, MASS.] [March 1865]

[MY DEAR FRIEND [HENRY JAMES]:]

Men with all their badnesses are so susceptible of goodness that simple sincerity will shame all their badness out of sight. Meet them on the ground of their best and they will give you no other ground to stand on. If I judged men only by their relations to my own self, I should hardly have a word to say. They may be ever so wrong-headed, but practically they always turn to me right-hearted. I only see what men are at their worst by looking at them as you look at faint stars—obliquely. What men are to their wives, to their dependents, that men are. They are capable of better things, but that they are. The time languishes because woman cannot reveal herself. The great burden of material life, which her shoulders were never made to bear, weighs down upon her, and the whole creation groans and travails in pain as a consequence. With the consent and by the interference of the great mass of men the ox, the mule, the draught horse is regnant in the female man, and the woman is held in abeyance. How *can* she reveal herself? If you will use fine gold for pots and kettles, how can you cause that they shall not be disguised with crock?

Look at me. I have friends on every side who delight in me, men and women who come to me for joy, and solace, and strength. Is it because I am better, or brighter, or stronger than other women? Not the least in the world. I am constantly meeting women whose shoes' latchets I am not worthy to unloose, but to whom nobody ever comes. It is solely because I have never been overborne by hard physical labor, nor undermined by the unspeakable disappointments of marriage. God has suffered me to keep my life in my own right hand. I have never been crushed—I have never been oppressed. These other women, better than I, with more capacity than I, with higher possibilities than I, are mere household drudges, insignificant wives, uncommanding mothers, because they are buried under an Ossa on Pelion piled, of degrading labor without supporting love.[14] They passed in their youth under the yoke of a man, and the yoke was hard and the burden heavy. And just as long as their necks are bowed to them, women cannot reveal themselves. The sole advantage that I have over other women is, that I stand in the sunshine. If I were married the chances are ninety-nine in a hundred that I should be digging in the dark, down in a cellar where all the dead-alive women are. People are accustomed to see beasts of burden, and, accordingly, when they see me, a woman, they are pleased with the novelty.

You understand, Mr. Henry James, I think you are deeply and thoroughly right in your main idea. I do not remember that I ever met a man, hardly a woman, whose underlying principle was so satisfactory, so ultimate, so restful as yours. So far as I come in contact with men, they unconsciously swerve into my orbit,—never mind if the metaphors *don't* "go on all fours,"—because I am a woman under full headway; and in the collision of sincerity with falsehood, or perhaps I ought to say error, the error must go down. When a man comes so near me that I can touch him, he cannot help himself, but turns into pure gold—or at least the pure gold that existed in him in solution is precipitated into visibility; and if I were a wandering Jewess, and could be the wife of every man I see, I never would touch pen to paper to reform the world. Mind, I could not have done it if I had married him before I had myself waked to consciousness, but I could do it now. But you see that is impossible; so I can only do the next best thing, and work for men and women at a disadvantage.

What woman does for you, Mr. James, is to "put your spiritual instincts on the research of infinite things" by her "formal loveliness, grace, and tenderness." But suppose by the severity of your exactions you mar her loveliness, maim her grace, and forbid her tenderness? Suppose you impel her downward so entirely that even her own spiritual instincts are well-nigh lost, and all her soul becomes of the earth, is it encouraging rivalry between the sexes for me to tell you so? When we see a man beating his wife, will you stand apart and talk to him of "vivified selfhood." and shall I flow around him in silver silence? Not a bit of it! I will double up my fist, and give him one good, sharp, stinging blow between his eyes, and if it knocks him down so much the better. Nine men out of ten are so pachydermatous that they don't know they are touched unless they are felled. Then, while he lies conscience-smitten, his wife may proceed to array herself in white robes, and his own outraged spirit shall return to him again. I will pour in oil and wine, you shall feed him with your heavenly manna, and presently we shall have him sitting with his wife clothed in fitting garments and in his right mind. But till the beast within him is stabbed, all your music of the skies is but as the clatter of sounding brass and tinkling cymbals.

Can you not see that I am as far as possible from instituting any rivalry between the sexes or aiding any battle? I am for peace, for harmony, for unity. I do believe that the world is a failure because it has been so exclusively man's world; but then I believe it would have been just as much a failure if it had been exclusively woman's world. The world's work needs to be done by man and woman together. But by world's work I do not mean simply digging canals and hewing stone, but making of earth heaven, which surely can be done, for the kingdom of God is within you. In science, art, politics, is there no spiritual truth and beauty hidden under all this coarse outward seeming? I verily believe there is, and that it will throw off its cerements and rise into lovely life when the virgin-born Messiah bids it come forth. In the treatment of science and politics the womanly element has had hitherto little part. We should have fared just as ill had the manly element been omitted; but when both are brought to bear on the same end, though not perhaps in the same way, we shall see how that which was so base and dull held in its ungainly bosom the very brightness of the firmament.

Is this rivalry between the sexes?

The thorn-tree will never produce figs, but since God made it, it must have its uses, which we will discover, and its beauty, which we may learn to love. The paving-stones will never be rubies, but they may become very precious stones when they bear up the feet that are swift to do only good. You say that men recognize women as God's shrine in our nature only, etc., etc., as they are content to make home sweet and holy. Content—*content*—why, it is the one sole longing and love of women to make home holy and sweet. They have no other thought or desire, and all that these women want is the possibility to make it so.

And I belong to the woman's rights women. I belong to all—to those who suffer, and those who, however, clumsily, are trying to mitigate suffering. The brawniest Amazon that ever stalked over the pavement, the vilest harlot that ever crouched in the cellars beneath it—I belong to them all. I have not gone through the world with my heart naked, shuddering against all the world's woes, and quivering with all its pain, that I should gather my skirts from the dust and walk softly away to green pastures and still waters. I am pure, I am blameless only just so far as I go down into these sad places and pour over them all a warm, human sympathy. If I hug my virtue, away in some vale of Tempe, I am of all creatures most vile.[15] What shall be my thank-offering to God for having set my feet on a dry place, if not unceasing effort to help all struggling souls to come up hither to me and breathe with me the pure air and stand by my side in the sweet sunshine?

[HAMILTON, MASS.] JUNE 30, 1865.

[MY DEAR MR. WOOD:][16]

A lady came to me in the cars and asked if this was Miss Hamilton? I said no. Had I been thought to resemble her? Not that I ever heard of! Oh! why she asked was because she was going to The Laurels, and she thought I might be going, too, and she feared she might have taken the wrong day. I said *I* was going to The Laurels, too, and it was all right. You should have seen the breathless attention and astonishment of Messrs. Benson and Cutler during the colloquy, which I maintained with the utmost frankness and gravity. "Why," said Mr. Benson when she had gone, "doesn't she mean Gail Hamilton?" "I don't know what she meant," I replied emphatically, "I only answered what she said." They agreed I should make a good lawyer. At Mr. Spalding's I found Lucy Larcom and a Professor Webster. After talking awhile he asked me if I lived in Newburyport. I said no, I lived in Hamilton. What! you are not Gail Hamilton? Oh! no, not at all. Well, I *was* entirely different from the idea he had formed—but being from the town of Hamilton he did not know but that, etc., etc. Lucy Larcom opened wide eyes at me, but I went on talking, and it all passed off. It was a fine day and we went to The Laurels in a steamer and two gondolas lashed to its sides. Maria Mitchell, the astronomer, was there, about fifty or so, iron gray hair in curls, dark and rather masculine complexion, fine eyes, peculiar mouth, rather full lips, talks rapidly and a little recklessly like me—saucy and witty, and funny and entirely original—and very natural—and gives you an idea of strength—not in the least seminary-ish, or teacher-ish, or fine lady-ish, or pedantic. Mrs. Oliver was there also, my Lynn friend, with Mrs. John B. Alley, Mrs. Bubier, sister of Mrs. Sewell Annable, Julia Hayes, Lucy Everett, Abner Goodell, and three hundred more, and Whittier. He was in tolerable health and good spirits—saw the [James T.] Fields at Campton, had a poem read, which I told him I could have written if I had only thought of it, and he wished I had read it. The number of my admirers was quite wonderful to see, but, as I remarked to Whittier, it is sometimes convenient to be lionized, because you get so well waited on. Miss Mitchell brought her niece to me, remarking that she was of the gushing age, and just silly enough to be enthusiastically carried away by me. Going home Professor Webster edged himself in by me and brought forward Professor Park's "respectable man," declaring that he supposed I denied my identity in the same way.[17] I assured him that I never denied my identity—that my name was on the town records and I always answered to it. Nevertheless he expressed his own and his wife's regard for me, and I sent her a spray of laurel. Mr. Todd was there and had sent me by letter the night before a five-hundred dollar Treasury note and a ten-dollar bill—but unfortunately not payable till two years after a treaty of peace between the United and the Confederate States.

[HAMILTON, MASS.] APRIL 13, 1867.

[TO MR. WILLIAM FRENCH?:][18]

"It is done. Clang of bells and roar of gun send the tidings up and down."

My dear
They are here.
But oh!
Woe! woe!
Is me
To see
Myself as others see me.

I dare say they are good likenesses, but it is cruel in you to want to perpetuate them. The good God made *me,* and we cannot help ourselves, but he never made photographs, and State sovereignty extends over them. They are good pictures as art. I have not shown them and shall not show them to any one. On no account let Mrs. F. see them, and above all things keep me from being hung on the public gallows. Believe me if I ever hear of these being seen anywhere, if they ever get into so small a public, it will be a lasting annoyance to me. My only objection is that they look just like me, and when I wish to be transparent and see only life and the world, why should you seize and fix me, an opaque body, to "stain the white radiance of eternity" withal?[19] Now, I beg you at once to destroy them body and soul,—negative and positive,—and write and tell me so. Then let us saints forget we have bodies till we are good enough to go to heaven and be clothed upon with immortality.

I shall not go to Boston again to have my picture taken till it is warm enough to wear a white dress so I need not be obliged to discard my own clothes and be folded in a rag that has wrapped Egyptian mummies in Thebes' street three thousand years ago, for aught I know. I think that is one reason I looked so cross. I felt uncomfortable and ill-placed, and then I am cross besides, and my pitch-forked vision does not mend the matter. Do try and hunt up those missing photographs. Do I look like that, I wonder? I stay at home among mine own people and am full of other things and forget all about myself till I go out into the world, and then every once in a while I somehow get a glimpse of facts and am scared back again. This photograph is one of the glimpses.

Mr. Fields wants me to have the book—a few chapters—printed in the "Atlantic," before publishing in book form.[20] He affirms that it is capital, and that when he is reading it he has to roll himself up into a ball and roll round the street to relieve himself. I don't think very favorably of his plan, and I hardly think I shall agree to it. I think it will have more dignity as a book than as a series of articles. Mr. Foster came over and planted peas, and we had a long conversation on intellect, ambition, books, social differences, in which we agree to a charm, both of us being eminently sensible.

[HAMILTON, MASS.] JUNE 17, 1867.

[MY DEAR MR. WOOD?:]

Just as we were sitting down to dinner the bell rang, and Professor and Mrs. Stowe appeared at the door. They had ridden from Andover to Georgetown, and from G. here, and were to go back to G. to dinner at five. They stayed till near four o'clock. The first half hour I did not like her. After she came out to her lunch she glowed up and was very simple, natural, agreeable, and entertaining. About half an hour before she went away she gave out again and was silent, but I understood it and did not mind. He rallied her and declared she had not come up to his expectations. She told me coming out that the fact was she had talked just as much as she could, but of course as she had come twenty-five miles she was tired. She is plain at first sight, but not after five minutes. Her face is very attractive and her smile charming and sometimes very expressive. When she was silent it said a great deal. She said Professor Stowe was gone to Canada before she got home from Florida and she had not seen the critter since February. They are not going to sell their Hartford house, but only going to Florida, winters. She says he has been round at a great rate trading on female sensibilities over going to Florida, and making people think he was the most abused man in the world. They are evidently very happy together.

[HAMILTON, MASS.] MARCH 23, 1868.

[MY DEAR MR. WOOD:]

Your characterization of Dickens tallies admirably with that of another friend of mine, but did not you enjoy his reading? I did, and mean to hear him again. I wish you were here to go with me, and then you could amuse yourself between whiles with raving against Boston infidelity. I have had a little experience of it in one shape lately. I discovered quite accidentally that ten per cent. on the retail price of books is the minimum price paid to authors. As my books have brought me only from six and two-thirds to seven and one-half per cent. I laid the case before a lawyer friend, who has made investigations among the book men, which results in a conviction that I have been underpaid, and I have broken off connection with my publishers. Of course, it was not a thing to be lightly done, and I have not done it lightly. It began in December, and is only just completed—and hardly that. But where I have been on terms of such intimate friendship I cannot come down to mere business relations. Mr. ——— [Fields] had the matter entirely in his own hands. I never questioned, or proposed, or bargained, and that he should have gone on, year after year, paying me less than a new author has, paying me from one-third to one-half less than the lowest market price, is not a thing to be overlooked. I desire you not to speak of this to any one. There is no occasion as yet for its being known. I should not have told you, only I thought it probably must one day come out, and you might feel aggrieved at knowing it only as the general public knows it. I have acted in this according to the advice of learned and apparently disinterested friends.

[HAMILTON, MASS.] MAY 11. [1868.]

[MY DEAR MR. WOOD:]

It is not simply because a personal relation is at an end that I discontinue a business relation. Mr. ——— [Fields] has not merely vanished from my regard so that the place which once knew him knows him no more. He dug his way out with a rough and relentless spade, so that the soil all along is loosened and the ground treacherous, and I know not in what pit I should sink if I walked that way. And in his wild journey-work he upturned so many earth-worms and unearthed venomous creeping things and revealed nests of unclean and hateful birds till I turn away shuddering, and want that chasm to be filled with gravel and covered with loam and veiled with turf, and until the grass grows green and the dandelions shine above it I shall not feel that the earth is sweet and wholesome again. I have no indignation towards Mr. ———. There is no Mr. ———. He is evaporated. He squirmed out of my sight one day, and in his stead I saw some one before me with a mean face and ophidian eyes and puny voice uplift, who would have pulled the thunderbolts of Jove down upon me and did not see that they were knitting-needles forged in his own small smithy, and back-acting machinery at that. *That* is not the man I cared for at all. The man I cared for has departed this life. He never came into it. He never was born. I am not half so vexed with Mr. ——— as I am with myself. He could not be, but I ought to have seen. I had eyes to begin with. And I worshipped a golden calf. I did not think he was a lion, but I did think he was a sprightly, agreeable, amusing, and friendly and virtuous beast. When he began to bleat, I found he was a jackal.

We have but one mail a day, and if I were writing to Jerusalem my letters would go to Boston first. All letters come to me at nine in the morning. All letters go from me to Boston at 12 M. by mail. But possibly I can mail this at the station, which is why I write with a running pen, and I will give you the rest when I see you, but you must see for yourself simple—*sine plica* as you are, that this is no matter of sentiment but of fact. What little sentiment there was died out long ago from loss of blood which never was red. And I don't believe it is for my money interest, anyway, to stay with them.

My house is all cellar over garret and a lime-kiln at that. A furnace was put in yesterday, and the house was not burnt down last night. I had nine men at work yesterday,—in three sets,—and I—I beg your pardon—I—bossed them all! Now don't lay that word up against me, and I wish I never had anything to do but order men round! One of my nine men is in a constant drunkenness, and gives me more trouble than the other eight.

HAMILTON, MASS., SEPTEMBER 7, 1877.

MR. H. L. ENSIGN, *Managing Editor "Alliance"*:

[. . .] I always lay out my work by reducing my editors to subjection. It is impossible to accomplish anything so long as an editor is liable to pop up at the critical moment with a will of his own; when he is properly subjected the rest is easy!

[. . .] The only reason that I cannot form an alliance offensive and defensive with you is because you are poor, and I am a saint and martyr to the one fixed principle never to write except for the highest price. I know nothing of your finances except what may be inferred from the nature of things, but a religious and radical and new newspaper, it stands to reason, cannot be rich, so I rub my hands together in the most unscriptural manner and say, Depart in peace, be ye warmed and filled, but give you not that which is needful. When your ship comes home from sea, oh! whistle and I'll come to you, my lad! But so long as you cultivate literature on a little oatmeal, bless you, my children, bless you, but leave me my fatted calf!

With heroic self-denial,

Always truly,

M. A. D.

[CLIPPING.]

At the founding of the American Authors' Society Grace Greenwood—Mrs. Lippincott—told a pathetic story of swindling from which there seems to be no redress, and Gail Hamilton sent to Mrs. Hodges a letter which is no less entertaining than suggestive. Here it is:

[SPRING 1891.]

DEAR MADAM: I thank you very much for the honor of the Vice-Presidency which you wish to confer upon me, but I must continue to decline it for the simple reason that I should not be able to perform any service.

I will do a great deal better for you than that. I will send you a "Battle of the Books" which will show you that I was fighting for your Authors' Club while you were all rocking in your respective cradles.

When your combination has learned that book by heart and is ready to pass a competitive examination on it, *you* will know whether *I* fear to "jeopardize personal interests by open movement," or "shrink from responsibility."

If you think I am a little inclined to be skeptical as to results, you will not wonder when I tell you that in this very history of my Holy War, though I was previously assured that a sale of one thousand copies would pay costs, and though some fifteen hundred copies were sold, the facts and the figures were somehow twisted into such a contra-dance as to put me seven hundred and fifty dollars on the debit side, above all product of sales, for "expenses of publication!"

I admit that I am skeptical of results. I have lately published a book—"A Washington Bible Class." It has been a great literary success. I speak as a fool, but ye have compelled me. It has received the highest commendation from the highest literary and even theologico-scientific authorities in the country. It has been discussed in the pulpits and distributed in the Sunday-schools. An *édition de luxe* of seventy-five copies has been issued by private beneficence for private circulation. Now, though I speak great swelling words to the publishers of being satisfied with nothing less out of the book than my house and barn repainted, and a wind-mill for the well, and a new harness for St. Cuthbert,—the best family horse in Essex County, and not for sale, either, and *such* an appetite, eating me out of house and home every minute of his dear life,—yet, speaking as a wise man confidentially to the Authors, I confess that in spite of your efforts and mine, I shall be surprised if the author receives as much money for the brain-work of the book as the publishers receive for the de luxe work. With best wishes.

GAIL HAMILTON.

COUNTRY LIVING AND COUNTRY THINKING

PREFACE

I KNOW that I can bear censure; I think I could endure neglect: but there is one thing which I will never forgive, and that is, any encroachment upon my personality. Whatever an author puts between the two covers of his book is public property; whatever of himself he does not put there is his private property, as much as if he had never written a word. I do not say, that any information which may be gathered, or any conjecture which may be hazarded, concerning the man or the woman who stands behind the mask of the author, may not be a lawful theme of conversation, if people are interested enough to make it so; but the appearance of any such information or conjecture in any public print, whether in the form of book-notice or news-item, I consider an unpardonable impertinence.

As this seems to me a matter of serious importance in the minor moralities, and one in which this people is verily guilty, I desire to be clearly understood. If any person writes a book or an article, and prefixes his name, he, in a manner, makes an unconditional surrender of himself. The public has perhaps the shadow of a right to ascertain and announce his birth-place, his residence, his wife, the color of his eyes, the length of his beard, the precocity of his childhood, the college at which he was graduated, the hotel in which he is spending the summer months, and similar items—startling, if true—which are so dear to the public. But if he withholds himself, and writes under the signature of Apsby Jones, you, my dear

Public, have no right or title to him. That is an indication that he wishes to remain unknown. You should respect his reticence. Though you may have heard from your brother-in-law or your grandmother that Apsby Jones is a Mr. Jonathan Jenkins of Kettleville, refrain scrupulously from printing that report; for in the first place, you have probably been misinformed,—Jonathan Jenkins is not the man at all, and is made to feel extremely uncomfortable; and, in the second place, if he were the man, it would be shamefully impolite in you to rend away the veil in which he chose to drape himself. You may criticise his book to the top of your bent, but don't meddle with him. No matter if he was your schoolmate, no matter if he descended from a French refugee, no matter if he made a speech at your picnic; you be quiet about it,—at least till he is dead. Doubtless he was very glad to have his book published, but doubtless he has insurmountable objections to being published himself.

This is a preface, Public, and you will readily see that I cannot talk as freely as I should like, because it will never do to put you in an ill-humor at the beginning; but you must know, yourself, that you are very much given to illegal gossip. You have a *cacoethes* print*endi.* The moment you get hold, by fair means or foul, of the outermost fibre of the shred of the husk of the semblance of a fact, you go straightway and put it in the newspapers. You are not so much to blame. Your fathers did it before you, and I don't suppose you were ever told that it was ill-bred; but it is. Please not do it again. Be very sure to know whether the name on the title-page is a pen-name or a baptismal name. If it is the former, confine your remarks to the book and its relations; if it is the latter—you cannot do better than follow the same course.

I most eagerly desire, O Public, your good opinion, and especially your friendly feeling. I shall count it one of the greatest happinesses of my life if I succeed in pleasing you, and one of the greatest misfortunes if I do not. But if you commit this sin against me, I will never forgive you! Or, since that may be unscriptural, I will forgive you just enough to save my own soul, but not enough to be of any use to you.

Country Living and Country Thinking

MY GARDEN

I CAN speak of it calmly now; but there have been moments when the lightest mention of those words would sway my soul to its profoundest depths.

I am a woman. You may have inferred this before; but I now desire to state it distinctly, because I like to do as I would be done by, when I can just as well as not. It rasps a person of my temperament exceedingly to be deceived. When any one tells a story, we wish to know at the outset whether the story-teller is a man or a woman. The two sexes awaken two entirely distinct sets of feelings, and you would no more use the one for the other than you would put on your tiny teacups at breakfast, or lay the carving-knife by the butter-plate. Consequently it is very exasperating to sit, open-eyed and expectant, watching the removal of the successive swathings which hide from you the dusky glories of an old-time princess, and, when the unrolling is over, to find it is nothing after all, but a great lubberly boy. Equally trying is it to feel your interest clustering round a narrator's manhood, all your individuality merging in his, till, of a sudden, by the merest chance, you catch the swell of crinoline, and there you are. Away with such clumsiness! Let us have everybody christened before we begin.

I do, therefore, with Spartan firmness, depose and say that I am a woman. I am aware that I place myself at signal disadvantage by the avowal. I fly in the face of hereditary prejudice. I am thrust at once beyond the pale of masculine sympathy. Men will neither credit my success nor lament my failure, because they will consider me poaching on their manor. If I chronicle a big beet, they will bring forward one twice as large. If I mourn a deceased squash, they will mutter, "Woman's farming!" Shunning Scylla, I shall perforce fall into Charybdis.[1] (*Vide* Classical Dictionary. I have lent mine, but I know one was a rock and the other a whirlpool, though I cannot state, with any definiteness, which was which.) I may be as humble and deprecating as I choose, but it will not avail me. A very agony of self-abasement will be no armor against the poisoned shafts which assumed superiority will hurl against me. Yet I press the arrow to my bleeding heart, and calmly reiterate, I am a woman.

The full magnanimity of which reiteration can be perceived only when I inform you that I could easily deceive you, if I chose. There is about my serious style a vigor of thought, a comprehensiveness of view, a closeness of logic, and a terseness of diction, commonly supposed to pertain only to the stronger sex. Not wanting in a certain fanciful sprightliness which is the peculiar grace of woman, it possesses also, in large measure, that concentrativeness which is deemed the peculiar strength of man. Where an ordinary woman will leave the beaten track, wandering in a thousand little by-ways of her own,—flowery and beautiful, it is true, and leading her airy feet to "sunny spots of greenery" and the gleam of golden apples, but keeping her not less surely from the goal,—I march straight on, turning neither to the right hand nor to the left, beguiled into no side-issues, discussing no collateral question, but with keen eye and strong hand aiming right at the heart of my theme. Judge thus of the stern severity of my virtue. There is no heroism in denying ourselves the pleasures which we cannot compass. It is not self-sacrifice, but self-cherishing, that turns the dyspeptic alderman away from turtle-soup and the *pâté de foie gras* to mush and milk. The hungry newsboy, regaling his nostrils with the scents that come up from a subterranean kitchen, does not always know whether or not he is honest, till the cook turns away for a moment, and a steaming joint is within reach of his yearning fingers. It is no credit to a weak-minded woman not to be strong-minded and write poetry. She could not if she tried; but to feed on locusts and wild honey that the soul may be in better condition to fight the truth's battles,—to go with empty stomach for a clear conscience' sake,—to sacrifice intellectual tastes to womanly duties, when the two conflict,—

> "That's the true pathos and sublime,
> Of human life."[2]

You will, therefore, no longer withhold your appreciative admiration, when, in full possession of what theologians call the power of contrary choice, I make the unmistakable assertion that I am a woman.

Hope told a flattering tale when, excited and happy, but not sated with the gayeties of a sojourn among urban and urbane friends, I set out on my triumphal march from the city of my visit to the estate of my adoption. Triumphal indeed! My pathway was strewed with roses. Feathery asparagus and the crispness of tender lettuce waved dewy greetings from every railroad-side; green peas crested the racing waves of Long Island Sound, and unnumbered carrots of gold sprang up in the wake of the ploughing steamer; till I was wellnigh drunk with the new wine of my own purple vintage. But I was not ungenerous. In the height of my innocent exultation, I remembered the dwellers in cities who do all their gardening at stalls, and in my heart I determined, when the season should be fully blown, to invite as many as my house could hold to share with me the delight of plucking strawberries from their stems and drinking in foaming health from the balmy-breathed cows. Moreover, in the exuberance of my joy, I determined to go still further, and despatch to those doomed ones who cannot purchase even a furlough from burning pavements baskets of fragrance and sweetness. I pleased myself with pretty conceits. To one who toils early and late in an official Sahara, that the home-atmosphere may always be redolent of perfume, I would send a bunch of long-stemmed white and crimson rose-buds, in the midst of which he should find a dainty note whispering, "Dear Fritz: drink this pure glass of my overflowing June to the health of weans and wife, not forgetting your unforgetful friend." To a pale-browed, sad-eyed woman, who flits from velvet carpets and broidered flounces to the bedside of an invalid mother whom her slender fingers and unslender and most godlike devotion can scarcely keep this side the pearly gates, I would heap a basket of summer-hued peaches smiling up from cool, green leaves into their straitened home, and with eyes, perchance, tear-dimmed, she should read, "My good Maria, the peaches are to go to your lips, the bloom to your cheeks, and the gardener to your heart." Ah me! How much grace and gladness may bud and blossom in one little garden! Only three acres of land, but what a crop of sunny surprises, unexpected tenderness, grateful joys, hopes, loves, and restful memories!—what wells of happiness, what sparkles of mirth, what sweeps of summer in the heart, what glimpses of the Upper Country!

Halicarnassus was there before me (in the garden, I mean, not in the spot last alluded to).[3] It has been the one misfortune of my life that Halicarnassus got the start of me at the outset. With a fair field and no favor I should have been quite adequate to him. As it was, he was born and began, and there was no resource left to me but to be born and follow, which I did as fast as possible; but that one false move could never be redeemed. I know there are shallow thinkers who love to prate of the supremacy of mind over matter,—who assert that circumstances are plastic as clay in the hands of the man who knows how to mould them. They clench their fists, and inflate their lungs, and quote Napoleon's proud boast,—"Circumstances! I *make* circumstances!" Vain babblers! Whither did this Napoleonic idea lead? To a barren rock in a waste of waters. Do we need St. Helena and Sir Hudson Lowe to refute it?[4] Control circumstances! I should like to know if the most important circumstance that can happen to a man is not to be born? and if that is under his control, or in any way affected by his whims and wishes? Would not Louis XVI. have been the son of a goldsmith, if he could have had his way? Would Burns have been born a slaving, starving peasant, if he had been consulted beforehand? Would not the children of vice be the children of virtue, if they could have had their choice? and would not the whole tenor of their lives have been changed thereby? Would a good many of us have been born at all, if we could have helped it? Control circumstances, forsooth! when a mother's sudden terror brings an idiot child into the world,—when the restive eye of his great-grandfather, whom he never saw, looks at you from your two-year-old, and the spirit of that roving ancestor makes the boy also a fugitive and a vagabond on the earth! No, no. We may coax circumstances a little, and shove them about, and make the best of them, but there they are. We may try to get out of their way; but they will trip us up, not once, but many times. We may affect to tread them under foot in the daylight, but in the night-time they will turn again and rend us. All we can do is first to accept them as facts, and then reason from them as premises. We cannot control them, but we can control our own use of them. We can make them a savor of life unto life, or of death unto death.

Application.—If mind could have been supreme over matter, Halicarnassus should, in the first place, have taken the world at second-hand from me, and, in the second place, he should not have stood smiling on the front-door steps when the coach set me down there. As it was, I made the best of the one case by following in his foot-steps,—not meekly, not acquiescently, but protesting, yet following,—and of the other, by smiling responsive and asking pleasantly,—

"Are the things planted yet?"

"No," said Halicarnassus.

This was better than I had dared to hope. When I saw him standing there so complacent and serene, I felt certain that a storm was brewing, or rather had brewed, and burst over my garden, and blighted its fair prospects. I was confident that he had gone and planted every square inch of the soil with some hideous absurdity, which would spring up a hundredfold in perpetual reminders of the one misfortune to which I have alluded.

So his ready answer gave me relief, and yet I could not divest myself of a vague fear, a sense of coming thunder. In spite of my endeavors, that calm, clear face would lift itself to my view as a mere "weather-breeder"; but I ate my supper, unpacked my trunks, took out my papers of precious seeds, and, sitting in the flooding sunlight under the little western porch, I poured them into my lap, and bade Halicarnassus come to me. He came, I am sorry to say, with a pipe in his mouth.

"Do you wish to see my jewels?" I asked, looking as much like Cornelia as a little woman somewhat inclined to dumpiness can.[5]

Halicarnassus nodded assent.

"There," said I, unrolling a paper, "that is *Lychnidea acuminata.* Sometimes it flowers in white masses, pure as a baby's soul. Sometimes it glows in purple, pink, and crimson, intense, but unconsuming, like Horeb's burning bush.[6] The old Greeks knew it well, and they baptized its prismatic loveliness with their sunny symbolism, and called it the Flame-Flower. These very seeds may have sprung centuries ago from the hearts of heroes who sleep at Marathon; and when their tender petals quiver in the sunlight of my garden, I shall see the gleam of Attic armor and the flash of royal souls. Like heroes, too, it is both beautiful and bold. It does not demand careful cultivation,—no hot-house tenderness—"

"I should rather think not," interrupted Halicarnassus. "Pat Curran has his front-yard full of it."

I collapsed at once, and asked, humbly,—

"Where did he get it?"

"Got it anywhere. It grows wild almost. It's nothing but phlox. My opinion is, that the old Greeks knew no more about it than that brindled cow."

Nothing further occurring to me to be said on the subject, I waived it, and took up another parcel, on which I spelled out, with some difficulty, "*Delphinium exaltatum.* Its name indicates its nature."

"It's an exalted dolphin, then, I suppose," said Halicarnassus.

"Yes!" I said, dexterously catching up an *argumentum ad hominem,* "it *is* an exalted dolphin,—an apotheosized dolphin,—a dolphin made glorious. For, as the dolphin catches the sunbeams and sends them back with a thousand added splendors, so this flower opens its quivering bosom and gathers from the vast laboratory of the sky the purple of a monarch's robe, and the ocean's deep, calm blue. In its gracious cup you shall see—"

"A fiddlestick!" jerked out Halicarnassus, profanely. "What are you raving about such a precious bundle of weeds for? There isn't a shoemaker's apprentice in the village that hasn't his seven-by-nine garden overrun with them. You might have done better than bring cart-loads of phlox and larkspur a thousand miles. Why didn't you import a few hollyhocks, or a sunflower or two, and perhaps a dainty slip of cabbage? A pumpkin-vine, now, would climb over the front-door deliciously, and a row of burdocks would make a highly entertaining border."

The reader will bear me witness that I had met my first rebuff with humility. It was probably this very humility that emboldened him to a second attack. I determined to change my tacties, and give battle.

"Halicarnassus," said I, severely, "you are a hypocrite. You set up for a Democrat—"

"Not I," interrupted he; "I voted for Harrison in '40, and for Fremont in '56, and—"

"Nonsense!" interrupted I, in turn; "I mean a Democrat etymological, not a Democrat political. You stand by the Declaration of Independence, and believe in liberty, equality, and fraternity, and that all men are of one blood; and here you are, ridiculing these innocent flowers, because their brilliant beauty is not shut up in a conservatory, to exhale its fragrance on a fastidious few, but blooms on all alike, gladdening the home of exile and lightening the burden of labor."

Halicarnassus saw that I had made a point against him, and preserved a discreet silence.

"But you are wrong," I went on, "even if you are right. You may laugh to scorn my floral treasures, because they seem to you common and unclean, but your laughter is premature. It is no ordinary seed that you see before you. It sprang from no profane soil. It came from the—the—some kind of an office at WASHINGTON, sir! It was given me by one whose name stands high on the scroll of fame,—a statesman whose views are as broad as his judgment is sound,—an orator who holds all hearts in his hand,—a man who is always found on the side of the feeble truth against the strong falsehood,—whose sympathy for all that is good, whose hostility to all that is bad, and whose boldness in every righteous cause, make him alike the terror and abhorrence of the oppressor, and the hope and joy and staff of the oppressed."

"What is his name?" said Halicarnassus, phlegmatically.

"And for your miserable pumpkin-vine," I went on, "behold this morning-glory, that shall open its barbaric splendor to the sun and mount heavenward on the sparkling chariots of the dew. I took this from the white hand of a young girl in whose heart poetry and purity have met, grace and virtue have kissed each other,—whose feet have danced over lilies and roses, who has "known no sterner duty than to give caresses," and whose gentle, spontaneous, and ever-active loveliness continually remind me that of such is the kingdom of heaven."

"Courted yet?" asked Halicarnassus, with a show of interest.

I transfixed him with a look, and continued,—

"This *Maurandia,* a climber, it may be common or it may be a king's ransom. I only know that it is rosy-hued, and that I shall look at life through its pleasant medium. Some fantastic trellis, brown and benevolent, shall knot supporting arms around it; and day by day it shall twine daintily up toward my southern window, and whisper softly of the sweet-voiced, tender-eyed woman from whose fairy bower it came in rosy wrappings. And this *Nemophila,* 'blue as my brother's eyes,'—the brave young brother whose heroism and manhood have outstripped his years, and who looks forth from the dark leafiness of far Australia lovingly and longingly over the blue waters, as if, floating above them, he might catch the flutter of white garments and the smile on a sister's lip—"

"What are you going to do with 'em?" put in Halicarnassus again.

I hesitated a moment, undecided whether to be amiable or bellicose under the provocation, but concluded that my ends would stand a better chance of being gained by adopting the former course, and so answered seriously, as if I had not been switched off the track, but was going on with perfect continuity,—

"To-morrow I shall take observations. Then, where the situation seems most favorable, I shall lay out a garden. I shall plant these seeds in it, except the vines and such things, which I wish to put near the house to hide as much as possible its garish white. Then, with every little tender shoot that appears above the ground, there will blossom also a pleasant memory, or a sunny hope, or an admiring thrill."

"What do you expect will be the market-value of that crop?"

"Wealth which an empire could not purchase," I answered, with enthusiasm. "But I shall not confine my attention to flowers. I shall make the useful go with the beautiful. I shall plant vegetables,—lettuce, and asparagus, and—so forth. Our table shall be garnished with the products of our own soil, and our own works shall praise us."

There was a pause of several minutes, during which I fondled the seeds, and Halicarnassus enveloped himself in clouds of smoke. Presently there was a cessation of puffs, a rift in the cloud showed that the oracle was opening his mouth, and directly thereafter he delivered himself of the encouraging remark,—

"If we don't have any vegetables till we raise 'em, we shall be carnivorous for some time to come."

It was said with that provoking indifference more trying to a sensitive mind than downright insult. You know it is based on some hidden obstacle, palpable to your enemy, though hidden from you,—and that he is calm because he knows that the nature of things will work against you, so that he need not interfere. If I had been less interested, I would have revenged myself on him by remaining silent; but I was very much interested, so I strangled my pride and said,—

"Why not?"

"Land is too old for such things. Soil isn't mellow enough."

I had always supposed that the greater part of the main-land of our continent was of equal antiquity, and dated back alike to the alluvial period; but I suppose our little three acres must have been injected through the intervening strata by some physical convulsion, from the drift, or the tertiary formation, perhaps even from the primitive granite.

"What are you going to do?" I ventured to inquire. "I don't suppose the land will grow any younger by keeping."

"Plant it with corn and potatoes for at least two years before there can be anything like a garden."

And Halicarnassus put up his pipe and betook himself to the house,—and I was glad of it, the abominable bore!—to sit there and listen to my glowing schemes, knowing all the while that they were soap-bubbles. "Corn and potatoes," indeed! I didn't believe a word of it. Halicarnassus always had an insane passion for corn and potatoes. Land represented to him so many bushels of the one or the other. Now corn and potatoes are very well in their way, but, like every other innocent indulgence, carried too far, become a vice; and I more than suspected he had planned the strategy simply to gratify his own weakness. Corn and potatoes, indeed!

But when Halicarnassus entered the lists against me, he found an opponent worthy of his steel. A few more such victories would be his ruin. A grand scheme fired and filled my mind during the silent watches of night, and sent me forth in the morning, jubilant with high resolve. Alexander might weep that he had no more worlds to conquer; but I would create new. Archimedes might desiderate a place to stand on, before he could bring his lever into play; I would move the world, self-poised.[7] If Halicarnassus fancied that I was cut up, dispersed, and annihilated by one disaster, he should weep tears of blood to see me rise, Phoenix-like, from the ashes of my dead hopes, to a newer and more glorious life. Here, having exhausted my classics, I took a long sweep down to modern times, and vowed in my heart never to give up the ship.

Halicarnassus saw that a fell purpose was working in my mind, but a certain high tragedy in my aspect warned him to silence; so he only dogged me around the corners of the house, eyed me askance from the wood-shed, and peeped through the crevices of the demented little barn. But his vigilance bore no fruit. I but walked moodily "with folded arms and fixed eyes," or struck out new paths at random, so long as there were any vestiges of his creation extant. His time and patience being at length exhausted, he went into the field to immolate himself with ever new devotion on the shrine of corn and potatoes. Then my scheme came to a head at once. In my walking, I had observed a box about three feet long, two broad, and one foot deep, which Halicarnassus, with his usual disregard of the proprieties of life, had used to block up a gateway that was waiting for a gate. It was just what I wanted. I straightway knocked out the few nails that kept it in place, and, like another Samson, bore it away on my shoulders. It was not an easy thing to manage, as any one may find by trying,—nor would I advise young ladies, as a general thing, to adopt that form of exercise,—but the end, not the means, was my object, and by skilful diplomacy I got it up the back-stairs and through my window, out upon the roof of the porch directly below. I then took the ash-pail and the fire-shovel, and went into the field, carefully keeping the lee-side of Halicarnassus. "Good, rich loam" I had observed all the gardening books to recommend; but wherein the virtue or the richness of loam consisted I did not feel competent to decide, and I scorned to ask. There seemed to be two kinds: one black, damp, and dismal; the other fine, yellow, and good-natured. A little reflection decided me to take the latter. Gold constituted riches, and this was yellow like gold. Moreover, it seemed to have more life in it. Night and darkness belonged to the other, while the very heart of sunshine and summer seemed to be imprisoned in this golden dust. So I plied my shovel and filled my pail again and again, bearing it aloft with joyful labor, eager to be through before Halicarnassus should reappear; but he got on the trail just as I was whisking up-stairs for the last time, and shouted, astonished,—

"What are you doing?"

"Nothing," I answered, with that well-known accent which says, "Everything! and I mean to keep doing it."

I have observed, that, in managing parents, husbands, lovers, brothers, and indeed all classes of inferiors, nothing is so efficacious as to let them know at the outset that you are going to have your own way. They may fret a little at first, and interpose a few puny obstacles, but it will be only a temporary obstruction; whereas, if you parley and hesitate and suggest, they will but gather courage and strength for a formidable resistance. It is the first step that costs. Halicarnassus understood at once from my one small shot that I was in a mood to be let alone, and he let me alone accordingly.

I remembered he had said that the soil was not mellow enough, and I determined that my soil should be mellow, to which end I took it up by handfuls and squeezed it through my fingers, completely pulverizing it. It was not disagreeable work. Things in their right places are very seldom disagreeable. A spider on your dress is a horror, but a spider out-doors is rather interesting. Besides, the loam had a fine, soft feel that was absolutely pleasant; but a hideous black and yellow reptile with horns and hoofs, that winked up at me from it, was decidedly unpleasant and out of place, and I at once concluded that the soil was sufficiently mellow for my purposes, and smoothed it off directly. Then, with delighted fingers, in sweeping circles, and fantastic whirls, and exact triangles, I planted my seeds in generous profusion, determined, that, if my wilderness did not blossom, it should not be from niggardliness of seed. But even then my box was full before my basket was emptied, and I was very reluctantly compelled to bring down from the garret another box, which had been the property of my great-grandfather. My great-grandfather was, I regret to say, a barber. I would rather never have had any. If there is anything in the world besides worth that I reverence, it is ancestry. My whole life long have I been in search of a pedigree, and though I run well at the beginning, I invariably stop short at the third remove by running my head into a barber's shop. If he had only been a farmer, now, I should not have minded. There is something dignified and antique in land, and no one need trouble himself to ascertain whether "farmer" stood for a close-fisted, narrow-souled clodhopper, or the smiling, benevolent master of broad acres. Farmer means both these, I could have chosen the meaning I liked, and it is not probable that any troublesome facts would have floated down the years to intercept any theory I might have launched. I would rather he had been a shoemaker; it would have been so easy to transform him, after his lamented decease, into a shoe-manufacturer,—and shoe-manufacturers, we all know, are highly respectable people, often become great men, and get sent to Congress. An apothecary might have figured as an M.D. A green-grocer might have been sublimated into a merchant. A dancing-master would flourish on the family records as a professor of the Terpsichorean art. A taker of daguerrotype portraits would never be recognized in "my great-grandfather *the artist*." But a barber is unmitigated and immitigable. It cannot be shaded off, nor toned down, nor brushed up. Besides, was greatness ever allied to barberity? Shakespeare's father was a wool-driver, Tillotson's a clothier, Barrow's a linen-draper, Defoe's a butcher,

Milton's a scrivener, Richardson's a joiner, Burns's a farmer; but did any one ever hear of a barber's having remarkable children? I must say, with all deference to my great-grandfather, that I do wish he would have been considerate enough of his decendants' feelings to have been born in the old days when barbers and doctors were one, or else have chosen some other occupation than barbering. Barber he did, however; in this very box he kept his wigs, and, painful as it was to have continually before my eyes this perpetual reminder of plebeian great-grand-paternity, I consented to it rather than lose my seeds. Then I folded my hands in sweet, though calm satisfaction. I had proved myself equal to the emergency, and that always diffuses a glow of genial complacency through the soul. I had outwitted Halicarnassus. Exultation number two. He had designed to cheat me out of my garden by a story about land, and here was my garden ready to burst forth into blossom under my eyes. He said little, but I knew he felt deeply. I caught him one day looking out at my window with corroding envy in every lineament. "You might have got some dust out of the road; it would have been nearer." That was all he said. Even that little I did not fully understand.

I watched, and waited, and watered, in silent expectancy, for several days, but nothing came up, and I began to be anxious. Suddenly I thought of my vegetable-seeds, and determined to try those. Of course a hanging kitchen-garden was not to be thought of, and as Halicarnassus was fortunately absent for a few days, I prospected on the farm. A sunny little corner on a southern slope smiled up at me, and seemed to offer itself as a delightful situation for the diminutive garden which mine must be. The soil, too, seemed as fine and mellow as could be desired. I at once captured an Englishman from a neighboring plantation, hurried him into my corner, and bade him dig me and hoe me and plant me a garden as soon as possible. He looked blankly at me for a moment, and I looked blankly at him, wondering what lion he saw in the way.

"Them is planted with potatoes now," he gasped, at length.

"No matter," I returned, with sudden relief to find that nothing but potatoes interfered. "I want it to be unplanted, and planted with vegetables,—lettuce and—asparagus—and such."

He stood hesitating.

"Will the master like it?"

"Yes," said Diplomacy, "he will be delighted."

"No matter whether he likes it or not," codiciled Conscience. "You do it."

"I—don't exactly like—to—take the responsibility," wavered this modern Faint-Heart.

"I don't want you to take the responsibility," I ejaculated, with volcanic vehemence. "I'll take the responsibility. You take the hoe!"

These duty-people do infuriate me. They are so afraid to do anything that isn't laid out in a right-angled triangle. Every path must be graded and turfed before they dare set their scrupulous feet in it. I like conscience, but, like corn and potatoes, carried too far, it becomes a vice. I think I could commit a murder with less hesitation than some people buy a ninepenny calico. And to see that man stand here, balancing probabilities over a piece of ground no bigger than a bed-quilt, as if a nation's fate were at stake, was enough to ruffle a calmer temper than mine. My impetuosity impressed him, however, and he began to lay about him vigorously with hoe and rake and lines, and, in an incredibly short space of time, had a bit of square flatness laid out with wonderful precision. Meanwhile I had ransacked my vegetable-bag, and, though lettuce and asparagus were not there, plenty of beets and parsnips and squashes, etc. were. I let him take his choice. He took the first two. The rest were left on my hands. But I had gone too far to recede. They burned in my pocket for a few days, and I saw that I must get them into the ground somewhere. I could not sleep with them in the room. They were wandering shades, craving at my hands a burial, and I determined to put them where Banquo's ghost would not go,—down.[8] Down accordingly they went, but not symmetrically nor simultaneously. I faced Halicarnassus on the subject of the beet-bed, and though I cannot say that either of us gained a brilliant victory, yet I can say that I kept possession of the ground; still, I did not care to risk a second encounter. So I kept my seeds about me continually, and dropped them surreptitiously as occasion offered. Consequently, my garden, taken as a whole, was located where the Penobscot Indian was born,—"all along shore." The squashes were scattered among the corn. The beans were tucked under the brushwood, in the fond hope that they would climb up it. Two tomato-plants were lodged in the potato-field, under the protection of some broken apple-branches dragged thither for the purpose. The cucumbers went down on the sheltered side of a wood-pile. The peas took their chances of life under the sink-nose. The sweet-corn was marked off from the rest by a broomstick,—and all took root alike in my heart.

May I ask you now, O friend, who, I would fain believe, have followed me thus far with no hostile eyes, to glide in tranced forgetfulness through the white blooms of May and the roses of June, into the warm breath of July afternoons and the languid pulse of August, perhaps even into the mild haze of September and the "flying gold" of brown October? In narrating to you the fruition of my hopes, I shall endeavor to preserve that calm equanimity which is the birthright of royal minds. I shall endeavor not to be unduly elated by success nor unduly depressed by failure, but to state in simple language the result of my experiments, both for an encouragement and a warning. I shall give the history of the several ventures separately, as nearly as I can recollect in the order in which they grew, beginning with the humbler ministers to our appetites, and soaring gradually into the region of the poetical and the beautiful.

BEETS.—The beets came up, little red-veined leaves, struggling for breath among a tangle of Roman wormwood and garlic; and though they exhibited great tenacity of life, they also exhibited great irregularity of purpose. In one spot there would be nothing, in an adjacent spot a whorl of beets, big and little, crowding and jostling and elbowing each other, like schoolboys round the red-hot stove on a winter's morning. I knew they had been planted in a right line, and I don't even now comprehend why they should not come up in a right line. I weeded them, and though freedom from foreign growth discovered an intention of straightness, the most casual observer could not but see that skewiness had usurped its place. I repaired to my friend the gardener. He said they must be thinned out and transplanted. It went to my heart to pull up the dear things, but I did it, and set them down again tenderly in the vacant spots. It was evening. The next morning I went to them. Flatness has a new meaning to me since that morning. You can hardly conceive that anything could look so utterly forlorn, disconsolate, disheartened, and collapsed. In fact, they exhibited a degree of depression so entirely beyond what the circumstances demanded, that I was enraged. If they had shown any symptoms of trying to live, I could have sighed and forgiven them; but, on the contrary, they had flopped and died without a struggle, and I pulled them up without a pang, comforting myself with the remaining ones, which throve on their companions' graves, and waxed fat and full and crimson-hearted, in their soft, brown beds. So delighted was I with their luxuriant rotundity, that I made an internal resolve that henceforth I would always plant beets. True, I cannot abide beets. Their fragrance and their flavor are alike nauseating; but they come up, and a beet that will come up is better than a cedar of Lebanon that won't. In all the vegetable kingdom I know of no quality better than this, growth,—nor any quality that will atone for its absence.

PARSNIPS.—They ran the race with an indescribable vehemence that fairly threw the beets into the shade. They trod so delicately at first that I was quite unprepared for such enthusiasm. Lacking the red veining, I could not distinguish them from the weeds with any certainty, and was forced to let both grow together till the harvest. So both grew together, a perfect jungle. But the parsnips got ahead, and rushed up gloriously, magnificently, bacchanalianly,—as the winds come when forests are rended,—as the waves come when navies are stranded. I am, indeed, troubled with a suspicion that their vitality has all run to leaves, and that, when I go down into the depths of the earth for the parsnips, I shall find only bread of emptiness. It is a pleasing reflection that parsnips cannot be eaten till the second year. I am told that they must lie in the ground during the winter. Consequently it cannot be decided whether there are any or not till next spring. I shall in the mean time assume and assert, without hesitation or qualification, that there are as many tubers below the surface as there are leaves above it. I shall thereby enjoy a pleasant consciousness, and the respect of all, for the winter; and if disappointment awaits me in the spring, time will have blunted its keenness for me, and other people will have forgotten the whole subject. You may be sure I shall not remind them of it.

CUCUMBERS.—The cucumbers came up so far, and stuck. It must have been innate depravity, for there was no shadow of reason why they should not keep on as they began. They did not. They stopped growing in the prime of life. Only three cucumbers developed, and they hid under the vines so that I did not see them till they were become ripe, yellow, soft, and worthless. They are an unwholesome fruit at best, and I bore their loss with great fortitude.

TOMATOES.—Both dead. I had been instructed to protect them from the frost by night and from the sun by day. I intended to do so ultimately, but I did not suppose there was any emergency. A frost came the first night and killed them, and a hot sun the next day burned up all there was left. When they were both thoroughly dead, I took great pains to cover them every night and noon. No symptoms of revival appearing to reward my efforts, I left them to shift for themselves. I did not think there was any need of their dying in the first place; and if they would be so absurd as to die without provocation, I did not see the necessity of going into a decline about it. Besides, I never did value plants or animals that have to be nursed, and petted, and coaxed to live. If things want to die, I think they'd better die. Provoked by my indifference, one of the tomatoes flared up, and took a new start,—put forth leaves, shot out vines, and covered himself with fruit and glory. The chickens picked out the heart of all the tomatoes as soon as they ripened, which was of no consequence, however, as they had wasted so much time in the beginning that the autumn frosts came upon them unawares, and there wouldn't have been fruit enough ripe to be of any account, if no chicken had ever broken a shell.

SQUASHES.—They appeared above-ground, large-lobed and vigorous. Large and vigorous appeared the bugs, all gleaming in green and gold, like the wolf on the fold, and stopped up all the stomata and ate up all the parenchyma, till my squash-leaves looked as if they had grown for the sole purpose of illustrating net-veined organizations. In consternation I sought again my neighbor the Englishman. He assured me he had 'em on his, too,—lots of 'em. This reconciled me to mine. Bugs are not inherently desirable, but a universal bug does not indicate special want of skill in any one. So I was comforted. But the Englishman said they must be killed. He had killed his. Then I said I would kill mine, too. How should it be done? O, put a shingle near the vine at night, and they would crawl upon it to keep dry, and go out early in the morning and kill 'em. But how to kill them? Why, take 'em right between your thumb and finger and crush 'em!

As soon as I could recover breath, I informed him confidentially, that, if the world were one great squash, I wouldn't undertake to save it in that way. He smiled a little, but I think he was not overmuch pleased. I asked him why I couldn't take a bucket of water and dip the shingle in it and drown them. He said, well, I could try it. I did try it,—first wrapping my hand in a cloth to prevent contact with any stray bug. To my amazement, the moment they touched the water they all spread unseen wings and flew away, safe and sound. I should not have been much more surprised to see Halicarnassus soaring over the ridge–pole. I had not the slightest idea that they could fly. Of course I gave up the design of drowning them. I called a council of war. One said I must put a newspaper over them and fasten it down at the edges; then they couldn't get in. I timidly suggested that the squashes couldn't get out. Yes, they could, he said,—they'd grow right through the paper. Another said I must surround them with round boxes with the bottoms broken out; for, though they could fly, they couldn't steer, and when they flew up they just dropped down anywhere, and as there was on the whole a good deal more land on the outside of the boxes than on the inside, the chances were in favor of their dropping on the outside. Another said that ashes must be sprinkled on them. A fourth said lime was an infallible remedy. I began with the paper, which I secured with no little difficulty; for the wind—the same wind, strange to say—kept blowing the dirt at me and the paper away from me; but I consoled myself by remembering the numberless rows of squash-pies that should crown my labors, and May took heart from Thanksgiving. The next day I peeped under the paper, and the bugs were a solid phalanx. I reported at head-quarters, and they asked me if I killed the bugs before I put the paper down. I said no, I supposed it would stifle them,—in fact, I did not think anything about it, but if I had thought anything, that was what I thought. I was not pleased to find I had been cultivating the bugs and furnishing them with free lodgings. I went home, and tried all the remedies in succession. I could hardly decide which agreed best with the structure and habits of the bugs, but they throve on all. Then I tried them all at once and all o'er with a mighty uproar. Presently the bugs went away. I am not sure that they would have gone just as soon, if I had let them alone. After they were gone, the vine scrambled out and put forth some beautiful, deep-golden blossoms. When they fell off, that was the end of them. Not a squash,—not one,—not a single squash,—not even a pumpkin. They were all false blossoms.

APPLES.—The trees swelled into masses of pink and white fragrance. Nothing could exceed their fluttering loveliness or their luxuriant promise. A few days of fairy beauty, and showers of soft petals floated noiselessly down, covering the earth with delicate snow; but I knew, that, though the first blush of beauty was gone, a mighty work was going on in a million little laboratories, and that the real glory was yet to come. I was surprised to observe, one day, that the trees seemed to be turning red. I remarked to Halicarnassus that that was one of Nature's processes which I did not remember to have seen noticed in any botanical treatise. I thought such a change did not occur till autumn. Halicarnassus curved the thumb and forefinger of his right hand into an arch, the ends of which rested on the wrist of his left coat-sleeve. He then lifted the forefinger high and brought it forward. Then he lifted the thumb and brought it up behind the forefinger, and so made them travel up to his elbow. It seemed to require considerable exertion in the thumb and forefinger, and I watched the progress with interest. Then I asked him what he meant by it.

"That's the way they walk," he replied.

"Who walk?"

"The little fellows that have squatted on our trees."

"What little fellows do you mean?"

"The canker-worms?"

"How many are there?"

"About twenty-five decillions, I should think, as near as I can count."

"Why! what are they for? What good do they do?"

"O, no end. Keep the children from eating green apples and getting sick."

"How do they do that?"

"Eat 'em themselves."

A frightful idea dawned upon me. I believe I turned a kind of ghastly blue.

"Halicarnassus, do you mean to tell me that the canker-worms are eating up our apples, and that we shan't have any?"

"It looks like that exceedingly."

That was months ago, and it looks a great deal more like it now. I watched those trees with sadness at my heart. Millions of brown, ugly, villanous worms gnawed, gnawed, gnawed, at the poor little tender leaves and buds,—held them in foul embrace,—polluted their sweetness with hateful breath. I could almost feel the shudder of the trees in that slimy clasp,—could almost hear the shrieking and moaning of the young fruit that saw its hope of happy life thus slowly consuming; but I was powerless to save. For weeks that loathsome army preyed upon the unhappy, helpless trees, and then spun loathsomely to the ground, and buried itself in the reluctant, shuddering soil. A few dismal little apples escaped the common fate; but when they rounded into greenness and a suspicion of pulp, a boring worm came and bored them, and they too died. No apple-pies at Thanksgiving. No apple-roasting in winter evenings. No pan-pie with hot brown bread on Sunday mornings.

CHERRIES.—They rivalled the apple-blooms in snowy profusion, and the branches were covered with tiny balls. The sun mounted warm and high in the heavens, and they blushed under his ardent gaze. I felt an increasing conviction that here there would be no disappointment; but it soon became palpable that another class of depredators had marked our trees for their own. Little brown toes could occasionally be seen peeping from the foliage, and little bare feet left their print on the garden-soil. Humanity had evidently deposited its larva in the vicinity. There was a school-house not very far away, and the children used to draw water from an old well in a distant part of the garden. It was surprising to see how thirsty they all became as the cherries ripened. It was as if the village had simultaneously agreed to breakfast on salt fish. Their wooden bucket might have been the urn of the Danaïdes, judging from the time it took to fill it.[9] The boys were as fleet of foot as young zebras, and presented upon discovery no apology or justification but their heels,—which was a wise stroke in them. A troop of rosy-cheeked, bright-eyed little snips in white pantalets, caught in the act, reasoned with in a semicircle, and cajoled with candy, were as sweet as distilled honey, and promised with all their innocent hearts and hands not to do so any more.

Then the cherries were allowed to hang on the trees and ripen. It took them a great while. If they had been as big as hogsheads, I should think the sun might have got through them sooner than he did. They looked ripe long before they were so; and, as they were very plenty, the trees presented a beautiful appearance. I bought a stack of fantastic little baskets from a travelling Indian tribe, at a fabulous price, for the sake of fulfilling my long-cherished design of sending fruit to my city friends. After long waiting, Halicarnassus came in one morning with a tin pail full, and said that they were ripe at last, for they were turning purple and falling off; and he was going to have them gathered at once. He had brought in the first-fruits for breakfast. I put them in the best preserve-dish, twined it with myrtle, and set it in the centre of the table. It looked charming,—so ruddy and rural and Arcadian. I wished we could breakfast out-doors; but the summer was one of unusual severity, and it was hardly prudent thus to brave its rigor. We had cup-custards at the close of our breakfast that morning,—very vulgar, but very delicious. We reached the cherries at the same moment, and swallowed the first one simultaneously. The effect was instantaneous and electric. Halicarnassus puckered his face into a perfect wheel, with his mouth for the hub. I don't know how I looked, but I felt badly enough.

"It was unfortunate that we had custards this morning," I remarked. "They are so sweet that the cherries seem sour by contrast. We shall soon get the sweet taste out of our mouths, however."

"That's so!" said Halicarnassus, who *will* be coarse.

We tried another. He exhibited a similar pantomime, with improvements. My feelings were also the same, intensified.

"I am not in luck to-day," I said, attempting to smile. "I got hold of a sour cherry this time."

"I got hold of a bitter one," said Halicarnassus.

"Mine was a little bitter, too," I added.

"Mine was a little sour, too," said Halicarnassus.

"We shall have to try again," said I.

We did try again.

"Mine was a good deal of both this time," said Halicarnassus. "But we will give them a fair trial."

"Yes," said I, sepulchrally.

We sat there sacrificing ourselves to abstract right for five minutes.

Then I leaned back in my chair, and looked at Halicarnassus. He rested his right elbow on the table, and looked at me.

"Well," said he at last, "how are cherries and things?"

"Halicarnassus," said I, solemnly, "it is my firm conviction that farming is not a lucrative occupation. You have no certain assurance of return, either for labor or capital invested. Look at it. The bugs eat up the squashes. The worms eat up the apples. The cucumbers won't grow at all. The peas have got lost. The cherries are bitter as wormwood and sour as you in your worst moods. Everything that is good for anything won't grow, and everything that grows isn't good for anything."

"My Indian corn, though," began Halicarnassus; but I snapped him up before he was fairly under way. I had no idea of traveling in that direction.

"What am I to do with all those baskets that I bought, I should like to know?" I asked, sharply.

"What did you buy them for?" he asked in return.

"To send cherries to the Hudsons and the Mavericks and Fred Ashley," I replied promptly.

"Why don't you send 'em, then? There's plenty of them,—more than we shall want."

"Because," I answered, "I have not exhausted the pleasures of friendship. Nor do I perceive the benefit that would accrue from turning life-long friends into life-long enemies."

"I'll tell you what we can do," said Halicarnassus. "We can give a party and treat them to cherries. They'll have to eat 'em out of politeness."

"Halicarnassus," said I, "we should be mobbed. We should fall victims to the fury of a disappointed and enraged populace."

"At any rate," said he, "we can offer them to chance visitors."

The suggestion seemed to me a good one,—at any rate, the only one that held out any prospect of relief. Thereafter, whenever friends called singly or in squads,—if the squads were not large enough to be formidable,—we invariably set cherries before them, and with generous hospitality pressed them to partake. The varying phases of emotion which they exhibited were painful to me at first, but I at length came to take a morbid pleasure in noting them. It was a study for a sculptor. By long practice I learned to detect the shadow of each coming change, where a casual observer would see only a serene expanse of placid politeness. I knew just where the radiance, awakened by the luscious, swelling, crimson globes, faded into doubt, settled into certainty, glared into perplexity, fired into rage. I saw the grimace, suppressed as soon as begun, but not less patent to my preternaturally keen eyes. No one deceived me by being suddenly seized with admiration of a view. I knew it was only to relieve his nerves by making faces behind the window-curtains.

I grew to take a fiendish delight in watching the conflict, and the fierce desperation which marked its violence. On the one side were the forces of fusion, a reluctant stomach, an unwilling æsophagus, a loathing palate; on the other, the stern, unconquerable will. A natural philosopher would have gathered new proofs of the unlimited capacity of the human race to adapt itself to circumstances, from the *débris* that strewed our premises after each fresh departure. Cherries were chucked under the sofa, into the table-drawers, behind the books, under the lamp-mats, into the vases, in any and every place where a dexterous hand could dispose of them without detection. Yet their number seemed to suffer no abatement. Like Tityus's liver, they were constantly renewed, though constantly consumed.[10] The small boys seemed to be suffering from a fit of conscience. In vain we closed the blinds and shut ourselves up in the house to give them a fair field. Not a cherry was taken. In vain we went ostentatiously to church all day on Sunday. Not a twig was touched. Finally I dropped all the curtains on that side of the house, and avoided that part of the garden in my walks. The cherries may be hanging there to this day, for aught I know.

BUT WHY do I thus linger over the sad recital? *"Ab uno disce omnes."* (A quotation from Virgil: means, "All of a piece.") There may have been, there probably was, an abundance of sweet-corn, but the broomstick that had marked the spot was lost, and I could in no wise recall either spot or stick. Nor did I ever see or hear of the peas—or the beans. If our chickens could be brought to the witness-box, they might throw light on the subject. As it is, I drop a natural tear, and pass on to

THE FLOWER-GARDEN.—It appeared very much behind time,—chiefly Roman wormwood. I was grateful even for that. Then two rows of four-o'-clocks became visible to the naked eye. They are cryptogamous, it seems. Botanists have hitherto classed them among the Phænogamia. A sweet-pea and a china-aster dawdled up just in time to get frost-bitten. *"Et præterea nihil."* (Virgil: means, "That's all.") I am sure it was no fault of mine. I tended my seeds with assiduous care. My devotion was unwearied. I was a very slave to their caprices. I planted them just beneath the surface in the first place, so that they might have an easy passage. In two or three days they all seemed to be lying round loose on the top, and I planted them an inch deep. Then I didn't see them at all for so long that I took them up again, and planted them half-way between. It was of no use. You cannot suit people or plants that are determined not to be suited.

Yet, sad as my story is, I cannot regret that I came into the country and attempted a garden. It has been fruitful in lessons, if in nothing else. I have seen how every evil has its compensating good. When I am tempted to repine that my squashes did not grow, I reflect, that, if they had grown, they would probably have all turned into pumpkins, or if they had stayed squashes, they would have been stolen. When it seems a mysterious Providence that kept all my young hopes underground, I reflect how fine an illustration I should otherwise have lost of what Kossuth calls the solidarity of the human race,—what Paul alludes to, when he says, if one member suffer, all the members suffer with it.[11] I recall with grateful tears the sympathy of my neighbors on the right hand and on the left,—expressed not only by words, but by deeds. In my mind's eye, Horatio, I see again the baskets of apples, and pears, and tomatoes, and strawberries,—squashes too heavy to lift,—and corn sweet as the dews of Hymettus, that bore daily witness of human brotherhood.[12] I remember, too, the victory which I gained over my own depraved nature. I saw my neighbor prosper in everything he undertook. *Nihil tetigit quod non crevit.*[13] Fertility found in his soil its congenial home, and spanned it with rainbow hues. Every day I walked by his garden and saw it putting on its strength, its beautiful garments. I had not even the small satisfaction of reflecting that, amid all his splendid success, his life was cold and cheerless, while mine, amid all its failures, was full of warmth,—a reflection which, I have often observed, seems to go a great way towards making a person contented with his lot,—for he had a lovely wife, promising children, and the whole village for his friends. Yet, notwithstanding all these obstacles, I learned to look over his garden-wall with sincere joy.

There is one provocation, however, which I cannot yet bear with equanimity, and which I do not believe I shall ever meet without at least a spasm of wrath, even if my Christian character shall ever become strong enough to preclude absolute tetanus; and I do hereby beseech all persons who would not be guilty of the sin of Jeroboam who made Israel to sin,[14] who do not wish to have on their hands the burden of my ruined temper, to let me go quietly down into the valley of humiliation and oblivion, and not pester me, as they have hitherto done from all parts of the North-American continent, with the infuriating question, "How did you get on with your garden?"

MEN AND WOMEN

I HAVE READ that a stranger, passing through certain portions of New Hampshire, was deeply impressed with the rocky nature of the soil and scenery, and inquired of a laborer whom he met, "What in the world can you raise in a country like this?" "We raise men, sir!" was the prompt reply. I am free to confess that this sounds to me very much like a made-up story; but it will answer my purpose just as well, which is simply to introduce the fact, that, not having found in agricultural pursuits that eminent satisfaction which I had pictured, I occasionally divert myself with speculations touching men and women. After close observation and mature deliberation, I have come to the conclusion that, on the whole, men occupy vantage-ground.

I like women. I love them. I glory in them. What sight can be more impressive than one of those magnificent creations we often read of, and occasionally see,—stately, grand, epic,—with the blackness and beauty of night in the matchless locks that sweep over the calm, still brow, and all the starry splendor of a thousand nights in the eyes that burn beneath? What can be more captivating than the opening life of a gay little blonde, from whose soft curls the flutter never quite dies out, whose dimpling smile is only less sweet than her tender pensiveness? Or, passing from these types of an extinct womanhood, whose departing left but few traces, we see every day pretty, graceful, and elegant women; some neat, simple, and indistinctly limned; some standing out in bold relief, with regal adornings; and in our daily walks we jostle against countless heroines,—self-sacrificing wives, devoted mothers, noble maidens, who bear a hidden grief, who wrestle with a secret foe, who silently, if need be, brave the sneer of the world, who will die and give no sign,—and we cannot choose but admire. Still, narrowing the question down to a point, this is the conclusion of the whole matter,—high or low, rich or poor, bond or free,

There is nothing so splendid as a splendid man!

I need not search the pages of history for facts to confirm my position. I need not point you to Mozart, king in the realms of song; to Napoleon, "wrapped in the solitude of his own originality";[1] to John Bunyan, standing alone on his Delectable Mountains: to Milton, thrusting his wives behind him when he entered Paradise. They are confessedly unapproached and inapproachable, and therefore would in no wise strengthen my case; for they are unique, not as regards women only, but the whole human race. To be a man does not necessarily imply to be a Milton. Eighteen hundred years furnished but one Napoleon. John Smiths are born, married, and die by the thousand, and nothing apparently can be more commonplace than their lives. What advantage, then, has John Smith over his wife? Precisely this. Commonplace as is the life of John Smith, the life of Mrs. J. S. is still more so. Small as are his advantages and opportunities, hers are incomparably smaller; and so, whether as a man I might have sat in kings' palaces, or ground in the prison-house of poverty, I put on sackcloth and ashes, bewailing my womanhood.

Now don't overwhelm me with a torrent of platitudes about woman's opportunities for self-sacrifice, moral heroism, silent influence, might of love, and all that cut-and-dried woman's sphere-ism; pray don't. I know all about it. I could write an octavo volume on the subject, with dedication, introduction, preface, and appendix; but just go to your window the next rainy day, and notice the first woman who passes. See how she is forced to concentrate all the energies of mind and body on herself and her casings. One delicate hand clings desperately to the unwieldy umbrella; the other is ceaselessly struggling to keep firm hold of the multitudinous draperies; and if book, basket, or bundle claim a share of her attention, her case is pitiable indeed. Down goes one fold upon the wet flagstone, detected only by an ominous flapping against the ankles when the garment has become saturated,—a loosened hold on the umbrella, of which it takes advantage, and immediately sways imminent over the gutter,—a convulsive and random clutch at the petticoats. The umbrella righted, a sudden gust of wind threatens to bear it away, and, one hand not being sufficient to detain it, the other involuntarily comes to the rescue,—sweep go the draperies down on the pavement; then another clutch, another adjustment,—forward! march!—and so on to the dreary, draggled end.

Stalk—stalk—stalk—comes up the man behind her. Stalk—stalk,—he has passed. Stalk—stalk—stalk,—he is out of sight before she has passed a single block.

Of course he is. One sinewy hand lightly poising his umbrella; waterproof overcoat "close buttoned to the chin"; tight-fitting trousers tucked into enormous India-rubber boots. What is the storm to him?

Is this a small matter? Beloved friend, smaller matters than these have swayed the world; and ten thousand such small matters mark the childhood, youth, and maturity of twice ten thousand small men and women.

It is a very small matter for John Smith to take a journey of six or eight hundred miles. He rushes home from his counting-room, office, or workshop, fifteen minutes before the train leaves, bids Mrs. S. put a clean shirt or two in his valise, takes a cold luncheon, kisses the children all round, and perhaps their mother, strides to the station, goes in at one end just as the engine is puffing out at the other, waits leisurely till the last end of the last car is opposite him, throws his valise on the platform, grasps the railing, vaults lightly up the steps, and in half a minute is talking unconcernedly with Mr. Jones, who has probably gone through the same performance, barring the last half-minute.

But if Mrs. John Smith wishes to pay a ten days' visit to her mother, sixty miles away, a fortnight is not too much time to devote to preparations. Her wardrobe is to be thoroughly overhauled; dresses selected, bought, made; a dressmaker consequently to be hunted up and engaged; old skirts adjusted to new basques; collars mended, whitened, and clear-starched; Mr. Smith's shirts, stockings, and handkerchiefs placed where he can lay his hands on them blindfolded, for no Smith ever yet conceived the idea of lifting up one thing to find another under it: the various strata of rocks being tilted, the genus Smith seems to have imbibed the opinion that bureau-drawers should be arranged on the same plan. Then there are the children to be seen to, the marketing to be arranged, Bridget to be admonished, and everything in general wound up to go ten days without stopping or derangement. Consequently, when the appointed morning comes, and with it the appointed coach, Mrs. Smith is not quite ready. With one cheek flushed, and no collar, she gives hurried directions, ties up brown-paper packages with nervous, trembling fingers, which packages no sooner receive the final jerk than they are discovered to be bursting out at both ends; scatters the young folks hither and thither, running down all who are not agile enough to get out of the way, and is only restrained from scolding outright by a dim vision of plunges down embankments, butting against opposing engines, splintered bridges, flying axles, and life-long separation from beloved ones, to which a railroad journey now-a-days renders one so fearfully liable. At length, the last knot is tied, the last kiss given, and Mrs. S., anxiously looking at her watch, stumbles over the hem of her dress into the coach, beseeching the driver to hurry. He politely says "Yes," but persistently drives "No." After what she considers unnecessary delay, she arrives at the station, hurries into the ticket-office, tries to hurry open her portemonnaie, but, as that is governed by the Medo-Persic laws of inertia and attraction, it refuses to be hurried.[2] Hurriedly she asks the ticket-master, "Is the train north gone?" His loud, clear, deliberate, "No, ma'am," startles her, and before she recovers herself, he has gone to the opposite window. She waits her turn again. "How long before it goes?" "Twen-ty—min-utes,—ma'am." With a sigh of mingled relief and weariness she sinks upon a sofa. Time would fail me to follow Mrs. S. on her devious way,—to note her anxious watch over "great box, little box, band-box, and bundle"; her uncertainty as to which train she is to take, and her incessant inquiries of every man who approaches; the intense unrest that looks out of her eyes, quivers on her lips, trembles in her hands, and flutters in every thread of her garments. All these things may only provoke a smile, but Mrs. J. S. is tragically in earnest.

Man, too, is independent. He goes where and when he lists. He need not be rich to gaze upon all the wonders of the New World, all the magnificence of the Old. He can shoulder his knapsack, and traverse the globe. Every spot consecrated by genius, patriotism, suffering, love, is spread out before him. Whatever of beautiful, grand, or glorious is to be found in art or nature, is his. He can people his brain with memories that will never die, adorn it with pictures whose colors will never fade, treasure up untold wealth for his soul to feed on in future years.

If the day's long toil leave him restless,—if throbbing heart or aching head crave a draught of pure elixir,—if the murmur of the waterfall, the glow of the stars, or the ever-new splendor of the moon lure him out into the night, he goes; and the hush and solitude bring him rest and healing; the night sweeps into his soul, and cools the fever in his veins. The world recedes. He stands face to face with God. He receives again the breath of life, and becomes a living soul.

Alas for a woman! She can never do a thing except gregariously. She has no solitude except in the house, which is no solitude at all. She is always at the mercy of others' whims, caprices, tastes, business engagements, or headaches. If she travels, she must partially accommodate herself to somebody's convenience. She must go in the beaten track. Her eyes must look right on, and her eyelids straight before her. There are no wild wanderings at her own sweet will, no experimental deviations from the prescribed route, no hazardous but delightful flying off in a tangent on the spur of the moment. She cannot separate herself from the past, slough off her identity, and become a new being in new scenes. She must take her old associations with her, and they are a robe of oiled silk, effectually excluding the new atmosphere which should penetrate to the very sources of life. She cannot enjoy in quietness and silence. She is one of a party, and must go into a rapture here and an ecstasy there, and give a definite reason for both. She must be wakened from a trance of delight by a lisped "How beautiful!" or a quotation from Byron, by some one whose knowledge of Byron is derived from a gilt volume of "Elegant Extracts," or the "American First-Class Book." It is very exasperating.

I remember well the agonizing stupidity of a journey which I once undertook with great expectations. Halicarnassus was obliged to leave me on the road, and I contemplated a solitary completion of my expedition with unbounded delight; but at the very last moment he hunted up an old schoolmate, a planter from the South, and consigned me to him, ready invoiced and labelled! I yielded with a resigned and quiet despair.

He proved to be a very sensible man, and slept most of the time, except when I spoke to him, which I did occasionally for the sake of seeing him jump. He knew that it was not polite for him to sleep, but he cherished the pleasing illusion that I did not know it, but fancied him lost in profound meditation. Bless his dear soul! If he only could have known that it was the most agreeable disposition he could possibly have made of himself,—though, as far as my observation goes, men certainly look better awake than asleep. Slumber is not becoming to the masculine gender. Look at the next man you see asleep in church. What absolute lack of expression; what falling jaws; what idiocy in the bobbing head; what lack-lustre vacancy about the eyes and in the eyes, when they slowly drag themselves open; how senseless are the fingers, and how, when he awakes, he half looks about, and then suddenly looks straight at the minister for two minutes, and pretends he has been awake all the time, just as if everybody didn't know. It is as good as a pantomime. But I was glad my fellow-traveller slept, for our attempts at conversation were really distressing to a sensitive mind. He had a habit of receiving my most trifling remarks with an air of deep solemnity, which was very provoking. It is bad enough to say foolish things, and to know they are foolish when you say them; but it is a great deal worse to have people think that you think you have said something wise. Then he never would understand what I said the first time; consequently it had to be repeated. Now, when you are putting about in distress for a remark, you do often seize hold of any platitude, and give it audible utterance, despising yourself all the while; but after it has done duty, and you have shoved it from you in disgust, to be forced to stretch out your hand and draw it back once more. Eheu! Our conversation might be daguerrotyped thus:—

I. "This is a fine country."

He. "Ma'âm?"

I. "This is a fine country, I said!"

He. "Yes, a very fine country!" Pause. Profound meditation on both sides.

I. "Is that an eagle?" (with an attempt at animation).

He. "Ma'âm?" (with a start, and wild, bewildered look).

I. "I asked if that was an eagle, but he is gone now!" (Of course he was,—a mile off.)

He. "I don't know, really. I didn't quite see him." Relapse into meditation.

I. "Do we change cars at B———?"

He. "Ma'âm?"

I. "Do you know whether we change cars at B———, sir?"

He. "I don't know, but I think we do. I will ask the conductor!"

I. "O, no! Pray don't, sir! I dare say we shall find out when we get there." Third course of meditation, and so on.

Whenever we did have to change cars,—and it seemed to me as if this occurred at irregular intervals of from ten to twenty miles—(I desire to enter my earnest protest against it. One is scarcely seated comfortably, with valise and satchel on the floor, shawl on the arm, and bundles tucked on the rack, before "Passengers for ——— change cars"; and up must come the satchels with a jerk, and down the bundles with a thud, and off we elbow our way through a crowd, across a dusty track, into another car, where the same process is repeated. When people are satisfactorily adjusted, why can't people be let alone?) As I was saying, whenever we had to change, he was sure to be sound asleep, and I would spare his feelings and not wake him, knowing that the people jostling against him in passing would do that, and suddenly he would rouse, gaze wildly around, and exclaim, "Are you going to get out?" as if all the commotion was caused by me; and I would turn from the window at which I had been steadfastly staring, and answer calmly, and as if I had just thought of it, "Perhaps we would better, sir; the people seem to be getting out!" And so, by constant watchfulness and studied forbearance, I managed to pick up his goods for him, and land him safely at H———, with great respect for his many virtues, and great contempt for his qualifications as guide and protector.

Yet I was currently reported to be travelling *under the care* of Mr. Lakeman of Alabama; as if I couldn't take care of myself fifty thousand times better than that respectable stupidity could take care of me.

Men are strong. They do things, and don't mind it. They can open doors in the dampest weather. They can unstrap trunks without breaking a blood-vessel, turn keys in a moment which women have lost their temper and lamed their fingers over for half an hour, look down precipices and not be dizzy, knock each other prostrate and not be stunned. You may strike them with all your might on the chest, and it doesn't hurt them in the least (I mean if you are a woman). They never grow nervous and cry. They go up stairs three at a time. They put one hand on a four-rail fence, and leap it without touching. In short, they do everything easily which women try to do and cannot.

Moreover, men are so "easy to get along with." They are good-natured, and conveniently blind and benevolent. Women criticise you, not unjustly, perhaps, but relentlessly. They judge you in detail, men only in the whole. If your dress is neat, well-fitting, and well-toned, men will not notice it, except a few man-milliners, and a few others who ought to be, and to whose opinion we pay no regard. If you will only sit still, hold up your head, and speak when you are spoken to, you can be very comfortable. I do not mean that men cannot and do not appreciate female brilliancy; but if you are a good listener, and in the right receptive mood, you can spend an hour very pleasantly without it. But a woman finds out in the first three minutes that the fringe on your dress is not a match. In four, she has discovered that the silk of your sleeves is frayed at the edge. In five, that the binding of the heel of your boot is worn out. By the sixth, she has satisfactorily ascertained, what she suspected the first moment she "set her eyes on you," that you trimmed your bonnet yourself. The seventh assures her that your collar is only "imitation"; and when you part, at the end of ten minutes, she has calculated with tolerable accuracy the cost of your dress, has levelled her mental eyeglass at all your innocent little subterfuges, and knows to a dead certainty your past history, present circumstances, and future prospects. Well, what harm if she does? None in particular. It is only being stretched on the rack a little while. You have no reason to be ashamed, and you are not ashamed. Your boots are only beginning to be shabby, and we all know the transitory nature of galloon. Your fringe *is* too dark, but you ransacked the city and did your best, "angels could no more."[3] You trimmed your bonnet yourself, and saved two dollars, which was just what you intended to do. "The means were worthy, and the end was won." Your lace is *not* real, according to the cant of the shopkeepers; but it *is* real,—real cotton, real linen, real silk, or whatever the material may be, and you never pretended it was Honiton or point;[4] and if lace is soft and white and fine, and sets off the throat and wrists prettily, I don't see why it may not just as well be made in America for two cents a yard, as in Paris for two dollars, or two hundred. In fact, this whole matter of lace is something entirely beyond my comprehension. Why, I have seen women who, in the ordinary affairs of life, were neat to a fault, just not fall down and worship a bit of dingy, old yellow lace, that looked fit for nothing but the wash-tub; and, when remonstrated with, excuse themselves by saying, "Why, it is fifty or five hundred years old"; which may be a very lucid explanation, but I cannot say I fully understand and appreciate it.

Men can talk "slang." "Dry up" is nowhere forbidden in the Decalogue. Neither the law nor the prophets frown on "a thousand of brick." The Sermon on the Mount does not discountenance "knuckling to"; but between women and these minor immoralities stands an invisible barrier of propriety,—waves an abstract flaming sword in the hand of Mrs. Grundy,—and we must submit to Mrs. Grundy, though the heavens fall. But who can reckon up the loss which we sustain?

"Dry up,"—a lyric poem is sealed in that Spartan conciseness. Only have eyes, and you shall see a summer brook murmuring through the greenwood; hushed into stillness where the shadows fall darkly, flashing right merrily where sunlight glints through the mermaiden tresses of the trees; mingling its low song with Nature's many-toned lyre; glassing in tricksy, ever-changing caricature the damp, soft mosses on its borders; dropping a deeper purple into the cups of bending violets; flinging a roguish little spray against the sober old rocks; cooing small white feet to tempt its limpid depths; frisking with young lambs in loving, cool embrace; curling around smooth-faced pebbles in perpetual overflow; singing, dancing, hurrying, scurrying, grave and gay, till the baleful dog-star rises, the loitering sun treads slowly through the brazen heavens, and the earth lies parched and panting in his fierce, fiery clasp. Then the brook-music dies away. Softly and more softly the ripples sing themselves to sleep. The thirsty lambs go sorrowing. The tender feet turn back mournfully. The white pebbles rise hot and hard. The mosses crisp and wither. The violets faint and fade. The last cool moisture breathes itself to heaven. Sweet life is quenched. The brook is—"dried up."

What equivalent can your drawing-room grammar furnish for such a "sunny spot of greenery"?

It would be easy to go through a long list of tabooed expressions and show how they are informed and vivified with feminine sweetness, brawny vigor, strength of imagination, the play of fancy, and the flash of wit. Translate them into civilized dialect,—make them presentable at your fireside, and immediately the virtue is gone out of them. Can the man who simply rebukes your proceedings compete for a moment with the man who comes down upon you like "a thousand of brick"? Would not myriads of men weakly agree to a compromise, who would start back in horror at the insinuation of knuckling to their opponents?

I should like to call my luggaage "traps," and my curiosities "truck and dicker," and my weariness "being knocked up," as well as Halicarnassus, but I might as well rob a bank. Ah! high-handed Mrs. Grundy, little you reck of the sinewy giants that you banish from your table! Little you see the nuggets of gold that lie on the lips of our brown-fisted, shaggy-haired newsboys and cabmen!

But if men, in their strength and courage and independence, are enviable, men in their gentleness are irresistible. You expect it in women. It is their attribute and characteristic. You do not admire its presence so much as you deplore or condemn its absence. But manly tenderness has a peculiar charm. It is the wild ivy shooting over the battlements of some old feudal castle, lending grace to solidity, veiling strength with beauty. And you meet it everywhere,—in the house and by the wayside, in city and country, under broadcloth and homespun. The best seat, the finest standpoint, the warmest corner, is not only offered, but urged upon a woman. You may travel from one end of the country to the other, and meet not only civility, but the most cordial and considerate kindness. You may be as ugly as it is possible for virtue to be, and tired and travel-stained and stupid, and your neighbor of a day will show you all the little attentions you could claim from a father or a brother. He will place his valise for your footstool and his shawl for your pillow, open or close your window-blind at every turn of the road, point out every object of interest, explain everything you don't understand, and do a thousand things to make your journey pleasant. The roughest laborer will step out ankle-deep in the "slosh" to give you a firm footing; and if you have the decency to thank him, his good-natured face will light up with as broad a smile as if you were doing him the greatest favor in the world. When a carpenter drags the heavy old road-gate—which he has just unhinged to mend—half a dozen rods, to lay it across a mud-puddle that a woman, to whom he never spoke before and probably never will again, may pass over dryshod, it is false to say that the age of chivalry is gone. Talk of Sir Walter Raleigh's gallantry! Say rather his shrewdness. Surely his was the most economical use to which cloak was ever put. What wonderful politeness was there in a risking a few yards of plush to win the smile of a sovereign whose smiles were "money and fame and troops of friends"?

I am aware that this universal politeness has passed under the ban of certain of my sex, who are pleased to consider and designate it as "doll-treatment," and resent it accordingly. They ask no favors, despise condescensions, and demand dues. Very well. They are doubtless conscientious. If I thought as they do, I should probably act as they do. Only I do not.

Even if this courtesy were a kind of *quid pro quo,*—a superfluity given for an essential taking away,—a Roland of kindness, thrust upon us for an Oliver of right, fraudulently kept back,—why, I am afraid I must make the ignoble confession that I—believe—I like the Roland better than the Oliver,—that is, if we cannot have both,—if rights preclude courtesy.[5] It is pleasanter, or, as Englishmen would say, "jollier," to sit by the flesh-pots of Egypt, than to starve legally in the promised land. Women would better improve the rights they have, a little more, before going mad after others that they know not of. It seems to me that I have business enough on my hands now to occupy three persons at least; and if men *will* be so good as to do the law-making, and stock-jobbing, and bribing, and quarrelling, and stump-speaking, I will be greatly obliged to them. It will give them employment, and take them off our hands for a good part of the day, which is very convenient. As the big man said, when asked why he let his little wife beat him, "It amuses her, and it don't hurt me."

This is not at all heroic, I know; and I suppose, if there was the least probability that anything would ever come of it, I could work myself up to the proper pitch of indignation, and prefer a crust of bread and the right of suffrage to enjoying the pleasures of slavery for a season. But Plato says it is an awful gift of the gods that we can become used to things; and I have become so used to this, that, notwithstanding an occasional spasm, really I am—pretty well, thank you, *but*—

I do not believe that the stream of kindness, which flows so continually from men to usward, has any such polluted source. It is not underhand, as some would have us believe, nor sinister. Men do not systematically oppress us. They mean well, only they are a little thick-headed. As soon as they see their way clear, they will walk in it. Meanwhile comes in this involuntary outgushing, this innate nobility of soul, this germ of the possible angel, which I pray God may spring up, and bud and blossom into glorious fruitage. Am I enthusiastic? I have a right to be. A nation of men loyal, not to grace, beauty, magnificence, but to womanhood, to the highest impulses of fallen human nature, to the love element of the universe, is a thing to be enthusiastic about. "I will indulge my sacred fury."

I have somewhere read that, in a part of the Jewish worship, the men say, "I thank thee, O God, that thou hast not made me a woman"; and the women devoutly and meekly follow, "I thank thee, O God, that thou hast made me as it pleased thee." The first is the language of nature, the second of grace. The first is physiology, and impracticable to us; the second, philosophy, and attainable. Let us take courage.

From the confession of faith which I have made, it will readily be inferred that I have no petty spite to gratify, but that I speak more in sorrow than in anger when I say that men do sometimes act like downright—persons devoid of sense (dictionary definition of a word which I refrain from using for courteous reasons), and it really is necessary to fall back on undisputed proofs of their common sense in other matters, to convince ourselves that this is only a *monostultitia.*[6]

I do not blame men for not understanding women. It is, perhaps, not in the nature of things. Two organisms so delicate, yet so distinct,—so often parallel, yet so entirely integral,—can perhaps never be thoroughly understood objectively. But I do blame them for obstinately persisting in the belief that they do when they don't. Instead of going quietly on their way, and letting us go quietly on ours, giving and receiving help when it is needed, and standing kindly aloof when it is not, they are continually projecting themselves into our sphere, putting their officious shoulders to our wheels, poking their prurient fingers into our pies. They seem to have no idea that there is any corner of our hearts so hidden that their halfpenny tallow-candles cannot illuminate it; and, at the first symptom of doubt, the tallow-candles are accordingly produced. Assuming that they are entirely conversant with woman's nature, conscious with all their stolidity that there is friction somewhere, and perfectly confident that they can tinker us up "as good as new," with the best of motives and the clumsiest of hands, they begin forthwith to hammer away, right and left, on the delicate wheels and springs, till we are forced to cry out, "Dear souls, we know you are good and honest and sincere. You would die for us; but your fingers are all thumbs. Let us alone!" Do you think they will? Not they. Undaunted by their want of success, apparently even unconscious of it, they ding on doggedly, and if continuity, persistence, inflexibility, and a continual harping on the same string, could have reformed us, we should have been reformed into the seventh heaven long ago. But God works by means. Water does not spontaneously run up hill. No combination of numbers can make two and two equal five. The strength of Samson would not enable a man to lift himself to the stars, by pulling at the strap of his boots. So the Conflict of Ages goes on.

O, if those who are at such infinite pains to teach woman her duties, and make her contented with her lot, would but stop a moment to take their reckonings, and compare notes! "Go to, brothers; we don't seem to get on very fast. There must be a screw loose somewhere. Let us investigate."

Do I flatter myself that what I may say will have the slightest tendency to modify the views or the practice of any one of my masculine readers, should I be so fortunate as to have any? Not in the least. Though I speak with the tongues of men and of angels, yet of six men who should do me the honor to read me, half a dozen, invited to deliver an address at the anniversary of a female boarding-school, would rise slowly in their places, smile down a bland and benignant compliment on the white-robed beauty before them, and glide gracefully into an oily eulogium upon woman's influence, her humanizing and elevating mission, promulgating the novel and startling theory that her power is in her heart, not in her arm; that she judges by intuition rather than induction; that her sphere is not on the rostrum, but by the fireside; that she is to rule by love, not by fear;—

interspersing some venerable fling at woman's-rights conventions and their strong-minded leaders, quoting with unutterable pathos,

"I called her angel, but he called her wife,"—

(Query: what right has any man to be calling another man's wife angel?)— and winding up gloriously in a metaphoric convulsion.

Do you ask me, then, why I write? Because I know that I shall be read by girls, and, as we have been told nine hundred and ninety-nine times, the girls of this generation are to be the mothers of the next, and I hope and believe that the few crumbs I cast upon the waters will be returned to me or mine after many days.

Boarding-school anniversaries are becoming a part of our institutions, and the above outline is no fancy sketch. I once heard a lecturer on such an occasion introduce such an address with the remark that he was left no choice. The subject was forced upon him by the nature of the case; and having thus apologized at the outset, he immediately struck the trail, and came in at the death handsomely. His voice was melodious, his accentuation perfect, his language elegant, his manner refined. He did in the best possible style what needed not to be done at all. And he knew that it needed not to be done. The very fact that he did apologize indicated that he saw the necessity of apologizing. It was as if he had said, "My dear girls, I know you are bored to death with people's telling you what your sphere is, but I must give the screw one more twist. I pray you try to bear it; for what the mischief is a man to talk about, if not this?" This would not have been dignified, but it would have been frank.

But I take issue on the fact. There is a choice of subjects. A man is not confined to this stupid treadmill. Girls can understand and appreciate a broader sweep of thought. One of the finest public addresses I ever heard was on such an occasion. I have forgotten the definite theme, but it treated of the cultivation of the beautiful, and, strange to relate, there was not in it, as far as I recollect, a single injunction to women to mind their own business. Truth obliges me to confess that, though all the good people admired it as very beautiful, they all added, "but not appropriate." In my opinion, however, it was appropriate. Instead of telling us to stop doing nothing, and refrain from doing the wrong thing, he showed us how to do a right thing; and no matter if people do find fault with a good lecture. It only proves that their taste is weakened by long disuse, and must be educated up to a higher level.

That villanous old woman-hater, Alexander Pope, avenged himself for the unpardonable superiority of Lady Mary Wortley Montagu's wit to his own, and her scornful and merry refusal of his proffered love,—one shrinks from profaning the sacred word by applying it to such mockery of the divine passion,—by pattering rhymes against the whole sex, as

> "Matter too soft a lasting mark to bear,
> And best distinguished by black, brown, or fair."[7]

The men of to-day, with all their boasted progress, seem to have gone but a step farther. They do indeed give us sufficient consistency to bear whatever impress themselves shall stamp, but acknowledge no inborn power of self-development. Singularly enough, there is a wonderful sameness in all their stamps. If we were what men have tried to make us, and only that, *a man X his mark* would be set upon us with the uniformity of the red cross on a flock of sheep. Now, if there were in our seminaries only one class of girls, and that a class reared in luxurious homes, and tempted by mere surfeit of idleness into forbidden paths, there would be more excuse for the monotone, though it would still be utterly ineffectual; but, collected as our New England schools are,—and I am speaking now of these particularly,—there is many and many a girl in them who has come from a home of poverty, some perhaps of ignorance, a few, alas! of vice. He who should be the stay and honor of his family is its weakness and shame. A frail girl, with a strong heart and a clear brain, throws herself in the breach. She studies with energy, purpose, and effect. She stands on the threshold of womanhood, and turns to take a last look at her girlish days. All the luring pictures spread out by a poetical speaker her woman's heart has already portrayed, and she knows that she must resolutely shut her eyes, and turn away from them. Maiden hopes, wifely trust, mother's love, are not for her. The sacred privacy and dear delights of home,

> "The graces and the loves that make
> The music of the march of life,"

she gazes upon with tear-dimmed eyes and pale lips; for between them and her rises a sad vision,—a care-worn mother tottering graveward, brothers and sisters who will rush into rude, ignorant and immature maturity but for her. Her path lies straight, but very rough. Duty points with stern finger, "This is the way, walk ye in it," and with silent heroism she presses the thorn to her heart, and gathers up her womanly robes, trembling, but unwavering. Have you no word for her? You roll out musical periods, exhorting her companions to be content with the love that waits to receive them with open arms: can you not speak a work of comfort to her for whom no arms shall ever be outstretched? Must she feel herself exiled from man's sympathy, because a man's sin forces her to assume a man's duty? The poor ye have always with you,—the orphaned, the unfriended, the faint-hearted. They stand alone, and see the jostling, eager, selfish crowds go by, and draw back, shrinking and shuddering, but have no sanctuary from the throng. Speak to *them.* Give them your sympathy. Show them the dignity of self-respect. From your wiser years and your larger experience, assure them that a crown of thorns nobly worn shall become a crown of rejoicing, to be cast before the Lord. Strengthen the weak hands and confirm the feeble knees, by telling them how duty is greater than pleasure, integrity better than happiness, and he alone rich who is "dowered with the hate of hate, the scorn of scorn, the love of love."[8] O men, O brothers, you talk of woman's influence, but you do not know your own. You cannot suspect how much a true woman dreads your sarcasm, who will yet, if need be, brave it unflinchingly,—how priceless is your sympathy and approbation to the heart that will yet throb just as highly without it. Cease to exhaust yourselves on those whose every step is watched and guarded by home affection, who face no sterner "duty than to give caresses," who neither need nor heed your injunctions, and turn to those whose weakness must be consolidated into strength, and to whom your appreciation would be as the breath of life.

Even those whom you do address are not benefited thereby. Upon the young girl about to leave school for her home of comfort and peace and plenty, you inculcate the duty of making home happy, because you think it is the most appropriate thing you can do. Very well, if you will only tell her how to do it. But you do not. You utter glittering and sounding generalities. You are definite in your directions only where her way is straight ahead. You bid her minister to the wants of her parents, to rock the cradle of their declining years gently, to tend the couch of sickness, to supply the wants of the poor, and be a useful member of society. To what end? All these things she is forward to do. She dusts the parlor, sees that the guest-chamber is aired, supplies the breakfast-table with flowers, reads to the one or two poor old women of the village, tends her garden, teaches in the Sunday school, and—what then? Half her time remains on her hands. Her soul is full of the nebulæ of great thoughts, lofty purposes. Can you help her resolve them into perfect, self-radiant, and radiating suns? From the chaos, as yet without form and void, will you teach her to evoke a world of symmetry and beauty, which God the Judge on the Last Day shall pronounce to be very good? You have a pleasant voice, and play well on an instrument, but "How shall I make my life noble?" is her eager cry. "How shall I wrest from every day the heroism that it holds? What shall I do with my Monday, and Tuesday, and Wednesday,—with my June and September?" Can you answer her these questions? Can you even mark off a section of the heavens, that she may sweep with her telescope, to find the answer? If you cannot, your words are as idle tales. You might just as well repeat your lecture as gay nuns do their prayers,—"Our Father, which art in heaven, &c., &c., &c., Amen." Of what conceivable use is it to tell her that a woman's place is the

> "Sweet, safe corner by the household fire,
> Behind the heads of children,"

when the very clay of which the bricks are to be made, with which the hearth is to be built, on which the fire is to be kindled, around which the children are to gather, behind whose heads she is to hide, is not yet dug! This mode of talking is all wrong,—to some useless, to others absolutely hurtful. I have not observed that American girls are generally too coy. They do not, to the best of my knowledge, evince any conventual epidemic, any unnatural repugnance to the society of men, any accountable reluctance to assume the duties of wife and mother. A respectable middle-aged gentleman, of rare intellectual endowment and excellent moral character, tells them, sonorously and seriously, that they will probably be married one day, and they would better be getting ready for it. He evidently thinks the sweet little innocents never heard or thought of such a thing before, and would go on burying their curly heads in books, and sicklying their rosy faces with "the pale cast of thought" till the end of time, if he did not stir up their pure minds by way of remembrance.[9] My dear sir, a good many of your artless hearers think of nothing else from morning till night. They talk of their wedding-ring long before they can give you a definition of the circle which is its form. They are firm believers in the truth of the principle, that it is better to be ready and not go, than to go and not be ready; and they have already decided to be married in church with the Episcopal form, because it is so much more impressive. To us who are behind the scenes, and know all this, your exhortations sound, to say the least, rather funny; and we cannot avoid the faintest *soupçon* of a suspicion that you are carrying coals to Newcastle.

"Of all the blind fanatics in this perverse world," says one writer, "your professed hater of fanaticism is the most inveterate and conspicuous; of all agitators, your determined foe to agitation is the most pestilent and effective. Many an excitement has been kept up long after it would have died a natural death, by the wrong-headed hostility of those who had determined and proclaimed that it should be suppressed *instanter.*" These men have profound faith in the *vis inertiæ.* Like the dog Noble, they believe that a squirrel once in a hole cannot by any possibility have got out again. If women are ever caught doing a foolish thing, men evidently fancy that they must be keeping up a steady doing it. Many years ago, women compressed themselves suicidally in steel and whalebone, and, though the custom is dead and buried beyond all hope of resurrection, there are men not a few who will go down to their graves in the firm belief that women are killing themselves off by thousands with tight lacing. Here and there a foolish girl is said to have been found on damp pavements with thin shoes. Corollary: no end of homilies on the folly and wickedness of sacrificing health to beauty. A handful of women have occasionally amused themselves by thrusting a long stick into the mud-puddle of society, and forthwith what a hubbub among the animalculæ! Fie! fie! Do men really believe that the mass of women are possessed with an insane and insatiable desire to distinguish themselves before the world? Nothing is farther from the truth. A decade of years may perhaps produce as many women who see fairer pictures than in the household fire, who find sweeter music than the lisping voice of childhood, but such cases are very rare. On the contrary, women need to be roused rather than repressed. They are far too apt to be content with small attainments and ignoble ends. This woman's rights agitation is but the natural reaction from frivolity, aimlessness, inanity. It is only a move too far in the right direction, or rather an injudicious means to compass worthy ends. I can far more readily sympathize with those who are, blindly and blunderingly it may be, but honestly, endeavoring to right the wrong, than with those who weakly acquiesce. When such things as these happen without comment,—that a school for boys and girls is changed into one for girls only, the boys being removed with their "excellent and efficient Principal" to another, and the girls remaining behind with their female assistant, who receives less than half the salary of her male predecessor,—when a father on his death-bed is allowed by law to bequeath the only child of his wife to strangers, and that child is torn from her widowed bosom, and all her prayers and tears and agony of love are of no avail,—do you wonder that a woman can help thinking, if she has any think in her? And if she be a woman of energy, accustomed to act as well as think, and if the men around her be stupid or indifferent, is it strange that, with her burning sense of wrong, her woman's intense hatred of injustice and sympathy with the oppressed, she should herself strive to redress the grievance? And if so be the reins shall slacken in her unwonted hand,—if her feeble fingers essay in vain to stay her steed of heaven,—if, on the sharp thorns or jagged rocks of some untrodden mountain-side, you shall see her womanhood lie, bleeding, shattered, formless,—you may weep and wail, but—mock, if you dare!

They, therefore, are right—right in their premises, though wrong in their conclusions—who dolefully affirm our Female Conventions and things of that ilk to be the sad results of our free society. They *are* the results of free society; just as the smoke and soot and cinders belched forth by George Stephenson's first locomotive engine were the results of the practical application of a great principle,—the might of matter quelled by the might of mind. But just as the more perfect elucidation of that principle converted this very smoke and soot into a motive power, so will free society, when it has learned wisdom, turn all this surplus activity into its proper channels, and make all things work together for good,—which is God.

Newspaper readers will perhaps remember a statement, originating, I am sorry to say, in Massachusetts, but copied by our enlightened free press as accurately, extensively, and intelligently as a flock of sheep follow their leader over the gap in a stone fence. I am sorry that I cannot give the paragraph exactly; the writer seemed to have bounced suddenly against the fact, that there are not so many marriages in the country as there used to be, and ought to be. Being greatly exercised thereby, he casts about for a cause and a remedy for this deplorable state of things. In a frenzy of haste, he seizes his cudgel, and bangs away at whatever comes within his reach; and, as he could not walk up and down the fine old high street of his native city without seeing troops of handsomely-dressed women, he "falls to" upon female extravagance. "I have found it! I have found it!" he cries with ill-concealed exultation; and his sorrow for the fact is for a moment overpowered by rapture at his own sagacity in discovering it. "It costs so much to support a wife, that is the reason why the young men don't marry. They feel that they must wait till their income is enough to maintain a wife in the style to which she has been accustomed. Girls think they must begin where their mothers leave off," &c. The mother, too, receives her share of the blame, and generally the lion's share; for it somehow happens in almost all these jeremiads, that the father comes off scot-free. Then statistics are duly produced to show the quantity of silks, laces, velvets, and feathers yearly imported, and the whole ends with a dismal groan over the degeneracy of the nineteenth century, and a prolonged howl for the melancholy prospects of the twentieth, in case there should be any twentieth.

Now this is an elevated way of treating the subject, is it not? Are we not placed in a dignified position? They come to us with a silk in one hand, and a husband in the other,—"Which will you choose? You can't have both. Come, now, there's a dear, wear calico, and it shall have a nice little husband, so it shall." Girls, don't do it! There are thousands more women than men in New England, and the chances are that you lose both husband and dress. The husband if you can, but at any rate make sure of the silk. It is your duty to dress as well and look as pretty as you can, consistently with your other duties. You are to be guided by what is right, not by what a rabble of men may like. And, above all things, don't retrench because men threaten not to marry you unless you do. Just let them try it, and see who will hold out the longest.

But, as a matter of fact, the statement is false,—at least to this extent, that women are, if anything, less extravagant than men. They dress up, not down, to their fathers', and brothers', and husbands' wishes. I do not believe there is one woman in five hundred in New England, who, if frankly informed of the sources and amount of her husband's income, would not cheerfully and handsomely bring her expenses within it. Women do undoubtedly spend a great deal of money; but if their fathers or husbands give it to them to spend, why should they be blamed? How many failures, I beg to know, have been laid on the shoulders of women the last few years? But when the numbers are counted up and handed in, will the statistician be so good as to tell us in how many cases the husband had been in the habit of making his wife conversant with the state of his affairs,—how many times the wife knew, or had any means of knowing, what the amount of her expenses for the year ought to be.

There are very few men who are capable of telling whether a woman is extravagant or not. It is very dangerous to attempt to judge the cost of her dress from its appearance. It is not the most showy things that cost the most, nor the most simple that cost the least. It is not the most elegantly, not even the most richly-dressed woman, who runs up the highest bill. I know women who tread royally in satin and velvet, who entertain magnificently, and give generously, who yet can economically, and do merrily, spend hour after hour in making mosquito-bars, covering ottomans, putting locks on doors, upholstering old chairs quite "as weel's the new," mending sewing-machines, and by thousands of ingenious and happy devices saving money from animal wants, to spend it in generous, intellectual, and social pleasures. If your lady-love's dress does not offend your taste, my fine fellow, never trouble yourself about its price; for the flounces which make you so uneasy are seven years old, and redeemed from a dress which her mother cast off when she went into mourning;—the velvet basque, which you must allow to be very becoming, is the joint product of two worn-out cloaks of her sisters;—the bonnet was made by herself from a lace veil that has been in the family for years, and all the while she was pricking her soft fingers over it, she smiled unconsciously at the thought of pleasing your eyes; and this is all the thanks she gets for it. Insensate! Look at her face. Is it blank? To her conversation. Is it stale, flat, and unprofitable? Find out the stuff of which she is made,—the texture of her soul. If there is a jewel, wear it on your brow and in your heart, though the casket be gold. If there is a treasure, make it yours, though the vessel be rarest Sevres China. If she does not love you enough to prefer poverty with you to wealth without you, her love is little worth. The fault is not that her purse is full, but that her heart is empty. You insult not womanhood merely, but human nature, by supposing that the incidents of life are more valuable than life itself. You discover innate meanness in that you can conceive of a love influenced by dollars and cents. What kind of affection, pray, is that which counts the cost, and coolly compares chances? If you are a true man and she is a true woman, you will so enfold her life, so fill her heart and her eyes, that she will have no power to perceive any lack. If you are not true, you have no right to marry her or any one else. Begone!

"But," moans our editor, "a man who finds he has married a wardrobe and a piano, and not a living, loving woman, is most egregiously taken in." Of course he is, and deserves to be. Why did he marry the wardrobe? Whose fault is it? The world was all before him. What right has any man to marry a woman before he knows whether she is a wardrobe or not,—where her dress ends and her soul begins? He has every opportunity for knowing; and if he does not choose to take the trouble, let him not complain. He at least has no cause to cry foul play. The game was not even, inasmuch as his superiority gave him the advantage; and if a man finds himself checkmated by a wardrobe, more shame to him, but don't let him come whimpering to us for pity and sympathy. I for one feel very much as did the old woman witnessing, with arms akimbo, the conflict between her husband and a bear, "Go it, husband! Go it, bear! *I don't care which beats!*"

"O, if parents in educating their daughters would but insist upon their having a reasonable notion of what it is to be a wife, rather than upon a smattering of French, and a little thrumming upon the piano, there would be such a revolution," continues our disconsolate author. (I should like first privately to put the question, whether any man ever wrote upon any subject connected with woman, without being sure, somewhere in the course of his article, to trot out that unflagging piano. I have heard many musical performances in my day, but I never was so tired of hearing any girl thrum upon a rosewood instrument, as I am of hearing men thrum on this imaginary one.) But what do you mean, you talkers and writers, in saying that girls should be educated to be wives and mothers? Is not a wife a woman? Is there any special course of instruction to be followed? Is not that education the best which most fully develops every power,—moral, mental, and physical? Womanhood is greater than wifehood. It comprehends and embraces it. The best woman will make the best wife. If the mind of a woman is dwarfed, and her faculties weakened by disuse, she will be an inefficient wife, because she is an inefficient woman. If, on the other hand, her mind is trained, her judgment cultivated, her powers developed, she will be adequate to any emergency as woman or wife. Soul is stronger than circumstance. If a girl is a fool in silks, will she be any the less a fool in calico? Does a feeble, frivolous nature grow strong and self-reliant, by being transferred from a palace to a cottage. What folly is this? Let girls be taught to make the most of themselves. Let them fulfil present duties, and the future will take care of itself. She who walks grandly as a woman will not walk unworthily as a wife. She who stands upright alone, will not drag her husband downward. She who guides her own life wisely and well, will not rule her household with an erring hand. Familiarity with the details of domestic management will be a help, but want of familiarity will not be an insurmountable obstacle.

I lay this down as a self-evident proposition: a woman of sense, married to the right man, can do anything.

But you, O maidens and matrons beloved, you are greatly to be blamed for this style of acting and tone of thinking. You care too little to be, and too much to seem. You must command, not ask, respect. You must not complain of contempt, so long as you are contemptible. There is no power to keep you permanently below or above your proper level. In this great rolling sea of society, you will sink or swim according to your specific gravity. If you are stupid and heavy, plump you will go to the bottom where you belong. If you are light and empty,—no cargo, no ballast, no rudder,—you will be tossed about by every eddy, aimless and useless, except as the toy of an hour. You must be well proportioned, well provisioned, with adequate machinery in good working order, if you would ride the waves proudly and make your haven successfully. Remember this. Whatever is done for you must be done by you. All real improvement must work from within outward. Woman's incapacity is the only real barrier to woman's progress. Whenever women show themselves able, men will show themselves willing. This is what you need,—strength, calibre. You do not set half enough value on muscular power. Æsthetic young lady-writers and sentimental penny-a-liners have imbibed and propagated the idea, that feebleness and fragility are womanly and fascinating. The result is, a legion of languid headaches, an interesting inability to walk half a dozen consecutive miles, a delicate horror of open windows, northwest wind, and wholesome rain-storms. There is no computing the amount of charming invalidism following in the wake of such a line as

"There is a sweetness in woman's decay,"—

a lengthened sweetness long drawn out by some compliant and imitative females. I do not, of course, refer to real invalids, who have inherited feeble constitutions, and, by unavoidable and often unselfish and unceasing wear and tear, have exhausted their small capital, and to whom life is become one long scene of weariness and pain. Heaven help them bear the burden; and they do bear it nobly, often accomplishing what ought to make their ruddy and robust sisters blush for shame at their own inefficiency. I mean women who have every opportunity to be healthy, but who are not healthy,—who are sick when it is their duty to be well. A woman of twenty, in comfortable circumstances, ought to be as much ashamed of being dyspeptic as of being drunk. Fathers and mothers, burdened with cares and anxieties, may neglect physiological laws without inpugning their moral character; but for a girl, care-free, to confess such an impeachment, is presumptive evidence of gluttony, laziness, or ignorance, and generally all three. This is not elegant language, I know; but when we have learned to call things by their right names, we shall have taken one step towards the millennium; and it is an indisputable fact, that a great majority of ailments arise from over-eating and under-exercising. The innumerable hosts of nervous diseases with which our women are afflicted are always aggravated, and often caused, by these indulgences. Women do not know this, and if they did, it would be of little use, so long as they consider illness one of the charms of beauty. Let the idea once get firm hold, that illness is stupid and vulgar, and a generation or two—nay, even a year or two—would show a marked change. If a woman is ill, let her take it for granted that it is her first business to get well, and let her forthwith set about it. A good stout will, a resolute purpose, would work wonders. "Few persons like sick people," says Charles Lamb; "as for me, I candidly confess I hate them." Whatever poetasters sing, you may depend upon it, a good digestion is "an excellent thing in a woman."

Health once re-established, let women next divest themselves of the idea that moral weakness is an essential attribute of a well-developed character. It is a pandering to masculine prejudices with which I have no patience. If there is anything more disagreeable than your strong-minded women, it is she who denounces them to ingratiate herself with men,—who obtrudes herself as not being one of them. Whenever prominent women are made the subject of conversation by men, if there is a possible peg in their character or course on which a commendation can be hung, be sure you hang it. Scold them or spurn them privately as much as you think they deserve, but defend them publicly as much as you can. Scorn the meanness of striving to attract men's admiration by affecting little weaknesses. "I dislike to travel alone," said a young lady; "I always feel as dependent as a child." Dependent on what? Whom? How? It is exceedingly disagreeable to be obliged to sit on the same seat with a person who evidently does not believe that man is an amphibious animal. It is not pleasant to elbow your way through a mob of vociferous hackmen. You feel safer and far more comfortable to be under the care of a good traveller; but that the necessity of independent and intelligent action should produce a feeling of dependence, indicates an unsoundness somewhere which should be looked after at once. I know no risks in ordinary travelling so great that one should prefer an indifferent companion to one's own society. I do not believe men apotheosize this amiable incapacity to the extent supposed; but what if they do? God does not. He gave every muscle and nerve, every power and faculty, to be used. He never intended that we should effervesce in a sigh, or collapse to a shadow. If men think so, it only shows that they need, as the Brahmin said, "to have a little more intellect put into them."

The old oak quivers through all its tremulous leaves at the passing of the softest summer breeze; but deep hidden in the heart of its greenness flows its sap of life; and away down under the ground spread out its roots of strength; and it stands the storms of a hundred years; nor does it murmur out a less delicious music in June, because the skirring blasts of December have no power to destroy. They make a great mistake, who think a strong, brave, self-poised woman is unwomanly. The stronger she is, the truer she is to her womanly instincts,—the more unswervingly does she point to the mysterious pole-star of her womanhood. A feeble soul loves, hates, wills, feebly. It is only those who have borne the burden and heat of the day who know the blessedness of the evening-tide. It is only those who have walked well, unsustained, who fully appreciate the unutterable happiness of leaning on a stronger arm. Love is like the cholera, dysentery, and other acute diseases. An emaciated, sickly nature takes it lightly, and recovers quickly; but with your generous, hearty, healthy, robust, vigorous souls, it goes hard. Ten to one if they ever recover; and when they do, they bear the scars for life. Do not, therefore, fear to be too strong. Be not afraid to grapple with the higher mathematics, lest you should be called strong-minded. "Sir!" thundered the rhinoceros-hided Ursa Major of the eighteenth century, "what harm does it do a man to call him Holofernes?"[10] What harm, indeed, in being called strong-minded? It is better than weak-minded. Do whatever you think, on mature deliberation, you ought to do. "Be sure you are right, and then go ahead." Never mind what men think about it. I do not mean that you are not to try or to wish to please them. It is both natural and proper. But do it honestly and openly. Have a benevolent desire to give pleasure, and it is very probable that the innocent desire to please will be gratified. If you cannot please without being false to yourself, you would better displease. Admiration gained by slurring over your convictions, or refraining from having any, is dearly bought. Best of all, take no thought of pleasing. Have no anxiety about it. Make yourself worthy of love, admiration, reverence, and you will always hold trumps.

"Woman's devotion" is another theme which has been run into the ground. Orators extol it. Editors paragraph it. Poets rhyme it, and women exemplify the old proverb, "Give a dog a bad name, and kill him." But devotion, of itself, has no moral character. It is simply stickiness, shared in common, and to a far greater degree, by oysters, molasses, blood-suckers, court-plaster, and officeseekers. Intelligent, voluntary devotion—devotion to a great principle endangered, to justice though obscured, to nobility though persecuted—is good. But a discerning public utters devout moral reflections over a wife's devotion to her scamp of a husband. He commits theft, and is thrown into prison; he is unkind and brutal in his treatment of her; or he is coolly indifferent to her happiness, and alive to the charms of other women,—but still she clings to him with all a woman's devotion.

Now I beg to ask this question. When a woman marries, what does she marry? Is it a coat, moustache, and umbrella? If it is, then so long as the coat, moustache, and umbrella are extant, she does well to devote herself to them with constancy and fervor. But if, as is popularly supposed, she marries a soul, a heart, a character, then, when she discovers that the soul rung false, the heart is not there, and the character assumed, I do not see what there is to cling to, nor where is the merit in clinging. You love what you think a man is, not necessarily what he is. You cherish reverently a lock of hair, because it once shaded the brow of an absent friend; but when you find that you have been deceived, and that it is only from the head of Tom, Dick, or Harry, who happened to be tonsured at the same time and place, you cast it from you in disgust. We admire Satan, appearing to us as an angel of light; but when the horns protrude, shall we still cling to them with woman's devotion? Heaven forbid! Do I then aver that a woman may break away from her marriage vows so soon as she becomes dissatisfied with her husband? No more than I would advise you to burn down your house because it is not built according to contract. You may alter it if you can, and if not, you must make the best of it as it is. But you need not admire and extol it, just as it would have been right for you to do if it really were what you wished and planned it to be. A woman judges wrong in the chief incident of her life. She makes a mistake, whose consequences are far-reaching, and very deplorable, but she must bear them. Her husband's neglect or refusal to fulfil his part of the contract does not justify her non-fulfilment any further than is necessary. I say *than is necessary,* for the promise is of such a nature that I do not see how it is in her power to keep the whole of it, and, consequently, what is the possible use of making it. She vows to love, honor, and obey; but love and honor do not depend on the will. You cannot love a man if he has not the qualities which inspire love, nor honor him when he ceases to be honorable. God, it is true, commands us to love him; but his character is such that it needs only be considered to be adored. Man is a long way from Divinity, and our feelings towards him cannot be bespoken beforehand. They are entirely contingent on his deserts, which are variable. Therefore, a woman promises to do what is quite beyond the sphere of her volition, and she can neither keep nor break her promise. But for her own soul's sake she must maintain her integrity. She must be faithful and just and gentle and blameless. If she does more than this,—if she is so unfortunately constituted that she still prostrates herself before the fragments of her broken and debased idol,—she is to be pitied. She is not to be praised.

[. . .] I [also] have little faith in dying for love. I have, however, great faith in moping one's self to death out of spite, or stubbornness, or false shame. If I am wrong, I am sorry—or glad; perhaps I ought to be glad. At any rate, I am in just that state of mind in which I ought to be under the circumstances. If I have injured any one's feelings by my unbelief, I most humbly beg pardon. I dare say I shall die of unrequited love myself some day. It would be no more than strict poetic justice. "Doubtless God might have made a better berry than a strawberry, but doubtless God never did."[11] Doubtless there might be such a thing as dying for love, but doubtless there never (or seldom) was. In point of fact, there is not a great deal of marrying for love. Not that I suppose all marriages are mercenary. Far from it. But people marry for a thousand things,—money not only, but a home, beauty, genius, because others do, because it is respectable, convenient, &c. Some of these motives are objectionable, some perhaps not. When a poor girl, after laying the worn-out bodies of her father and mother in the grave, sees no prospect before her but unremitting toil, loneliness, poverty, and death in the dreary end, and marries the kind old physician who has tended her parents without prospect of reward; who has been the witness of her assiduity, watchfulness, generosity, good cheerful sense, and real worth, and feels that she would shed upon his widowed hearth something of the light of other days, I am far from blaming her. She is not false to her noblest nature, although perhaps, in the dreams of her early and happy girlhood, his was not the arm she looked to lean on. He will love her with a fatherly love; she will return it with grateful affection, and therefore her walk in life will be higher, her ends nobler, her benevolence more expansive, her womanhood better developed. Though the ecstatic glow that flushed her morning sky, when

"Life went a-Maying,
With Youth and Hope and Poesy,"[12]

may have faded; yet a calm serenity—"the sober certainty of home-felt bliss"—will enwrap her in a holy atmosphere, soft, hazy, and warm-tinted, as the beautiful Indian-summer.

When a young man is captivated by the fall of a graceful shoulder, or the twirl of a tiny toe, and on the strength of it marches straightway to church, and there promises to love and cherish, I shall not forbid the banns:

> "Honored well are charms to sell,
> If priests the selling do";—[13]

or, if more practical, and with an eye to the windward, he notes that the pretty silk is not new, but simply colored, turned upside down, wrong side out, with new fringe and trimmings, and new waist and sleeves, and bethinks himself how, under such management, his narrow cottage walls would stretch away into stately halls,—if he can secure the fair artisan he is doubtless lucky. I do not object. Their talk will be of bread and butter, the baby's teething, and the price of turnips; but let them marry. I do say, however,—and am I not right?—this is not that resistless tide, which, gathering to itself the thousand streams that ripple through the quiet meadows of life, sweeps suddenly over the heart, bearing down all the old landmarks of pride and prejudice; not that raging and quenchless fire which consumes the dross of selfishness, and fuses into a glowing devotion every power, thought, faculty, and purpose; not that great, deep, absorbing, passionate, deathless love, which, having once passed into a soul, can go no more out forever.

I could wish that women were happier. This may appear a needless wish to those who look only on the surface; but below the smoothly-flowing surface there is an undercurrent which the world knoweth not of. There is a restlessness, an unuttered discontent, a vague longing, which frets and wears away the cheerfulness and happiness of life, particularly in the young. It is involuntary, unsought, resisted, but all-powerful. Ah! the capacity for suffering that there is in girls,—the capacity, too, for enjoying and for acting. It is weighed and measured by those who are armed for the conflict, girded for the race, but for whom no conflict and no race ever wait. It is the slow wasting away of powers that have nothing to grasp; the silent, subtle corrosion of a heart turned in upon itself. O girls, everywhere waiting and watching for a day that never comes, I have seen you. I know you. I have followed you through the dreary days that dragged their slow length along. I know how the tramp of the monotonous years seems to you the dead march of your young aspirations,—how the pulse of your heart grows fainter and fainter, beneath the swelling fountain of tears.

> "My heart, and hope, and prayers, and tears,
> Are all with you, are all with you,"

and therefore I have a right to bid you take heart and hope, for this very unrest is a sign. It is the beating of your soul against its prison-bars. It is a token from above,—a voice from the unseen world, bidding you come up higher. It tells you of a level you have not yet reached; of energies not yet developed; of a life not yet rounded off to full perfection. Your soul is unconsciously sending out feelers, and they find nothing to grasp. The world is six thousand years old, but it has not yet learned to use its resources. It knows not what to do with you, and you know not what to do with yourselves. Your pastors and teachers exhort you to fear God and keep his commandments; and you try to do it. But that does not fill the void, does not stop the aching, nor soothe the unrest. No, and it never will. People may talk as much as they choose about the power of religion, but it will not satisfy your hungry heart, any more than it will your hungry stomach. God has given to every appetite its appropriate food, to every emotion its corresponding object. He has given us means and ends, but we blindly work at cross-purposes, and take wrong means for right ones, making his word of none effect by our traditions. When we ask him for bread, he gives us bread; his children, in all kindness, but ignorantly, give us oftentimes a stone. Do not reproach or think meanly of yourselves for not being happy. If you were absorbed in dress, visiting, pleasure-seeking, you would have no discontent; but would it be better so? If you were identified with any great work, anything which could enlist your whole being, you feel that it would be different; but women seldom have a great work to do. Their work is great only in its results, in the spirit with which it is done. It is a vast conglomeration of little things. You are where God has placed you, or suffered you to be placed, and for our purposes now it is all the same. If, in truth as in poetry, love could take up the harp of life, and smite on all the chords with might, then this chord of self would, trembling, pass in music out of sight, and this would be better. This self-abnegation is perhaps indispensable to womanly completeness. Until this chord has been touched, there is no diapason. The depths of the soul are unstirred. There is a power lying waste, a fountain sealed. No character can be perfect which is not symmetrical. You may, you ought to love Christ with an overmastering love, but the two are entirely distinct. One cannot take the place of the other. Every earthly affection should indeed be baptized in the heavenly,—but only baptized, not transmuted. I do not think God ever intended it should be.

Have I found you a remedy? No, certainly. I have only pointed out what would be a remedy if found, but no searching will ever bring it. It comes unsought, if it comes at all. What good have I done you, then? None at all so far; but here is the point where I wish to utter a note of warning. Here is where you are in danger of mistaking the seeming for the real. Faint and famishing, you will eagerly pluck the fair-looking apple, and it will turn to dust and ashes in your mouth. You would better have died of starvation. Because God has made you so that love is your life and breath, and you pant and gasp without it, you are not to inhale a foul malaria, under the mistaken impression that it is mountain air. If it be pure, the more you breathe of it the better, only be sure it is pure. Therefore, do not love indiscriminately. An over-ripe apple falls at the first gust, whether into lily-white hands or on the unheeding ground. Do not you so; nor be content with a slight preference,—a pale, nerveless, flickering, uncertain emotion, that brings as many misgivings as heart-throbs. I have heard of girls pausing on the threshold of an engagement, "at a stand to know what to do"! Never allow yourself to be in such a position. If you don't know what to do, it is the very strongest of all providential indications that you are to do nothing. By all means, give yourself the benefit of the doubt. "Friendship with all, entangling alliances with none," is a good motto for women as well as for nations. Faithfully adhered to, it will keep you free from those little attachments which insensibly but surely fritter away your power to form a lasting and noble one; while it will no more prevent your soul from going out to meet its lord and king, when his trumpet sounds, than the seven green withes had power to restrain the Hebrew athlete when his spirit returned to him, after its ignoble sleep on a treacherous bosom.[14]

Do not affect a motive in love. It is not a question of motive, but of fact. I have no faith in marrying to do good. The end does not sanctify the means. If you do all the good you can with your own individuality, I do not believe God will hold you responsible for anything more. Nor, in my opinion, does the respectability of the sinner diminish the enormity of the sin. I have known missionaries, excellent men, bury their poor wives in Hindoo jungles, and return to America to replace them, just as madam sends for a China teacup to replace the one broken by a careless servant. Men and women combine with Nature to abhor a vacuum, and the missionary's loss is often far more easily made up than madam the housekeeper's. Mysterious wheels, wires, and pulleys are set in motion by a clique of mothers in Israel behind the scenes, the result of which is, that some unoffending, benevolent, and practical Miss Brown finds herself suddenly precipitated, *nolens volens,*[15] (generally *volens,*) into the arms of the good missionary;—he congratulating himself on the success of his business transaction; she consoling herself that she has gained an excellent husband, and done God service, thereby killing two birds with one stone; and the mothers aforesaid rejoicing in their skillful matrimonial diplomacy. Now I affirm that it is miserable business the whole of it. It may be good manœuvring, where all manœuvring is out of place. It is an unholy traffic, though all the traffickers be members of an orthodox church in good and regular standing. It is transferring to the head what comes under the jurisdiction of the heart. The parties concerned may "live happily ever after," but they have no right to expect it. Of course, if a woman marries a missionary because she loves him, even though her love sprang up on his first Transatlantic appearance as a widower, and goes to Boorioboola Gha with him, because she would rather do it than stay at home without him, there is not the slightest objection; she is quite right; only let her say so honestly, if she feel called upon to say anything. But when she explains her marrige by enlarging on her sense of duty, the poor little children who stand in such pressing need of a mother's care, the heathen who are perishing for lack of knowledge, why then, I say, if these really are her motives, she is wrong,—just as truly, though not perhaps as greatly, wrong as she who follows the glitter of gold. Let her take a lesson from Jane Eyre and St. John, since she has failed to learn it from her Bible. If the claims of the heathen urge her so irresistibly, let her go to them untrammelled. The cause of God is not so desperate that it needs to be propped up by a falsehood.

Nor do I believe in marrying because, as I have frequently heard alleged, a woman's nature is such that she "must love somebody." In the first place, the implied fact is a convenient little fiction. There is no sort of necessity for your "loving somebody." It may be very pleasant to do so; it may be very distressing not to do so; but it is not immediately fatal. Even if it were, never mind. Remember Pompey's sublime words, "It is necessary for me to go; it is not necessary for me to live." Death comes to all, and the world does not need your bodily presence so much as it needs your moral heroism. If you die rather than live falsely, you will enrich it by one great example. Moreover, granting that you "must love somebody," does it inevitably follow that you "must love" a grown man in possession of a respectable yearly income? Look abroad at the orphans, thousands upon thousands, fatherless, motherless, to whom your love would be as the dew of Hermon.[16] Christ's little ones are all around you,—the ignorant, the uncared-for, the outcast. Lavish on them your irrepressible affection. The sunshine of love might melt the ice in which their better nature is incrusted, and warm into healthy, vigorous growth the wasting germ of many a virtue. The idea, girls, the *idea* of sacrificing your whole life to a so-so sort of person, for the sake of having "somebody to love," in a world so full of children that the most excruciating hand-organ will in two minutes block up the sidewalk in any portion of any city with admiring throngs of white-headed urchins!

To marry for a home or for happiness is little better. A home purchased by the sale of yourself is a dear bargain, and happiness is the most uncertain shadow you can pursue. It is incidental. It comes upon us unexpectedly; but if we set out determinately and definitely in pursuit of it, it generally leads us into bogs and quagmires, and leaves us there. [. . .]

I know, therefore, or no reason why a woman should marry, except because she cannot help it,—because "the spirit of life which dwelleth in the most secret chambers of the soul, all trembling, speaks these words: 'Behold a god more powerful than I.'"

If your love raises and exalts you, if it helps you on your heavenward way, if it brings you nearer to God, if it strengthens you to brave endurance, stimulates you to heroic action, and makes all greatness possible; if, in one word, it possesses itself of you, and sweeps you up and out from the finite to the infinite, as a wave bears seaward the strong swimmer, powerless,—you are safe.

[. . .] Because you can't get what you want, don't throw away what you can get. Squeeze out of the world all the juice there is in it. It is a mistake to suppose that you must be either at the brow or at the foot of the hill. There are many steps between, some of which command a charming view, and all a new horizon. Because you are not particularly happy, don't condemn yourself to particular misery. It is possible to sleep soundly, eat heartily, and be on the whole very comfortable, without being in a rapturous frame of mind. Only, when you are simply comfortable, don't pretend that you are tremendously happy. There is nothing to be gained by the deception; and if there were, you don't want to gain it. Do with your might whatsoever your hand finds to do. Sympathize largely. Don't merely try to feel, but feel. Associate with children, not to harass them by continually setting them right,—which is of no use, since they will inevitably and immediately fall back into their original sin,—but make yourself one with them. Nothing pays so well. I think it is the easiest of all ways to amuse yourself and benefit others. But don't confine yourself to any one class. Whenever anybody's orbit intersects yours, make something come of it. Sink a shaft wherever there is the least probability of water. Find out the secret place where abideth the soul of your Irish "girl." See if there may not be something in common between you and your washerwoman, your seamstress, your chambermaid, your cook. If there is a single plank in their platform on which you can stand, join hands thereon, and give one throb to the heart of humanity. Do not wait supinely for opportunity, but go out and seek her in the highways and hedges. Be alive at every pore. Make your soul great with unceasing benevolence. Make common cause with virtue against temptation, with goodness against wickedness, with right against might. If truth is solvent in falsehood, precipitate the truth, and cast out the false. Do not be intimidated because human nature is not every inch a saint, nor cajoled because it is not every inch a satan. This great world is a powerful diluent. Accustom yourself to analyze, and, having decided deliberately, maintain stoutly. However weak, unpopular, or ridiculed the just cause may be, let it find in you an unflinching and impartial supporter;—impartial, for women are too apt, having once espoused a cause, to cling to it "with woman's devotion," right or wrong; or, having rejected it, to fancy no good thing can come therefrom. If you approve one thing and condemn another, both of which Mrs. Grundy alike condemns, don't abstain from saying so for fear of being called inconsistent. If to-day you approve any measure which yesterday you condemned, don't be afraid to say so for fear of being deemed fickle. Is it not Ruskin who says that he has little faith in an opinion till he has changed it three times? Pope asks what changing the mind is, but saying we are wiser to-day than we were yesterday. And Ruskin again bids us say what we think to-day in words as hard as cannon-balls, and say what we think to-morrow in words just as hard, no matter if one assertion flatly contradict the other. Consistency is the bugbear of small, inactive minds.[17] A living soul, grappling with the great truths of the present, has no leisure to go digging among last year's ruins to see whether the two sets dove-tail exactly. Let bygones be bygones. Let the dead past bury its dead. A sincere and honest life will arrange itself. All opinions and beliefs, intelligently and conscientiously adopted, will group themselves into a beautiful mosaic, which you cannot now see because you are too near, and must behold one at a time; but when a stand-point in the other world gives you the proper focal distance, you will behold, with wonder and admiration, how the most diverse and the most similar were alike necessary to form a perfect and artistic whole. [. . .]

But unhappiness cannot be prevented or exterminated by a "whereas, be it resolved" alone. Action is not more the chief part of an orator than of every other human being. It is the necessity of every noble nature. Change is the essence of life, and action is continuous change,—wise action, continuous advancement. Whether grief be real or imaginary,—and imaginary grief *is* real,—employment is an excellent specific. Ah! that is the very thing you want,—something definite to do. Well, there is the school-house, which ninety-nine girls in a hundred enter, not because they feel that they have any particular call that way, but because it seems to open the only loop-hole of escape from inanity. That you have no taste for the work is the smallest possible objection. Good, honest people, reasoning *a priori,* affirm that no one can be a good teacher unless he loves teaching. Educational conventions and professional periodicals reiterate the statement, till they perhaps come to believe it themselves; but it is only a popular fallacy. In all my life, I have known but one woman who really loved teaching for its own sake. Some of the best teachers—the most respected and the most beloved—have adopted it because it was the only work that offered; and, hating it most heartily, have accomplished it most successfully. But it is far more probable that, being young and inexperienced, you fancy teaching will be the "*open sesame*" to Paradise,—or a triple coat of mail against all the ills that flesh is heir to; but you may as well undeceive yourself at once. You think it will give you the great desideratum,—employment, occupation, something to think about. Yes, it will, indeed; so much, that, if you do all that you see standing in need of doing, you will require the strength of Hercules and the days of the planet Jupiter. If you are strong and healthy, you will have the satisfaction of spending five or six of the best years of your life in a school, and at the expiration of that time be allowed to leave with honor, a pale face, disordered nerves, tired brain, and shattered constitution. The labor required in ordinary schools of the higher class is such, that I think a woman of average physical strength cannot spend more than four consecutive years in them without breaking down. The draughts on the vital energy are so unceasing, that the supply cannot equal the demand, and the fountain is exhausted. Of course I refer only to teachers of conscience and character. An inefficient, commonplace routinist can drone on in the same rut, *ad infinitum,* and perhaps give complete satisfaction to an astute public. So, if you have been tenderly nursed and nurtured, if you have indulged an appetite for sick headaches, if you have been trained in the belief that rest should follow labor, and that the best work can be performed by the best-conditioned animal, engage to "wash for the ladies" at sixpence an hour, or enter a bookbindery and be paid by the job, or dig clams on the sea-shore and sell them in the shell, (which I always fancied must be a delightful occupation,) or hire yourself out as nursery-maid to nine small children, but don't enter a public school,—and a private school is no better, and a great deal worse, since the former only devours you piecemeal, but the latter swallows you whole, body and soul.

But you think it will be so delightful, so *juvenescent,* to be surrounded by happy, joyous, bounding children. You can quote reams of poetry on the subject,—

"A beautiful, and happy girl,"—
"Child amid the flowers at play,"—
"A simple child,
That lightly draws its breath,"—
"A baby in a house is a well-spring of pleasure," etc.,—[18]

all of which I am not prepared to contradict; but a hundred and fifty babies in a house, together, representing every stage of infancy, from the bread and molasses of three years old, to the nuts and apple coquetry of thirteen, will make larger draughts on your patience than on your poetry, and exercise your judgment more than your imagination. You must divest yourself, as soon as possible, of the idea that all children are little white-winged angels, with golden curls and rose-bud lips. You must prepare yourself for diamonds in the rough, and sometimes for the rough without the diamond. Even where there is a diamond, you must not expect to polish it in the twinkling of an eye. Perhaps it will not flash its full lustre till the hand that first made way for its gleaming has crumbled into dust. We have all read any number of stories about hordes of ferocious boys, who have organized successful and successive rebellions, and ejected a long line of male dynasties from the professional chair, but who have suddenly been brought to roar you as gently as any suckling dove, by the apparition of a sweet-faced, low-voiced woman. Now, I know that calmness and gentleness and firmness will work wonders, where passion and violence and storm have been only abbots of misrule,—and of the whole circle of things that may happen to you, this may happen; but I would not advise you to set your heart upon it. If you begin with the practical, at least, if not theological belief, that the children of men are deceitful and desperately wicked, prone to evil as the sparks are to fly upward, you will be happily disappointed, if you are disappointed at all. Expect to meet wormwood, senna, and Epsom salts; and if you do find the land overflowing with milk and honey, you will be doubly delighted. Be prepared to employ sternness of tone, severity of manner, and anything else that may be necessary; and if a fair trial convince you that music has charms enough to soothe the savages, why then all you will have to do will be to sing with all your might and main.

I hope you will not be shocked, and think I recommend you to turn into a kind of ogress, with the appetite of the Wantley dragon, whose ordinary dessert was

"Poor children three,
That could not with him grapple,
But at one sup he ate them up,
As one would eat an apple";[19]

nor into a modern Medusa, with power to transform the trembling urchins to stone by a look. I only wish to give you a hint of unpleasant possibilities, so that, if your Spanish castle should fall, it may not bury you in the ruins. As the Cat observed to the Ugly Duckling, "I say disagreeable things, but it is for your good." I take it for granted that your own hearts will teach you enough of love, and the spirit of meekness; that your woman's nature makes it incumbent on one to exhort you to let justice temper mercy, rather than mercy temper justice.

There are other stones of stumbling, against which you may as well be forewarned. Every community that has emerged from a state of barbarism is infested with excellent and exemplary individuals, leaning to the "goody—good," accustomed to take things on trust, who will embrace every opportunity to speak a word, in season and out of season, especially out of season, on the fearful and weighty responsibilities of your position. I advise you, as a friend, not to listen to them. The comparative amount of your responsibility and mine, his, hers, or its, is a thing not cognizable by human eyes.

It is not necessarily the man who comes in contact with the largest number of people who exercises the most influence. It may be so, but it does not follow, and we do not know whether it is or not. When John Bunyan was cast into Bedford jail, there were doubtless many pious souls who mourned that the zeal and power of his best years should be thus wasted; yet through those prison-walls there streams a light which will grow brighter and brighter, till lost in the glory of the Celestial City.[20] Every person is responsible for all the good within the scope of his abilities, and for no more,—and none can tell whose sphere is the largest. A mother, tending her child in the quiet seclusion of a Virginian home, sees no foreshadowing of a mighty destiny, yet there comes a day when an empire's fate trembles in the tiny hand now clasping hers. It is therefore impertinent to assume that the responsibility of teachers, or of any one class of people, is greater than that of any other. The only difference is, that one influences at first hand, another at second or third. At every foot-fall, we set in motion a chord whose trembling thrills ten thousand more, and will quiver on eternally. Every thought and word and deed of every human being is followed by its inevitable consequence; for the one we are responsible; with the other we have nothing to do.

You will also probably encounter a great many deprecatory remarks, concerning superficial knowledge, a smattering of the sciences, &c. Fond mammas will think they are making a display of great and judicious wisdom, in exhorting you to render their infants thorough masters of whatever study they pursue. Now I think superficial knowledge is a very good thing; and, for my own part, I should be only too glad to be well-smattered. In the first place, complete mastery by school-children of any one study is a moral impossibility; not only from the organization of our school system, but from the very structure of the human mind. Take geography, one of the earliest and perhaps the simplest studies attempted. Childish capacity cannot seize it in all its bearings, nor is the attempt to present them wise. Many things are taught to children which they would be far better left to find out for themselves. Let them grow up to their difficulties naturally, instead of having difficulties thrust upon them from without. If you lead them tenderly up to a fact, they will quite probably be indifferent, or but partially interested; but if they run against it, they will not leave it till they have found whence it came, and why it is there. School life should be considered only a preparatory course. It is a means, not an end. It is what you work out of their minds, and not what you put in, that is of importance. If a boy, at the end of his school days, has learned how to study, if he has acquired mental, moral, and physical self-control, his career is a success, no matter how many or how few *things* he knows. Of all the knowledge learned, he may have forgotten the greater part; but the wisdom which that learning brought him is his inalienable estate. You must be content to lodge the seed, for April rain and May sunshine and June warmth are necessary to bring it to perfect fruitage. You may drive the nail, but time alone can clinch it.

This charge of superficial knowledge is so often brought up against women, that I may be pardoned for pursuing it a little further, and asking how many *men* there are in America whose knowledge of things generally extends far beyond a smattering? I have something more than a suspicion that, if the principle should obtain that we are to know nothing of a science unless we know that science thoroughly, the sphere of our knowledge would suffer a sudden collapse. Is it indeed desirable that we should be entirely ignorant of the history of Greece, unless we can become imbued with the spirit of her golden age,—entirely conversant with her literature, her antiquities, her topography, her climate, her Fauna and Flora,—know precisely what tide of religious emotion it was that swept over her, bearing on its crested wave the Parthenon,—what silent influence of sun and shade and dew and rain centred on the germ that sprung up into that magnificent outgrowth of national eloquence, whose fruit was Demosthenes and his immortal compeers? Shall we not trace the long wanderings of the heroic Ten Thousand, and share their madness of delight, when, from the heights of the Sacred Mountain, their eyes beheld the sparkle and glow of the Euxine Sea; or watch "Idalian Aphrodite beautiful" flush from the ocean foam, to live in marble forever; or dream in the shadow of Olympus, to the music of that harp whose strings have not yet ceased to quiver,—because, forsooth, we do not know in what city Homer was born, or even whether there was any Homer at all; what force of nature the poetic mind of early Greece symbolized in the Cytherean myth; what wire-pullers, lobby-members, or Hellenic Maintenon moved the lever that thrust the Persians and the Greeks in each others' faces?[21] Nay, verily. The world grew nearly six thousand years before it flowered in Linnæus, yet every child in our village school-houses will listen with appreciative eagerness while you point out to them the different parts of a common pea-blossom, stamen, pistil, keel, wings, and banner; every eye will sparkle, and every little listener become a practical botanist, and bring you specimens from every kitchen garden in the neighborhood[22] The Old World of his birth and the New World of his adoption alike contend for Agassiz; but on shady Saturdays in May, every brook in New England is fringed with ichthyologists in jackets, who will tell you the habitat, the breathing apparatus, the locomotive power, of trout and roach and shiner and sucker for miles around.[23] A life-time is not too much to spend in the investigation of the structure of the earth; but in three months an intelligent boy can learn enough of "rock and tree and flowing water" to give a new interest and beauty to every landscape on which his manhood's eye may rest. Many men have a specialty, something towards which they are drawn by an irresistible impulse, and to which they devote themselves with eager and delighted zest. Shall they therefore be ignorant of everything else? Many more have no specialty. They have an accumulative, analytic, and critical power, and roam at large through many fields. They make no new discoveries, and establish no new generalizations, but they are delightful companions, the appreciative welcomers and true interpreters of the Master Spirit when he comes. None, so far as I know, are thoroughly versed in all branches of knowledge; few, in any one; but many, very many, are sufficiently conversant with a large variety to realize the words of the poet,

"My mind to me a kingdom is."[24]

I have by no means exhausted the possible exasperations which society in general will give you, if you decide to teach. The man who makes your shoes thinks it incumbent upon him to learn the trade; the woman who trims your bonnets finds it necessary to serve an apprenticeship; but the world at large, collectively and individually, considers itself abundantly qualified to make suggestions, offer opinions, and pass judgment on so simple and easy a matter as teaching; nor will any motive of delicacy prevent its doing so. You will also have the satisfaction of knowing that you, devoting the prime of your life, are receiving from one to three fourths as much money as a boy preparing for his junior examination would receive in the same situation; or a graduate, laying up money for his medical or theological lectures. The subject grows too rapidly under my hand, and I believe I shall have to devote a separate treatise to its discussion; but I must show you a few gleams from the "Sunny Side," before I pass on.

In the first place, if you wish to love and to be loved, it offers you delightful opportunity. You will bind fresh young hearts to your own, with a tie that time only strengthens and hallows. They are too far removed from you to see your faults, and they will leave you before they have acquired discernment enough to do so. Consequently, you will be enshrined in their memories, haloed with a glory that is less of your deserts than of their imaginings. They will see what you aim to be, rather than what you are. They will mark your standard, and not your inability to reach it. You will be associated with their purest thoughts and ambitions, their most innocent joys and simplest pleasures,—with all that in after days they will sigh to remember,—with the dew and freshness of their morning. You will also be doing godlike work,—moulding mind, fashioning material which is indestructible. You will see your influence, as you go on from day to day, in the awakening interest, the brightening eye, the more thoughtful brow, the kinder hand, and warmer heart; and below the surface, below all that you can see, the train you have set in motion is going noiselessly on. Without sound of hammer or axe, there is rising a beautiful temple, meet residence for the indwelling of the Holy Spirit. A lovely, gentle woman, who went to heaven long ago, probably never dreaming of the work she had done, perhaps weeping that she had been but an unprofitable servant, changed the current of at least one life, turning it from the valley of the Shadow of Death, through the pleasant land of Beulah;[25] and now, years after, a young man, her pupil, writes thus tenderly of her: "She has a place in my soul, a little inner room, where once dwelt passion, gloom, and chaos; but when she opened it, she gently arranged it, dispelled the gloom that obscured the window, and till I fall asleep her face shall ever meet me there, with all I hold most dear."

To be thus treasured up, not in one soul, but in many souls; to live, not your own life only, but hundreds and hundreds of other lives, perhaps wiser, purer, or happier than yours; to be woven in with the warp and woof of boyhood's strong, firm web; to gleam and flash through the finer, subtler texture of girlhood;—this is your "exceeding great reward."

Girls generally have more or less taste for writing. If we could believe critics on the subject, they take to poetry as naturally as ducks to water; but we do not believe critics, because they write from theory; not from observation, and know little about the inner life of girls,—actual, everyday girlhood. Of all those who are unfitted by their organization for a life of inactivity, by their moral sense for frivolity, by their position, possessions, or taste for manual labor, by far the larger part will turn to the schoolroom rather than to the pen. Still there are, in the aggregate, many who cast wistful and furtive glances towards authorship. It is to them a

> "Shadowy isle of Eden, lying in dark purple spheres of Sea,"—

a Land of Promise, wreathed in golden mist, indistinctly limned, but wondrous fair. To the high-spirited and finely-strung it proffers mental work and pleasurable excitement behind an impenetrable veil. To the poor and struggling it is a mystic Aladdin's lamp, flashing before their dazzled eyes the gleam of gold, paving their way to happiness with pearls and diamonds.

Undoubtedly these castles in the air are not "the baseless fabric of a vision," but, like our thrilling novels, are founded on fact, perhaps on just about as large a proportion of fact. There is a charm about writing. I can conceive of few things more delightful than to see one's self right-angled off in oblong form, on fine white paper, with broad margins, clear type, Russian calf, and illustrations by Darley.[26]

If your cistern is over-full, a newspaper is a very convenient faucet, if you can unscrew it. I know that editors complain bitterly of the multitudinous pipes directed to their sanctums, and the "weak, washy, everlasting flood" with which they are inundated; but I would not hold back on that account. What is the use of having newspapers, pray, if you cannot write for them? Do dry-goods clerks complain because their counters are continually strewed with silks and muslins,—because they are constantly obliged to arrange, and derange, and rearrange? Why, it is their business. It is a sign of prosperity. A shop whose shelves were always in order would be apt to close business in a month, and a newspaper which is not sufficiently alive and active to draw into its vortex a host of spirits from the vasty deep around it, will soon stagnate into decay and death. Besides, how small a portion of the whole suffering is borne by the editor. It is absolutely appalling to think of the hopes and fears, the aspirations and dreams, the anxieties, tears, and heart-throbs, the watching, waiting, and disappointment, shut up in the "dark drawers" of editorial tables,—those terrible Black Holes of literature. And the worst of it is, that in the great majority of cases the execution is merited. I suppose it does sometimes happen that wheat and chaff are alike condemned. In fact, I know it does. If you should be impertinent, and ask me how I know, I should follow the example of the

Autocrat of the Breakfast Table, and simply say, "*Nullum tui negotii.*"[27] Still, as I was remarking, if your poem is not printed, there is a presumption, at least, that it was not worth printing.

Men talk as if it were a sin to write, unless the writing be of the very highest order. But are all preachers Pauls? all soldiers Bonapartes? all actors Garricks? all statesmen Washingtons? Shall a woman not dance unless she have the heels of an Ellsler, or sing without the voice of a Lind, or paint without the pencil of an Angelo? Would it even be better so? Is there not many a man whose pulses thrill to the notes of "Yankee Doodle," who would sit calm and impassive under "Casta Diva"?[28]

A certain reviewer said of a certain writer, that her poems had done positive harm,—they had weakened the English language and perverted the English taste; that it would really be better if she had never taken a pen in her hand; and then he pronounced an anathema on the whole race of feminine rhymers. Nonsense, again! Is the English language more important than the English heart? Is the marble statue which the skillful artist carves with his chisel of greater moment than the living soul which he is to shape, "not for an age, but for all time,"—ay, and for all eternity? All over the green fields of England, and under the blue skies of America, hearts have throbbed and eyes have filled with tears at a woman's simple songs. Of what use is it, then, for a critic to rise up in his self-conceit and say, "This is not poetry; this is all sentiment; it ought not to be written; it is not Miltonian nor Spenserian nor Virgilian nor Dantesque; it is not written according to the rules of high art."

You may tell a mother that her child's features are not Grecian, that his skin is browned and freckled by sun and wind, that his hair is coarse and his form ungainly; but will she clasp him to her bosom with any the less tenderness, or will she thenceforth cease to whisper his name in her morning and evening prayer? The object of poetry is to please—and whom? Not the elegant, the cultivated, the delicately-nurtured, merely; but the poor, the homely, the ignorant, as well. It is to polish the rough, to refine the vulgar, to ennoble the commonplace, to scatter pearls before those who find the path to heaven among the untrodden ways of life. Go to now, fools, and slow of heart to believe! There must be vessels of honor and vessels of dishonor. All stars have not the same glory; but one star differeth from another star in glory. Homer wrote the Iliad, and Florilla Flowerdale writes a Sonnet to a Dew-drop; and though the soul of the one be the basin of an ocean, and that of the other a gill dipper, they are both full. There is but one Chinese wall, but there are many stone fences; and they are entirely effectual in keeping the cows from the meadow and the sheep from the corn. There are but few St. Paul's Cathedrals, but white spires peer heavenward from every valley; and wayworn feet tread cheerily thitherward, and many souls are refreshed and gladdened. The nightingale is the sweetest of all birds, but we could ill spare from our woodland chorus the notes of the robin, the hum of the bee.

No little confusion of ideas prevails as to what constitutes useless and useful, light and heavy literature. There are many who open their damp *Gazettes, Journals, Chronicles, Couriers,* and plod through miles of dry, dusty, dreary political editorials, going to show that the country will sink to remediless ruin if Jenkins is elected town-clerk, but will rise to untold heights of glory should the spotless Muggins radiate his splendor from that lofty station; and they fancy themselves patriotic, absorbed in noble themes, interested only in what is excellent and of good report. Or they plunge into the foreign news columns, litter their brain with the grand dinner given by the Legation on somebody's birthday, or the astute prophecies of some mercantile agent, whose historical knowledge is bound up in Whelpley's Compend,[29] concerning the ultimate fate of Italy, the far-reaching designs of Louis Napoleon, and the balance of power in Europe; and don't *think,* probably, but have a kind of pleasant, unconscious *feeling,* that they are employing their vast intellect on abstruse and weighty matters. Or they watch the light-heeled Blondin on his tight rope,[30] admire the financial operations of enterprising scoundrels, marvel at the manifold and ingenious crimes brought to light in New York, and call this "intelligent," "well-informed,"—"keeping up with the times"; while they pass over the stories, the essays, the poetry, to their wives and daughters, as light reading, quite too small for the attention of their stupendous minds.

But a story or a poem may comprehend the whole duty of man. I have read such a one. I recollect "Herman, or Young Knighthood,"[31] which contained not only more wit, but more wisdom,—not only more beauty, but more grandeur,—not only more play of fancy, more power of imagination, more directness of purpose, more felicity of expression, and more elegance of diction, but more knowledge of human nature, more soundness of judgment, grander conceptions of human aspirations and human capacity to love and to suffer, to enjoy, to act, to die, and to rise again,—a vaster sweep of thought, broader generalization, more comprehensive views, more logical and accurate reasoning, nicer analysis, and a higher standard of Christian manhood,—than you will find in a column of your "solid reading" that would reach from Maine to Georgia.

People *must* live their life, one way or another,—on battle-field or quarter-deck; in cabinet, laboratory, pulpit, or nursery. Boys expend theirs on Virgil and candy; men, on farm and ledger, with a small surplus that goes to liquidate the claims of Smith and Jones to the suffrages of an enlightened community. Girls read Lalla Rookh,[32] crotchet lamp-mats, write interminable letters to immortal female friendship, and so manage to drain off their spare life, till, in the course of human events, it runs naturally to housekeeping and babies, and takes the whole force to keep the mill a-going.

But sometimes the farm and nursery and workshop do *not* use up all the fluid; then, according as it makes for itself a channel, or is pent up in too narrow bounds, you have Shakespeare chaining the ages to his triumphal car, or Chatterton flinging down life at sixteen years as a burden too heavy to be borne. You have Raleigh, leaving the apple-orchards of beautiful Devon for an unknown Land of Faery, a new Jason, wandering world-wide for a golden fleece; Spenser, walking with Genii in enchanted woods, and weaving a mightier spell than they; Burns, upheaving not only the soil with his plough, but the land with his song; Browning, voicing on her many-stringed lyre the "Cry of the Children" who pass through the fire to Moloch; Brontë, chained to her desolate rock, and eating her own heart out with a sharper than Promethean torture; Stowe, throwing open to the shuddering day a sepulchre full of dead men's bones, and all uncleanness; Sappho, harping her own requiem on the Leucadian cliff; Socrates, calmly quenching with hemlock the life that would no otherwise be stayed; Dante, gazing in rapt beatific vision on the glorified face of Beatrice; Galileo, spinning the world around in spite of the pious dunces who sat on it in solemn conclave to hold it down; Kane, walking in silence with the Spirit of Storms; Paul, transported with a holy ardor, denouncing woe to himself if he rein in the fiery words that leap to his lips; David, the stripling, ruddy, and of a beautiful countenance, changed by the spear-touch of an heroic purpose from the dreaming shepherd-boy to the champion of Israel; and William of Orange, and Alfred the Great, and Milton, and Tasso, and Napoleon, and Homer, and Mozart.

Corollary 1. Everybody has just so much life to live, and if it is damned up in one direction it will overflow in another.

Corollary 2. Greatness, heroism, glory, spring from what is left over and above necessity. That is, some people have just soul enough for salt. You cannot conceive a further diminution of their mental endowments unattended by immediate physical decomposition. Of course they have nothing to spare for fame. But the highest must have body as well as the lowest intellect. The body is the strong cord which keeps the "animula vagula blandula" from flying off in a tangent.[33] They cannot live in a state of pure mind, any more than the others can live in a state of pure matter. Consequently, there is a plane on which they both meet, and that plane is bread and butter. But the one never soars above it, while the other never remains upon it. Herein consists the difference between the two. It is from the latter, roaming about in the empyrean, that we get our grandeur and sublimity, our pathos and poetry.

Corollary 3. Female authorship, instead of being deprecated, ought to be encouraged as the great safety-valve of society; and those who ridicule and oppose it show themselves far behind the age in endeavoring to put down such an army with no better weapon than that wherewith Samson slew a thousand Philistines fifty centuries ago.[34]

Many a woman with no pretensions to genius walks her daily round, fulfils all wifely duties, seems contented and happy in her home of peace and plenty, who is nevertheless sometimes lonely and dispirited. There are glimmerings of somewhat higher; shadowy remembrances of girlish aspirations and heroic purposes; a sad and eager questioning—"Is *this* all?"—to the heart that vouchsafes no reply. This feeling can find no vent like poetry or music. If from the keys of her piano or the strings of her harp her troubled spirit, Saul-like, shall find rest, it is well; but if she have no spell to evoke the genius of song, why should you forbid her to give expression by rhythmic cadence to the feeling which, unvoiced, will be crushed back into the soil whence it sprang, to moulder and decay, and cast a mildew and blight on all the graces, virtues, and affections which should adorn and beautify life? The little poem may be simple in thought and rugged in outline; it may be at once consigned to the silence of a secret drawer; but the longing is gratified, the pent-up mind has found an outlet, and the weary woman goes on her way rejoicing. Years afterward, when the hand that wrote it is cold in the grave, a daughter's eyes, it may be, will fall upon it, and a page of that mother's history, hitherto all unrevealed, be suddenly illuminated; and between the daughter on earth and the mother in heaven there will be another and a golden link, which the world knoweth not of.

Girls, do not be deceived. Write. Write poetry,—write in rhyme,—if it is only

"One, two,
Buckle my shoe;
Three, four,
Open the door."

Form the habit. It is often convenient. It is a refuge from ennui. It may do good. Any one of you who refrains from writing for fear of ridicule, is a coward. Don't be a coward. There is not much to a woman at best. She is not expected to have physical courage; but if she has not moral, pray, what has she? The more a man tells you not to write, the more do you write. By this I do not mean to say that you must immediately publish a volume of "Something, and other Poems," though even that I advise you to do, if you feel disposed and can afford it. It is better than to be talking scandal or making flounces. Would-be critics lament pathetically or satirize mercilessly this "rushing into print." It is mere selfishness on their part. You might rush elbow deep into a batter pudding, or bury heart and soul and mind, beyond all hope of disinterment, beneath a confused rubbish of unmended stockings, or by a letter of recommendation become the fifth wife of some hard-worked, hard-working, broken-down, and worn-out missionary, and they would not lift a finger to prevent. No, girls; no. If your heart is stirred within you to write, write! If you can find an editor or publisher who is willing to print for you, print! Somewhere in the world, a heart-string may tremble to your feeble and unsteady touch, with a strange bliss. I do not suppose a line of poetry was ever written, from the New Hampshire bard's

> "The beauties of nature, I positive declare
> The beauties of nature are very rich and rare,"

to the stately hexameters of Britain's sturdy old Republican, which did not bear a message of joy or consolation to some of God's children,—whose coming was not watched for, perhaps, by many loving eyes, and gazed at with untiring satisfaction.[35] Never be concerned about readers. You will, at all events, read it yourself, and, better than all, you will appreciate it. Your darling Arabella will read, admire, and very probably cut it out and place it in her scrap-book. What is fame, more than this?

If you are a little inclined to egotism, and tolerably imaginative, you can trick yourself out in all sorts of Protean shapes; serve yourself up in as many different disguises as a French cook does a *ragoût;* and, at the same time, preserve the most rigid reticence; because no one knows how much is memory and how much is imagination. Or if you have acquired the habit of entertaining views of things, it gives you an excellent opportunity to exhibit them; and of the many comfortable things in the world, one of the most comfortable is to give your views. It is so agreeable to say things, when you have things to say. Your opinions may not be very striking, or original, or important; still it is a relief to express them. No matter if they have been said fifty times before; you never said them. They must go through the crucible of your brain before they can be efficient in preventing a congestion from plethora of ideas. The stream may have meandered down the mountains of life a thousand years, and heaped together priceless diamonds and ingots of gold, and yet fail in that fertilizing power more valuable than all, till it sweeps along the rich alluvial deposits that lie in the green meadows of your own soul. It does not satisfy your craving for the "delicacies of the season," to know that salmon and peas have been eaten since the world began.

In so far as literature seems to you a royal road to fame and fortune, let me entreat you not to be deceived. If you have been put through Watts's "Sixteen Rules for Gaining Knowledge and Mental Improvement," as thoroughly as I, I shall not need to say, "Be not so weak as to imagine that a life of learning is a life of laziness and ease." But, besides good Dr. Watts's exhortations, the testimony of the great mass of writers proclaims,

> "Hard the labor, small the gain,
> Is in making bread from brain."

I have seen, in several modern American novels, certain counter statements. Brilliant but obscure young women are represented as having surreptitiously sprung a book upon an unsuspecting public, and being summarily overwhelmed with money, and fame, and troops of distinguished friends and patrons. I know that charming Fanny Burney did really smuggle her Eveline into the world without even the complicity of "Daddy Crisp," and that there presently fell upon her listening, straining, but scarcely expectant ear, a rustling among the mulberry-trees; coaches blocked up the way to the circulating libraries; Burke sat up all night to watch the adventures of a young lady upon her first entrance into the world; fops levelled their glasses; women of fashion patronized the shrinking authoress; and the brutal, benevolent "Great Cham" coiled his huge arm thrice about her slender wrist, and bound her to him forever.[36] Nor have I any doubt that, notwithstanding Campbell's savage toast, publishers are often honest, upright, excellent men, many of whom would gladly bind up the wounds and bruises which their own hands have been forced to inflict.[37] There are individuals among them—several I know—who are perfect pinks of disinterested kindness, full of good works and alms-deeds. Still, I think I do not err in affirming that, as a class, they are not largely addicted to sending huge rolls of spontaneous bank-bills to anonymous correspondents. When you hear of men's receiving twenty, forty, or a hundred dollars a page, and twenty and forty thousand for a volume of history or romance or science, don't think of the forty dollars simply, but of the forty years of daily and nightly toil, research, study, thought, contrivance, experiment, disappointment, discouragement, vexation, and heartache that have preceded them.

> "The crowd, they only see the crown,
> They only hear the hymn;

They mark not that the cheek is pale,
And that the eye is dim."

Do you prize the crown so highly, that you will bear the cross? To be purified by the poet's fire, will you endure the anguish of the burning? Do you worship the goddess with so true a faith, that you will offer up yourself at her shrine?

There are obstacles without as well as within. A certain prejudice against female writers "still lives." It is fine, subtle, impalpable, but real. It is like the great ocean of air that wraps us round. A little of it cannot be seen; it is only in mass that it becomes visible. It is like a far-off star; look straight at it, and it is not there; look askance, and it twinkles and winks at you again. It is like the Indian in warfare; it never meets you face to face, and takes fair aim, but, darting behind shelter, sends a shot obliquely. It is also like the Devil; resist it, and it will flee from you. It is indeed vanishing every day; and as woman gravitates to her proper place, and the elements cease to be agitated, it will entirely disappear. Like other fashions founded on whim, caprice, or injustice, and not on the eternal fitness of things, it will go from master to man, from man to scullion, from scullion to the dogs. It has already begun its downward progress. Large-hearted and large-brained men, the monarchs of thought, have flung it clean off. The ranks below them, men of small capacities but unbounded ambition, who see in women their own rivals,—who fear, and justly, too, that a fair field and no favor would oust them from seats they have questionable claim to fill and infinite difficulty to hold,—have caught the flimsy, floating thing, and see but darkly through its tremulous shimmer; and, with limbs tangled in its fair, strong, invisible meshes, walk stumbling and uncertain. So long as you will lend yourself to the amusement of these men,—be witty, playful, piquant, affectionate, and saucy; dance and sparkle along their ascending pathway; circle, as brilliant a satellite as you please, round themselves, the central, acknowledged sun,—they will shine down on you the most benignant and complacent condescension. But once undertake to set up for yourself; get the troublesome idea into your head, that that head was given you for something more than a series of fireworks; tell them seriously that you have been thinking whether all play may not make Gill a mere toy, just as it does Jack, and whether there may not be something in the world for you to do,—whether the purling, singing, happy brook, that now only freshens the violets on its banks, may not, by widening and deepening the channel, be made subservient to nobler and not less pure uses,—whether the same vivacity, compactness, and power that enliven the social circle, and fling a charm around a few favored lives, may not gleam on a broader sphere with no diminished lustre, soften the harsh outline of some unwelcome truth into grace and loveliness, light up some sombre picture with golden tints, polish some hidden blade—rusty, disused, and rusty because disused—into Damascene gleaming, suppleness, and sharpness, and restore it once more to the armory of God,—and lo! our respected friend, who, whilom, found no words so sweet as fitly could express his love, complacence, interest in your weal, admiration of your character, and pride in your reputation, cools suddenly down to zero, leans leisurely back in his comfortable study-chair, strokes caressingly his black moustache, and, with eyes turned contemplatively ceiling-ward, and infinite and pitying forbearance of voice and manner: "Yes" (with an inflection indicative of mental and subjective interrogation),—"yes" (falling inflection; interrogation not satisfactorily answered). "You may be able to effect something. There are very respectable authors among women." (Magnanimous concession!) "There is no doubt that the thing is overdone. Still—" and here, or a minute after, at furthest, he will cut an intellectual pirouette, and, with a most frank, arch, and engaging smile, inform you that, after all, he would "rather see a ring on your third finger than an ink-spot on your first." Stupid!

You will often see the outcropping of this feeling in the criticisms of women's books; not that just and generous criticism which discriminates between the evil and the good, condemns the one without rancor, and applauds the other without servility, but that half-flattering, half-contemptuous, and wholly contemptible notice, whose compassionate blame and condescending praise are alike insulting. Such was the revenge of some of our sleek, respectable, self-admiring male writers, when Aurora Leigh dashed in upon their fancied security, and shivered her most knightly yet right womanly lance against their time-honored commonplaces.[38] What a shaking of the dry bones there must have been, indeed, under the hoofs of her high-mettled steed! But as soon as their spirits returned to them again, they fell a-babbling of Socialism, and Fourierism, and Chartism, and "all the others that end in" ism; and there was poetry in the book, *but* there was a deal of obscurity; and there was felicity of expression, *but* there was occasional awkwardness; and there were a great many things, *but* there were also a great many others; and, on the whole, Aurora Leigh must be pronounced a failure. Self-blinded! If Aurora Leigh be a woman's failure, what would a woman's success be?

Sometimes this prejudice takes the form of disinterested counsel, paternal and affectionate advice; but through the lion's skin, the long ears reveal indubitably the true nature of the animal. "Aspiring sisters," says the domestic brute before alluded to, "why is the tone of your lucubrations always so mournful? If you must write, write cheerfully. Don't let every song be a dirge. We want to be amused when we read" (there is the ear again); "consume in private your private griefs." Not a doubt of it. Beyond cavil, it would be vastly agreeable to our private Neros,—Heaven be praised that they are few, I know that there are some,—who harry the life out of wife and child, who are tyrants without the fear of assassination, because their victims are too good, or of public opinion, because the thing is done in a corner, or of the law, because it takes no cognizance of soul-murder,—doubtless it would be vastly agreeable to them, that women should endure uncomplainingly. No voice louder than theirs in praise of her sweet self-abnegation and silent fortitude, or in deprecation of publicly-displayed sorrow, when, in song or story, the minor key of sadness, the outburst of long-pent-up anguish, or the unmistakable wail of a broken heart, sends home to their own breasts the prophet's stern charge, "Thou art the man." Consume in private your private griefs! No. Take them in a bundle, and bear them to the highest mountain-top; ring the church-bells, hoist the flags, beat the drums, and let the whole world see the bonfire; and if the flame scorches our sensitive friends, let them stand back. Why should they flutter about it, if they don't want their wings singed?

Do all or any of these things move you? Do you fear to launch your bark on so unquiet a sea? Do you shrink from the lion without, lest you should be slain in the street? Then by all means remain within doors, and hold your peace. Do not fancy that you would achieve immortality, if you only had the chance,—that you would soar sunward, if your wings were not pinioned. Genius is expansive, irresistible, and irresistibly expansive. If it is in you, no cords can confine it. A good book will get itself written. Authorship is not a thing to be quietly chosen, as circumstance may determine. It chooses you; you do not choose it. Did Mrs. Browning sit down in her little back parlor, and wonder whether she would better fashion a song, or devote herself exclusively to Robert's shirts and stockings? And, observing that she had facility in language, familiarity with the classics, knowledge of human nature, and abundant leisure, did she forthwith seize her pen, and tell us

> "how a fairy bride from Italy,
> With smells of oleander in her hair,
> Was coming through the vines"?

I trow not. I rather believe that her spirit groaned, being burdened,—that she was but an unwilling Sibyl, lashed on, foaming, by a fierce Apollo. Currer Bell trod in agony the desolate heaths of Haworth, till the consuming fire burned deep scars in her tortured soul, before Jane Eyre leaped, full armed, not from her throbbing brain alone, but from her riven heart.[39]

If prejudice, ignorance, or sloth pile a Hill Difficulty which you hesitate to scale; if indifference, neglect, or rebuff quench your spirit's flow; if encouragement and appreciation must be the Aaron and Hur on either side, without whose aid your failing hands droop, nerveless;[40] if you fear to speak out boldly your convictions lest you forfeit approbation; if peace and smiles and sunshine seem to you more desirable than truth; if you are not in and of yourself sufficient to yourself; if a mind conscious of rectitude, of upright intentions, and honorable performance, is not to you a sufficient guerdon,—you may be

> "A perfect woman, nobly planned,
> To warn, to comfort, and command,"[41]

but lyre and tripod are not for you. The world awards its meed of praise to no uncertain claimant. Only to him that hath shall be given. You go out on a mission of high emprise, with scrip and staff and "sandal shoon," and there are few to say, "God bless you." You return in purple and scarlet and fine linen, with gilded chariot and horse of Arabia, and the world comes out to meet you, with timbrels and dancing, and ministers unto you a triumphal entrance. I do not say that this is wrong; only that it *is.* You must conquer Fate, before Fate will bow the knee. You must prove your royal blood, before you can wear the royal crown; and that perhaps so late that it will only press, cold and heavy, on aching brows.

Watchman! What of the night? The morning cometh.

It is not for the generation among whom Elizabeth Browning has sung, and Charlotte Brontë spoken, and Harriet Hosmer chiselled, and Rosa Bonheur painted, and Mary Lyon taught, and Florence Nightingale lived, to despair of woman's achievement of her highest destiny. In whatever direction you choose to walk, you will find that a firm footfall has preceded yours; that a strong hand has hewed down the giant trees, and cleared away the tangled undergrowth, so that the forest which once required all a man's strength and a woman's fortitude, a child may thrid unharmed. Thus do the strong bear the burdens of the weak. Thus have noble women made straight, in the desert, a highway for our God. "Inasmuch as ye have done it unto one of the least of these my brethren, ye have done it unto me." The costly step has been taken.

But let us not suppose that generous ends can be attained only on the mountain-top. To but few is strength given to climb its ragged sides, and clearness and breadth of vision to take in the broad sweep of its low-lying landscape. Down in the valley there is work to be done,—humble, yet divine; small in the germ, yet great in the unfolding. However simple or however difficult, however obscure or however prominent the work may be, matters not, provided it be God's appointed work. It is better to rule a household well, than a kingdom ill.

"He that sweeps a floor as to God's law,
Makes that and the action fine."[42]

The ring on a child's finger is as perfect a circle as the zone of this round world. The Dairyman's Daughter "just knew, and knew no more, her Bible true," lived out her brief and simple life, and was not, for God took her.[43] But from her humble island home her voice still speaks comfort and hope to the ends of the earth.

Here and there, both in the beaten paths and the untrodden ways, on the lowlands and the uplands of life, I meet an angel,—not in white robes, garlanded with roses, and winged for Heaven, but plain in calico, it may be, or grand in velvet. I recall now the face of one whose life is to me a constant gospel. A slight, pale girl, orphaned, homeless, neglected by those who should have watched her young years tenderly, she yet seems to have drawn to herself, by some magnetic power, all the good of all the persons by whom she has been surrounded, and to have fed her own soul thereon. She went to school, bearing in her mean and scanty dress, her thin cheeks, and hard hands, the marks of poverty and toil; and wild, thoughtless, elegantly-dressed, and carefully-nurtured girls hushed their heedless sarcasm, softened their merry voices, and spoke to her with love, and of her with tears. Shrinkingly sensitive to their opinions, tremblingly alive to her own disadvantages, conscious as she must have been that she served a hard taskmaster, no word of complaint ever passed her lips. Always cheerful, modest, happy, willing to be pleased, grateful for kindness, and patient of any chance neglect, you might have supposed her entirely insensible to the motives and feelings that influence ordinary girls, were it not for the occasional quiver of the lip, the quick, nervous gesture, the moistened eye, and faltering tone. She left school with disease lurking in her system, slowly and surely undermining the citadel of life; but she kept up her courage. She had no idea of dying till her hour should come, and, as long as she should live, she determined that her living should bring forth fruit. She earned money enough to transport herself to a climate which was pronounced favorable to her health; there, in wild backwoods, among a rough people, who had forgotten, if they ever knew, the common refinements of life, she opened a school. From her rude home she wrote merry letters, describing her adventures and her circumstances. There was no talk of self-denial, the greatness of sacrifice, the hardship of missionary life. Over all the harsh outline, and the harsher filling in, she threw the veil of her playful fancy, and few heard the mournful undertone that thrilled through the gay, sprightly song. The new scenes and the softer air did not have the desired effect, and a short time since she wrote to a friend: "I have moved from a small, quiet school to a large, rollicking, frolicking, fun-loving one. I am happy; I think I ought to be. Every one is kind. But I am quite puzzled. I don't know just what to do. If I am to teach much longer, it would be better for me to return to New England, and go to school awhile. I have earned enough to keep me at school a year or so, and I do believe I am willing to exert myself to the utmost to improve. But, then, this cough increases. It may not be long before it will have an end. If I go to New

England, I may spend all the life left me in *acquiring* knowledge, and so lose the opportunity for usefulness that I might have if I remained here. Now the question is, "Which will bring the largest pile of wood,—the dull axe for six hours, or the sharp one for two?"

This is what I mean by heroism. This young girl standing at bay, watching what she believes to be the approach of inevitable death, asking for no rest from toil, no indulgence for weakness and weariness, no sympathy in loneliness, but only striving to know how the little life that remains may be turned to the best account. Brave heart! on the wings of this soft south-wind, that murmurs of violets in the ear of winter, I send you greeting. In your far-off home my voice may never reach you; but if by any chance your eyes should fall upon these words, know that my soul does willing homage to yours, and forgive these few sentences, for the love and reverence that prompted them.

"None but thou and I shall know."

I remember another, a stranger in a strange land; an exile from the home of her fathers; a fair-haired and blue-eyed girl, a warm-hearted and whole-souled woman; of exquisite sensibility, refined taste, and elegant culture; a lover of song and grace and beauty in any guise; a man in strength, a martyr in endurance; performing a father's duty to children not her own; fighting the battle single-handed, and no holiday contest, but a life-and-death struggle with the wolf at the door; welcoming the cold embrace of Duty as smilingly as if it were the warm clasp of Love; eager eyes and ears wide open to the green fields, the upspringing daisies, the note of bee and bird, yet swerving not a hair's breadth from the rocky path which her aching feet most resolutely tread; and where I see her footprints, I know it is holy ground.

And yet another face shines on me through the night,—a face over which the Angel of Sorrow has swept his wing in passing, and saddened into a beauty that is not of the earth. You, looking, see only dark eyes that flash laughter, love, or tears; a delicate cheek, that pales and flushes at your words; red lips, whence drop rare gems of wit and wisdom. These are there, and I see them; but beyond these, and deeper than these, I see a soul that has been weighed in the balance and not found wanting; a heart that has been wrung by sorest anguish, and only grown more pitying and tender; a hand that has touched every note from highest to lowest, and learned to strike from earthly chords most heavenly harmonies; a woman who has said to wealth and station and ease, "Get thee behind me!" and, mailed in her own integrity, has dared opposing fate. It is these, and such as these, that

"show us how divine a thing
A woman may be made."[44]

They redeem their sex from the charge of frivolity, inanity, and feebleness, revealing to us the capacities that lie hidden in her heart of hearts; and it is because I have witnessed such noble living, such "extraordinary, generous seeking," that I believe in woman; and when I see life going to waste,—when I see a woman's soul bent on ignoble ends, frittered away on trifling toys, finding content and happiness in things that perish with the using,—I feel, not contempt, not anger, but sadness and sore regret:—

"The pity of it, Iago, the pity of it."[45]

I mourn for gold grown dim, and fine gold changed,—for fields white to harvest, and the reapers disporting among flowers,—for a world lying in ignorance and wickedness, and the power that should raise and redeem it, and fit it once more for the footsteps of its Lord, spending its strength for naught.

O, if this latent power could be aroused! If woman would shake off this slumber, and put on her strength, her beautiful garments, how would she go forth conquering and to conquer,—how would the mountains break forth into singing, and the trees of the field clap their hands,—how would our sin-stained earth arise and shine, her light being come, and the glory of the Lord being risen upon her!

One cannot do the world's work; but one can do one's work. You may not be able to turn the world from iniquity, but you can at least keep the dust and rust from gathering on your own soul. If you cannot be directly and actively engaged in fighting the battle, you can at least polish your armor and sharpen your weapons, to strike an effective blow when the hour comes. You can stanch the blood of him who has been wounded in the fray,—bear a cup of cold water to the thirsty and fainting,—give help to the conquered and smiles to the victor. You can gather from the past and the present stores of wisdom, so that, when the future demands it, you may bring forth from your treasures things new and old. Whatever of bliss the Divinity that shapes our ends may see fit to withhold from you, you are but very little lower than the angels so long as you have the

"Godlike power to do,—the godlike aim to know."

You can be forming habits of self-reliance, sound judgment, perseverance, and endurance, which may one day stand you in good stead. You can so train yourself to right thinking and right acting, that uprightness shall be your nature, truth your impulse. His head is seldom far wrong whose heart is always right. We bow down to mental greatness, intellectual strength, and they are Divine gifts; but moral rectitude is stronger than they. It is irresistible,—always in the end triumphant. There is in goodness a penetrative power that nothing can withstand. Cunning and malice melt away before its mild, open, steady glance. Not alone on the fields where chivalry charges for laurels, with helmet and breastplate and lance in rest, can the true knight exultantly exclaim,

"My strength is as the strength of ten,
Because my heart is pure,"[46]

but wherever man meets man, wherever there is a prize to be won, a goal to be reached. Wealth and rank and beauty may form a brilliant setting to the diamond, but they only expose more nakedly the false glare of the paste. Only when the king's daughter is all glorious within, is it fitting and proper that her clothing should be of wrought gold.

From the great and the good of all ages rings out the same monotone. The high-priest of nature, the calm-eyed poet who laid his heart so close to hers that they seemed to throb in one pulsation, yet whose ear was always open to the "still sad music of humanity," has given us the fruit of his life-long wisdom in these grand words:—

"True happiness abides with him alone
Who, in the silent hour of inward thought,
Can still respect and still revere himself."

Through the din of twenty rolling centuries pierces the sharp, stern voice of the brave old Greek: "Let every man, when he is about to do a wicked action, above all things in the world stand in awe of himself, and dread the witness within him." All greatness and all glory, all that earth has to give, all that heaven can proffer, lies within the reach of the lowliest as well as the highest; for He who spake as never man spake has said that the very "kingdom of God is within you."

Born to such an inheritance, will you wantonly cast it away? With such a goal in prospect, will you suffer yourself to be turned aside by the sheen and shimmer of tinsel fruit? With earth in possession and heaven in reversion, will you go sorrowing and downcast, because here and there a pearl or ruby fails you? Nay, rather, forgetting those things which are behind, and reaching forth unto those which are before, press forward. Discontent and murmuring are insidious foes; trample them under your feet. Utter no complaint, whatever betide; for complaining is a sign of weakness. If your trouble can be helped, help it; if not, bear it. You can be whatever you will to be. Therefore, form and accomplish worthy purposes. If you walk alone, let it be with no faltering tread. Show to an incredulous world

> "How grand may be Life's might,
> Without Love's circling crown."

Or if the golden thread of love shine athwart the dusky warp of duty, if other hearts depend on yours for sustenance and strength, give to them from your fulness no stinted measure. Let the dew of your kindness fall on the evil and the good, on the just and on the unjust.

Compass happiness, since happiness alone is victory. On the fragments of your shattered plans and hopes and love, on the heaped-up ruins of your past, rear a stately palace, whose top shall reach unto heaven, whose beauty shall gladden the eyes of all beholders, whose doors shall stand wide open to receive the wayworn and weary. Life is a burden, but it is imposed by God. What you make of it, it will be to you, whether a millstone about your neck, or a diadem upon your brow. Take it up bravely, bear it on joyfully, lay it down triumphantly.

MY BOOK

FROM SKIRMISHES AND SKETCHES

THE TROUBLE about biographies is that by the time they are written the person is dead. You have heard of him remotely. You know that he sang a world's songs, won victories, founded empires, did heroes' work; but you do not know the little tender touches of his life, the things that bring him into near kinship with humanity, and set him by the household hearth without unclasping the diadem from his brow, until he is dead, and it is too late forevermore. Then with vague restlessness you visit the brook in which his trout-line drooped, you pluck a leaf from the elm that shaded his regal head, you walk in the graveyard that holds in its bosom his silent dust, only to feel with unavailing regret that no sunshine of his presence can gleam upon you. The life that stirred in his voice, shone in his eye, and fortressed itself in his unconscious bearing can make to you no revelation. It is departed, none knows whither. He is as much a part of the past as if he had tended flocks for Abraham on the plains of Mamre.[1]

This, when biographies are at their best. Generally, they are at their worst. Generally, they do not know the things you wish to learn, and when they do, they do not tell them. They give you statistics, facts, reflections, eulogies, dissertations; but what you hunger and thirst after is the man's inner life. What use is it to know what a man does, unless you know what made him do it? This you can seldom learn from memoirs. Look at the numerous brood that followed in the wake of Shelley's fame. Every one gives you, not Shelley, but himself, served up in Shelley sauce. Think of your own experience: are not the vital facts of your life hermetically sealed? Are you not a world within a world, whose history and geography may be summed up in that phrase which used to make the interior of Africa the most delightful spot in the whole atlas—"Unexplored Region"? One person may have started an expedition here, and another there. Here one may have struck a river-course, and there one may have looked down into a valley, and all may have brought away their golden grain; but the one has not followed the river to its source, nor the other wandered bewilderingly through the valley-lands, and none have traversed the Field of the Cloth of Gold.[2] So the geographies are all alike, boundaries, capital, chief towns, rivers. And what is true of you is doubtless true of all. Faith is not to be put in biographies.

Whether you were susceptible of calmness or were deeply turbulent,—whether you were amiable, or only amiably disposed,—whether you were inwardly blest and only superficially unrestful, safely moored even while tossing on an unquiet sea,—what you thought, what you hoped, how you felt, yes, and how you lived and loved and hated, they do not know and cannot tell. A biographer may be ever so conscientious, but he stands on the outside of the circle of his subject, and his view will lack symmetry. There is but one who, from his position in the centre, is competent to give a fair and full picture, and that is your own self. A few may possess imagination, and so partially atone for the disadvantages of position; but, a thousand to one, they will not have a chance at your life. You must die knowing that you are at the mercy of whoever can hold a pen.

Unless you take time by the forelock and write your biography yourself! Then you will be sure to do no harm, inasmuch as no one is obliged to read your narrative; and you may do much good, because, if any one does read it and become interested in you, he will have the pleasing consciousness of living in the same world with you. When he drives through your street, he can put his head out of the carriage-window and perhaps see you just going in at the front gate. Also, if you write your biography yourself, you can have your choice as to what shall go in and what shall stay out. You can make a discreet selection of your letters, giving the go-by to that especial one in which you rather—is there such a word as spooneyly?—offered yourself to your wife. Every word was as good as the bank to her, for to her you were a lover, a knight, a great brown, bearded angel, and all metaphors, however violent, fell upon good ground. But to the people who read your life you will be a trader, a lawyer, a shoemaker, who pays his butcher's bills and looks after the main chance, and the metaphors, deprived of their fire, but retaining their form, will seem incongruous, not to say ridiculous. I do not say that your wife's lover and knight and angel are not a higher and a better, yes, and a truer you, than the world's trader and lawyer; still your love-letters will probably be better off in the bosom of the love-lettered than on a bookseller's shelves. Besides these advantages, there is another in præ-humous publication. If you wait for your biography till you are dead, it is extremely probable you will lose it altogether. The world has so much to see to ahead that it can hardly spare a glance over its shoulder to take note of what is behind. Take the note yourself and make sure of it. You will then know where you are, and be master of the situation.

I purpose, therefore, to write the history of my life, from my entrance upon it down to a period which is within the memory of men still living. In so doing, I shall not be careful to trace out that common ground which may be supposed to underlie all lives, but only indicate those features which serve to distinguish one from another. Everybody is christened, cuts his teeth, and eats bread and molasses. Silently will we, therefore, infer the bread and molasses, and swiftly stride in seven-league boots from mountain-peak to mountain-peak.

I was born of parents who, though not poor, were respectable, and I had also the additional distinction of being a precocious child. I differed from most precocious children, however, in not dying young, and that opportunity, once let slip, is now forever gone. I believe the precocious children who do not die young develop into idiots. My family have never been without well-grounded fears in that line.

Nothing of any importance happened to me after I was born till I grew up and wrote a book. Indeed, I believe I may say even that never happened, for I did not write a book. Rather a book came to pass,—somewhat like the goldsmithery of Aaron, who threw the ear-rings into the fire, and "there came out this calf!"[3] I went out one day alone, as was my wont, in an open boat, and drifted beyond sight of land. I had heard that shipwrecked mariners sometimes throw out a bottle of papers to give their friends a clew to their fate. I threw out a bottle of papers, less out of regard to friends than to myself. They floated into a printing-press, and came forth a book, whereon I sailed safely ashore, grateful. Alas! in another confusion will there be another resource?

It is this book which is to form the first, and quite possibly the last chapter of my life and sufferings, for I don't suppose anything will ever happen to me again. To be sure, in the book I have just been reading a girl marries her groom, leaves him, rejects two lovers, kills her husband, accepts one lover, loses him, marries the second, first husband comes to light again and is shot, marries second husband over again, and goes a-journeying with second husband and first lover, first cousin and two children, in the South of France, before she is twenty-two years old. But in my country girls think themselves extremely well off for adventures with one marriage and no murder. But then the girls in my country do not have the murderous black eyes which shine so in romances.

My book being fairly set a-going, of course you wish to know what came of it. Do not pretend you don't care, for you know you do. Only look not too closely at me, or you will disconcert me. Veil now and then your intent eyes, or my story will surely droop under their steadfastness. Look sometimes into yonder sunset sky and the beautiful reticulations drawn darkly against its glowing sheets of color. You will none the less listen, and I shall all the more enjoy.

You have read much about the anxieties, the forebodings, the anticipatory tremors of new authors. So have I, but I never felt them,—not a single foreboding. I was delighted to write a book, and it never occurred to me that everybody would not be just as delighted to read it. The first time my book weighed on me was one morning when a meagre little letter came to me, which turned out to be only a card bearing the laconic inscription,—

"Twelve copies 'New Sun' sent by express, with the compliments of the Publishers."

The "New Sun" was my book. I put on my hat and walked straightway up to the hole in the rock, about a mile around the corner, where the expressman always leaves my parcels, and took up the package to bring home. It was very heavy. I balanced it first on one arm and then on the other, until, as the poet has it,—

"Both were nigh to breaking."

Then I lifted it by the cords, but they cut my fingers. Then I remembered the natural law, that internal atmospheric pressure prevents any consciousness of the enormous external pressure exerted by an atmosphere forty-five miles thick, and applied the law, saying, "These books all being inside of my head, of course I shall not feel them on the outside." So I put the package on my head, and walked on, making believe I was in a gymnasium, keeping a sharp watch fore and aft, and considering the distant rumbling of wheels a signal for dousing my colors. In my country people do not carry their burdens on their heads, nor would they be likely to account for me on the principles of Natural Philosophy. I might have been apprehended as a lunatic, but for my timely caution.

Thus the "New Suns" came home and were speedily stripped of their dun wrappings. I lingered over them, admiring their clear type, their fragrance, their crispness. I opened them wide, because they would open so frankly. I delighted myself with their fair smoothness. And then I began to read. I am ashamed to say I never read a more interesting book!

How very true it is that suffering is about equally distributed, after all! If you do not have your troubles spread out, you have them in a lump. The furies may seem to be held in abeyance, but they will only lay on their lashes all the harder when they do come. My unnatural calmness was succeeded by a storm of consternation. I pass over the few days that followed. If you ever put yourself into a pillory in the night just to see how it seemed, and then found yourself fastened there in good earnest, and day dawning, and all the marketmen and shopkeepers up and stirring, and everybody coming by in a few minutes, you will not need to ask how I felt. When you write a book, you are quite alone and your pen is entirely private; but when it comes to you so unquestionably printed, and inexorable, and out-of-doors—Ah, me! It did not seem like a book at all,—not at all the abstraction and impersonality that were intended, but a concrete person walking out into the world with malice aforethought.

But though a writer is before critics, did it never occur to you that the critics are just as much before the writers? A critic's talk about a book is just as truly a revelation of the critic as the writer's talk in the book is a revelation of the writer. One man gives you an opinion that implies attention. He does not go into the depths of the matter, but he tells you honestly what he likes and what he does not like. This is good. This is precisely what you wish to know, and will indirectly help you. Another, from the steps of a throne, in a few sentences, it may be, or a few columns, classifies you, interprets you not only to the world, but to yourself; and for this you are immeasurably glad and grateful. It is neither praise nor censure that you value, but recognition. Let a writer but feel that a critic reaches into the *arcana* of his thought, and no assent is too hearty, nor any dissent too severe. Another glances up from his eager political strife, and with the sincerest kindness awards you a nice little bon-bon, chiefly flour and water, but flavored with sugar. Thank you. Another flounders in a wash of words, holding in solution the faintest salt of sense. Heaven help him! Another dips his spear-point in poison and lets fly. Do you not see that these people are an open book? Do you not read here the tranquillity of a self-poised life, the inner sight of clairvoyance, the bitterness of disappointed hopes and unsuccessful plans, the amiability that is not founded upon strength, the pettiness that puts pique above principle, the frankness that scorns affectation, the comprehensiveness that embraces all things in its vision, and commands not only acquiescence, but allegiance, the great-heartedness that by virtue of its own magnetism attracts all that is good?

When my poor little ewe-lamb went out into the world, I did not fear any shearing it might encounter in America. I do not mind my own countrymen. I like them, but I am not afraid of them. Two elements go to make up a book: matter and manner. The former, of course, is its author's own. He maintains it against all comers. Opposition does not terrify him, for it is a mere difference of opinion. One is just as likely to be right as another, and in a hundred years probably we shall all be found wrong together. But manner can be judged by a fixed standard. Bad English is bad English this very day, whatever you or I think about it; and bad English is a bad thing. When I know it, I avoid it, except under extreme temptation; but the trouble is, I do not know it. I am continually learning that words in certain relations are misplaced where I never suspected the smallest derangement, and, no doubt, there are many dislocations which I have not yet discovered. So far as my own people are concerned, I do not take this to heart,—because my countryman very likely perpetuates three barbarisms in correcting my one. He knows this thing that I did not, but then I know something else that he does not, and so keep the balance true. Moreover, my America, if I use bad English, whose fault is it? You have had me from the beginning. The raw material was as good as the average; why did you not work it up better? I went to the best schools you gave me. I learned everything I was set to learn. You can nowhere find a teacher who will tell you that I ever evaded a lesson. I was greedy of gain I spared neither time nor toil. I lost no opportunity, and here I am, just as good as you made me. So, if there is any one to blame, it is you, for not giving me better facilities. The Children's Aid Society warned New York a dozen years ago that a "dangerous class of untaught" pagans was growing up in her streets; but she did not think it worth while to arouse herself and educate them, and one morning she found them burning her house over her head. You too, my country, have been repeatedly warned of your dangerous class, a class whom, with malice aforethought, you leave half educated, and, from ignorance, idle,—and now comes Nemesis! New York had a mob, and you have—me.

The real ogres were those terrible Englishmen. I was brought up on the British Quarterlies. Their high and mighty ways entered into my soul. I never did have any courage or independence, to begin with; and when they condescended to tread our shores with such lordly airs, I should have been only too glad to burn incense for a propitiation. So impressive was their loftiness, their haughty patronage, that their supercilious sneers at our provincialism were heart-rending. I came to look at everything with an eye to English judgment. It was not so much whether a book or a custom were good as whether it would be likely to meet with English approval. To be the object of their displeasure was a calamity, and at even a growl from their dreadful throats I was ready to die of terror.

But it so happened that by the time my book was set afloat, the Reviewers had lost their fangs. The war came, and they went over to the enemy, every one: "North British," "London Quarterly," "Edinburgh," and even the liberal "Westminster," had but one tone. "Blackwood" was seized with an evil spirit, and wallowed foaming. The English people may be all right at heart. Their slow, but sure and sturdy sense may bring them at length within hailing distance of the truth. Noble men among them, Mill and Cairnes and Smith and their kind,[4] made their voices heard in the midst of opposing din, even through the very pages which had rung with Southern cheers: but it is not the English people who make up the Quarterly Reviews. It was not the voice of Mill or Cairnes that answered first across the waters to the boom of Liberty's guns. When our blood was hot and our hearts were high, and sneers ten thousand times harder to bear than blows, we found sneers in plenty where we looked for Godspeed. It may not have been the English heart, only the English head. But we could not get at the English heart, and the English head was continually thrust against ours. The fires may have burned warmly on many a hearth, but we could not see them. The only light that shot athwart the waters was from the high watch-towers, and it was lurid. This wrought a change. The English may put on airs in literature; for our little leisure leaves us short of repose, and it would be strange indeed, if their civilization of centuries had not left its marks in a finer culture and a deeper thought. But when, leaving literature and coming down into the fastnesses of life, they gave us hatred for love, and scorn for reverence,—when they sneered at that which we held sacred, and reviled that which we counted honorable,—when, green-eyed and gloating, they not only saw through their glasses darkly, but all things were distorted and awry,—when devotion became to them fanaticism, and love of liberty was lust of power,—did virtue go out of them, or had it never been in? This, at least, was wrought: when one part of the temple of our reverence was undermined, the whole structure came down. They who showed themselves so morally weak cannot maintain even the intellectual or aesthetic superiority which they have assumed. Henceforth their blame or praise is not what it was. When a man rails at my country, it is little that he rails at me. If they have called the master of the house Beëlzebub, they of his household would as soon be called little flies as anything else.

(As a matter of fact, I do not suppose my little venture has ever been heard of across the ocean. You think it is very presumptuous in me ever to have thought of it; but I did not think of it. I was only afraid of it. Suppose the British Quarterly has not vision microscopic enough to discern you; you like to know how you feel in a certain contingency, even if it should never happen. Besides, so many strange things arise every day, that incongruity seems to have lost its force.)

But if we only did reverence England as once we reverenced her, this is what I would say:—"Upon my country do not visit my sins. Upon my country's fame let me fasten no blot. Wherever I am wrong, inelegant, inaccurate, provincial, visit all your reprobation upon me,—

'Me, me, adsum, qui feci; in me convertite ferrum,
O Angli! mea fraus omnis,'—[5]

upon me as a writer, not upon me as an American. Do not regard me as the exponent of American culture, or as anywhere near the high-water mark of American letters. If you will see the highest, look on the heights. If you look at me, look at me where I am: not among those whose infancy was cradled in art and luxury, whose life from the beginning has been carefully attuned to the finest issues, who for purity of language and dignity of mental bearing may throw down the gauntlet to the proudest nation in the world,—but among those wild children of the soil who take its color, who share its qualities, who give out its fragrance, who love it and lay their hearts to it and grow with it, rocky and rugged, yet cherish, it may be hoped, its little dimples of verdure here and there,—who show not what, with closest care, it might become, but what, under the broad skies and the free winds and the common dews and showers, it is. Our conservatories can boast hues as gorgeous, forms as stately, texture as fine as yours; but don't look for camellias in a cornfield."

Does this seem a little inconsistent with what I was saying just now to my home-made critics? Very likely. But truth is many-sided, and one side you may present at home and the other abroad, according to the exigencies of the case, without being inconsistent.

O England, England! what shall recompense us for our Lost Leader?[6] Great and Mighty One, from whose brow no hand but thine own could ever have plucked the crown! Beautiful land, sacred with the ashes of our sires, radiant with the victories of the past, brilliant with hopes for the future,—

"O Love, I have loved you! O my soul,
I have lost you!"

Ah, if these fatal years might be blotted out! If we could stand once again where we stood on that October day when the young Prince, whose gentle blood commanded our attention, and whose gentle ways won our hearts, bore back to his mother-land and ours the benedictions of a people! Upon that white-faced shore I shall one day look, but woe is me for the bitter memories that will spring up for the love and loyalty so ruthlessly rent away!

So I borrow your ears, my countrymen, and tell you why it is impossible to defer to you as much as one would like. Partly, it is because you talk so wide of the mark. It may not be practicable or desirable to say much; but so much the more ought what you do say to be to the point. A good carpenter needs not to vindicate his skill by hammering away hour after hour on the same shingle; but while he does strike, he hits the nail on the head. Moreover, you show by your remarks that you have such—such—well, *stupid* is what I mean, but I am afraid it would not be polite to employ that word, so I merely give you the meaning, and leave you to choose a word to your liking—notions about the nature, the facts, and the objects of writing. Look at it a moment. With your gray goose-quill you sit, O Rhadamanthus, and to your waiting audience pleasantly enough affirm that I have "taken Benlomond for my model."[7] But when I happen to remember that the larger part of my book was written and printed not only before I had ever met Benlomond, but before he had ever been heard of in this country at least, what faith can I have in your sagacity? And when, remembering those remarkable coincidences which sometimes surprise and baffle us, which in science make Adams and Le Verrier discover the same planet at the same time without knowing anything of each other's calculations, and which in any department seem to indicate that a great tide sweeps over humanity, bearing us on its bosom whithersoever it will, so that

> "God's puppets, best and worst,
> Are we; there is no last nor first,"—[8]

I institute an examination of Benlomond to discover those generic or specific peculiarities which are supposed to have made their mark on me, why, I find for resemblance, that the situations, look you, is both alike. There is a river in Macedon; there is also, moreover, a river in Monmouth; 't is as like as my fingers to my fingers, and there is salmons in both!

Have I taken Benlomond for my model? But why not Josephus and

Ricardo and François and Michel, any and all who have poured their fancies and feelings into this mould?[9] Why select the last disciple and ignore the first apostle? Many prophets have been in Israel whom I resemble as much, to say the least, as this Benlomond. Is it not, my friend, that, in the multitude of your words and ways, you have not found time to renew your acquaintance with these ancient worthies, and so their features have somewhat faded from your memory? But Benlomond came in but yesterday, and because he is a newspaper-topic, him you know; and because at the first blush you doubtless can read that there is a river in Monmouth and also a river in Macedon, and salmons in both,—'t is as like as my fingers to my fingers, and Monmouth was built on the model of Macedon! Ah, my eagle-eyes, Judæa, too, had its Jordan, and Damascus its Abana and Pharpar, and little Massachusetts its Merrimac, which,

> "poet-tuned,
> Goes singing down his meadows."

But Judæa did not type Damascus. The Merrimac bears not the sign of Abana, nor was Abana born of Jordan: all, obedient to the word of the Lord, trickle forth from their springs among the hills, and wander down, one through his vineland, one through his olive-groves, and one to meet the roaring of the mill-wheel's rage.

I lay no claim to originality. I know full well that the soil has been tilled and the seed scattered of all that is worthy in the world. Where giants have wrestled, it is not for pigmies to boast their prowess. Where the gods have trodden, let mortals walk unsandalled. The lowliest of their learners, I sit at the feet of the masters. To me, as to all the world, the great and the good of the olden times have left their legacy, and the monarchs of to-day have scattered blessings. Upon me, as upon all, have their grateful showers descended. My brow have they crowned with their goodness, and on my life have their paths dropped fatness. Dreaming under their vines and fig-trees, I have gathered in my lap and garnered in my heart their mellow fruits.

> "With them I take delight in weal
> And seek relief in woe,
> And while I understand and feel

How much to them I owe,
My cheeks have often been bedewed
With tears of heartfelt gratitude."

But though with gladness I render unto Cæsar the things that are Cæsar's, he shall not have that which does not belong to him. Neither Benlomond, nor any living man, nor any one man, living or dead, has any claim to my fealty, be it worth much or little. If I cannot go in to the banquet on Olympus by the bidding of the master of the feast, I will forswear ambrosia altogether, and to the end of my days feed on millet with the peasants in the Valley of Tempe.[10]

Then, changing ground, you smile and shake your head and say, "It is all very well, but it has not the element of immortality. Observe the difference between this writer and Charles Lamb. One is ginger-pop beer that foams and froths and is gone, while the other is the sound Madeira that will be better fifty years hence than now."

Well, what of it? Do you mean to say, that, because a man has no argosies sailing in from the isles of Eden, freighted with the juices of the tropics, he shall not brew hops in his own cellar? Because you will have none but the vintages of dead centuries, shall not the people delight their hearts with new wine? Because you are an epicure, shall there be no more cakes and ale? Go to! It is a happy fate to be a poet's Falernian, old and mellow, sealed in *amphoræ,* to be crowned with lindon-garlands and the late rose. But for all earth's acres there are few Sabine farms, whither poet, sage, and statesman come to lose in the murmur of Bandusian founts the din of faction and of strife; and even there it is not always Cæcuban or Calenian, neither Formian nor Falernian, but the *vile Sabinum* in common cups and wreathed with simple myrtle, that bubbles up its welcome.[11] So, since there must be lighter draughts, or many a poor man go thirsty, we who are but the ginger-pop of life may well rejoice, remembering that ginger-pop is nourishing and tonic,—that thousands of weary wayfarers who could never know the taste of the costly brands, and who go sadly and wearily, will be fleeter of foot and gladder of soul because of its humble and evanescent foam.

Ginger-pop beer is it that you scoff? Verily, you do an unconsidered deed. When one remembers all the liquids, medicinal, soporific, insipid, poisonous, which flood the throat of humanity, one may deem himself a favorite of Fortune to be placed so high in the catalogue. Though upon his lowliness gleam down the rosy and purple lights of rare old wines aloft, yet from his altitude he can look below upon a profane crowd in thick array of depth immeasurable, and rejoice that he is not stagnant water nor exasperated vinegar nor disappointed buttermilk. Nay, I am not only content, but exultant. It may be an ignoble satisfaction, yet I believe I would rather flash and fade in one moment of happy daylight than be corked and cobwebbed for fifty years in the gloom of an unsunned cellar, with a remote possibility, indeed, of coming up from my incarceration to moisten the lips of beauty or loosen the tongue of eloquence, but with a far surer prospect of but adding one more to the potations of the glutton and the wine-bibber.

And what, after all, is this oblivion which you flaunt so threateningly? Even if I do encounter it, no misfortune will happen unto me but such as is common unto men. Of all the souls of this generation, the number that will sift through the meshes of the years is infinitesimally small. The overwhelming majority of names will turn out to be chaff, and be blown away. I shall be forgotten, but I shall be forgotten in very good company. The greater part of my kinsfolk and acquaintance, your own self, my critic, and your family and friends, will go down in the same oblivion which ingulfs me. When I am dead, I shall be no deader than the rest of you, and I shall have been a great deal more alive while I *was* alive.

I am not afraid to be forgotten. Posterity will have its own soothsayers, and somewhere among the stars, I trust, I shall be living a life so intense and complete that I shall never once think to lament that I am not mulling on a book-shelf down here. Besides, if you insist upon it, I am not going to be forgotten. You know no more about it than I do. Knowledge is not always prescience. "This will never do," ruled Jeffrey from his judgment-seat.[12] "Order reigns in Warsaw," pronounced Sebastiani.[13] "I have now gone through the Bible," chuckled Tom Paine, "as a man would go through a wood with an axe on his shoulder, and fell trees. Here they lie, and the priests, if they can, may replant them. They may, perhaps, stick them in the ground, but they will never make them grow." But Wordsworth to-day is reverenced by the nation that could barb no arrow sharp enough to shoot at him. The evening sky that bends above Warsaw is red with the watch-fires of her old warfare bursting anew from their smouldering ashes. And the oaks that doughty Paine fancied himself to have levelled show not so much as a scratch upon their sturdy trunks. Nay, I do not forget that even Charles Lamb was fiercely belabored by his own generation. So, when upon me you pass sentence of speedy death, I assure you that I shall live a thousand years, and there is nobody in the world who can demonstrate that I am in the wrong. Even if after a while I disappear, it proves nothing; you cannot tell whether I am really submerged, or only lying in the trough of the sea to mount the crest of the coming wave. Till the thousandth year proves me moribund, I shall stoutly maintain that I am immortal.

Concerning Charles Lamb the less you say the better. It is easy to build up a reputation for sagacity by offering incense to the gods who are already shrined. Of course there is a difference between us. A pretty rout you would make, if there were not. But, for all your adoration of Charles Lamb, I dare say he would have liked me a great deal better than he would you. Would? Why should I intrench myself in hypothesis? *Does* he not? When I knock at the door of the Inner Temple, does he not fling it wide open, and does not his face welcome me? When the red fire glows on the hearth, have I not sat far into the night, Bridget sitting beside me with heaven's own light shining in her beautiful eyes, and above her dear head the white gleam of guardian angels hovering tenderly,—herself a guardian angel now? And when Elia arches his brows, and lowers at me his storm-clouds, which I do not mind for the sunshine that will not be hidden behind them,—when in the sweet play of June lights and shadows, and the golden haze of Indian-summer, I forget even the kingly words that go ringing through the land, waking the mountain-echo,—when I look out upon this gray afternoon, and see no leaden skies, no pinched and sullen fields, but green paths, gem-bestrewn from autumn's jewelled hand, and warm light glinting through the apple-trees under which he stood that soft October day, till

> "Conscious seems the frozen sod
> And beechen slope whereon he trod,"—

O Alexander, stand out of my sunshine with your bugbear of a Charles Lamb! "I have heard you for some time with patience. I have been cool,—quite cool; but don't put me in a frenzy!"

When you have satisfied yourself with the limiting, you begin on the descriptive adjectives, and pronounce me egotistical. Certainly. I should be unlike all others of my race, if I were not. It is a wise and merciful arrangement of Providence, that every one is to himself the centre of the universe. What a fatal world would this otherwise be! When one thinks what a collection of insignificances we are, how dispensable the most useful of us is to everybody, how little there is in any of us to make any one care about us, and of how small importance it is to others what becomes of us,—when one thinks that even this round earth is so small, that, if it should fall into the arms of the sun, the sun would just open his mouth and swallow it whole, and nobody ever suspect it, (*vide* Tyndall on Heat,)[14] one must see that this self-love, self-care, and self-interest play a most important part in the Divine economy. If one did not keep himself afloat, he would surely go under. As it is, however disagreeable a person be, he likes himself,—however uninteresting, he is interested in himself. Everybody—you, my critic, as well—likes to talk about himself, if he can get other people to listen; and so long as I can get several thousand people to listen, I shall keep talking, you may be sure, and so would you. You are just as egotistical as I am, only you will not own it frankly, as I do. True, I might escape censure by using such circumlocutions as "the writer," "the author," or, still more cumbrously, by dressing out some figure, calling it Frederic or Frederika, and then, like the Delphic priestesses, uttering my sentiments through its mouth, for the space of a folio novel; but it would be my own self all the while. Besides, in order to get at the thing I wanted to say, I should have to detain you on a thousand things that I did not care about, but which would be necessary as links, because, when you have your man, you must do something with him. You cannot leave him standing, without any visible means of support. One person writes a novel of four hundred pages to convince you in a round-about way, through thirty different characters, that a certain law, or the mode of administering it, is unjust. He does not mention himself, but makes his men and women speak his arguments. Another man writes a treatise of forty pages, and gives you his views out of his own mouth. But he does not put himself into his treatise any more than the other into his novel. For my part, I think the use of "I" is the shortest and simplest way of promulgating one's opinions. Even a *we* bulges out into twice the space that *I* requires, besides seeming to try to evade responsibility. Better say *"I"* straight out,— *"I,"* responsible for my words here and elsewhere, as they used to say in Congress under the old *régime.* Besides being the most brave, "I" is also the most modest. It delivers opinions to the world through a perfectly transparent medium. "I" has no relations. It has no consciousness. It is a pure abstraction. It detains you not a moment from the subject. "The writer" does. It brings up ideas entirely detached from the theme, and is therefore impertinent. All you are after is the thing that is thought. It is not of the smallest consequence who thought it. You may be certain that it is not always the people who use "I" the most freely who think most about themselves; and if you are offended, consider whether it may not be owing to a certain modern morbidness of taste in the reader as much as to egotism in the offender.

Remember, also, that, when a writer talks of himself, he is not necessarily speaking of his own definite John Smithship, that does the marketing and pays the taxes and is a useful member of society. Not at all. It is himself as a unit of the great sum of mankind. He means himself, not as an isolated individual, but as a part of humanity. His narration is pertinent, because it relates to the human family. He brings forward a part of the common property. He does not touch that which pertains exclusively to himself. His self is self-created. His imaginative may have as large a share in the person as his descriptive powers. You do not understand me precisely? Well, what is to be done about it?

You think me arrogant. You would think so a great deal more, if you knew me better. At heart I believe I incline very much to the opinion of a friend of mine, that, "after all, nobody in the world is of much account but Susy and me,"—only in my formula I leave out Susy. Think not, therefore, solely of the arrogance that is revealed, but also of the arrogance concealed, and in consideration of the greater repression pardon the great expression. It is not the persons who sin the least, but those who overcome the strongest temptations, who are the most virtuous. People endowed by nature with a sweet humility do not deserve half the credit for their lovely character that those who are naturally selfish and arrogant often deserve for being no more disagreeable than they are. Yes, it must be confessed, you are right in attributing arrogance,—though, after this meek confession and repentance, if you do not forgive me freely and fully, for past and future, your secondary will be a great deal worse than my original sin;—but you never would accuse me of "an arrogance that disdains docility," if you could see the mean-spirited way in which I sit down by the side of an editor and let him *ram-page* over my manuscript. Out fly my best thoughts, my finest figures, my sharpest epigrams,—without chloroform,—and I give no sign. I have heard that successful authors can always have everything their own way. I must be the greatest failure of the age.

"It will be much better to omit this," says the High Inquisitor, turning the thumb-screw.

"No," I writhe. "Take everything else, but leave that."

"I am glad to see that you agree with me," he responds, with Mephistophelian courtesy; and away it goes, and I say nothing, thankful that anything is left.

"Revealing somewhat of the arrogance of success," you comment, directed by your Evil Genius, upon that especial chapter which was written in a gully of the Valley of Humiliation, when I was gasping under an Ætna of rejected manuscripts,[15]—when there was not a respectable newspaper in the country by which I had not been "declined with thanks,"—when, in the desperation of my determination, I had recourse to bribery, and sent an editor a dollar with the manuscript, to pay him for the fifteen minutes it would take to read it. (*Mem.* I never heard from editor, manuscript, or dollar.) No, it may be arrogance, but it is not the arrogance of success. Whatever it was, it was in the grain. And, to look at it in another light, I cannot have been "spoiled by the indulgent praise which my early efforts received," because I have always been praised,—

"Like to the Pontic monarch of old days,
I fed on poisons, till they had no power,
But were a kind of nutriment."[16]

The earliest event I remember is being presented with two cents by one of the "Committee" visiting the school. And if I could stand two cents in my helpless infancy, don't you suppose I can stand your penny-a-lining now I am grown up? I may have been spoiled, or I may not have been worth much to begin with; but the mischief was all done before you ever heard of me. Confine yourself to facts: dismiss conjectures. State actions: shun motives. Give results: avoid causes, if you would insure confidence in your sagacity.

Furthermore, you say that with abundant denunciation of present evils, my book contains no practical suggestions for their removal,—and this in face of the fact that, as Chaucer would say, it sneweth in that book of practical suggestions. But they are so simple that you make no account of them. So Naaman of old went to Elisha to be healed of his leprosy, expecting the prophet to come out and work a miracle with great pomp and solemnity, as was befitting the state of the Lieutenant-General of the army of Syria.[17] And when Elisha did not so much as go to the door, but sent a servant to advise the great man to wash himself, no wonder he went away in a rage. That was a practical suggestion, indeed! However, when he suffered his wrath to subside and did as the prophet bade him, his flesh came again like unto the flesh of a little child. So if you, august complainer, will but be docile, and not insist upon being told to do some great thing that shall overturn the foundations of society, but will be content to go into your own family circle and do the seven and seventy times seven little things that I counsel you to do, you will become sweet and pure and innocent like a little child, and every one will love you, especially they which are of your own household; nor will you ever again find either lack or need of practical suggestions.

There is also a kind of stock criticism on which a large class of critics do a flourishing business. It is no new thing, for the Abbot Trublet well described it a hundred and fifty years ago.[18] "He (the critic) has also general forms of censure and commendation, composed wholly of terms of art. He is particularly fond of such as dispense with the detail of proofs, and are most proper to make you sensible of his superiority over the author he pronounces upon. For instance, one of the most common judgments he passes upon works just published is that they have nothing new in them;" to which the modern critic has learned to add "nor do they present old things with any new force." Another general form has already been referred to, that of holding up an author of established reputation with the discriminating and scholarly command to "see the difference." "Compare with Kingsley and note the difference."[19] "Compare one of these Essays with those of the 'Country Parson' and you will note a vast difference."[20] "Compare the 'Religio Medici' with the 'New Sun' and the immense superiority of the former over the latter will be apparent at once,"—a form of criticism safe and therefore sagacious.[21] Or, again we are informed that "this book might have been compressed into one half or one third or—the vulgar fraction expanding into whatever infinite decimal the critic may choose—the space it occupies. Very true. It might not have been written at all, while you are about it; as country children amuse themselves with improving on the old adage,

> "He that would thrive
> Must rise at five."

By adding

> "He who'd thrive more
> Must rise at four."
>
> "He who the best would be
> Must rise at three."

And so on, till they arrive at the conclusion,—

> "He who would get ahead
> Must never go to bed."

It must be confessed that these people are wise in their generation; for, to write a real criticism, to set the strength or weakness of a book in such clear lights that all may see it for themselves, to pronounce judgment with such weight that the decision shall be final, is a work of high art. It requires skill, learning, power, genius, attention. It creates risk and involves responsibility; while any noodle can make a general statement which all the other noodles shall receive as pure gold. But though such criticism may be indulged in to almost any extent, and with entire impunity, not every one can condense it into the elegant compactness of that writer who closes a protest against the verbiage of a certain author with the assertion, that "she has a *fatal* facility of expression *that will yet be the death of her!*"

But all else will I forgive and forget, if you will not tell me to stop writing. *That* I cannot and will not do. You may iterate and reiterate, that the public will tire of me. I am sorry for the public, but it is strong and will be easily rested. Sorry? No, I am not; I am glad. I should like to pay back a part of the weariness which the public has inflicted on me in the shape of lessons, lectures, sermons, speeches, customs, fashions. Why should it have the monopoly of fatiguing? Minorities have their rights as well as majorities. The spout of a tea-kettle is not to be compared, in point of bulk, to the tea-kettle, but it puts in a claim for an equal depth of water, and Nature acknowledges the claim. I cannot think of reining in yet. I have but just started. And everything is so interesting. Nothing is isolated. Nothing is insignificant. Everything you touch thrills. It seems to matter but little what you look at: only look long enough, and a life, its life, springs up. You see that it has causes and consequences, dependencies, bearings, and all manner of social interests; and before you know it, you have become involved in those interests and are one of the family. For the time, you stake all on one issue, and contend valiantly. As soon as that is decided, and you stop to take breath a moment, something else comes equally interesting and seeming equally important, and again your lance is in rest. When it comes to the *quantities* of morals, there is not much difference between one thing and another. And you ask me to fold my hands and sit still? Not I. I promise to do the best I can, but I shall do it. There are rows of blocks standing around the walls of my studio, waiting to be chiselled. They will not be Apollos,—but even Puck is a Robin Goodfellow,[22] since,

"In one night, ere glimpse of morn,
His shadowy flail hath threshed the corn
That ten day-laborers could not end."

And I shall not confine myself to my sphere. I hate my sphere. I like everything that is outside of it,—or, better still, my sphere rounds out into undefined space. I was born into the whole world. I am monarch of all I survey.[23] Wherever I see symptoms of a pie, thither shall my fingers travel. Wherever a windmill flaps, it shall go hard but I will have a tilt at it.[24] I shall not wait till I know what I am talking about. If I did, I never should talk at all. It is a well-known principle in educational science, that the surest way to learn anything is to teach it. How fast would Geology get on, if its professors talked only of what they knew? Planting their feet firmly on facts, they feel about in all directions for theories. By carefully noting, publishing, comparing, discussing their uncertainties, they presently arrive at a certainty. Horace might advocate nine years' delay.[25] He was building for himself a monument that should defy the rolling years. He was setting to work in cool blood to compass immortality, and a little time, more or less, made no difference. Apollo and Bacchus could afford to wait.

Beautiful daughters of beautiful mothers will exist to the world's end, and their praises will always be in order. But when, unmindful of the next generation, which will have its books and its memories, though you are unread and forgotten, mindful only of this generation which groans and travails in pain, you look on suffering that you yearn to assuage, danger of which you long to warn, sadness which you would fain dispel, burdens which you would strive, though ever so little, to lighten, delay, even for things so desirable as complete knowledge and perfect polish, becomes not only absurd, but impossible. Better shoot into the cavern, even if you do not know in what precise part of it the dragon lies coiled. The flash of your powder may reveal his whereabouts to a surer marksman. A transient immortality is of no importance; it is of importance that hearts be purified, homes made happy. Is that ignoble? Very well. But the noblest way to benefit posterity is to serve the present age,—to serve it by doing one's best, indeed, but by doing it now, not waiting for some distant day when one may do it better. A writer deserves no pardon for careless or hurried writing. As much time as he has mental ability to spend on it, so much time he should devote to it. But then speed it on its way. Shut it up for a term of years, and you will perhaps have a manuscript that says *begin* where it used to say *commence,* but in the mean time all the people whom you wished to save have died of a broken heart,—or lived with one, which is still worse. Besides, even for improvement, it is better to publish your paper than to keep it in the drawer. There, all the amendments it can receive will come from the few feeble advances in knowledge which you may be so fortunate as to make. But print it and every one immediately gives you especial attention and the benefit of his judgment. If you should happen to serve in the right wing of Orthodoxy, you will have the inestimable boon of the freest criticism from the left wing. And it is the religious newspapers for not mincing matters! Between Jew and Gentile hostility is the normal condition of things, and is carried on peaceably enough; but when Jew meets Jew, then comes the tug of war! These people obey to the letter the Apostolic injunction, and confess your faults one to another with a marvellous relish, which must furnish to the unbelieving world a lively commentary on the old text, "Behold how these Christians love one another!"[26] When their own list of your shortcomings is exhausted, ten to one they will take up the parable of somebody else; and if little Johnny

Horner sitting in the corner of his sanctum has not room in his crowded columns for the whole pie in which his brother Horner has served you up, never fear but he will put in his thumb and pick out the plums to enliven the feast withal.

One blemish which grievously annoys the bishops and other clergy is irreverence. Like their Oriental prototypes, they meet the exhortation to be of good cheer with an outcry that the exhorter blasphemeth. They are shocked with the contempt which is shown for the Divine record, with the irreverent use of Bible language. They evidently judge according to Dr. Johnson's standard: "Campbell is a good man,—a pious man. I am afraid he has not been in the inside of a church for many years; but he never passes a church without pulling off his hat; this shows he has good principles."[27] They are of their father the Jew, who would not trample on a piece of paper lest it might contain the name of Jehovah, but who scrupled not to stone His prophets and crucify His Son. Yet though their hearts are stirred within them at liberties taken by lay writers, they are not only not shocked, but on the contrary they quite—if I may use so secular a word in so sacred a connection—chuckle over it, when such liberties emanate from clerical sources. Nobody professed himself shocked when a religious newspaper told us, with great glee, how, when a certain Dr. S. was first settled in Hartford, "Dr. Bellamy, feeling a deep interest in the success of the church in this favored spot, resolved to visit the youthful pastor, and 'see if he would do.' On arriving at the residence of his young brother, which was a new house and nicely furnished, Dr. Bellamy remarked, as Mr. S. met him at the door, 'So you have got your house all swept and garnished.' 'Yes, yes, Dr. Bellamy, all ready for evil spirits,—walk in, walk in.' We need not add, that Dr. Bellamy, after a hearty laugh, remarked, 'He'll do, he'll do.'"[28]

The same paper tells of Mr. Leifchild's "journey from Bristol to Wells in company with Mr. Hall, who was a great smoker. He descended at a blacksmith's shop to relight his pipe. Making his way to the forge, he jumped aside with unwonted agility, when a huge dog growled at him. When he returned to the carriage, Mr. Leifchild observed, 'You seemed afraid of the dog, sir.' Mr. Hall instantly rejoined, 'Apostolic advice, sir, Beware of dogs.'"[29]

The Remarker is the head and front and both wings of the Orthodox army. It is so intensely religious a newspaper that it cares little to have a long list of subscribers, but is deeply anxious to have them of sound Orthodox piety,—which is a thing to be admired (at) in this Mammon-worshipping age, and furnishes a touching illustration of the manner in which Providence tempers the wind to the shorn lamb. Now one would not wish, even if it were possible, to be any more pious than the Remarker, for fear he might die young. Yet the Remarker tells us a story of Father Hill, of Mason, N.H., who "had a parsonage full of young children":—

"The Rev. William M. Rogers of this city was once on a visit to that brother minister. The boys and girls were in full glee around him, when he quietly remarked, that he never knew before the full meaning of the Psalmist, where he says that 'the little hills rejoice on every side.'"[30]

And it not only tells the story without any apparent horror of the Scriptural quip, but adds, that we may be sure of its truth, "We had this from the Rev. Timothy Hill, one of the juvenile group, for many years since a Western missionary."

But if it is meet and right for the clergy to wrest the words of the Divine record away from their Divine meaning, can it be a high crime for the laity to apply their Divine meanings to common things? If a clergyman may make a joke from the Bible whenever he can think of one, may not a layman use a phrase from the same source when it comes to him? If a minister may manufacture puns, may not a man borrow pungency? or are we to return to the good old times, and have the Bible once more chained to the pulpit?

But a thing truly wonderful to see is the manner in which the hostility aroused by my book swallows up all lesser hostilities. The chronic enmity between different divisions of the Church Militant disappears at its coming, and "The Remarker" and "The Furnace" lie side by side in melodious concord,—which is such a reconciliation as has rarely been seen since the day when Herod and Pilate were made friends together.[31] The Furnace is indeed pathetic in its aversion. It is little to say that it disapproves; it cannot even tolerate me when mingled with, and, it might be hoped, modified by, other ingredients in the "Oceanic Miscellany," and insists on being warned against my approach that it may parry the blow. In pity for its woes, permit me to announce that there is a plan on foot, either to issue for its use an expurgated edition of the "Oceanic Miscellany," comprising only the most Elegant Extracts, or else to hoist a little black flag when I am coming, that the Reverend Mokanna may have time to put on his silver veil and so the gales of heaven shall not visit his face too roughly.[32] Next, and with no unequal steps, comes "The Noticer," a paper which, apparently finding it impossible to become thoroughly regenerate, long ago gave up the attempt in despair, and now regularly divides itself off into a sort of Holy and Profane State. Unfortunately, in its eagerness to embrace a fancied opportunity to despatch a provincial victim and several metropolitan brethren at one fell swoop, it left a bar down or a gate open, and so permitted—unconsciously let us hope—a rather profane little fib or two to stray over upon the holy side. But to use its own brilliant and startling language, which, it congratulates itself those who have once heard will never forget, "Doctors differ. Editors differ. Good men differ,"—a "logical division" of mankind which, so far as one may judge from "The Noticer," complies strictly with Whately's third rule for Division, viz. the Parts or Members must not be contained in one another.[33] However, since nobody supposes difficulty of perception to be incompatible with goodness of heart, and since we permit a pious soul to puff itself out a good deal beyond its due dimensions without forfeiting its right of passage through the strait gate, we may also admit that a good man who differs so widely from other good men as to be careless of truth, is like Kinglake's Gladstone, a good man—in the worst sense of the term![34]

It will readily be inferred that, after all this banning with bell, book, and candle, it only remains to sigh with penitent Pet Marjorie, "My character [sic] is lost among the Braehead people. I hope I will be religious again, but as for regaining my charecter I despare [sic] for it." However, I shall keep on writing,—hit, if I can, miss, if I must, but shoot any way. There is a great deal of firing that kills no men and breaches no walls, but it worries the enemy. John Brown did not in the least know what he was doing. His definite attempt was a fatal failure; but the great and guilty conspiracy behind, of which he saw nothing, was smitten to the heart under his random blows; his sixteen white men and five negroes, flung blindly and recklessly against the ramparts of Slavery, were but the precursors of that great host, black and white, which has since gone down, organized and intelligent, to tread the wine-press of the wrath of God.

I fear I am committing the rhetorical error of comparing small things with great; but, if Virgil could bring in the Cyclops and their thunderbolts to illustrate his bees, and Demetrius Phalereus justify it, you will hardly count it a capital offence in me,—and I don't much care if you do, if I can only convince you that I am not going to be silent because I do not know the Alpha and Omega of things. I do not pretend to be logical, or consistent, or coherent. Nature is not. A forest of oaks burns down or is cut down, and do oaks spring again? No. Pines. Logic is baffled, but the land is bettered. A field of corn is planted, and Nature does not set herself to protect it, but sends a flock of crows to devour it; the farmers grumble, but the crows are saved alive. Freezing water contracts awhile, and then without any provocation turns about and expands; if your pitcher stands in the way, so much the worse for the pitcher, but the little fishes are grateful; and with all her whims and inconsequences, Nature gets on from year to year without once failing of seed-time and harvest, cold or heat. How is it with you and your logic, you men who have been to college and discovered what you are talking about? You who discuss politics and decide affairs, are you not continually accusing one another of sophistry, inconsistency, and shying away from the point? Take up any political or religious newspaper, and see, according to their own testimony, how deficient in logic are all these logic-mongers,—how all the learned and logical are accused by other learned and logical of false assumptions, of invalid reasoning, of foregone conclusions, of pride and prejudice and passion. One would say that the result of your profound researches was only to make you more intensely illogical than you could otherwise be.

> "As skilful divers to the bottom fall
> Swifter than they who cannot swim at all,
> So in the sea of sophisms, to my thinking,
> You have a strange alacrity in sinking."
>
> (*Ego et Dorset fecimus!*)[35]

Sure I am, my humble ability in the way of unreason can never compass fallacies so stupendous as those which you attribute to one another; and I will none of your logic, but will rather rest content with the advantage, that, when I write nonsense, I know it is nonsense, while you, pardon me, write it and think it sense. But your thinking so does not make it so, and you will not rule me out of court on the strength of it. In the domain of letters is none but Squatter Sovereignty. In literature, though not in morals, might makes right. If you are cultivating the soil to its utmost capacity, I shall not meddle; but if it seems to me that you are letting it lie fallow while I can draw a furrow to some purpose, you need not warn me off with your old title-deeds; *in* my ploughshare shall go. To a better farmer I will yield right gladly, but I will not be scared away by a sign-board.

When you learnedly assert that my induction is meagre, I am the farthest in the world from contradicting you. Nay, I am ready to confess not only that it is meagre, but that there is no induction at all. For, look you, induction is for hidden, not for obvious truth. If I wished to convince you, or to satisfy myself, that the earth's centre is a mass of fire, I should produce a sufficient number of caloric facts to give the statement a stable basis. But if my design were to arouse you to a true sense of earth's beautiful summer greenness, I should not go plucking grass in all directions, but should merely show you a blade or a leaf to illustrate what I meant by "green," and bid you use your own eyes for the rest. If the earth is indeed not green, but blue, my judgment pays the penalty; but there is no induction about it.

Nor need you go very far out of your way to affirm that I have not the requisite experience for writing on such and such topics. As a principle, the remark is absurd. Cannot a doctor prescribe for typhus fever, unless he has had typhus fever himself? On the contrary, is he not the better able to prescribe from always having had a sound mind in a sound body? As a fact, my experience in those things concerning which you allege its insufficiency has never been presented to you, and its discussion is therefore entirely irrelevant. If my statements are false, they are false; if my arguments are inconclusive, they are inconclusive: disprove the one and refute the other. But whether this state of things be owing to a want of experience, or inability to use experience aright, or any personal circumstance whatever, is a matter in regard to which all the laws of courtesy forbid you to concern yourself.

You are sometimes so good as to inform me that I am exhausting my resources, and in over-anxious kindness declare even that I have exhausted myself. Not a bit.

"It is no task for suns to shine,"

though the sputtering little tallow candle can hardly be expected to believe it.

And pray, Gentle Critic, do not tell me that I must be content simply to amuse, or *must*—anything else. Must is a hard word; be not too confident of its power. I feel a grandmotherly interest in the world and its ways; and much as I should like to amuse it, I shall never be content with that. You may not *like* to be instructed, my dear children, but instructed you shall be. You read long ago, in your story-book, that little Tommy Piper did not want his face washed, though he was very willing to be amused with soap-bubbles; but his face needed a washing, and got it. I come to you with soap-bubbles indeed, but with scrubbing-brushes also. If you take to them kindly, it will soon be over; but if you scream and struggle, I shall not only scrub the harder, but be all the longer about it.

Sometimes grave refutations are very amusing. It is astonishing to see how crank-proof sundry people are. Everything seems to them on a dead level of categorical proposition. They walk up to every statue with their measuring-line of *Barbara, Celarent, Darii, Ferioque Prioris,* and measure them off with equal solemnity, telling you severely that this nose is far longer than the classic rule admits, and this arm has not the swelling proportions of life,—never seeing, that, though another statue was indeed designed for an Antinoüs, this was never meant to be anything but a broomstick dressed in your grandfather's cloak, with a lantern in a pumpkin-shell for a head. O the dreariness of having to explain pleasantry! of dealing with people who do not know the difference between a blow and a "love-pat," between Quaker guns and an Armstrong battery, between a granite paving-stone and the moonshine on a mud-puddle!

But they make up for it by turning your wisdom into wish-wash; as Charles Lamb atoned for reaching his office late in the morning by leaving it early in the afternoon. Your sense must be solemn and stationary in order to be recognized. They cannot conceive that it may toss like the buoy on the tide, and yet be moored to foundations firm as the perpetual hills. On the whole

"The Robin sings in the elm;
The cattle stand beneath
Sedate and grave, with great brown eyes,
And fragrant meadow breath.

"They listen to the flattered bird,
The wise-looking stupid things!
And they never understand a word
Of all the Robin sings."[36]

But the great consolation both for my critics and myself is, that we shall gradually get used to each other. At least, I shall furnish them abundant opportunity to get used to me. There are many books still to come,—a treatise on the Curvature of the Square,—a Dissertation on Foreign Literature,—two or three novels,—a book on Human Life, that is going to turn the world upside down,—a book on Theology, dull enough to be sensible, that is going to turn it back again,—and a bandboxful of children's stories. And when these are disposed of, I dare say I shall turn the glass and begin again.

Truly there was no need of saying all this; but when they droop their fair large ears, my gentle joy, so temptingly within hand-reach, who can restrain himself from filliping them? But I take no liberties with leviathan. Good and friendly souls, Greathearts who might crush me and do not, I should like to thank you, but perhaps you do not care. Yet bear with me a little longer in my folly; and, indeed, bear with me for the sake of the weak. Many and many there may be to whom the meat of your metaphysics is indigestible and unpalatable, but who find strength and cheer in the sincere milk of such words as I can give. To you who have already set your feet on the high places, that may be but a bruised reed which is a staff to those who are still struggling up.

Of the blessings which my book has brought me,—blessings of inward wealth that cannot be so much as named,—blessings so rich, so divine, that I sometimes think nothing ever was so beautiful as to have written a book,—I may not speak; but I trust that when all this frightful glare of day, all this rough litter, and jar, and deafening din of work shall be overpast,—when the serene Night beckons to me, and I go on into her fragrant silence and her sweet sheltering darkness,—I shall bear with me some memories that were not all of earth; some pure delights that shall glow through the charmed air, soft as night's dewy breath and lasting as her stars.

A BATTLE OF THE BOOKS

I

EDITOR'S INTRODUCTION

THE PAPERS comprising the following narrative, called "A Battle of the Books," were found in my state-room after a violent storm, during a long and dangerous sea-voyage which I was once forced to undertake. They were much stained with salt-water, but were for the most part legible. The name of the author or compiler is not given; but I judge, somewhat from the chirography, chiefly from incontestable internal evidence, that the writer is a woman. As this evidence will unfold itself to the reader in the course of the narrative, I shall not dwell upon it; nor is it, indeed, a matter of importance, except that it bears upon the question of the participation in the government by both sexes. Viewed from that point, it shows with great force the inability of women to understand affairs, and the groundlessness of the present clamor for a change of status. It proves beyond question that all that women need do is to trust, and all that men care to do is to protect.

The date given is of the last century, but of its accuracy I am not assured. The manuscript is soiled, and stained, and shabby enough; but the storm which brought it to my feet would account for that. There are references, allusions, and even names which point to a time far within the memory of men still living; but this is not conclusive, since I believe, according to the best scriptural exegesis, the name of a historical person in a book, as, for instance, that of Cyrus in Isaiah, does not determine the date, so much as the nature of the writing, simply changing it from history to prophecy. No one, in reading this story, will suspect it of scriptural inspiration; but may not the writer have been in that state which is sometimes called clairvoyant, and which is perhaps but a preternaturally acute condition of the intellectual perceptions, wherein the logic of events is so plainly seen that the future is as clear and certain as the past, and that which is to happen seems as much a matter of fact as that which has happened? If the human mind can calculate an eclipse of the sun, with entire accuracy, three thousand years beforehand, why should it be thought a thing incredible that the human heart should be able to calculate some of the incidents of an eclipse of faith a hundred years in advance?

But as upon the question of authorship, so upon that of chronology, I conceive the strongest evidence to be internal. The state of society described in this narrative is surely no nearer than a hundred years. It chronicles an age of barbarism, when author and publisher were natural enemies, and relieved the monotony of their lives by petty skirmishing or pitched battles with each other. This age, happily for us, has passed away, and exists only in tradition. Whether from the universal softening of manners which accompanies the introduction of Christianity, and in which both publishers and authors may be supposed to have shared, or from that equally universal brightening and quickening of the intellect which attended the Renaissance, and which may have enabled even publishers to see how he that watereth shall be watered also himself,—certain it is that these times of turbulence are gone, and we have peace. No longer does the wily publisher lie in wait, seeking what chance he may have to devour his author. Rather he woos him to receive his dues, wins open with gentle urgency the hand no longer grasping, but modest and reluctant, and presses into it the crisp, abundant bills. No longer do authors shamelessly drink toasts to the despotic emperor to whose thousand crimes is linked the one virtue of having hanged a bookseller.[1] On the contrary, they raise their harps and join voices to sing their benefactor's praise. Who has not seen in all the newspapers the affecting tale of the great house of Fields, Osgood, & Co.,—*nomen clarum et venerabile,*[2]—on whom has fallen the mantle of Ticknor & Fields?

"Fame spread her wings, and with her trumpet blew"

the story of their having offered payment to an author, which he declined to receive because he had once had money for the writing. "But," replied the firm, "we intend to use the article for a book. We make a profit on both. Why should you hesitate to take pay?" "I am sure I ought not to take it," said the author; "I should not if I acted according to my ideal. I don't believe it is honest to take money twice for the same piece of work." "But do," replied the publisher; "we insist upon it as our right;" and insist he did, till the author coyly yielded. History is silent from this point, but the imagination fondly stoops to trace the scene. Undoubtedly this prince of publishers, like Mr. Pecksniff when blessing Martin Chuzzlewit for hating him, "waved his right hand with much solemnity. . . . There was emotion in his manner, but his step was firm. Subject to human weaknesses, he was upheld by conscience."[3]

Hear also what the "Atlantic Monthly" says: "There are no business men more honorable or more generous than the publishers of the United States, and especially honorable and considerate towards authors. The relation usually existing between author and publisher in the United States is that of a warm and lasting friendship,—such as . . . . now animates and dignifies the intercourse between the literary men of New England and Messrs. Ticknor & Fields. . . . . The relation, too, is one of a singular mutual trustfulness. The author receives his semi-annual account from the publisher with as absolute a faith in its correctness as though he had himself counted the volumes sold. . . . We have heard of instances in which a publisher had serious cause of complaint against an author, but never have we known an author to be intentionally wronged by a publisher. . . . How common, too, it is in the trade for a publisher to go beyond the letter of his bond, and after publishing five books without profit, to give the author of the successful sixth more than the stipulated price."

Time and scissors would fail me to cull from the journals all the ingenious and touching paragraphs which show how the eminent publishers referred to do good by stealth and blush to find it fame.

Doubtless similar illustrations might also be drawn in great numbers from other sources, were ordinary publishers in the courtly habit of keeping a historian to record their royal deeds. But enough has been said to show that the publishers of to-day have become evangelized, and no longer seek every man his own, but every man the things of another. I infer, therefore, without hesitation, that the dates of the following papers are correct, and that, notwithstanding a certain confusion in the nomenclature, the state of things they describe, belongs exclusively to the good old times of a hundred years ago.

Joined to the main body of the narrative were injunctions the most imperative regarding its publication. But even had I chosen to disregard these, there are other reasons which might have impelled me to the same course. As one sitting by his own fireside glows with a deeper content for the sound of the storms without, so we, who live in this golden age of love, may all the more rejoice, seeing how they let their angry passions rise in the brave days of old.

I would say, then, borrowing the language of an old Sunday-school hymn:—

"Authors, attend, while I relate
A new and simple story;
'Twill teach your hearts with thankfulness
To praise the Lord of glory"

that the lines have fallen to you in pleasant places, and that you receive your goodly heritage without having to fight for it.

II

AUTHOR'S INTRODUCTION

WHEN IN THE COURSE of human events, it becomes necessary for an author to dissolve the bands which have connected him with his publishers, a decent respect for the opinions of mankind requires that he should declare the causes which impel him to the separation.

The war between authors and publishers has been a conflict of ages.

On the one side, the publisher has been looked upon as a species of Wantley dragon, whose daily food was the brain and blood of hapless writers.

> "Devouréd he poor authors all,
> That could not with him grapple;
> But at one sup he ate them up,
> As one would eat an apple."[4]

On the other side, the author has been considered, like Shelley, "an eternal child" in all that relates to practical business matters, and a terrible child at that,—incapable of comprehending details, and unreasonably dissatisfied with results. A definite illustration will sometimes throw more light on a general principle than reams of abstract discussion. But in matters of this sort, definite illustrations are very hard to come at. In any case of trouble between author and publisher, it is for the interest of the latter that it be kept as quiet as possible. Even if he be unquestionably right, and the difficulty be owing solely to the author's inexperience and impracticability, the ill odor of having had a quarrel will hardly be neutralized by any knowledge of its causelessness. The sympathy of the public is more likely to be with the author than with the publisher.

The author also is held to silence by various considerations. The difficulty of getting at the real state of the case, and the misgiving which results from it; the always unpleasant nature of the controversy; the obtrusion of one's private affairs, as if it were a theme of general interest; the uncertainty of any good to be obtained; the fatigue and disgust of the quarrel itself,—a thousand circumstances combine to make it appear altogether easier and better to let the matter go than to take the trouble of any adequate presentation or explanation of it. But as he is never quite satisfied, he can never quite let it go; and though there come not a real thunder-storm crashing among the hills, but clearing the skies, there are low mutterings and occasional flashes, which betoken a signal discontent of the elements.

Thus exists the chronic feud between authors and publishers; partly traditional, partly experimental; a matter often for outward jest, but quite as often of deep and serious import. It is a sort of bushwhacking, in which every man whacks on his own account, and frequently does not know that there is any other bushwhacker than himself. So the warfare goes on, but to no end. Nobody learns wisdom from another man's experience, because the other man keeps his experience to himself.

I propose to supply what the theologians call a "felt want," and to become the historian of a contest all of which I saw, and part of which I was. From the confusions of long misunderstanding I would fain evolve an intelligent and lasting peace. "When," in the language of Dr. Johnson, "I am animated by this wish, I look with pleasure on my book, however defective, and deliver it to the world with the spirit of a man that has endeavored well." If it be instigated by any other motive than pure benevolence, the fact will doubtless appear in its progress. Should my little cask of oil be poured out in vain upon the stormy waters,—should I, instead of soothing their rage, be whelmed beneath it,—there remains the consoling assurance that no one else is involved in my fate.

It would be hypocritical to apologize for the intrusion of private affairs upon the public notice, when it is notorious that there is nothing the public so dearly loves, nothing upon which it so eagerly fastens, nothing which it so greedily devours, as private affairs. Indeed, the privacy of affairs seems to be sometimes the only element of interest they possess, and the delight which the public finds in them is proportioned to the amount of good manners it was necessary to sacrifice in order to get at them.*

I give fair warning that this narration is not intended to be of interest or value to any but authors and publishers. A log-book is not generally considered very entertaining reading, yet it may be scanned with great eagerness by those who are following the track it chronicles. This is simply the log-book of a desperate voyage, a careful knowledge of which may prevent many a young mariner from being drawn into it himself.

---

*The most casual observer will readily see that this strain of remark can refer only to a far distant past. If our age is remarkable for any one thing, it is for a delicate reticence regarding what is not lawfully, and by divine right, its own.—*Note by Editor.*

III

RISE AND PROGRESS OF SUSPICION IN THE SOUL

MY RELATIONS with the house of Brummell and Hunt began somewhere about the year 1760.[5] Until 1768 these relations had always been agreeable. I seemed to be living in an orchard of pomegranates, with pleasant fruits. I thought, as Mr. Tennyson remarked to the lily, "there is but one" publishing house, and that is the house of Messrs. Brummell & Hunt. All others were to me outside barbarians, mercenary hirelings, mere hewers of wood and drawers of water. Messrs. Brummell & Hunt published on high moral grounds, from love of literature and general benevolence. Gingerbread followed their virtue, indeed, but had no part nor lot in it. My dealings were with Mr. Hunt, and the business aspect of our connection came to be nearly lost sight of behind the veil of friendship. Money arrangements I left entirely to him. I never stipulated for anything, either on books or magazine articles. I considered that he best knew the money value of these things, and that, as we are constantly told, the interest of author and that of publisher are one. He accordingly paid me whatever he chose, and I was entirely satisfied.

One day in December, 1767, happening to want more money than was due me,* I recollected having seen, a few weeks before, an article in the "Segregationalissuemost,"** on the "Pay of Authors," which said:—

"In regard to books, the common percentage paid by publishers to average writers is *ten per cent. upon the retail price of the book;* the copies given to the press for notice not being included in the estimate. Thus, for an edition of a volume whose retail price is $1.00, the account would be made

---

*A circumstance which at once relegates this story to the last century.—*Note by Editor.*

**Proof that this paper belongs to an age when people had time to pronounce long words.—*Ed.*

up thus: Suppose 1,000 copies to be printed, of which 90 are distributed to the press, and otherwise given away for notice, and the balance sold, the publishers would owe the author (1,000−90=910 copies, at 10c. each) $91.00. And so proportionately for larger works at costlier prices."

Without the least presentiment of anything uncanny, I made the following reference to it in a letter to Mr. Hunt. This extract unfolds the beginning of sorrows.

"Now see, in the 'Segregationalissuemost,' this very morning, I saw an article about the pay of authors, in which it said that the ordinary price for average authors was ten per cent. on the retail price of the book; but according to my account I don't have ten per cent. I only have somewhere about seven or eight per cent. Looking in my papers, I find that all the contracts I have are only for fifteen cents on the two-dollar volumes, which certainly is not ten percent. except the first contract for 'City Lights,' which says ten per cent., but the bills or accounts, or whatever it is, are made out for that,—not at ten per cent., but, just as the other, fifteen cents on the volume. At least, this is the way I make it out; but I am not good at figures, and may have made some mistake. However, here are the papers, and you can see for yourself, or I will show them to Judge Dane when I go to Athens. I don't like to talk about it here at home any way. But perhaps you will know all about it from what I have said, and perhaps it is all right. But certainly I am an 'average writer,' and you are an 'ordinary publisher,' not to say extraordinary! And I want all the money I can possibly get and more too! Especially—dollars by and by.[6]

"It just occurs to me that you may possibly think that I think that *you* have been falling into temptation! My dear friend and fellow-sinner, if you should stand up with both hands on your heart, and swear that you had cheated me, I should not believe you. I should say, 'Poor fellow, work and worry have done their work. His brilliant intellect—I saw a lovely private asylum in Corinth. I would go there and spend the summer!'

"Yours, sane or insane,

"M.N."

I waited nearly two weeks, and then, receiving no reply to this letter, I wrote to my friend, Mr. Jackson, a book-publisher of Corinth, asking him several questions, but avoiding as far as possible any personality, or giving rise to any suspicion. I hoped he would think I was merely collecting information. On the 16th of January, nearly three weeks after my letter was sent, came a reply from Mr. Hunt, in which the only reference to my inquiry was:—

"I have not answered your last letter, touching the terms expressed in the contracts; for you and I went over that matter once, and it was with your entire concurrence with our views, based upon the present state of trade and manufacture, that the amount was decided on. When you come to town, we will go all over it again, and it will be again settled to your entire satisfaction."

This reply did not meet my question. I was aware that I had concurred in their views, as my name on the contract showed it. But I was not aware of ever having gone over the matter; and I did not care for a second settlement while I was as yet unassured of a first. I wrote again, replying also to an invitation by telegram received the same day from a member of Mr. Hunt's family.

"MY DEAR MR. HUNT:

That is great of you to come down here with a gay letter, and utterly blink out of sight the fact of your having made me wretched for three weeks by not writing. *Of course* I concurred in your views. If you had said to me, 'Owing to the state of trade and manufactures, all the trees are now going to be bread and cheese, and all the rivers ink,' I should have said, 'Yes, that is a very wise measure.' I don't remember ever talking the thing over with you, but I dare say I did,—or, rather, you talked, and I nodded, as usual! And of course I agreed; for here are the contracts that say so, and if I don't know what is in those contracts and accounts, it is not for want of patient industry. If I had as many dollars as I have pored over those miserable papers the last two weeks, I would build a meeting-house. Don't you see the trouble lies back of the contract? Why did you *wish* me to be having seven or eight per cent. when other people are getting ten? If it was because I was not worth more, you need not be afraid to say so. I can bear a great deal of rugged truth. But why am I not worth more, when there is not a paper of any standing in the country, to put it rather strongly, that has not applied to me to become a contributor, offering me my own terms? Does not that show that I have at least a commercial value? Writing books seems a more dignified thing than writing newspapers, but in point of money there is no comparison to be made.* I could have got five times as much by putting 'Cotton-picking' in the form of letters as I have from the book.

"When day after day went by, and you did not write, I came to the conclusion that your High Mightiness was standing on your dignity, and then *I* was indignant too. I can always be a great deal more angry with any one than any one is with me, and I always *will* be. And I said last week, 'If he does not write me by Saturday, I will do something.' And what I did was—write to Mr. Jackson. Now you will perhaps be vexed at this, but you have no right to be. Do you think I am going to die, and give no sign? Mr. Jackson is an older friend than you,—I said an older soldier, not a better!—and then you did not write. I did not mention your name, nor say anything about myself or my affairs, only asked some general questions. I tell you this because your letter was good-natured. If it had been cross, I would not tell you anything; and if you will be as perplexed and uneasy for three weeks as I was, and not do anything worse than that, I will award you a gold medal. Mr. Hunt, you ought never under any circumstances to be angry with me. In your large circle of friends you may have scores who will bring you more personal revenue; but for the quality of loyalty 'pure and simple,' you will not find many who will go beyond me. I may be infelicitous and inexplicable in demonstration, but I was never anything but thoroughly true in mood.

"The telegram came this morning in due season. A thousand thanks for her kind remembrance, but of course I was not going to Athens with your letter staring me in the face.[7] Talking it over is the very thing I don't want to do. There is nothing to be talked over. There are the papers. I admit them all. But when ——— takes you to task for some misdemeanor,—and if ever you go to the good place, it will be because that woman has pulled you through,—you don't say, 'What are you talking about? When I offered myself to you, did you not say you would have me

*This was in reference to Mr. Hunt's repeated injunctions that I should write only books.

for better, for worse; and are you not perfectly satisfied?' She was satisfied then according to her lights, but doubtless she has thought twenty times since she might have done better. Any way, you don't 'dast' ask her and see. Now my case is not parallel. 'England, with all thy faults, I love thee still.'[8] I cannot conceive of anybody being a better publisher than you, because you don't seem like a business man, but a friend. But here is the fact that I want (so much) and I have only (so much) to get it with, and sales falling off, and I getting on what is sold less than an unknown author gets on his first book. Can you tell me in a month whether the new book is going to sell or not? I have another children's book nearly ready, but I suppose decency demands an appreciable interval between two issues. Do you suppose the unpopularity of my doctrines has anything to do with it? If it has, I will thunder them out harder still. If I must go down, I will go down, like the *Cumberland,* with a broadside volley.[9]

"Of the books I want I don't know how many,—a dozen or two. If people won't buy them, I will give them away, for read them they shall. . . .

"I will now close this short note with the reflection which I have often made,—Be good, and you will be happy. And never bring up against me a concurrence of views at any past time as a fortification against *discur*rence in the present. And if that is, like Saint Paul, hard to be understood,—good enough for you for not writing me sooner, and throwing me into such a perturbation. Remember always the difference between the assent of indifference and the assent of conviction. Whatever I agreed to in times past was because I had no interest whatever in the subject, and supposed it was all according to the laws of the Medes and Persians.[10] Now that ruin gapes before me, and I am, after all, only the law unto myself, it makes no atom of difference to me that I have not been fighting you the last century—steady.

"While I am in a spasm of comparative serenity, I will declare and affirm that you are and always have been one of the kindest, brightest, and most agreeable of men; that you never said to me a word of compliment, or silliness, or impatience, or anything that wounded me,—and Heaven knows you have said bad things enough,—and this you may cut out, and show to men and angels when we come to blows. The worst thing I ever knew you to do was not answering my last letter, and then *aggravating* me by coming down as breezy and cheery as if nothing had happened. Give my love to ———. She deserves a better fate, but I don't know that I can do aught to forward it."

Mr. Hunt's reply to this letter was through another person; in which reply the only response to my letter was:—

"I sent off my telegram with perfect unconsciousness of your state of mind, or of the fact that there was any business unsettled which might be talked about. Your note last night was a surprise, and your non-appearance a disappointment. . . .

"Do you forget that a certain friend of ours cannot write a word with his own hand?[11] Do you wonder, matters having been many times explained, that he thought they must sooner or later explain themselves through your memory?

"*We* forget how in a retired life things work in the mind, and you must therefore forgive the apparent neglect of one who is overwhelmed by letters and people from day's beginning to day's end."

This reply was not soothing. The suggestion that one is morbidly suffering mole-hills to rise into mountains is not flattering to his intellectual calibre. Nor is it agreeable to be assigned the part of one who had been so given to dissatisfaction that it was not worth while to try to quiet him again. One thing I did learn from it,—that Mr. Hunt did not design to answer my question.

I none the less desired an answer. I thought if I could not secure it, perhaps some one else could. Mr. Dane was an old friend of Mr. Hunt's, and a friend of mine. His office was but a short distance from Mr. Hunt's. He had chanced to write me some excellent advice about saving money just before,—without, however, any knowledge of this affair. I wanted somebody's opinion, and I could not talk about the matter. I therefore wrote to Mr. Dane a letter of self-justification, not to say glorification,—saying:—

"You think, perhaps, because I have once or twice lost a few things, therefore I take no heed of anything. On the contrary, there is probably no one in the land who, on the whole, is more careful, systematic, and provident than I! Truth! . . . There is no such thing as independence, or dignity, scarcely honesty, without money. Perhaps that is putting it a little too strong, but at any rate *impecuniosity* is a constant temptation.

"I should have . . . more if I had had ten per cent. on the books, as the 'Segregationalissuemost' said the other day was the custom for new authors. I don't. I have only fifteen cents on a two-dollar book, and ten cents on a dollar-and-a-half book, which is not nearly ten percent.; and if you can tell me any reason why I should not have as much as an unfledged author, I wish you would put up your patents and do it. . . . I want money just now extremely. If I had a few thousand dollars, I could benefit some very excellent persons certainly, and in all probability should lose nothing myself, but in the course of a few years, by the time I should want my money at least, have it all back. I *can* take up bonds to be sure, and I rather think I shall; but as a general thing, one never wants to meddle with money that is settled. Don't you think I talk sensibly? Don't you take back your insinuations about my loose habits of expenditure? Unthrift, reckless expenditure, improvidence, indicate an organic defect of character. But I will not sacrifice the present to the future. 'The present, the present, is all thou hast for thy sure possessing.' Whenever I see an imminent need, I will not pass it by on the score of laying up for a rainy day. For, don't you see, when the rainy day comes, I may not be here to be rained on, while to my friend the rainy day is already come. I will enjoy money as I go along,—not in so reckless a way as to involve the necessity of one day imposing a burden upon others. And of all enjoyment, I know of none so delightful and inexhaustible, and I may say so marvelous, as to see the amount of relief, the quantity of sunshine and help, put into another's life by the judicious bestowal of even a very little money.*

---

*The editor cannot allow this sentiment to go out into the world unchallenged. To him few things are more marvelous than the amount of provender which the ill-favored and lean-fleshed kine will consume without giving any sign of feeding. Poverty, or incapacity, which in this country is the almost inseparable companion of permanent poverty—poverty is a sort of Chatmoss into which cart-loads of gravel may be upset without giving any solid foundation to build on.

"Did you ever see such a letter as this? It is full of me, me, me, *and* me's money; but you began it. Your letter came down upon me just when I have been full of perplexity for more than a month, and you see I have not strength enough to keep myself to myself. You will of course consider this all confidential. You better make sure of it by destroying the letter as soon as you have read it. Yes, by all means. Seems as if this letter was sort of virtuous. But you know I am not virtuous at all. And don't misconstrue me about the books. Mr. Hunt has always been everything that was generous and friendly, and I do not permit myself to admit for a moment, even to myself, that everything is not just as it should be. But that paragraph in the 'S.' induced me to examine my own papers,—joined with my great longing for money just now,—and I did not and do not understand it. Happily, it is not necessary I should. Perhaps that refers chiefly to the great Corinthian publishing houses.

Mr. Dane to M. N.

"TEN PER CENT. was a fair amount—I mean ten per cent. on the retail price—for B. & H. to pay you. When they put their dollar books up to two dollars, whether they should pay you the same percentage, should depend on their profits, and should be a matter of honor with them. Probably at first they did not double their profits with their price, but now I have no doubt they do, and more too. Still you are very much in their hands, and it is very disagreeable for you to help yourself. If the sale fell off with increase of price, although the profit per volume was at the same percentage, they would make less money by doing less business.

"Did you make any contract with them ever, and what was it?

"I don't believe anybody ever gets less than ten per cent. on *the price;* but it may be on the wholesale price, which is forty per cent. off the retail—*i.e.* a book that retails at $1.40 is wholesaled at $1.00. Pardon me, but I never imagine that a woman comprehends what per cent. means! Yes, your principles are good, but your practice is probably very deficient."

Horace Greeley was as true as the multiplication-table when he said that people generally earn money as fast as they have the ability to expend it judiciously.—*Ed.*

M. N. to Mr. Dane.

"I AM GOING to finish up about *my* business now, and then I shall not ever mention the subject again. But I did want to talk with somebody about it, having so little reliance on my own judgment. And your letter came just then, and so I wrote. I have never mentioned it to another soul. Confucius is a great deal better friend to me than you ever were or ever will be, but somehow I could not speak to him about it.[12] I don't want to *speak* to any one. Besides I was afraid he would take up against Mr. Hunt.

"I have looked into my papers, but I cannot make much out of them. . . . I never thought the first thing about it till I saw in the 'S.' what I told you before—and I hardly thought of it then, but several weeks after, when I wanted money, and my account for this year was less than I expected, I hunted up the old 'S.' to see if I had read it right, and then I wrote to Mr. Hunt without thought of there being anything wrong, but asking him how it was. I supposed there was some *modus operandi,* . . . and wanted to know what. It was nearly three weeks before he wrote again, and then came a pleasant letter; but all he said about mine was—(then follows an account of the correspondence.)

"Now I must confess I feel next door to being insulted. I hate to use the word, but there it is. ——— is as innocent and as good as an angel, and does not in the least know what she is writing about. But all that Mr. Hunt ever said to me on the subject, or I to him, did not occupy five minutes, and he never spoke but once. That was years ago. It must have been before the second contract was made. He said that owing to the fluctuations of the market, the uncertainties arising from the war, or something of that sort, they were going to give their authors a fixed sum—fifteen cents per volume—instead of a percentage. It was at a time when prices (of books) were changing from one dollar and a quarter to two dollars, but I don't know exactly when. I assented of course; I neither knew nor cared anything about it. I had no interest in it. And that is all that has ever passed between us. Even now I have not the least fault to find if I am on the same footing as others. But why does he not say so? Do you think I am entirely unreasonable in being dissatisfied? I wish you would tell me if you think so, for it is like death almost to think it possible that Mr. Hunt should be in the wrong. I have had the most implicit confidence in him. I like him so much that I hate to hear a word said against the 'Adriatic,' or anything that he is concerned in. I would have been delighted to write for him for nothing if he had needed the money, and asked me. . . . Mr. Hunt's last letter to me by ——— was January 18. I did not reply to it, and so the matter stands. I shall never say or do anything more about it. You cannot conceive how distasteful it is to me. Nothing in all my life—literary—ever touched me so nearly. If I had lost every speck of money that I had—twice over—it would not have so disheartened me. Confidence must be entire, or it is nothing. Do not you ever speak to any one of this. . . . I shall never mention it. A dead friendship is as sacred as a dead friend.

(But if your dead friend will not rest quietly in his grave, but persists in stalking up and down the earth, scaring the timid, oppressing the weak, and boasting all the time his own beneficence, you may presently learn with Browning, that even

"Serene deadness
Tries a man's temper.")

"Now I hope I have not overwearied you with my tiresome letter. You need not be afraid of a repetition of it. In fact, there is nothing more to say,—which you will perhaps think the strongest security of all. I hope that you are good,—at least that you are content with nothing less than good,—which is the highest that any of us can go, I fancy. I think you had better burn this letter too. It will be safest."

Mr. Dane to M. N., February 4

"LET US TRY your case by admitted principles. Inasmuch as you put yourself into Mr. Hunt's hands to do what was right, he was bound to pay you as much as others receive upon whose winnings the same profits are made. This is Law, Gospel, & Co. If he did more, it would be generosity; if less, meanness or worse.

"He agreed for ten per cent. on the 'City Lights,' and pays you fifteen cents per copy, which is exactly right if it retailed at one dollar fifty cents; and he pays you the same on the rest, I understand you.

"Whether he was reasonable in asking you to assent to the fifteen cents per copy depends on his sales. If they were very small, he would make less than if large. I suppose you own the copyright, but he owns the stereotype plates, which cost the same whether many or few copies are printed. If when paper, and so forth, increased in value, he increased the price *pro rata,* and the sales continued the same, he made a larger profit, and should pay you more; that is, your percentage should continue as large. Now, if he sends you any proper accounts of sales, they will tell the story as to the number of copies sold, but not whether they cost fifty or a hundred per cent. more than formerly. Jackson or any book-publisher would know as to that.

"It would seem that you have received the minimum price, according to Jackson and the Segregationalissuemost, and my own notions. Your books are well printed on tinted paper, and your *notions* may have abridged the profits. I mean you may have required expensive editions, more so than was profitable; but I think not. Will you just show me your contracts and accounts of sales. . . . I am bound professionally to secresy, and my habits are fixed, so that I tell nobody other people's affairs.

"It is due to Mr. Hunt that you investigate the matter to some conclusion. . . . Mr. Hunt mistook your position. Your ready assent to his proposition and your confidence in him, which rendered any sharp bargaining unnecessary on your part, was interpreted as inability to comprehend matters of business; and so they said you understood it once, and will again when you are where you can be talked to. You gave no heed to what was said, and it is a waste of ink to write it all out!

"But you and I know better. Your mind is logical, and your simplicity as to business a sham."

M. N. to Mr. Dane

"THANK YOU for your letter. . . .

"Second, I don't know whether the sales were large or small. Enormous I should say, considering the quality of what was sold; but I don't know what would be considered large as compared with other books. I remember that the 'New Zealander,' a good while ago, said that for any book not a novel five thousand was a success; and I think all mine, or nearly all, have come up to that, and some must have gone beyond it.

"Third, I do not know who owns the copyright or the stereotype plates. I never heard anything about either.

"Fourth, I am perfectly willing to push the matter to any agreeable conclusion; but suppose I inquire around among the publishers, and find that I have been underpaid, what do I gain? No money, for that is all past and gone. Will it give me back Mr. Hunt? Does that strike you as sentimental? It does me. Nevertheless, that is what it means.

"Next, it is very cool in you, if the mercury *is* below zero,—when you have always been telling that a woman has no logic, and that *I* have no logic, and other similar endearments,—to turn around now and quietly speak of my logical mind as if you had been preaching it up all your life. *I* knew it, but it is a good deal to have you even indirectly confess it. As for business, if I chose to turn my attention to it, I have no doubt I could master all its details, just as I could in cooking. But if you have a cook or a publisher for the express purpose of doing the business for you, what is the use of perplexing yourself about it?

"I am purposing to go to Athens next Saturday. I will gather up my papers and take them to you, if you will burden yourself with them, but it is a thankless task. . . . But I really do not want to talk about it.

"I had yesterday a hearty sort of letter from Mr. Hunt. He says that an unusual interest ever since the day of publication of 'The Rights of Men' was evident on all hands; that elaborate newspaper notices have followed the book in profuse showers; and though business is singularly slow this season, he thinks it will have a good sale. He also says, 'When you come again, remember if there are any business matters to be set right, we are to do it then,' and 'When the juvenile book is ready, pray send it, for it takes some time to have illustrations made, and we are even now preparing for autumn.'

"Now that does not read like a man who is conscious of anything blameworthy. It would be impossible he should go on talking as pleasantly, and cheerily, and carelessly as if nothing had happened, if anything *had* happened. Doesn't it look so to you? And why should it be? Brummell and Hunt are famous for their generosity and liberality, and what motive could they have in changing their course for me? It seems to me like an ugly dream. I wish I never had thought of it at all. They could not have been any worse off, and I might have been better."

Mr. Dane to M. N.

"YOU THROW yourself unreservedly into the arms of your publishers. Few of us can safely be trusted so far. Mr. Hunt has apparently given you the minimum share, but I do not know even that, and you don't without inquiry. . . . What I should do is this,—satisfy myself that he is probably keeping too large a share, then say to him frankly, in what form you please, that it seems so, and ask him to explain. As a business matter, it is proper. As between friends, it is due to friendship. What right have you to listen to the suggestions of the adversary, and give your friend no hearing? That you don't know much of your affairs is evident, because you don't know who owns the copyright or the stereotype plates. I do happen to know, for I asked Hunt once if you retained the copyrights, and he said you did. The accounts which he should render you will show exactly the sales. Of course Mr. H. will answer verbally your letter when you meet. Why not tell him frankly just as you tell me? Don't hesitate to let me do whatever you wish done, only I don't want to be officious."

IV

DECLARATION OF WAR

MR. DANE, at my desire, and without mentioning any names, went to several publishers in Athens, and was told by all whom he saw that ten per cent. on the retail price was the author's customary share of the profits. He was referred to Mr. Campton, of the firm of Murray & Elder, as being the person who knew more about these things than any man in Athens. Mr. C. said the same thing. I immediately wrote to Mr. Hunt, February 11:—

"In reply to the suggestion in your last letter, that I should send my juvenile book, I am forced to say what I never thought to say, that I cannot see how it will be for my interest that you should publish any more of my books. Unhappily, it is not necessary that I should give any explanation, since the reason, if it do not exist to your own knowledge and by your own arrangement, does not exist at all."

M. N. to Mr. Dane

"THIS, YOU SEE, is a little different from what I spoke of, but what is the use of keeping up appearances? If he has done what he seems to have done, there is no possible way of getting over it, and I may as well meet it face to face at once. If he takes no notice of this note, or if he asks an explanation, I shall refer him to you, and you may do whatever you think best. If he thinks this an unfriendly course, I think it is for him to show that any other was possible. Certainly, I tried hard enough to keep the matter between ourselves alone. Sometimes I feel indignant, but somehow the uppermost feeling is a sense of loss. There weighs upon me a burden, as if some great calamity had befallen. Unless he may yet show something that has hitherto not appeared, giving a new light."

M. N. to Mr. Dane, February 15.

"MR. HUNT shows an indifference quite in harmony with the theory that his friendship for me is founded on his business relations. In fact, it seems that business relations and friendly relations are alike unimportant to him, for he has taken no notice whatever of my letter. Of course, I shall not be careful to preserve what he values so lightly; yet I would rather err on the side of caution than of recklessness. It is possible my letter may have been missent, or that he is out of town. Of course, when our breach becomes public, it can never be healed; and I therefore do not wish it to pass beyond us till there is no possibility of doubt. I therefore will write another note, and inclose it in this letter. If you see no objection, I should like to have you mail it to him in Athens. Then I will wait one week more. The week after, that is, the week commencing February 23, I shall wish you to call upon Mr. Hunt and get all the money, etc., of mine which he holds."

Mr. Dane to M. N.

"I AM GRIEVED and sorry with you at the thing. I thought Mr. Hunt would hasten, at the suggestion of any real dissatisfaction, to satisfy you. . . . Yours, inclosing a note to him, just came. I know that suspense to you is very trying, and I want you to do all that is possible to keep the trouble where it is; and I would therefore have you send him the note which you inclose, before you suggest me or any one else as a disjunctive conjunction. . . ."

The note to Mr. Hunt simply said that I had received no answer to my last note; that, indeed, no answer was necessary, but I should be glad to know he had received it; and that, as it was hardly probable two successive letters should go wrong, if I did not hear from him, I should assume that he had received both notes.

M. N. to Mr. Dane, February 19.

"NO LETTER has come. . . . There is no use in waiting. I do not understand Mr. Hunt's course, nor do I care to understand it.

"The more I think of it, the more I am inclined *not* to have you do anything about the past. Let the dead bury their dead. It will be only a disagreeable personal affair, whose sole satisfaction will be the money. It will in effect be arguing and claiming a greater value than he has set upon me. For my part, I would a great deal rather let it all go. You just call and get the money that the account says is due. Make as much of a settlement as can be settled; and if he chooses to let everything remain as it is, I choose it also. If he can afford to dispense with an explanation, so can I."

I had given to Mr. Dane an order upon Mr. Hunt for what money of mine he had in his possession.

Mr. Dane called for the money on the 24th of February, and on the same day,—but whether before or after Mr. Dane's call, I can only infer,—Mr. Hunt wrote to me:—

"DEAR M. N.:—

"On my return home on Saturday, I found your note without date, informing me that you had received no reply to your 'note of last Tuesday.' I have not replied to your note of February 11th, because I could not understand the purport of it, and hoped you might be in town soon to explain it.

"In the last letter I received from you, some days before the note referred to above, written in the old friendly spirit and faith, you tell me you have a juvenile book nearly ready, and ask if it shall be sent for publication. I reply, please send it at once; and then comes your note of the 11th inst., with this passage in it: 'I cannot see how it will be for my interest that you should publish any more of my books. Unhappily, it is not necessary that I should give any explanation, since the reason, if it do not exist to your own knowledge, and by your own arrangement, does not exist at all.' Now there must have been something in my note to you (to which this note of February 11th is a reply) which has offended you; else why this sudden change from the sentiments in your long and friendly letter to those of the unhappy note of February 11th? Now, pray let us understand each other; and in all kindness, I ask you to tell me the ground of your sudden dissatisfaction.

"Very sincerely yours,

"R. S. HUNT."

Mr. Hunt's ignorance in face of my letters, his absolute inability to conjecture in what direction the trouble lay, his misgiving that some unremembered sentence in his letter had offended me, seemed to me not a little remarkable. I wrote again.

M. N. to Mr. Hunt

"MY DEAR MR. HUNT:—

"It is an unpleasant story to tell, but since you desire it I will repeat it.

"You recollect the letter I wrote you some time last December, and the question I asked you in it. The 'long and friendly letter,' of which you speak, told you of my waiting, and of my writing to Mr. Jackson. Mr. Jackson's letter confirmed the statement of the Segregationalissuemost. He said, 'There is a custom of the trade which obtains for the first venture of an author unknown to fame, to receive ten per cent. on the retail price of the books after the first thousand copies are sold. . . . As to the price per volume of M. N.'s works, I should think twenty to twenty-five cents per volume would be the fair copyright. Sometimes a moderate copyright makes larger sales by enabling the publishers to give larger discounts to the trade,' etc., etc. I still supposed there was some good reason for my receiving a lower rate than any he mentioned, and in my long letter I tried to make clear to you the point which I wished settled. In your reply, you said, by E———, 'Do you wonder, matters having been many times explained, that he thought they must sooner or later explain themselves through your memory? *We* forget how, in a retired life, things work in the mind,' etc., etc. My memory is not wont to play me false; and so far from matters having been many times explained, they have not been explained at all. I have never so much as sought any explanation till now. Never but once has the subject been referred to between us. That was years ago, soon after the publication of 'City Lights,' and while prices were as yet unfixed. You then said, of your own accord, that owing to fluctuation of prices and general uncertainties, you were making arrangements with your authors to pay them fifteen cents a volume instead of a percentage. To this I readily assented. All that you said did not take five minutes, and all that I said did not amount to five words. I had a great deal more faith in your honorable intentions toward me than I had in my literary power to serve you. I had far more anxiety lest I should make you lose money, than I had lest you should make me lose it.

"I decided that if I were indeed brooding in a retired life over a trifle, it was time to refer the matter to some one whose life was not retired, and who was better able than I to judge. I gave the whole matter to Hon. Mr. Dane. He made inquiries among the publishers, without using your name, or in any way bringing you in question; and as the result of his investigations, he reports ten per cent. on the retail price as the very lowest paid to the author. One publisher told him that they considered a book that was not worth to its author ten per cent., was not worth publishing.

"How, then, could I avoid the conclusion that you have been paying me all these years from one fourth to one third less than the lowest market price? For, notwithstanding the fixed sum was to avoid a change, change has not been avoided. When a book was published whose retail price was one dollar and fifty cents, the author's part went down to ten cents. That is, the author's price was fixed against a rise, but flexible toward a fall.

"Is not this enough to explain my 'change of sentiment' and my 'sudden dissatisfaction?'

"Mr. Hunt, I cannot talk of this. I have suffered a loss that money cannot measure, nor words express. The writing of this letter is the most painful work my pen has ever done. My faith in you was perfect, and my friendship boundless, and it has all come to this.

"I was thoroughly identified with you. I counted your prosperity mine. Not a word of praise or censure was passed upon you that I did not feel. Had your needs demanded it, I would gladly have offered twice, and thrice, and four times any reduction, and have reckoned it only pleasure.

"If I have failed to make anything clear, you can refer to Mr. Dane. No one but himself knows anything about it; but how can it be kept longer? And yet how can it be told?"

When Mr. Hunt rendered my account, and paid my money to Mr. Dane, I found that they had allowed ten per cent. on the new book, "Rights of Men."

Mr. Hunt did not reply to my letter, but sought an interview with Mr. Dane, of which the latter gives the following account:—

"ATHENS, *March* 2d, 1768.

"I have had a long talk with Mr. Hunt; longer than I can write. He asked me at first what you wished; said he had a long letter from you, referring him to me, etc. I told him that it seemed to you, as it did to me, strange that, while almost any author was receiving ten per cent. on sales, you were allowed much less, and that was what had not been explained. He expressed all through the greatest regard for you, and surprise that you should have so little confidence in him. I told him I should be very glad to be able to assure you that he had done everything toward you that his confidential relations required, and that I felt sure it was best, in every business point of view, that he should continue your publisher.

"He said your books are published more expensively than most books; that a great deal has been always expended for advertising; that it costs, for instance, $1,000 for one page of the 'Adriatic,' ——— copies being printed; that they employ one man at a yearly salary of ——— dollars to attend to having their books properly noticed in the papers; that all the machinery for a large sale is expensive; that they make forty per cent. discount to the trade—more on large orders; that Mr. Somebody makes estimates of the actual cost of books published, and submits them to him, and did so with yours, and so a fair price was fixed; that you have made more out of the books than the publishers, and that they could not and cannot afford to pay more than what has been allowed; and upon my suggestion that more had been allowed on 'The Rights of Men,' he said that was a thin book, and took but little paper, and so cost less. He says others will pay you much more for a single work in order to get you, but thinks the style, etc., would not be satisfactory, etc. In short, Mr. H. claims that in all respects, they have done their best as publishers and friends for your reputation and pecuniary interests in the long run.

"Mr. H. said he was sorry you did not call as he suggested, and talk about the matter; that he should never cease to be your friend—'I wish you would tell her so;' that in your letter you had almost charged him with dishonesty, which certainly you could not mean, etc. Upon my inquiry, he said they made less on the books at the present high prices, but he gave me no special estimates. He said he had arranged with other authors at a specified price per copy, but did not tell me what price. As the interview was at his request, I had no demands to make, and could do little but hear him. I told him I should write you to-day, placing the matter before you as he presented it; that I could not, without inquiry, say to you that I was or was not satisfied that all was right, but should be very glad to see your pleasant relations continue; and so it ended."

This explanation was not satisfactory. If my books were published more expensively than most books, Mr. Hunt should have told me before. When the first one was to be published, he asked what style I should like, and suggested that of the "City Curate." I preferred "Sir Thomas Browne."[13] He made no objection, nor even hinted that it was more expensive than the other. He wrote to me, "It will be a beauty, and look like 'Sir Thomas Browne,' in its red waistcoat." And again: "I am glad you like the costume into which we put your first-born." The following books were simply published in uniform style with the first, and nothing was ever said about it between us. As to the cost of advertising, why should it cost him more to advertise than it did other publishers, or more to advertise me than other writers? What, again, had I to do with the cost of the machinery for large sales, or with the rate of discount, unless they were gotten up and arranged solely or chiefly on my account? In that case I must indeed have been disastrous to my publishers, for I cannot think my sales have been exceptionally large. The reason alleged for the increased price allowed on "Rights of Men," seemed trivial. True, it was but a thin book, and took but little paper, and so cost less. But it was not so thin a book as "Holidays," on which they allowed me but ten cents, while on "Rights of Men," accounted for after I had begun to look into the matter, they allowed fifteen cents. Yet both books were sold at the same retail price,—one dollar and fifty cents. "Rights of Men" was one hundred and forty-four pages thinner than "Winter Work," one hundred and twenty-three pages thinner than "Cotton-picking," ninety-eight pages thinner than "Old Miasmas." Those books were sold at a retail price of two dollars, while this was one dollar and a half. On those books they allowed me seven and a half per cent., while on this they allowed me ten per cent.

But "Old Miasmas" is one hundred and fifty-one pages thinner than "City Lights;" "Cotton-picking" is one hundred and twenty-six pages thinner than "City Lights." All three of the books are sold at the same retail price,—two dollars. And on all three I was allowed but seven and a half per cent. That is, while all goes smoothly, a thinness of one hundred and fifty-one pages is of no account. It neither makes the price of a book less to the buyer, nor the pay of a book greater to the author. But when ripples begin to rise, a thinness of ninety-eight pages makes the buyer's price less by fifty cents, and the author's pay greater by one-fourth. Thinness, thou art a jewel!

One thing more: as these books are published in uniform style, if they are published more expensively than most books, they must have been so published in the beginning. Therefore the relative pay of the author should then have been less. But the first contract is made out according to the usual custom, at ten per cent. on the retail price. When the author was unknown and the sale uncertain, he received ten per cent. After he became known, and the risk, one would suppose, must have been diminished, he went down to six and two-thirds per cent. Great is the mystery of publishing!

Thinking it possible the smallness of sales might have something to do with it, I wrote to Mr. Dane:—

"I can't tell a lie, pa. I wish I was satisfied, but I am not. If Mr. Hunt had said this to me in the first place, I dare say I should have been. The best light is this: that I asked him a question to which, for three months, he made no reply. You asked it, and he answered at once. This, however, is a slight matter. I can talk about it, and scold him for it, and, without ever forgiving him, live on in perfect good-humor. It is a surface matter, and if this is all it is nothing.

"But I cannot thoroughly feel that this is all, and I cannot be the same without feeling so. Mr. Jackson knew the style of the book, so did Mr. Campton, and they knew the expenses of printing; and if Mr. Hunt had so much regard for me as he thinks he had, why did he let me go on making myself wretched for weeks, when an hour's time would have set everything at rest? He who really regards me, will regard my whims as well as my wants. And this was not a whim, either; it was a sensible and natural question. Mr. Hunt is mistaken in supposing I did not mean what I seemed to mean. I did mean just that. If I had meant less, I should have felt less. I am not a simpleton to break my heart over a difference of opinion. . . .

"I do not think it necessary to apply to any others than Marsh & Merriman, and Mr. Campton. If they think everything is as it should be, then be it resolved that it is. Enough testimony is as good as a feast. Why should others pay me more for a single work in order to get me? Can they afford to pay more than he? But there is no good in talking upon uncertainties. When we have found out any actual data, we can cipher on interminably. I trust you are pleased with the prospect. I do not think it is of any use to stop here, because inwardly I am no more content than I was when I began—not so much, in fact. I am at one of those places where it is easier to go forward than backward. Indeed, from this point it is impossible to go back to where I was when I started.

"Having slept over it, it occurs to me to say that I think you better see Mr. Campton and perhaps no one else. . . . I am afraid it will somehow get out."

Mr. Dane took my accounts to Mr. Campton and laid the facts before him, making thus the matter personal for the first time. He reported:—

"I have had a long talk with Mr. Campton, and stated to him all that Mr. Hunt said as reasons for his course, as well as what the sales had been, etc. He says your books are not within his—Murray & Elder's—usual line of publication, but he knows all about them. He says nobody would ask you to receive less than ten per cent. on the retail price, and any publisher in Athens will give you more for anything you may offer, and that now you ought to receive for all past sales at that rate on all the books, and that you would be entitled to that even on a book where only two thousand copies sold.

"Mr. Campton measured and counted the pages, etc., in your books, and figured the cost and all the items. At outside present prices it costs to compose and stereotype such a book, $1.25 a page, or $500 for 400 pages. That is the whole outlay for the plates ready to print. After that, the books cost, all told, say 52 cents per copy.

"The publisher receives, including what he retails and gives away, an average of $1.20 per copy on the whole editions.

"Such books of 400 pages cost each copy:—

Paper and press-work, ...	.24
Binding, ...	.23
Stereotype plates, $500, 10,000 copies, each, ...	.05
	.52
Retail price, ...	$2.00
40 per cent. off, ...	.80
	$1.20
	.52
	.68

Of which the publisher has	.53
The author	.15

"Old Miasmas" has only 310 pages, and so costs less by 25 per cent. Mr. C. says the books can be made at 15 per cent. less than these estimates, but he wanted to keep within bounds. . . . The advertising, etc., are part of the usual machinery of all publishers. He says B. & H., so far from making unusual discounts to the trade, have recently published a list prescribing so little discounts that 'the trade' are offended."

I also directed Mr. Dane to write to some of the Corinthian publishers to ascertain their custom. He wrote to Pearville & Co., and received the following reply on March 20:—

"DEAR SIR,—In reply to your favor of 18th, beg to say that, in the absence of any agreement, we should pay to the author 10 per cent. on the retail price for all copies sold. This on $2.00 would give the author 20 cts.; and 1.50, 15 cts. per copy.

"Very respectfully, B. PEARVILLE & CO."

My confidence in Mr. Hunt was lost, and I was too much disheartened to do anything more except to close my connection with the firm, so far as I could. I wrote to Mr. Dane:—

"Do not *you* be disturbed by this unhappy complication. If you do, I shall be *désesperé* indeed. There is nothing to be done between Mr. Hunt and me. There is nothing between us worth preserving. . . . The case has been presented to him. He is not inclined to do anything, and I certainly cannot press him. Either he feels that he is right or that he is wrong. If the former, any proceedings on my part will only bring on active antagonism. If the latter, the consciousness of it is penalty severe enough to atone for all. Moreover, so far as I am concerned, no money could make amends for what it would cost me; and in fact, having lost so much, I think I rather enjoy losing the money too. . . . I would not see Mr. Hunt any more. Let it all go."

EDITOR'S NOTE: Chapters V–IX continue with the story of the dispute, which I summarize here using real names. Although Dodge expressed a willingness to drop the whole thing after these first frustrating months, her anger was rekindled soon after when she discovered that Hawthorne's widow Sophia was having similar problems because of Nathaniel's contracts with Fields. Adding insult to injury, Dodge was rudely ousted as a contributing editor of the firm's Our Young Folks *(not, incidentally, at Field's behest). Subsequently, both Fields and his partner James Osgood visited Dodge to try to charm her out of her complaints, but to no avail. As the dispute continued over the next year, Dodge solicited information from other writers, while Ticknor and Fields launched a public relations campaign in the press. After months of wrangling, the two sides brought the dispute to informal arbitration in front of a three-person board. Dodge's defense, recorded in the book, included all the evidence she had gathered from other writers as well as a meticulous presentation of all her correspondence and dealings with the publishers. At the end of her presentation, she asked for back payments on the books for which she had not received 10 percent royalties, plus 7 percent interest on the amount. She also claimed $3000 for the expenses of preparing her case. In their ruling the referees did not actually accuse the publishers of wrongdoing—just lax business practices—and awarded her only $1250. But they did order that in the future she was to receive 10 percent on the retail prices of her books.*

X

SOBER SECOND AND THIRD THOUGHTS

HAVING TRESPASSED so far on the patience of the reader, I may as well presume a little farther, and indulge in a few reflections.

First, from the investigations and observations of the last two years, I infer that authors are very much to blame in their business dealings. By their inexactness, their indifference, their unreasonable and indolent trust, and their excessive monetary stupidity, they not only become an easy prey of, but they offer a direct temptation to the cupidity of publishers. Not a single author to whom I appealed showed the slightest reluctance to answer my questions, nor, I may almost add, the slightest ability to answer them adequately. For instance, the points I wished to ascertain were whether a writer was paid by percentage or by a fixed sum: what was the percentage and what the fixed sum: and whether during or subsequent to the year 1764 any change was made in the mode or rate of payment.

See now how charmingly the authors met my points.

Says one, "Brummell and Hunt never published but ——— with me and I received on this the usual beggarly percentage;" leaving me entirely in the dark as to what was the beggarly percentage.

Says another: "What terms do I make with B. & H.? Yes, with all my heart. In regard to ———, they print and sell and allow me a certain sum on all copies sold;" but with the greatest inclination in the world giving me no hint of the amount of that "certain sum."

Says another: "Brummell & Hunt have, I believe, allowed me ten per cent. on the retail price of my books. That was the first arrangement at least, but I must confess I never look at their statements of account."

Says a fourth: "I have always received a percentage. . . . I remember no change in 1764, unless that B. & H. about that time (perhaps earlier) without my asking it, raised the sum they paid me for ———, etc. . . . The interests of authors and publishers are identical—a fact which they understand better than we do."

Yet the firm testified of this very writer that they had written agreements to pay him percentage, and that when prices advanced they waived the percentage, and paid him a certain (lower) sum per volume.

A fifth says: "I have not the least objection in the world in replying to your letter in the most straightforward way. . . . I have been contented with ten per cent. on the retail price of my printed books."

Yet the written contracts of this writer showed every variety of arrangement from twenty per cent. downward.

A sixth says: "Messrs. B. & H. have published four books for me. . . The three first named sell for $1.25, and I receive twelve cents each copy.

But Messrs. B. & H. affirmed that these books sold for $1.50 each.

A seventh says: "I did not send your letter to ———, for the reason that she does not know as much as you do about the subject of its inquiry. The most she could tell you would be, that now and then there comes a bit of paper very neatly and tastefully diversified by red and blue lines, and dreadfully complicated by sundry hieroglyphics, which she has been told are figures, and that a check embellished with one of the rows of figures accompanies it. . . . I have an impression that years ago, when ——— was taking such sesquipedalian strides to public favor, Mr. Brummel told me that after the number of copies sold had reached a certain point, the author received a reduced percentage, and I think I remember wondering by what perversion of commercial philosophy, an article of which fifty thousand copies could be sold, was worth less, proportionally, than one of which only five thousand could be bartered, for of course the ratio of cost decreased with every successive thousand manufactured."

Here, it will be perceived, is a faint glimmer of sense, which will be completely extinguished by the next extract.

"——— said you made a mistake in thinking yourself differently used from the rest of the writing craft, and explained that the profits of the author did not keep up the same proportion in repeated editions, but went to pay the increased circulation. For his part he would rather be more poorly paid for the sake of being more widely read."

Must not that have been an explanation worth having? It is not difficult to conjecture the source whence that form of explanation originated, for another letter says, "Mr. ——— went to see Mr. Hunt. . . . Mr. Hunt expressed great regret that it had all happened; said 'Rights of Men,' had done more for your reputation than any other book; that you made more than the publishers did, etc., and that they thought better to have a low per cent. and large sales, than the contrary; though I don't see what a low per cent. paid to the author has to do with large sales, if the price of the book is kept high to purchasers."

The fact, is that as a bad woman is said to be a great deal worse than a bad man, so a man innocent of business capacity, is far more innocent than any woman can be. A woman may be never so silly but there is generally a substratum of hard sense somewhere. A man may be never so wise, and yet completely destitute of this practical ability. It is largely in behalf of these helpless, harmless, deluded, and betrayed gentlemen, that I have felt called to take up arms. What sword would not leap from its scabbard to maintain the cause of the weak and the wronged?

But though I admit and lament that authors are unpractical and unbusiness-like to the last degree, I must affirm that they have less inducement to be business-like and less opportunity to be practical than any other class of persons. Suppose a writer sets out with the determination to be prudent and sagacious, where shall he begin? If a farmer has a bushel of potatoes to sell, he knows, or can learn in a moment, precisely their market value. The Early Rose has its price, and the Jackson White has its price; there is no room for doubt, or misgiving, or mistake. But the author has not and cannot have the least notion of the market value of his products. He does not even know their intrinsic value. He does not know whether he has raised an Early Rose or a dead-and-gone Chenango. He may have spent his strength on what is absolutely unsalable. His work is production, but for its worth he must depend solely on the word of those who buy and sell. After a while he does indeed arrive at something like a scale of value, but he never reaches such a degree of certainty as to feel assured of any special piece of work. Every one must be judged by itself. Five successful books are no absolute guaranty that the sixth will not be worthless.

It seems to me, also, that there is no business in which so few checks exist as in that of publishing. An author, we will say, agreed to receive ten per cent. on the retail price of all copies of his works that are sold, but he has literally nothing but the publisher's word by which to know how many copies are sold. The manufacturer knows how many he has made, but it would be offensive to ask for the manufacturer's accounts, and moreover he would probably not render them if asked. He would consider it as betraying the secrets of the trade, or the trust of his employers, or otherwise impertinent and unwarranted. Of course a false return of sales would be fraud, and somewhat complicated fraud; but human ingenuity combined with human depravity has been known to surmount obstacles to crime as formidable as these, and the danger of detection is infinitessimally small. If there be any such thing in arithmetic as the Double Rule of Three,—and I seem to have a vague impression that there is,—it may well be brought to the solution of the problem: if a publisher may for years safely disregard, not to say violate, the condition of a contract which an author has before his eyes in plain black and white, how long may another publisher safely falsify accounts which an author never sees, and which he could not understand if he should see? I have no doubt that in nine cases out of ten, and perhaps also in the tenth, the returns of sales are as accurate as the moral law. What I maintain is, that the author, be he wise as

Solomon, has no means of knowing whether they are or not, while the manufacturer of all other goods knows precisely how much raw material goes into the mill and how much of the manufactured article comes out.

If the author, instead of receiving a percentage, takes half profits, he is even more at the mercy of the publisher. In the very outet the wildest theories prevail as to what constitute profits, and though the author may make heroic struggles to be exhaustively mathematical, the probabilities are that the only draught made upon his science will be the very simple effort of dividing by two whatever sum the publisher has chosen to figure up. The plan adopted by actors and actresses, to take half the gross receipts, is far more simple and sensible.

It is true that an author may take advantage of competition and seek a second market if the first prove unsatisfactory, but it is also certain that he cannot do this to any effective extent without serious injury to himself. All the skill, the vitality, the invention, the thought, which he brings to the disposition of his wares is so much taken from his producing power. He ought to be wholly free to do his best work. He ought to be able to concentrate himself on his writing. If he must turn aside to study the state of the market and superintend the details of sale and circulation, that necessity will surely tell in the deterioration of his works; and even at that cost he will not be so good a business manager as one who is to the manner born. It is a very pretty thing to be a poet-publisher—in the newspapers, but if the poet's imagination happens to get loose among the publisher's facts, it makes sad work, and it is not merry work when the publisher crops out in the poet's verses.

What then remains? It has been proposed that authors combine and form a publishing-house by themselves, publishing their own books and receiving their own profits. This plan looks simple enough, but I must confess it seems to me chimerical in the last degree. Excepting the temptations of their trade, doubtless a hundred publishers are as honest as a hundred authors, and surely they have a great deal more business sagacity. But as soon as authors turn publishers they fall into all the publisher's temptations without acquiring his business power; so that when you have chemically combined author and publisher you have an amalgam wholly and disastrously different from either of the original simples, namely, a publisher minus his common sense.

No, the publisher is not an artificial member of society. Like all other middle-men he meets a real want. He exists because in the long run it is cheaper and better for writers to employ him than to do his work themselves. Of course, the wiser and more righteous he is, the better he answers the end of his creation; but with all his imperfections on his head, he is better than nobody. A man may as well undertake to build his house with his own hands to save himself from the short-comings and extortions of carpenters, as to manufacture and distribute his own books to save himself from the extortions of publishers. We may send missionaries among them, we may gather them in to our Sunday-schools, but we need not think to exterminate them.

Authors may form publishing houses, and those houses may be successful, but if so it will be simply by adopting substantially the methods of successful publishing-houses already established. It seems to me easier and more economical to let such institutions spring from the soil, rather than attempt to construct them out of material which has already been organized into another form of life.

Shall we then take the publisher *cum grana salis*,[14] and try to guard our interests by keeping a strict look-out? We must turn publishers ourselves to make it of any account. A detective, to be worth anything, ought to be at least as wily as the rogue he watches, and to be so he must give his mind to it, and if he give his mind to that, wherewithal shall he set up any other business? An author need not rush in among publishers as Cincinnati swine are said to invade the streets with whetted knives, crying "come and eat me"; but if he on the contrary objects, steadfastly and stoutly, to being devoured, he does not know where his vulnerable point is, and cannot therefore arm himself against attack. He is not and cannot become, consistently with the proper pursuit of his own profession, sufficiently acquainted with the details of publishing to know whether a measure proposed by a publisher be or be not fair. For instance, the publisher contracts to pay ten per cent. on the retail price of a sixty-two cent book. A war comes, bringing high prices, and the book goes up to a dollar and a quarter. The publisher continues to pay the author ten per cent. of sixty-two cents, making no reference to the increased price. The author presently chances to discover it, and remonstrates. The publishers say curtly, "You will make the price of the book so large that it will have no sale," oblivious to the fact that it is not the author but themselves who have raised the price of the book. He replies that the price is not his affair; he must insist upon the contract. The publishers yield, and the author is apparently victorious. But when a second author brings up this case as a reason why he should receive his percentage, the publishers reply, "True, we did continue percentage because he insisted, but, as a warning, the book had a very poor sale." But what effect on the sale can the author's twelve and a half, instead of six and a half cents have if the price to the buyer is the same? Until some better answer is given I shall believe that the sale diminishes because the publisher chooses it; because he prefers to sacrifice a small sum on a single volume as a warning to contumacious authors, rather than encourage rebellion by continuing to receive profits of which he must divert a larger share to the author. If he can, by one or two examples, show restive writers that the question is not between six and a half cents and twelve and a half cents on a thousand books, but between six and a half on a thousand, and twelve and a half on a hundred, the sum he sacrifices in showing it is not a bad investment.

Since, then, the publisher has matters within his own grasp so entirely that what he is forced to pay with one hand he can easily pluck with the other, I do not clearly see the advantage to be gained by insisting on any special bargain with him. Perhaps I do not quite know what I am talking about. I suspect, on the whole, I do not. But my remarks are all the more valuable for that. If, after two years of clapper-clawing among a quartette of cats, a mouse is still unskilled in feline ways, in what state of helplessness must be those unadventurous little things who have never left their holes?

But there are the books of the firm which the suspected publisher opens to you with a frankness of innocence that ought to disarm and convince the most hardened unbeliever. Any demur is met by an invitation to come and look at "the books." The trail of the Serpent is over all the rest of the world, but "the books" have escaped the contamination of original sin and shine with the purity of Paradise. Burglars blow open safes, banks and directors and cashiers and tellers come to grief, but "the books" always tell the truth, the whole truth, and nothing but the truth. Notwithstanding which I, from the beginning, instinctively gave those "books" a wide berth. They were to me like the "magick bookes" of Spenser's hermite.[15] "Let none them read." That "the books" are not always "reliable gentlemen" will have been inferred from the account which they professed to have sent me, and which was—lost in the mail. That "the books" are not always intelligible witnesses would appear, could we know how many unwary persons have gone to them in pursuit of knowledge, and found the difficulty insurmountable. "We had the books here," said one benighted author of no mean repute, "and I examined them, and Kate examined them, and Frank examined them, and the Major examined them, and we could make nothing of them." That the books have been made to do yeoman's services in this battle has already been seen, and by various tokens it would seem that they have not yet been dismissed the service. Only to-day a letter says, "But the account of the sales of your book and the sums paid you for them, as I derived them from the books of Mr. Hunt, convinced me that whatever the bargain might be you had a better one than *I* had. I have half profits—you have had more."

That is what "the books" say unquestionably; but what a stiff-necked and perverse author refuses to believe without further proof. When a publisher shows me receipted bills for the sums he has actually paid in manufacturing and publishing my books, and for the sums he has received from their sale, I will—take them to an expert for examination; but when he proposes to set me down before a mighty maze of figures, which for aught that appears, may all have been conjured up by his imagination, and begs me to deduce from them any conclusion whatever, I decline with thanks. That contention I leave off before it be meddled with. It is not necessary to be a Solomon in order to know enough to keep away from figures which it is necessary to be a Solomon to understand, and which when understood are much like the "litle flyes cal'd out of deepe darkness dredd" by the hermite before referred to, and which—

"Fluttering about his ever-damned hedd,
Awaite whereto their service he applyes,
To side his friendes, or fray his enemies."

There remains also to the wronged or suspicious author recourse to the law or to the more informal arbitration, but this also is vanity. To me a lawsuit seemed utterly intolerable, but my experience of arbitration was so repulsive, and is so hideous in memory—and this solely from the nature of things, since, alike from the referees and from Messrs. Parry and Markman who, like St. Paul, were the chief speakers, on the other side, I met only courtesy—that a lawsuit seems attractive in comparison; but if I had instituted a lawsuit, without doubt adverse fate hereafter, would have been implored to take any shape but that! If two parties are really bent on getting at the vital facts, presenting absolute truth, securing exact and essential justice, nothing can be more to the purpose apparently than a reference to disinterested, non-professional, intelligent, and friendly persons; but two parties honestly bent on such an object would probably have nothing to quarrel over. Even if they have it is not certain that the informal is better than the formal mode of settlement. If there are no facts to be hushed up, a legal investigation will do no harm; if there are facts to be hushed up, a legal investigation is necessary. We look at the law as at best a clumsy round-about way of arriving at just conclusions—a method full of ingenious devices to entangle and confuse witnesses and make the worse appear the better reason. We take the informal arbitration as a short cut to the desired goal. On the whole I am inclined to think that the law is the shortest cut in the known world. The rules which obtain in courts of justice and which seem to the unprofessional mind a mere medley of arbitrary vexations and restrictions, are the result of the experience of ages, and with all their short-comings and their long-comings do probably present the most expeditious and unerring mode of reaching truth which human wit and wisdom have yet devised. If so we cannot depart from them without loss. In ridding ourselves of their clumsiness we rid ourselves also of their effectiveness. We rend away the red tape, but the package immediately falls apart into a worthless heap of memoranda. You avoid a lawsuit because of the publicity and multiplicity and infelicity of lawyers, witnesses, judge, and jury. You adopt a reference because it dispenses with all these and goes straight at the heart of things. But you find by experience that unless your opponent wishes it you may not get at the heart of things at all. In a lawsuit you can enforce measures; in a reference you are dependent upon courtesy. Your opponent presents only that which is good in his own eyes. He produces what he chooses; he withholds what he chooses. To be sure you do the same; but you, angel that you are, have nothing to hide, while he, the fiend! has all manner of wiles and wickedness to conceal. If now you were in court, politeness and impertinence would be equally and wholly out of the question. It is the duty and delight of lawyers to find out everything—and such is the depravity of the legal heart, it is especially their duty and delight to ferret out what the opposite party desires to conceal. It is not what a man wishes and means to say, but everything which he can be made to say, that a lawyer wants. His hand can put aside the proffered "books," and grab the books which are withheld. He does not permit the opposite parties to select and exclude witnesses, but goes out into the highways and hedges and compels to come in whom he wants. The law winds a long way round, but it sets you down as near your journey's end as the nature of things permits. A private reference takes a short cut, but it has no inherent power to carry you far from your starting-point. Arbitration has the advantage in respect of privacy, and that is an advantage not to be overestimated. Still, if there is anything to choose when both are intolerable, it seems rather worse to speak yourself before five men, than to have some one else to speak for you before five hundred. It matters not how wise, how impartial, referees may be, their jurisdiction is necessarily limited, and they cannot go beyond it to compel, or extort, or present. They must judge on what is spontaneously set before them. If to avoid trouble and unpleasantness be your object, it is better to submit to everything and keep out of strife altogether. If you set out to accomplish an end, it is better to shut eyes and ears to disagreements, and take the road which common experience designates as the surest and safest in the long run.

But I most heartily advise writers in general to do neither. So far as the improvement of one's fortune goes, nothing is more futile. One should be exact, prompt, methodical, and intelligent so far as possible. He will thus exert a salutary influence over his publisher, and will be far more likely to receive his dues than if he believes "in uninquiring trust" and lives wholly by faith. But it is better for his purse to take what a publisher chooses to give than to make an ado about it afterwards. Even if successful in regard to the particular sum he claims, it is at a cost of time and trouble altogether disproportionate to it. He plays an unequal game at best, because the publisher's business goes on serenely, during all the difficulty, while the author's must be at a stand-still. The very instrument that he uses in defending his works is the instrument which he ought to be using in producing them. Even as a pecuniary transaction it is far more profitable to sow seed for future harvests than to spend strength in trying to secure the gleanings of last year's growths. The money proceeds of the insurrection, whose history has been given in these pages, was twelve hundred and fifty dollars. The whole amount claimed to make up ten per cent. was about three thousand dollars, and considering that my whole plan of proceedings was demolished in the beginning, and that the case had to present itself, as one may say, smothered in a mass of irrelevant details, and deprived of much that was to the purpose, I reckoned myself extremely well off. But even had the whole sum been awarded, it would have been no very munificent compensation for eighteen months of literary labor, apart from the fact that the labor was of a kind for which no money could compensate. In its baldest shape, the results of a year and a half of work were twelve hundred and fifty dollars, or little more than one third of what was claimed on previous work. I think myself therefore justified in asserting that though quarreling with your publishers may be very good as a crusade, it is a very poor way of getting a living.

Let me here correct an impression that seems to prevail somewhat extensively as to the rewards of literary life. It certainly has its rewards, and of the most delightful kind. What joys it may bring in the higher walks I do not know, but even on the lower levels, I should like to live forever—a thousand years to begin with, at any rate. I could speak as enthusiastically as a certain popular writer, "once more famous than now," "Of all the blessings which my books have brought me,—blessings of inward wealth that cannot be so much as named,—blessings so rich, so divine, that I sometimes think nothing ever was so beautiful as to have written a book."[16]

But so far as literature pays cash down it is not to be compared to—shoemaking, for instance. The daily papers have been circulating a paragraph to the effect that a recent popular book had gone to a second edition and that its author had already received from it twelve thousand dollars. I am not prepared to deny the statement; but I know an author of nine books, not it is to be hoped on the same footing of intrinsic merit, but books which have travelled up to nine, ten, and fourteen editions, whose author never has received and never expects to receive twelve thousand dollars on the whole lot.

Let nothing in this remark be construed into anything like complaint.

On the contrary, authors ought to be grateful to their publishers for allowing them so large a gratuity. As Mr. Parry remarked concerning the appropriation of an edition of fifteen hundred books to the use of the firm, they might have taken more if they had chosen. And when we reflect that not only do they bestow upon us these large sums of money, but, as sundry extracts in other parts of this volume show, they first manufacture for us the fame which brings the money, we are, in the language of the hymn, lost in wonder, love, and praise.[17] It must be heart-rending to fashion your graven image and then have that image turn upon you and demand a share of the profits!

Unhappily a dense ignorance upon this subject broods over the community, and there should be added to our literature an

Author's Catechism

1. *Question.* Can you tell me, child, who made you?

Answer. The great House of Hunt, Parry, & Co., which made heaven and earth.[18]

In controversies with publishers, the author is at a signal disadvantage by reason of the connection of publishers with the press. Publishers have the entrée of the newspapers by their advertising, and all in the way of business, it is the easiest thing in the world to give public opinion a tilt in the desired direction without the least suspicion on the part of the reader, or any more collusion on the part of the editor than is implied in a good-natured relinquishment of a few lines of editorial space. Here, we will say, is a house which advertises to the extent of hundreds, perhaps thousands of dollars in a single paper. In connection with an extraordinary advertisement, it hands to the editor an extraordinary paragraph, celebrating its more extraordinary virtues. The advertisement goes in among the advertisements, and the eulogy goes in among the editorials and becomes the voice of the paper. Nobody is hurt, and the firm is greatly helped in building up for itself name and fame. When the Athenian newspapers glow with reflections upon the inability of authors to understand the details of publishing and the unimpeached and unimpeachable honor of the house of Hunt, Parry, & Co., not half a dozen readers suspect that those reflections are anything but the spontaneous tribute of a grateful people to the eminent firm in question. Nobody suspects that behind all the glitter and glory some pestiferous little author is poking an inquisitive finger in among those details, is indeed questioning that unimpeached and unimpeachable honor, and that this beating of gongs is but Chinese strategy on the part of the attacked, to scare away the impertinent foe. I can make no avowal on this head, having nothing but internal evidence to go upon: but applying the rules of Scriptural exegesis, it seems to me that we attribute to the four Gospels a divine origin on less evidence than we may attribute to these eulogies a common origin.

For instance, during that portion of the sidereal year known throughout the solar system as Jubilee week, the press of Athens burned with enthusiasm for the house of Hunt, Parry, & Co.

"The broadside advertisement," says one, "with which the renowned publishing house of Messrs. Hunt, Parry, & Co. salute the country in this jubilee time on another page of this morning's Post, will excite universal attention and remark. It details the literary achievements of this enterprising firm during the last year and a half in a form that is both novel and impressive. Where are the publishers on this continent who within that term have presented to the reading public works from (how many?) different authors, nearly all of whom are living celebrities? It would be glory enough for any firm to have announced original works from less than one fourth that number of well-known authors. Read the glittering roll of names as they are presented. In poetry, L., T., L., B., and W. Of novelists, D., T., S., H., H., R., and G. And of essayists, travellers, writers on natural history and science, such a shining company of men and women of genius as will make book-shelves brilliant for all time to come. But these publishers have not compromised quality with quantity. They hold up to their high standard in every essay in which they engage. Nor are they in any sense such devotees of Mammon as to think it possible to build a lasting reputation on anything less substantial than true honor in dealing as well as indisputable worth in selection.

"Their shelves and counters are an embarrassment of literary riches. Such a display of the ripest fruits of culture, taste, judgment, enterprise, and business sagacity cannot be surpassed. Their wonderful march to their eminent and leading position as publishers has given an excellent example to the country in refining and solidifying the common rules of business in their own field, and elevating and dignifying a branch of trade than which not one is clothed with nobler and purer associations. From this house, also, go forth a quarterly, two monthlies, and a weekly magazine, any one of which would add lustre to the repute of the publishers. None but sound and sweet literature comes from hence. It is the aim of the firm to keep the fountain clear from which such incessant streams of influence are to flow. American authors contribute in large store to the rich treasury of its productions, while foreign, and especially British writers supply in large degree the stores of reading, which are the recreation and delight of cultivated people everywhere."

And thus another paper takes up the parable:—

"Our first page to-day is entirely devoted to a remarkable advertisement, which tells the story of rare business enterprise, and is filled to overflowing with attractive announcements. But it is for characteristics other than these that it will command attention and really deserve study. Within a year and a half, Hunt, Parry, & Co. have given to the public works from the pens of two score of authors, American and English, almost all of them living and of widest popularity. To represent in print a half-dozen of the most prominent on the list might be the making of any firm; to take care of the whole of them would seem to be an embarrassment of riches. But the establishment has done and is doing this, with unremitting energy and in good style. We need not take room to run over the long and brilliant catalogue; a glance at the eight columns will reveal a galaxy of shining names. Observe the poets,—T., B., L., and L., W., and the rest; count up the novelists—S., T., D., R., G., H., and others of the tribe; consider the array of essayists, travellers, and naturalists, men and women of mark; and then ask whether Hunt, Parry, & Co. are surpassed by any of their contemporaries in their numerous issues, taking quantity, quality, and variety into the account. In offering this broadside programme of their performances, as bookmakers and booksellers, to the crowds of Jubilee week, they put forth a statement of indisputable facts; give a transcript of the record of the volumes they have issued, and their relations to eminent writers.

"Their achievements imply something more than an immediate and exclusive eye to the main chance. It is evident that the honorable pursuit of profit is not with them the sole consideration. (O that it were!) They desire to connect their names with good literature, advanced thought, and the intellectual progress of the age. They would be known for their taste and liberal policy as well as for their mercantile success; acting upon the principle that character as well as money is worth earning in the pursuits of trade and commerce. Without entering into comparisons, thus much is fairly to be inferred from their extended advertisement. It tells of results which imply the existence of the qualities we have attributed to them; for without such qualities such results could not have been attained. The evidence of culture, judgment, sagacity, energy, boldness, tact, skill, and whatever else goes to the building up of a publishing house known at home and abroad for its magnitude and the extent and variety of its ventures, is literally such that he who runs may read and see that it is beyond controversy. This is not extravagant praise or mere compliment; but simply the statement of the truth as made manifest by the facts.

"In this general reference to Messrs. Hunt, Parry, & Co., we must not, in passing, omit an allusion to their periodicals. To them the public are indebted for the maintenance of the oldest Greek Quarterly, the agreeable and fresh weekly selections of 'Every Tuesday,' the wide circulation and high character for ability, diversity, and independence of the 'Adriatic Monthly,' and that leading magazine of its class, 'The Buddhist.'

"In thus calling attention to a publishing house whose imprint is known wherever the Greek language is spoken or read, we are pointing to what is one of the leading concerns in a most important branch of the business of the city, of which others besides its proprietors may well be proud. Not only has it grown with the growing culture of the country, but it has encouraged home authors, and spread far and wide the best productions of the best writers on the other side of the Atlantic; thus giving it a claim to honorable consideration as holding a high place among the beneficent agencies of the advancing civilization of the world."

And a third chimes in:—

"The firm of Hunt, Parry, & Co., now almost as familiar to the public under the new name as under the old colors with which it sailed so long, has been a bulwark and a rallying point for our literature, on which book buyers as well as book writers depended for many years. It has always been active, but never so active as now. In another part of this paper, this house advertise their principal publications for the past eighteen months. With little more amplification than a catalogue, the list fills a very considerable space; but it is when we come to appreciate quality as well as quantity that its full importance is realized. No other Athenian house could bulletin such a list of authors, beginning with L., and ranging along the varied types of our literature, from W., S., H., H., and L., to P., H , and A. Nor can any house exhibit such a list of English writers, with the added merit of the authors' sanction, as T., B., H., E., D., and R.

"Periodicals have come to be recognized as necessary tenders to the business of every book firm; but the monthlies and the quarterly, etc., etc., etc.

"Whatever may be the differing opinions after the experiences of this week, upon the commercial position and prospects of Athens and the success of her musical experiments, there can be no dispute as to our preëminence among Greek cities as a literary centre. Even Corinthians, bitterly as they may sneer at our Jubilee, are forced to read the works of Athenian authors and to supply their libraries with Athenian books. It would be impossible to estimate approximately the influence in producing the literary character of the city, its clustering of authors, its tone of society, of one great publishing house; but unquestionably that influence is very great."

An ill-timed modesty on the part of the firm of Hunt, Parry, & Co. has apparently prevented the publication of the fact, but it is well known in Athenian social circles that the eclipse which made the last summer famous, and which elicited so much interest throughout the scientific world, was not owing to the interposition of the moon between our planet and the sun, but was chiefly due to the temporary disappearance from this continent of the senior partner of the house of Hunt, Parry, & Co.

I do not say that the extracts which I have quoted, and others which I might quote, emanated from the same pen, or that that pen was held in the interest of Hunt, Parry, & Co., but I do say that on any other theory the correspondence of thought, of illustration, and even of language is not a little remarkable.

And if this theory be correct, if the house which has perhaps the reputation of being the most liberal, the most generous, and the most refined publishing house in this country, has attained that reputation by assiduously blowing its own trumpet while assiduously strangling its own authors, of what value is reputation?

A novel and striking illustration of my theme has just come to hand in the publication of Miss Mitbridge's "Letters."[19] In 1754 she writes of Mr. Hunt: "He is a partner in the greatest publishing house of Greece, and the especial patron of ———, whom he found starving, and has made affluent by his encouragement and liberality, for the great romancer is so nervous that he wants as much kindness of management, as much mental nursing as a sick child. I have never known a more charming person than Mr. Hunt."[20]

The author of whom Miss Mitbridge refers is the author of whose real or supposed wrongs I have before spoken. If these publishers were indeed so liberal towards him, the unanimity with which that author's family and friends agree in attributing to them the contrary policy is a singular proof of ingratitude to benefactors; and Mr. Hunt may well exclaim with the Prophet of old, "I have nourished and brought up children, and they have rebelled against me."

I do not know what force these adulatory remarks may have upon the minds of others, but my experience and my information are such that whenever I see in the newspapers a fresh ascription of praise to the liberality of this house, I immediately infer that the screw has been given another turn on some unlucky author. The firm appears to me in the similitude of evil-minded hens cackling their noisy cut-cut-cut-ca-dah-cut over each new-laid egg, designing to conceal from an uninquiring public that, like those laymen denounced by Isaiah, they "hatch cockatrices' eggs;

he that eateth of their eggs dieth, and that which is crushed breaketh out into a viper."[21]

At a later period these general paragraphs began to converge around a particular point, and snugly nestled in among the literary items of religious newspapers may be found such announcements as this:—

"The public is threatened with a new book by the once redoubtable M. N., in which she is to narrate her tribulations, real or imaginary, with the eminent publishers, Hunt, Parry, & Co. Authors are very apt to have extravagant ideas of the popularity and profits of their books, unmindful of the fact that, generally, they are indebted to their publishers for a large proportion of their fame, and it will take several books to convince the public that H., P., & Co. deal unfairly with their authors. Thus far, H., P., & Co. have kept quiet during M. N.'s attacks, but we hope the time will come when they will vindicate themselves."

And almost simultaneously, in another quarter of the heavens, appears a similar turtle-dove, its pin-feathers developed into well-defined plumage, but unquestionably a bird of the same brood:—

"M. N., once more famous than now, had a little 'unpleasantness' with her publishers, Hunt, Parry, & Co. In plain words, she accused them of cheating her out of some thousands of dollars by making false returns of sales of her books. Like many authors, she had become inordinately vain, and had extravagant ideas of the popularity of her books, and was, as is too often the case, unmindful of the fact that a large portion of what fame she then had (but has now lost) was made for her by these self-same publishers. She had a quarrel with them of eighteen months standing, but they would not even appear in self-defense; what man would want to have an open quarrel with a woman? To any one acquainted with the details of book publishing, the charge she brings against H., P., & Co. is simply absurd; and besides, no business man would ever dare to suspect this publishing house to attempt such a system of petty cheating, and which, if attempted, would involve an amount of detail inconsistent with the end to be reached. H., P., & Co. are above the taint of suspicion. The truth is, M. N.'s books did not sell so well as she expected, and her pride (and her pocket) had a fall. It is known to us that an enormous outlay in advertising failed to make a remunerative sale on her last book. It fell dead on the market. It is now very quietly rumored that she has written a little volume which she proposes to call 'Little Men,' in which she describes her tribulations with the house of H., P., & Co. . . . M. N., you had better not! the public will not believe you."

The public will at least believe that, though a once redoubtable author, like Giant Pope in the Pilgrim's Progress, by reason of age, and also of the many shrewd brushes that he met with in his younger days, be grown crazy and stiff in his joints, he can at least sit in his cave's mouth, grinning at publishers as they go by, and biting his nails, because he cannot come at them![22]

It is not probable that these later paragraphs were actually written by the rose, but by some one who lives near the rose, and who takes roseate views of the situation.

When one has been introduced behind the scenes, these little touches go for what they are worth, but outside, they unquestionably, if imperceptibly, affect public opinion, and like an army of moral polyps build high the walls of lofty Rome. (A new species of polyps, the naturalist will say, but it answers my purpose.)

But while recognizing, to its fullest extent, the great power and prestige of a flourishing publishing house, and the great risk a writer runs in opposing it, I cannot bring myself to accept its invincibility, or its infallibility, or its indispensability. Of course a good reputation is, or ought to be, the sign of a good character; but a thing which is wrong is wrong, whatever be the reputation of him who does it. A charge of wrong is to be met by denial. It is not to [be] dazzled out of sight in a general brilliancy. When the course of our true love ceased to run smooth, I supposed my pebble was the only obstacle which my publishers' rivulet had ever known, and I was dismayed accordingly. But if all the rocks I have since discovered could be cast into one heap, we should have a bigger monument than Joshua made to mark the passage of Jordan.[23] But the monumenteers suffer in silence or speak with a bated breath that cannot be heard outside their own circle, while the flourishing firm keeps up such a continuous tooting with its rams' horns as would have flung flat the walls of Jericho had they been twice as stout as they were.[24] Undoubtedly it is not wise always to make an outcry over your follies or misfortunes. Neither is it wise always to go through the world with a chip on your shoulder, challenging people to fillip it off. Yet we all admit that there are times when short, sharp, and decisive resistance to aggression is the wisest plan. So also is there a time to speak as well as a time to refrain from speaking. There may be dignity, there may be generosity, there may be prudence, or pusillanimity, or selfishness in silence. There may be all in speech. Of this I am certain, if any of those writers who have escaped harm by their own skill, or any of those who have thought to escape further harm by silence had but given warning of the existence of rocks, some of us, with less skill, would have avoided that vicinage and might have had smooth sailing through the whole voyage. By their silence they have not only indirectly contributed to our disaster, but they have actually strengthened against us the hands of our natural foes, the publishers. They make it possible for a newspaper to say, in reference to the present difficulty, "As the house (of H., P., & Co.) has been in thriving existence for more than a quarter of a century, and has never before quarreled with an author,—or more correctly speaking, never had an author quarrel with it,—there will be a general disposition," and so forth. They thus directly increase the resistance which any succeeding author must overcome. "Nothing," says "The Nation" newspaper of January 13, 1770, in harsher language than I care to use, but we must take language as we find it,—"Nothing so promotes swindle as the readiness of the victims to pocket their losses, go their way with a sickly smile, and let the rogues begin again." But of course this must be left for each person to decide for himself. It is only that if one feels moved in the spirit to bear witness against wrong in any of the relations of life, there is nothing in the height, or depth, or breadth, or brilliancy of any reputation to overawe him. Nothing is real but the right. There is no life but in truth. When faith is lost, when honor dies, the man is dead. Dead? He never was born. There never was any such person. He was a mirage, an apparition. The stars dim twinkle through his form.

As to the harm that may accrue to an author from adopting the course which he counts wise, it seems to me entirely insignificant. Nobody expects to go through the world intact, but we all expect to do that which presents itself to be done. If a writer has life in himself he will not easily die. If he has not life in himself the sooner he dies the better. If there is no life outside one charmed circle,

"Then am I dead to all the globe,
And all the globe is dead to me."

Nothing is indispensable but a mind at peace with itself. It is pleasant to celebrate the glory of those you love, but better trudge comfortably across country on foot and alone, with all your worldly goods knotted up in a yellow bandana than ride unwillingly behind anybody's triumphal car.

So then, while it is undoubtedly best as a general thing for an author to live at peace with publishers, and sinners, there is also no reason why he should not make war if it is borne in upon him to do so.

But the only royal road to justice is for authors, in the beginning, to be intelligent, prompt, exact and exacting on all business matters which come within their scope. This seems a little thing, but it would work a revolution in the literary world. Let writers deal with publishers, not like women and idiots, but as business men with business men. If an author chooses to relinquish all pecuniary rewards from his books and to make an outright gift of the profits to his publishers, he may leave the whole matter in their hands; but if he condescends to take any part in the spoils, he thereby becomes a business partner, and the only question is whether he shall be a good business man or a poor one. By not being prompt and intelligent, by neglecting to secure or to examine his accounts, or to correct them when they are wrong, or to understand them when they are obscure, he does not approve himself an unmercenary person; he simply shows himself to be shambling and shiftless, and puts a direct temptation in his publisher's path. Many a servant would be honest if her careless mistress would not leave money lying about. Had I but used the ordinary care and caution which a lawyer, or a merchant, or a marketman brings to his business, this trouble doubtless would never have happened, and we should all have been the happier for it. The simple consciousness on the part of a publisher, that an author is observant of what is visible, will have a tendency to make him exact and upright concerning what is invisible. An author should so order his affairs that a publisher must make an effort to be dishonest. On the contrary, he so neglects them that a publisher must make an effort to be honest. Confidence and trust are excellent things and never more excellent than when they have a solid basis of paper and ink. Do the best he can there will still be points enough for the author to exercise his trust on, but to do business wholly on the trust system is utterly childish. No confidence can be more complete than was mine, and none apparently can be founded on a more honorable reputation. The confidential, friendly way of conducting affairs is pretty and sentimental, grateful to one's indolence and vanity and over fastidiousness, and confirmatory of one's conviction that he is too dainty and delicate to touch a bargain with the tips of his fingers. But in fact we all do take money for our work when we can get it; we want just as much money and money just as much as other people—rather more—and, in sober truth, the friction, the sacrifice of delicacy in keeping your money affairs straight from day to day, is not for a moment to be compared to the delicacy which may be sacrificed by leaving them at the mercy of others. You run well for a while, but a day of reckoning is almost sure to come. The thriftless, hap-hazard way of bargaining or not bargaining, common among literary people, is the fruitful parent of uneasiness, anxiety, disappointment, and bitterness, before which delicacy must be rudely and ruthlessly brushed.

It is the same with women as with men, for in literature as in the gospel, there is neither male nor female. When a woman does any work for which she receives money she becomes so far a man, and passes immediately and inevitably under the yoke of trade. She has no right to demand a favorable judgment of her work because she is a woman, nor has she the least right to require that chivalry shall come in to help fix or secure her compensation. Trade laws know no more of gallantry than trade winds—and it is well they do not. Individuals and societies wheedle and flatter and threaten and torture according to the fashion, or passion, or panic of the hour, but under it all, the great, pitiless, unseen, inexorable law of the world holds from age to age, never relaxing its grasp, never revoking its decree, deaf to the wail of weakness, dumb to the cry of despair, forever and forever teaching with unrelenting persistency, *by* unrelenting persistency, the good and wholesome lesson that will be taught no other way. Under this law there is no sex, no chivalry, no deference, no mercy. There is nothing but supply and demand; nothing but buy and sell. To him who understands it, and guides himself by it, it is a chariot of state bearing him on to fame and fortune. To him who does not comprehend it and flings himself against it, it is a car of Juggernaut, crushing him beneath its wheels, without passion, but without pity.

EXPLANATORY NOTES

Editor's Note: The annotations that follow identify many, though not all, of the quotations and allusions in Dodge's work. Some that are not identified can be easily traced in encyclopedias or dictionaries. Other passages proved to be too obscure to trace for this printing. In most of these cases, however, the meanings of the unidentified passages, if not their sources, are apparent from the context.

The quotations and allusions demonstrate Dodge's extensive knowledge of the Bible, classical literature, Shakespeare, eighteenth- and nineteenth-century poetry, and western civilization. The use of frequent quotations and allusions is common in the essays of the nineteenth century, even in those addressed to the general public, so Dodge was not unusual in adopting this style. In her work, the number of quotations and allusions varied from piece to piece, depending on audience and purpose. She used this citation style to illustrate her points, to strengthen her arguments, and to demonstrate her knowledge of the world. In "My Book" this style implicitly provides another defense of the value of her literary work.

GAIL HAMILTON'S LIFE IN LETTERS

1. The Kansas-Nebraska Act passed on 30 May 1854 affirmed the concept of popular sovereignty over the issue of slavery in the new territories. It eventually

led to the bloody confrontations of the late 1850s in Kansas between proslavery and antislavery forces.

2. "He rolls it under his tongue as a sweet morsel" is from Matthew Henry (1662–1714), *Commentaries* (1708–1710), *Psalms* 36.2.

3. "Sitting, and clothed, and in his right mind" (Mark 5.15) refers to the madman after he was cured by Jesus.

4. Here the author is referring to the *National Era*, an antislavery newpaper published in Washington, by Gamaliel Bailey (1807–59). Issued from 1847 to 1860, it included literary works by many leading writers of the day. The paper always struggled financially, a point mentioned in the next letter.

5. Actually, she was probably earning $600 as a teacher at this time.

6. The *Independent* was a leading Protestant paper that published fiction and poetry along with religious and national news from December 1848 to October 1928.

7. This line is quoted from George Gordon, Lord Byron (1788–1824), "English Bards and Scotch Reviewers" 399.

8. These initials refer to Mr. T. W. T. Curtis, principal at Hartford High School, where Dodge taught from 1855 to 1858.

9. Grace Greenwood was the pen name of the journalist and lecturer Sara Jane (Clarke) Lippincott (1823–1904). She published widely in the *National Era, Saturday Evening Post, New York Times,* and *Independent. Greenwood Leaves* (1850) was a best seller. With her husband, she began one of the first children's magazines, *Little Pilgrim* (1853–75).

10. The term "cacoethes scribendi" is in a passage by Juvenal (AD 60–c. 130) which speaks of the "itch of writing": "An inveterate itch of writing, now incurable, clings to many, and grows old in their distempered body" (*Satires* 7.51). Women in the nineteenth century were sometimes accused of suffering from the disease. Catharine Sedgwick (1789–1867) explored the meaning of authorship in women's lives in a short story entitled "Cacoethes Scribendi" (1830), reprinted in Fetterley, *Provisions.*

11. The *Congregationalist,* a Protestant paper of news and literature, was published in Boston between May 1849 and May 1867. Henry Martyn Dexter (1821–90), clergyman and author, was its editor-in-chief from 1856 to 1890.

12. When Gamaliel Bailey died, his wife struggled to keep the *National Era* going, but unsuccessfully. She was unable to pay Dodge for her contributions.

13. Dodge's friendship with the philosopher Henry James Sr. (1811–82) was confined to their correspondence, which was quite lively.

14. Ossa and Pelion are mountains in Thessaly. In the *Odyssey* 11.315, giants

tried to scale heaven by placing Pelion on Ossa for a ladder. The expression, "heaping Pelion upon Ossa" means adding difficulty to difficulty, embarrassment upon embarrassment.

15. The Vale of Tempe is a valley in Thessaly between Olympus and Mt. Ossa. It is known for its beauty, birdlife, and cool shade

16. George Wood (1799–1870) was a close friend of Dodge. They had met in Washington. He worked for the federal government and wrote fiction, including *Peter Schlemihl in America* (1848) and *The Gates Wide Open* (1869), playing on the popularity of *The Gates Ajar* (1868) by Elizabeth Stuart Phelps (Ward).

17. This is reference to Edwards A. Park (1808–1900), theologian and professor of Christian theology at Andover Seminary, who apparently referred to himself in lectures as the "respectable man."

18. William French was the Boston lawyer and friend who eventually helped Dodge with her case against Fields.

19. "Life, like a dome of many-coloured glass, / Stains the white radiance of Eternity" was written by Percy Bysshe Shelley (1792–1882), "Adonais," 52.

20. Dodge is referring to James T. Fields (1817–81), publisher of the *Atlantic Monthly* and many books by major writers of the nineteenth century.

COUNTRY LIVING AND COUNTRY THINKING

MY GARDEN

1. Scylla is a rock at the entrance to the straits between Sicily and Italy, opposite Charybdis. Charybdis is a dangerous whirlpool in a narrow channel (commonly identified with the Straits of Messina), opposite Scylla.

2. The passage referred to—"To make a happy fire-side clime / To weans and wife, / That's the true Pathos and Sublime / Of Human life"—is by Robert Burns (1759–96) in "To Dr. Blacklock."

3. Halicarnassus is the name of an ancient Greek city as well as that given by Dodge to a male character in several of her essays. The city's most famous ruler was the woman Artemisia, who served under Xerxes in the invasion of Greece in 480 BC. The Mausoleum of Halicarnassus, constructed c. 353–51 BC, one of the Seven Wonders of the World, has a frieze of the Greeks battling Amazons. The site was extensively excavated in 1856–57 and 1865. By using this name for her male character, Dodge may have hoped that her audience would remember the strength of women vis-à-vis men in the ancient city.

4. Sir Hudson Lowe (1769–1844) was the governor of St. Helena when Napoleon was exiled there.

5. Cornelia (second century BC) was married to Tiberius Gracchus and gave birth to the two famous tribunes, Tiberius and Gaius. She herself had a reputation as a fine letter writer and highly cultured woman. When a woman once asked to see Cornelia's jewels, she produced her two sons, saying, "These are my jewels."

6. Horeb is one name given to Sinai. The burning bush refers to Jehovah's appearance to Moses (Exod. 3.1–6) when God commanded him to go to Pharaoh to demand the release of His people.

7. Alexander the Great (356–23 BC) of Macedonia was one of the greatest generals in history and extended the Greek empire almost to India. Archimedes (287–12 BC) was the most famous mathematician and inventor in ancient Greece. He invented the Archimedes screw for raising water and developed many important mathematical formulas.

8. Banquo is the Scottish general in *Macbeth* by William Shakespeare (1564–1616). He is murdered by Macbeth because the witches prophesied that his issue would become kings. His ghost came back to haunt Macbeth at a great banquet.

9. This would have been a long time. According to Greek legend, the Danaïdes were punished for murdering their husbands by being condemned to the endless task of filling water in vessels with no bottom. See Homer's *Odyssey* 2.576–81.

10. Tityus was a son of Earth whom Odysseus saw in Hades. Two vultures tore at his liver as punishment for assaulting Leto, mother of Apollo and Artemis.

11. Here the author is referring to the views of the Hungarian patriot Lajos Kossuth (1802–94) and to Paul's "If one part suffers, they all suffer together" (1 Cor. 12.26).

12. "In my mind's eye, Horatio" is from Shakespeare's *Hamlet* I.ii.185. Hymettus is a mountain near Athens famous for its bees and marble.

13. The Latin means "he touched nothing that did not grow." Here Dodge has revised slightly the epitaph of Samuel Johnson (1709–84) on Oliver Goldsmith (1730–74): "Nihil tetigit quod non ornavit" meaning "he touched nothing that he did not adorn." See James Boswell's *Life of Johnson* 22 June 1776.

14. The sin would be forgetting the true God. Jeroboam (c. 931–10 BC) was a wealthy landowner and first king of Israel. He revolted against Solomon and was exiled to Egypt. He later incurred divine wrath for building idolatrous shrines in Dan and Bethel. His ascent to the throne by popular choice, not divine right, doomed his kingdom.

Explanatory Notes

MEN AND WOMEN

1. This quote is by Charles Phillips (1787?–1859) in *A Character of Napoleon Buonaparte* (1817).

2. Medo-Persic laws seem to refer to theories of physics from the time that the Medes joined the Persians under Cyrus of Anshan in 550 BC.

3. The passage referred to is "Who does the best his circumstance allows / Does well, acts nobly; angels could no more" by Edward Young (1683–1765) in *Night Thoughts* (1742–48).

4. Honiton lace was made in Honiton, Devonshire, England, starting in the seventeenth century. In the nineteenth century it had floral motifs joined to a net background. Its easy, natural style was very popular.

5. A Roland for an Oliver is retaliation equal to its provocation or a blow for a blow. Roland (d. 778 AD), the greatest paladin of Charlemagne, was known for his five-day combat with Oliver, in which neither was the winner.

6. This word is probably one of Dodge's own creations of a Greek word. It may mean "singular stupidity."

7. This line is from Alexander Pope (1688–1774), *Moral Essays* (1751).

8. The line comes from Alfred Lord Tennyson (1809–92), "The Poet."

9. This comes from *Hamlet* III.i.83. It occurs in the passage during which Hamlet contemplates suicide. "The pale cast of thought" is the fear about what might happen after death.

10. Boswell's father used to call Dr. Johnson "Ursa Major." Holfernes, a general serving Nebuchadnezzar, was killed by Judith; see the Book of Judith in the Apocrypha and Douay Bible. "What harm does it do a man?" suggests that it does not kill someone just to call him/her a name.

11. Actually the line reads: "Doubtless God could have made a better berry, but doubtless God never did." It is from Dr. William Butler (1535–1618) quoted in Izaak Walton (1593–1683), *The Compleat Angler* (1655).

12. This is a line from Samuel Taylor Coleridge (1772–1834), "Youth and Age."

13. These lines come from Nathaniel Parker Willis (1806–67), "Unseen Spirits."

14. This refers to the story of Samson and Delilah (Judg. 16.4–10). Samson was not restrained by the green branches.

15. *Nolens volens* (Lat.) means "willy nilly," "whether desired or not."

16. Hermon is a mountain mentioned in the Bible on the northern boundary of ancient Palestine. It experiences heavy precipitation.

17. Ralph Waldo Emerson (1803–82) said "A foolish consistency is the

hobgoblin of little minds" in "Self-Reliance," *Essays: First Series* (1841).

18. This last is a line from Martin Farquahar Tupper (1810–89), who wrote *Proverbial Philosophy* (1838), which was widely reprinted in the U.S.

19. This allusion is to an old story preserved in *Percy's Reliques* (1765), a collection of ballads and poems. The Wantley dragon represents a very greedy, unkind person.

20. John Bunyan (1628–88) was cast in Bedford jail for nonconformity to the Church of England from 1660 to 1672, during which time he wrote his spiritual autobiography. He was imprisoned for a second time in 1677. Soon after, he published *Pilgrim's Progress* (1678), probably begun during his first imprisonment and worked on in his second.

21. The Cytherean myth relates to the birth of the goddess Aphrodite who first landed at Cythera when she emerged from the sea. The reference to the Hellenic Maintenon suggests someone both revered and hated as much as Françoise d'Aubigné, marquise de Maintenon (1635–1719), who was the second wife of Louis XIV.

22. Carolus Linnaeus (1707–78), Swedish botanist, first established principles for defining and naming genera and species of organisms.

23. Jean Louis Rodolphe Agassiz (1807–73) was a Swiss-born U.S. naturalist, geologist and teacher.

24. Sir Edward Dyer (c. 1540–1607) wrote the poem entitled "My Mind to Me a Kingdom Is."

25. The land of Beulah is the place of rest enjoyed by Christians when their faith is strong and they have no doubts. In Bunyan's *Pilgrim's Progress* the pilgrims rest here after their pilgrimage and before death.

26. Felix O. C. Darley (1822–88) was well known for his illustrations in works by Irving and Cooper in the 1850s.

27. This line, meaning "it's none of your business," was said by Oliver Wendell Holmes (1809–94) in *The Autocrat of the Breakfast Table* (1858) when he was asked to report on what he talked about with the schoolmistress: "In this particular case, as I was allowed the privilege of walking alone with a very interesting young woman, you may allow me to remark, in the classic version of a familiar phrase, used by our Master Benjamin Franklin, *nullum tui negotii*" ("My first walk with the schoolmistress").

28. "Casta diva" is the name of Norma's aria with chorus in act I of *Norma* (1831) by Vincenzo Bellini (1801–35). The opera was performed in New York in English in 1841 and in Italian in 1843.

29. *A Compend of History from Earliest Times* (1808) by Samuel Whelpley

(1766–1817) was republished many times in the nineteenth century.

30. Charles Blondin (1824–97) was a French acrobat and tightrope walker who crossed Niagara River on a tightrope.

31. "Herman, or Young Knighthood," a serial novel, was published in the *National Era* at the same time as "Men and Women." It ran from 1 July 1858 to 7 July 1859.

32. *Lalla Rookh; an Oriental Romance* (1817) was written by Thomas Moore (1779–1852).

33. These words describing the soul are from Emperor Hadrian's address near death: "Dear little fleeting soul of mine, sometimes guest and comrade!"

34. This is a reference to Samson's physical strength.

35. Britain's sturdy old Republican may refer to Arthur Hugh Clough (1819–61) who is chiefly remembered as the author of hexameter verses, "The Bothie of Tober-no-Vuolich" (1848). I have not identified the reference to the New Hampshire bard.

36. Cham is an archaic term for khan. "That great Cham of literature" was a phrase used by Tobias Smollett (1721–71) in a letter to John Wilkes (1727–95), 16 Mar. 1759, when referring to Samuel Johnson. Johnson admired the author Fanny Burney (1752–1840).

37. When proposing a toast to Napoleon at a literary dinner, the British poet Thomas Campbell (1777–1844) said, "Gentlemen, you must not mistake me. I admit that he is the sworn foe of our nation, and if you will, of the whole human race. But, gentlemen, we must be just to our enemy. We must not forget that he once shot a bookseller." Campbell is also supposed to have said, "Now Barabbas was a publisher."

38. "Aurora Leigh" (1857), epic poem by Elizabeth Barrett Browning (1806–61), was important to many women as a demonstration of the greatness women could achieve as writers.

39. Currer Bell was the penname of Charlotte Brontë (1816–55), author of *Jane Eyre* (1847).

40. Aaron was brother of Moses and first high priest of the Hebrews; Hur was a prominent Israelite. Together they judged the people while Moses went up to Mt. Sinai.

41. These lines are from William Wordsworth (1770–1850), "She Was a Phantom of Delight."

42. This is similar to "Who sweeps a room as for Thy laws, / Makes that and th'action fine." These lines are from *The Elixir,* 1.19 by George Herbert (1593–1633).

43. *The Dairyman's Daughter* (1809) was a rustic moral tale by L. Richmond (1772–1827). It was very popular, selling two million copies in England, plus having extensive sales in America and elsewhere.

44. "Thou, while thy babes around thee cling, / Shalt show us how divine a thing / A woman may be made" comes from "To a Young Lady" by Wordsworth. It is significant that Dodge has left off the first line, thus suggesting there are many ways to be divine.

45. This line is from Shakespeare's *Othello* IV.i.205. Othello is referring to Desdemona's goodness. The pity is that she must be punished for her infidelity, even when she is so good.

46. These lines are from *Sir Galahad* (1842) by Alfred, Lord Tennyson (1809–1892).

MY BOOK

1. There is much known about Abraham who built an altar on the plains of Mamre in southern Palestine, but nothing known about his shepherd. See Gen. 18.

2. This description refers to the place near Calais where Henry VIII and François I of France met in 1520; François was trying to influence Henry to support him against Emperor Charles V. The place was so named because of the splendor of the tents and the wealth of the monarchs.

3. This was Aaron's excuse for the existence of the golden calf (Exod. 32.24).

4. Philosopher John Stuart Mill (1806–73) is known for his essays "Liberty" (1859) and "The Subjection of Women" (1869). John Elliott Cairnes (1823–75) was the author of *The Character and Logical Method of Political Economy* (1857) and several works on the slave question and American Civil War. Goldwin Smith (1823–1910) was a journalist who supported the cause of the North, as did the other two men, in the American Civil War and also supported the sentiment for independence in Canada. Many British people supported the South.

5. This passage is taken from Virgil's *Aeneid* (9.427–28). The original uses "Rutulians" instead of "Englishmen." It translates here as "On me, here I stand who did the deed—on me turn your sword. Englishmen, the fault is mine."

6. The Lost Leader is Abraham Lincoln (1809–65).

7. Rhadamanthus was the son of Zeus and Europa and the brother of Minos, king of Crete. Known for his justice and wisdom, he became one of the

judges of the infernal regions after death. Benlomond seems to be a made-up name here. Ben Lomond is a mountain in Scotland noted for its beautiful views from the summit.

8. John Couch Adams (1819–92) and Urbain J. J. LeVerrier (1811–77) both speculated on a new planet beyond Uranus in November 1845. The planet ultimately was named Neptune. These lines are based on "All service ranks the same with God— / With God, whose puppets, best and worst, / Are we; there is no last nor first" Robert Browning (1812–89), "The Pied Piper of Hamelin" 4.

9. Flavius Josephus (AD 37–c. 98) was a celebrated Jewish writer of history in the Roman times. David Ricardo (1772–1823), a Dutch Jewish economist, was known for *Principles of Political Economy and Taxation* (1817). Francisque-Xavier Michel (1809–87) was a French historian who wrote on medieval life and edited the newly discovered Oxford manuscript of the *Chanson de Roland.* François de Sales, Saint (1567–1622) was a religious moralist whose *Introduction à la Vie Dévote* (1609) was translated into seventeen languages and was a model for other books.

10. This is a humorous image here. See n. 15 to *Gail Hamilton's Life in Letters.*

11. The author is referring to various wines mentioned in classical literature. Caecubum was a marshy district in Latium famed for its wine. Calenum means of or belonging to Cales; Juvenal refers to its wine. Formianum was an estate near Formiae. Sabini, an ancient people of Italy, were northerly neighbors of the Latins. The Roman poet Horace (Horatius Flaccus, 65–8 BC) refers to their Sabinum wine and also mentions Falernian wine from the district between Volturnus and Mt. Massicus. Bandusia was a fountain celebrated in the *Odes* of Horace.

12. Francis Jeffrey (1773–1850) with Sydney Smith founded the *Edinburgh Review.* He was known as a stern but usually judicious critic.

13. Horace Sebastiani (1772–1851) was a French marshal and diplomat under Napoleon and later governments. He made this statement about Warsaw when he was minister of Foreign Affairs.

14. John Tyndall (1820–93), professor of natural history at the Royal Institution, did much in his writings to popularize science.

15. The Valley of Humiliation is a place in Bunyan's *Pilgrim's Progress* where Christian encounters a fiend named Apollyon. Aetna is a volcano in Sicily that figures in Roman legends.

16. Though I have not located the source of this quote, the ruler referred to is Mithradates VI (135–63 BC) who, as ruler of Pontus (northern Anatolia), successfully challenged Rome's hegemony in Asia Minor for a while. When he was on the verge of invading Italy, his troops revolted against him, so he tried to poison himself, but was unsuccessful. Dodge is implying that she had so much praise that it did not affect her.

17. This story is found in 2 Kings 5.1–19.

18. Abbé Nicolas Charles Joseph Trublet was a French author of many works, including *Essays Moral and Critical* (1744).

19. Charles Kingsley (1819–75), clergyman, novelist, and professor of history, wrote a wide variety of literary works and was a founding member of the Christian Socialist movement.

20. Country Parson was the pseudonym for Andrew Kennedy Hutchinson Boyd (1825–99), a minister at St. Andrews, Scotland, who wrote several very popular books including several volumes of *Recreations of a Country Parson* (1859, 1861, 1878) and of *Graver Thoughts of a Country Parson* (1862–65, 1875).

21. *Religio Medici* (1643) by Sir Thomas Browne (1605–82) was a confession of Christian faith and offered opinions on many secular and religious topics.

22. Puck was an evil or malicious spirit in popular superstition but from the sixteenth century onward was considered more of a mischievous goblin. He was also called Robin Goodfellow.

23. This is a transcendental sentiment; Dodge may have been comparing herself to Emerson here.

24. The author is comparing herself to the hero in *Don Quixote* (1605) by Miguel de Cervantes Saavedra (1547–1616).

25. Dodge is referring to how long Horace worked on his *Odes.* Actually, a period of eleven years (24–13 BC) separated the publication of the third and fourth volumes.

26. James 5.16 says "So confess your sins to one another" and Romans 13.8 says ". . . love one another."

27. Johnson was talking about Dr. John Campbell (1708–75), Scottish author and historian. See Boswell's *Life of Samuel Johnson* 1: 417–18 (1 July 1763).

28. Dodge is probably referring to Joseph Bellamy (1719–90), an associate of Jonathan Edwards and author of *True Religion Delineated* (1750). The Bible story referred to is in Matt. 12.43–45 and Luke 11.24–25: an unclean spirit returns to its house (person's body) to find it unoccupied, clean, and tidy. It goes to collect other evil spirits to come and settle in also. As a result, the house (person) is much worse off than it was before.

29. In Phil. 3.2 Paul cautions, "Beware of dogs! Watch out for people who are making mischief."

30. In *The Book of Common Prayer* 65.11, the psalm reads: "and the little hills shall rejoice on every side."

31. This reference to the time of Jesus's crucifixion is an interesting analogy to the author's own situation.

32. Mokanna was a repulsive impostor who posed as a prophet in "The Veiled Prophet of Khorassan" in Moore's *Lalla Rookh.*

33. Richard Whately (1787–1863) published works on philosophy and religion. He was a professor of political economy and an archbishop. His reputation rests on *Logic* (1826) and *Rhetoric* (1828).

34. Alexander William Kinglake (1809–91) was the author of *Eothen* (1844) and *Invasion of the Crimea* (1887). He did not entirely admire the liberal British statesman William Gladstone (1809–98), whom he once described as "a good man in the worse sense of the term, conscientious with a diseased conscience."

35. This is a little joke meaning "Dorset and I made this."

36. This poem by William Dean Howells (1837–1920) is entitled "The Robin and the Cows."

A BATTLE OF THE BOOKS

1. This refers again to Campbell's toast. See "Men and Women" at n. 37.

2. A name illustrious and venerable (Lat.).

3. This would be a rather hypocritical blessing since Pecksniff is a character in *Martin Chuzzlewit* (1843) by Charles Dickens (1812–70) who is described as "a drunken, begging, squalid letter-writing man" and as a "sleek, smiling, crawling abomination of hypocrisy."

4. This is an altered version of the poem in "Men and Women" at n. 19.

5. Brummell and Hunt stands for the firm of Ticknor and Fields. The senior partners were William D. Ticknor (1810–64) and James T. Fields. Throughout the following narrative Dodge has substituted fictional names or dashes for the actual people involved in her controversy. The following is a partial list of the actual persons, places, books, and magazines to which she refers:

Adriatic = *Atlantic Monthly*
Athens = Boston
Buddhist = *Our Young Folks*
City Curate = *Country Parson* (see "My Book" n. 20)
City Lights = *Country Living and Country Thinking* (1862)
Confucius = George Wood (see *Gail Hamilton's Life in Letters* n. 16)
Corinth = New York City
Cotton-picking = *Wool-Gathering* (1867)

(Mr./Judge) Dane = William French (see *Gail Hamilton's Life in Letters* n. 18)
Every Tuesday = *Every Saturday*, a magazine which reprinted European material
Greek Quarterly = *North American Review*
Holidays = *Gala-Days* (1863)
(Mr.) Jackson of Corinth = possibly James Derby, author of *Fifty Years among Authors, Books, and Publishers* (1884)
Little Men = *A Battle of the Books*
New Zealander = possibly *Harper's New Monthly Magazine*
Old Miasmus = *A New Atmosphere* (1865)
(Mr.) Parry = James R. Osgood (1836–92)
Pearville and Co. = Appleton and Company
The Rights of Men = *Woman's Wrongs: A Counter-Irritant* (1868)
Segregationalissuemost = *Congregationalist*
Winter Work = *Summer Rest* (1866)

6. Dodge told Fields in 1864 that she wanted to earn $10,000 someday. See *Life in Letters* 1: 410.

7. The woman referred to in the letter and to whom she sends greetings in the conclusion is Annie Fields (1834–1915), literary hostess, occasional author, and wife of James T. Fields.

8. This statement appears in William Cowper (1731–1800), *The Task* 2: "The Timepiece" 206.

9. The *Cumberland* was sunk by the Confederate *Merrimac* in March 1862.

10. These were the laws of the Persian Empire after 550 B.C. This was a stable empire that allowed a good deal of autonomy to the subject people, including the Jews who were allowed to rebuild their temple in Jerusalem. Thus, in this context, these would be laws beneficial to authors as well as publishers.

11. This note is from Annie Fields. The "friend of ours" is her husband, whose hand, I believe, was injured at the time.

12. She did not tell her good friend George Wood about the dispute until March 1868. See her letter to him republished here.

13. Sir Thomas Browne (real name) was a seventeenth-century author, more serious than the Country Parson (see n. 21 to "My Book"). She means to suggest that Browne's style would be more dignified than that of the "City Curate."

14. This Latin phrase means "with a grain of salt."

15. This situation comes from *The Faerie Queene* (1590, 1596) by Edmund Spenser (1552–99).

16. Dodge herself wrote this line in the conclusion of "My Book." The phrase "once more famous than now" comes from a newspaper article that she quotes later in this chapter in which she is similarly described.

17. "Lost in wonder, love and praise" comes from the hymn "Love Divine, All Loves Excelling" by Charles Wesley (1707–88).

18. During the year of their controversy the name of the publishing house changed from Ticknor and Fields to Fields, Osgood, and Co.

19. This refers to the writings of Mary Russell Mitford (1787–1855), the English author of *Our Village* (1832), *Recollections of a Literary Life* (1852), *Atherton and Other Tales* (1854) and other works. An edited edition of her letters was released in 1870.

20. Here Mitford is referring to Nathaniel Hawthorne, whose mistreatment at the hands of Fields had been described by Dodge in an earlier chapter.

21. This particular passage (Isa. 59.5) describes the evilness spawned by all who are vain, who lie, who cause mischief, and so forth; from evil comes more evil.

22. This refers to a character in Bunyan's *Pilgrim's Progress.* In the past he was powerful and put people cruelly to death but now is so old, he can only sit in his cave grinning at the pilgrims as they pass by, unable to go at them.

23. Joshua's monument of twelve stones, representing the twelve tribes of Israel, was set up in Gilgal as a reminder that God had held back the waters of the Jordan to allow the Israelites safe passage into their new land (see Josh. 4.1–24).

24. In Old Testament times Jericho was a flourishing city surrounded by powerful walls. When the Israelites encircled them and shouted, the walls fell down (see Josh. 6.1–27).